BEING

Jack Smith

SERVING HOUSE BOOKS

Being

ISBN: 978-0-9971010-1-0

Cover design: Walter Cummins

Serving House Books logo by Barry Lereng Wilmont

Published by Serving House Books
Copenhagen, Denmark and Florham Park, NJ
www.servinghousebooks.com

Member of The Independent Book Publishers Association

First Serving House Books Edition 2016

Jack Smith's fascinating new novel, *Being*, may be his "break-out" work. The prose pulls the reader deeper into the narrative with each phrase. One if its most intriguing merits is Smith's ability to create characters that can't be pinned down: are they crackpots, or are they serious people? Or are they both all at once? One thinks of Bellow's King Romilayu; and Nathaniel West can be invoked as well. (There's a touch of Terry Southern too.) There is much dialogue in this novel, and it is sprightly and meets Richard Yates' test: "Good dialogue reveals character; even better dialogue reveals more than the speaker might wish known."

The "square" protagonist Philip (he insists on being called by his formal name) is a magnet to a host of eccentric and beguiling characters, male and female, who insist on bending his ear as they seek to usher him into their often cheerfully absurd view of things—they convert Philip, one might say, as he stumbles about, looking for work: they attempt, often with comic results, to persuade and cajole him to join their dotty legions. They are all "operators," whether academics, salesmen, charming women, nuts and/or louts. His female characters are particularly beguiling. E. M. Forster notes that fiction's most salient value is making the reader want to find out "what happens next." This novel has that virtue—and is hilarious to boot.

—Geoffrey Clark, author of *Two, Two, Lily-White Boys*, *Wedding in October*, and *Necessary Deaths*

Being is Smith's third novel, and possibly his best, full of vitality, appetite, and wisdom. Philip, just out of college, sets off to find work, love, and happiness; his progress is as curious as it is tenacious, much like Alice's in Wonderland. Dialogue is Smith's forte, and as Philip encounters denizens of the adult world, they speak in varieties of jabberwocky. One is a Professor of Panegyrics at the local university, who wants him to do door-to-door surveys: "Everything is about happiness, Philip, and praise is a key cog, a fundamental mechanism of happiness." His encounters with women, their boyfriends and ex's, and a regional sales manager for hunting equipment are similarly muddled. Snowed in for a hotel tryst that lasts ten days, Philip digs out to search for more money and condoms, only to find the woman's loutish boyfriend in his place when he returns. Peripety prevails. Another woman tells him "I can't be part of a life that isn't taking me seriously." Wiser or not, Philip returns to the Professor's job finally, and Smith deftly pulls together the novel's philosophical ideas.

—DeWitt Henry, author of *Safe Suicide* and *Sweet Dreams*

Jack Smith's *Being* is a raucous existential romp through a proverbial house of mirrors where some, to their delight, will perceive Kierkegaard and/or Heidegger gazing back at them. Philip Fellows, a hapless Everyman who is *"running away from nothing,"* is on an ill-fated quest for fulfillment through meaningful employment and diverse erotic relationships while engaging with others similarly alienated as to the *whys* and *whats* of existence. A trenchant satirist, Smith deftly blends humor with pathos, and throughout the novel *Being*'s protagonist is shadowed by a stranger garbed in black who when confronted declares, "You are in despair, sir." The looking glass reflection Fellows cannot escape.

—Dennis Must is the author of several books. The most recent, *Hush Now, Don't Explain,* received the 2014 Dactyl Foundation Literary Fiction Award. *Going Dark: Selected Stories* is forthcoming in 2016 by Coffeetown Press, Seattle, Washington.

To Mary Jane Smith

Books by Jack Smith

Co-authored with Eddie J. Girdner. *Killing Me Softly: Toxic Waste, Corporate Profit, and the Struggle for Environmental Justice*, Monthly Review Press, 2002.

Hog to Hog, Texas Review Press, 2008.

Write and Revise for Publication: A 6-Month Plan for Crafting an Exceptional Novel and Other Works of Fiction, Writer's Digest Books, 2013.

Icon, Serving House Books, 2014.

Acknowledgments

I especially want to thank Geoffrey Clark, DeWitt Henry, Dennis Must, and Walter Cummins for their help and encouragement on this novel.

"This despair is a significant step forward."

—Søren Kierkegaard, *The Sickness Unto Death*

1

He heard the three knocks early on, the room pitch dark. He sat up and noticed the alarm clock: 3:12. Who would knock on one's door at this dark hour? It was winter, and Philip Fellows was too cold to answer the knock. He lay there, waiting for more knocks, but none came. If it was important enough, surely more knocks would soon come. Otherwise, it was the wrong door, or some prank.

When he was up at 6:30, dressing, he forgot about the knocks, but then when he stood at the window and looked down on the snow-covered sidewalk, he saw a man in a dark topcoat looking up at his window. Was it this man who had wanted to get his attention? Philip rapped at the window with his fist, but the man looked away and walked on.

Philip's eyes followed the measured steps of the man until he disappeared. Strange, wasn't it?

Three job interviews today. If he didn't get a job soon, he'd be evicted. He had so little money left and he'd have to save that for food.

He was hungry. He got his black suit, white shirt, and tie on, his coat on, pulled on his tall rubber boots, strapped his satchel on, and he exited his apartment. Down the hall, down the stairs.

God, it smelled. Out here it smelled worse than his apartment. It hit your nostrils with a stink of rotting garbage and something else—but what was it? Kerosene? No, but some sort of oily smell. It was hard to say.

A different apartment. Something civilized.

Please.

But unlikely.

He stepped outside.

A cold blast of air.

And this grinding poverty!

Forty-one dollars and thirty-nine cents in his checking account. Eighteen dollars and twenty-seven cents in cash. Both his credit cards maxed out.

My god, what to do? If he didn't find a job soon, what would he do? He couldn't, he *wouldn't* turn to his parents, six states away, his mother coiled up on the couch watching TV, a box of chocolate on the coffee table at a convenient reach, his father tied up in some sort of corporate meeting.

No, I would rather starve. He said it out loud. He kicked the snow. It was a half foot deep. There was something—what was it? Something ethereal about it. Or was that the right word?

White, he thought. So white.

He stopped off at the Jefferson House. He couldn't afford this, but ah, Sophia Cross, so delicious, he couldn't afford not to. He must at least have coffee, once he ran out of money for the pancakes. He must at least have coffee to be with Sophia Cross. When in her presence, her lovely looks permeated the place and his entire being, and he longed to be in her presence. Every morning, he made sure of it. At approximately this time.

At seven o'clock.

"You look very nice today," Sophia Cross said. "Why the suit?"

"A job interview." He felt a little fraudulent. A suit—this wasn't him. Yet he did feel rather sharp. Self-important? A man on his way up.

"Oh—well, good luck!"

"Thanks."

"I hope you get it."

The way she said that: bright, cheerful. It titillated him. "I do too!" he shot back.

"God, I hate to apply for jobs, don't you?" she bent over and whispered. Her breath was on his neck.

"Yeah," he said. "Yeah." He wanted her now. Now he must have her.

She took his order.

Pancakes, of course.

"You know," she said, "you really ought to eat something besides pancakes now and then!" She stood back, one hand on a hip.

"I know. I just like them."

"Well, there's nothing wrong with having what you like." She gave his hand a quick pat. What a buzz it gave him.

She took off. He watched her curvy hips swaying. He watched her hair and neck.

Oh, god. How he did want her. She was twenty-one, slim, with a full bosom, and Philip thought about those breasts every night before he fell asleep. They often popped up in his mind during the day, several times. Sometimes he was thinking about something entirely unrelated, like an exam he'd done well on back in college, or one he hadn't—at least not as well as he'd hoped—or his plans to get a different apartment, and then suddenly there they were: Sophia's breasts. Large, full, bountiful, more than a handful. He tried to imagine the size. Thirty-eight? Forty? It struck him that it wouldn't be wise to inquire about such a matter even if you got the girl's bra off. What would you say? "Uh, are you a thirty-eight . . . or perchance a forty? I would . . . just kind of like to know? You know?"

But there was a serious problem here: Sophia Cross was some other guy's girl. Some guy named Rod Busby, football player, boxer, frat jock. Busby was a business major and had a job lined up with his father when he graduated in the spring. Or, he'd told Sophia, maybe the CIA. *I just might give that a go*, he'd told Sophia, and she'd whispered it at Philip, and then gave it a horse laugh. He didn't want her to laugh like that. It ruined his ... well, he had to admit, his idealistic picture of her.

He was older than the two of them by a few years. He'd taken his B.A., but he still had no steady work. He really must have steady work to have Sophia Cross. This was beyond question. And he had come to this conclusion after months of love and lust: If he didn't have Sophia Cross, this would mean a very bad life. It was wrong, he thought, to be slated for a very bad life at his age, but clearly if he did not have Sophia Cross, he would be doomed to that very thing. He sometimes thought of it as misery. Yes, that was the right word. What other word was there? To love and love, and to lust too, yes, call it what it was—lust. And not find satisfaction. To be tormented by the sheer lack of this woman, her beauty, her mystery, the blood and breath of her deep sexuality—how could one, how could one possibly go on? There would be no happiness for him at all. How sad. How tragic.

When he thought of such misery, he thought of himself stuck in that cold, stinky apartment. The pea-green radiators. The ceiling with brown stained tiles dangling down. The kitchen with the grimy stove with two burners that didn't work.

No, he would not end up in such misery as that. There was so much more to him. More than to the likes of Rod Busby. He'd graduated in the top five percent of his class. He'd made straight A's in English. He read constantly. He could quote—he could quote a lot. English literature, and world literatures in translation. Poetry all over the place. He had written twenty poems himself, all revised. They would be published soon, he was sure. Give him a place to work, time to think, and a life of greater ease.

And he could tell Sophia Cross liked him. He could tell by her green eyes, the way they focused, the way they flashed.

She was making her way toward him now, a bright smile, with the coffee.

"Should I eat something else?" he asked. And then he was immediately sorry he'd asked. Because it was a sign of weakness. Declare what you want, and take it, as his father had said—never take the duck head. But pancakes?

"No, pancakes are fine. If you like pancakes, who am I?" She twirled, and he died inside at her unfathomable beauty.

He watched her again. He watched every move she made, the way her hips sinuously swiveled and swayed. Perhaps this was only lust, not love at all. If one were in love, truly in love, would he watch how his lover's hips sinuously swiveled and swayed?

Get the job. Get a good job, he told himself, an impressive one, suit and tie, polished black shoes, and you will steal Sophia Cross from that bastard Rod Busby. You will have unlimited sex with her. Yes, unlimited. You will live in that bed with that woman. When you aren't at work. How stupid it is to have to work. Damn. Son of a bitch.

His job interview for a magazine was still several hours off—at 1 p.m.

Time to relax. Take in Sophia Cross all you want.

Sophia Cross brought his pancakes. She stood there afterwards. Was she going to watch him eat? He hated to be watched. He worried about food on his lips, in the corners, smears of butter and syrup. A disgusting residue on his teeth. He worried about being gross. One of his greatest worries in life was being gross or at least appearing to be gross.

She got a look on her face. Had she guessed his thoughts?

"I have such a problem. Maybe you know."

"What? Know what?"

"Well. I can't talk *long*," she whispered.

"Oh."

"Maybe more later."

He could see the fat woman with the brown beetle glasses situated back toward the kitchen staring at them.

"Yes. Maybe later, then," he said. *Later*. The sound of the word pleased him. Later meant there would be a continuum, with her and him on it. *Later* meant development of some sort.

"I'll make it quick," she said. "My boyfriend—Rod . . . he shoved me. Hit me." Her voice choked up. She was about to cry. A finger dabbed one eyelash. Wasn't that a tear? He looked closely.

"What? Hit," he said. "My god. *Hit*. When?"

"I can't talk longer. I just had to tell someone. You're such a nice guy, and his friends, what a bunch of frigging crapheads, and—"

Oh, god, he didn't want her to use language like that.

"I know, I know," he said. "I want . . . I want to—"

"What?" she said.

"To help," he said. It was out of his mouth, and there was no taking it back.

"You do?" She turned to go. "I have to . . . but later. Later," she said, and she wiped a tear—a visible tear, yes—away, and he watched her hips sway and swivel as she returned to duty. And he wanted to reach around her from behind and cup her breasts, and kiss her neck—yes—and go further, much further. God, he thought, what if? What if?

A flash image of Rod Busby coldcocking him, but he put it away and began to butter his pancakes, then pour a good helping of syrup on them, then cut the stack into bite-size pieces. He was a neat person. He hated sloppiness. He hated ugliness in all its forms. For this reason, he especially hated where he lived. He hated the two rooms, no rug, junk furniture, ugly blond dresser with broken drawers, knobs off, vanity with cracked mirror, bare ceiling bulb hanging down from the dangling tiles. That stifling sewer odor, or whatever it was, hit you as soon as you entered the building. But until he got a job that paid, he would be reduced to this—to such dismal surrounds, to such penury. And perhaps worse than this if he didn't find a job soon. You couldn't be yourself if the world around you made you less than what you were. He'd argued this plenty of times and grew quickly impatient with those who said it was *your* fault, *your* fault if you didn't measure up.

Your fault? He had to laugh at that.

I've done every single frigging thing I can.

He watched her as he ate his pancakes. He could watch her all day, every minute of the day, and it would still not be enough. He wanted every inch of her, every inch for himself. He sometimes thought of her as a delectable food entrée. It disturbed him to think that Rod Busby surely had every inch of her. He wouldn't let himself imagine it. He put it out of his mind every time it surfaced. He could not stand the thought of Rod Busby feeling her, stroking her, running his hands over her curves, that supple flesh, and doing more than that—things he would not let his mind even start to imagine.

She was coming toward his table. He tried to keep his attention on her face, which was beautiful—and not on her body. He smiled as he put his fork down so that he would not be in the act of delivering a wad of pancake into his mouth as she approached the table. He took a sip of coffee. It was so good, that coffee. He preferred to think of her brewing it up herself, but he knew someone else did that. She waited tables, and that was all.

She brought the bill and laid it on the table. It was the usual—$7.37. It cost to eat, and he had but a week or more to live, it appeared.

"Forget what I said," she said to him, and laid her soft, pretty hand on his table. Her hand was so lovely. The delicacy of it, the fingers so proportionately shaped. The skin so smooth. The fingernails pink. Glowing. He imagined them in his mouth, but then checked himself. You mustn't, he thought. *You mustn't—you might reveal . . .*

"Why?" he said. "Did you—"

"Nothing's changed," she said. "Just me. I can't lay that on you. I'm sorry."

They had known each other for six months now, he the customer, she the waitress, but more than that: confidantes. He had told her of his job struggles. Of his dwindling money. Of his bad apartment. And he'd thought: *You shouldn't have.* Wouldn't she perceive this as a weakness? Rod Busby had it together. But Philip's openness had somehow struck a chord with her. She herself was open. She had told him of her college courses—all the woes, the small victories, the male professors who leered at her, the female professors who judged her. She had decided to drop out a semester. Maybe two. And then her boyfriend woes—that had come up almost right away. He had suggested right off that maybe she ought to forget that guy—really, forget him. Move on! But then she dropped the facts on him—Rod Busby's incredible strength, his raw aggressiveness, his ill-temper, one bloody fight she'd witnessed herself. That fist fight outside a bar—over her. *He put that poor man in the hospital*, Sophia had told him. *He broke his nose, and he broke three ribs.* She spoke of blood and pain, and whimpering. Here was the archetypal jealous jock, the cretin who pounded you to dust if you were stupid enough to be caught running off at the mouth. Philip had forgotten pricks like that still existed. Since college, he'd thought of the world as more civilized than that. But the barbarians were apparently at the gate.

Sophia started to leave, but he grabbed her hand. He'd never done that before. He surprised himself. But it felt so right.

She let him hold it. She squeezed his hand, just slightly.

"You're so nice," she said, and then took her hand away. "I wish all men were as nice as you." And then she left.

He tried not to watch her walking, but he couldn't help himself. It wasn't walking. What was it? It was something close to

15

swimming—lithe and graceful. He choked on it. How was it fair that you were brought into the world to suffer so? How was that fair at all?

But you saw it in male cats, didn't you? How they died for it. He'd seen it on a farm as a boy, out at a young friend's barn. "Like electricity," said his friend. "Poor sap is wired for it."

You get rid of Rod Busby, he told himself, and you will do yourself one huge favor. Keep it in mind, he thought. And he said it out loud when he was back on the sidewalk, wading through the snow.

2

At the public library, he ran into Adam Most, who all but lived there. A short weasel-faced man, he was in his late thirties, with two days growth of beard. Somehow it was always two days. Funny how he managed that. How *would* you manage that? The man talked fast. He made multiple gestures, gyrating about. Philip thought of him as a monkey in your face—always in your face. You couldn't sneak by him. He smelled you, or something. *I attract people like that*, Philip thought. *Why me?*

The man didn't work. He had some sort of government assistance. He had special funds. He was very vague about it all.

Adam Most was attempting to understand What Makes Man Tick. He was writing it all up in composition journals. He pigeonholed you so that you had trouble getting away, unless you didn't mind being rude, and Philip himself didn't like rudeness. He had made a point of not being rude ever, if he could manage it. This meant, sometimes, a herculean effort, especially with a bore, and a boor, like Adam Most. The man had used Philip as a sounding board on a variety of subjects: the circuitry of the brain, Chinese medicine, Japanese art, hedonism, theistic evolution, and parallel universes. There was a host of others too.

"Listen, Philip," he now said. "Listen. If you want to understand what makes man tick, you've got to get underneath all the social conventions. Peel them away. There are usually several layers. There can be countless layers. No one knows who he or she is because there are so many layers. Do you see what I mean?"

"Yes, I think—"

"You want to know one definite layer?"

"What?"

"It's society's tolerance for cruelty. If, now listen to me, if this *very* moment, there was to be a public execution in front of the library here—imagine that, if you will. Are you imagining it?"

"Yes."

"You've got it pictured."

"Yes." God, he thought, why? Why picture such a thing?

"Well, all right then. Imagine right now, we were all ushered out of this library because the occasion had come—to execute the so-called Criminal. The treasonous, you see. High treason. Imagine one of the most horrendous, most violent and most inhumane of executions—the drawing and quartering of the victim. I say victim, but I should say instead *human being*, or better yet, *person*. Have it? Have it fixed in your mind?"

"Yes. I do." Philip sought refuge. The restroom? A sudden need to urinate?

But the weasel had him locked in. Those eyes, and those monkey gyrations.

"I won't sink to enumerate each specific thing done to this poor sap—the hanging, almost to the point of death, the taking down, the disemboweling, the beheading—that's not my point. I will allow you to imagine the rest on your own."

"Thank you. But I'd rather not."

"But—but I do want to point out that each of us in this library, each of us, Philip, would assemble in front to witness the atrocity. We would be required to do so. And some, quite a large percent, would *want* to. Do you know why?"

"Why?"

"A spectacle. Everyone loves a spectacle. And do you know this? The executioners would not want to do this job. Some executioners, that is. They are required to do this job. And so what do we have? We have a spectacle. A spectacle which is at the cost of the victim, and we all participate. Some willingly, some out of curiosity, some out of fear of not participating, but we all do in fact participate. And for this we are all condemned, Philip. Utterly. I speak seriously, Philip. A man who watches, and does nothing, this man is condemned."

"To what?"

"Fill in the blank."

"I don't—I don't know," said Philip.

"Don't know what?"

"Well, if we ourselves would be condemned. Because what could we do?"

"Oh, but we must do something! We are our brother's keeper, Philip. We must take action. Even for the past, what occurred in the past—we are condemned. Yes."

"The *past?*"

Now he grabbed Philip by the shoulders. He sometimes did that.

"Yes. We must rectify the sins of the past—sins of that magnitude, such as the burning at the stake of Joan of Arc. Do you realize? Do you know that?"

"Her?"

"Yes."

"God, I . . . what have you been reading?" It was a mistake. Philip realized it as soon as it shot out of his mouth.

"Come," said Adam Most. "Please come."

The little man directed him to a table loaded down with books. "Torture," he said, "through the ages. Note this book, and this one, and this one as well. Torture. There's always a reason to torture, Philip, and each age has its reasons. Perhaps it's to dissuade others from regicide. Perhaps it's to terrorize a population. Perhaps it's for payback. Perhaps it's for the sheer deviltry. Some, you see—"

"I've got to go. I must, you see—"

Adam Most grabbed up a book. "Here, Philip, is a book you must read. You must read it."

"I will."

"Note the title."

He did. *Torture 101—A Thorough Analysis.* But he had to go now. He had to research a magazine on sailboating. He had to find out everything he could—skim several issues, look at the masthead, know some names, know the magazine's target audience, circulation, layout, graphics design, logo, and so forth.

He loaded Philip down with three torture books.

"Well," said Philip, "I guess I really need to—"

"See, you can't help but dig in pretty deep. Did you know that they used pincers to pull away flesh from the chest and thighs? And then poured in molten lead? Did you know that?"

"No," he said. "No I didn't." He did not want to know this.

"This has to be rectified," said Adam Most. "We can't let this ride."

"Really? What the hell, what the hell can you do—now?"

"Frightful, isn't it? How anyone, and I mean anyone, could take such pain? But they did—they did take that pain, Philip."

"God," said Philip.

"You bet, God," said Adam Most. "They did it in the name of God, some of them. Many of them."

"I know," said Philip. "I know that."

"Nothing we can do about it," said Adam. "It's too late. But still, we must—we must try. We must somehow." He waved a jittery hand at his stack of books. "I've got a lot more to read. I've just started. God, there is so much to read!"

"Good luck."

Philip turned and headed, or rather he flashed, to the magazine area. Lucky for him, they did carry the sailboating magazine. He'd checked a few days earlier, but didn't bother to do research until today.

Notes—notes were important. Write down key things on notecards, organize them, memorize, and practice.

He took notes quickly on the masthead. He skimmed articles.

He closed his eyes. *Get a picture. Get a picture of this thing in your mind.*

Okay. Got it.

Nine o'clock. Or almost.

He was about to exit—but then he realized: the three torture books he was sporting under one arm. Yes, he must check them out. He went to circulation. He dodged Adam Most somehow. He got them in his leather satchel.

He was soon on the street.

A shout.

"Hey! Hey, Phil!"

"What?"

He looked about.

"Are you going to ignore me?"

He spun around. Oh, my. Dick Hazzard.

"I yelled at you from across the street. You deaf? Or what?"

"No."

"What then? Your head on *crack*? Look, I need something. I need to borrow a little—if you don't mind."

"Borrow?"

"I'm broke. I need twenty. I can pay it back—in a week, maybe."

"What're you living on?"

He looked thinner to Philip. Dick Hazzard was thin, always thin, but his face looked hollowed-out. He looked sick. His eye sockets looked grayish green. It was that axe blade of a face he had that any hollowing-out made him look real bad. Once when he'd had the flu he looked on the verge of death. Dick Hazzard had once told him: *My gene group, man, we don't last long. So get what you can when you can. Right? Isn't that right?*

"Not much." Dick said.

"And you want to borrow twenty for what—for food?" He wanted to say *medicine*.

They'd moved up against a building, out of the way of passersby—and the cold wind.

Dick was kicking the snow. "Goddamn it, I hate this snow. When's winter going to be over, anyway?"

"I don't have much in the way of money myself," said Philip. "That's why I ask—"

"Goddamn it, I've got to have her, Phil. I'm about to lose her. I can feel it in my bones. She wants to throw a party. I need to buy some beer, chips—you know."

"Don't call me Phil. Would you please not?" He'd told Dick Hazzard this plenty of times, but it seemed to make so little difference. "It's *Philip*. You know that."

"Yeah—sorry. Okay? You know what?"

"What?"

"This girl I'm living with—Lisa Wing? Her uncle's funeral is today. How about that? She didn't like the man—hated him, as a matter of fact. And he's not really her uncle, anyway. But the thing is, she's roped me into going."

He didn't know the girl at all, and he was supposed to worry about this dead uncle, who wasn't even her uncle?

"Well," Philip said. "That's rough, huh?"

He was making out a check for twenty bucks. Now his life was down to a couple days, unless something changed fast. But he owed Dick Hazzard one, and they both knew it.

"Yeah, because if I don't, she's moving out on me. Says it's a matter of moral support. Pretty silly, isn't it? But you know women. Right over there—see that church?"

Philip looked across the street. It was an old red brick Methodist church. "Yes, I see it."

"That's where the funeral is, in a half hour. Want to come?"

Philip caught Dick's grin. "What? Are you serious?"

"What're you doing that's so important?"

"I'm not going to some funeral. Of somebody I don't even know! Hell!"

"You're dressed like it."

"I've got a job interview. Okay? Three of them."

"Come on. It won't take that long."

Dick's typical pushiness. Over practically anything. Everything. Philip had realized the importance of being assertive around Dick Hazzard—a control freak. Still, he liked him in spite of it all. He was hard not to like. He handed him the check for twenty.

Dick pocketed it without a word.

"Like I said, I've got a job interview."

"When?"

"In a few hours."

"*When?*"

"One o'clock."

"Hell, that's three hours—four. The funeral won't last more than thirty minutes. Come on."

"No! Are you out of your goddamn gourd? I'm not going to that funeral."

"Thirty minutes tops, Philip. Come on."

"How do you know?"

"I pinned her down. Thirty minutes tops. That's straight from her."

"How does she know?"

"That chick knows everything. Take it from me."

Philip shook his head. "No."

"Come *on*."

"No."

"Come *on*."

"And then you'd have to go up to the coffin afterwards, wouldn't you?"

"Not necessarily."

"Well, I'm not doing that!"

"Look, Philip, just do it for me, won't you?"

"No . . ."

"Look, she'll sit there and cry and all that, and it'll be embarrassing."

"What? I thought you said she didn't like the man."

"You know women. She'll cry anyway. I mean funerals—they bring out the worst, you know."

"Hell, no."

"Moral support, Phil. Moral support."

Philip observed the church. People were entering.

"Damn it, Dick."

"Please, goddamn it. I'm begging," said Dick. "You want me to *beg*? Jeez."

"No damn way."

"I did punch that guy out for you," said Dick, grabbing his arm.

"I just gave you twenty, and I can't afford it. I'm about to starve."

"Got three good ones in. Saved your ass, didn't I?"

"Yeah, yeah."

"Hey, there she is. Lisa Wing, my sweet love. A real looker, isn't she? Look at that. Really, take a good look. Man, I can't even believe—"

Dick Hazzard's standard line. He was always saying *I can't even believe*.

But she was a looker all right. Philip wanted to sit so that she was between the two of them. My god, she was a looker.

3

"**Y**ou didn't have to dress up so much," said Lisa Wing.

"A job interview. Believe me, I don't always—"

"And you're *here*? Ha!" She laughed. There was a giggly quality to her laugh he went for. It spoke of reserves of something. But he wasn't sure what they were.

The Methodist Church was sparsely populated with funeral attendees. Apparently this uncle person wasn't all that loved by anyone. How many? Fifteen? Twenty?

They sat toward the back.

Lisa Wing sat between him and Dick Hazzard. Ah! She seemed in a bright mood. She was fluttery like a bird. Spirited. He imagined her flitting about the church, gliding in for a landing.

He pumped her for information.

Her uncle, or non-uncle, was named Barnhart Bigfoot. What the hell kind of name was that?

"Maybe that's why I didn't particularly like that man," said Lisa Wing. "I mean, first off he wasn't even my *real* uncle, and second off, that name. I mean, *damn*."

Second off? "Yes," he said, "That's an odd one." And meanwhile his eyes roamed her. What gorgeous blond hair. What bright white teeth. What sensual lips, coated with pinkish purple. In the corner of her lips, on one side, it was too thick. He wanted to take his finger and gently wipe it off. Or lick it off. Yes, he did want to lick it off. She made him think of a lollipop.

"The thing is, it was more than the name, really. It was. He was *so* . . . abrupt. Rude, rude, rude. You say something . . . okay? And right off, he's on it like a sledgehammer or something."

Philip worried that others would hear. After all, the man *was* dead. Up there in that brown, polished casket. The man's remains. Though Philip didn't go for the word *remains*. It made you think of loose parts, an arm, a leg, a skull. Was the spirit of Barnhart Bigfoot hovering over the coffin?

It struck him that he might be eyeing the two of them, him and

Lisa Wing. He might be fixing his eyes right on them. But then, what eyes?

"I might have liked him," said Lisa, moving closer to him and whispering in his ear. He felt a wetness.

"Oh, yes," he said.

"I might have." Another whisper in his ear, breathy, wet: "But I didn't much care for the way he *presented* himself. You *know*? You know what I mean?"

"I *do*," he said. His eyes were on that casket, and above it, but the rest of him was feeling Lisa Wing in his blood, bones, and sinews.

"Oh, god," Lisa Wing said. "Oh, god." She slumped back in the pew.

He felt her body tight against his. He imagined her suddenly getting on his lap, wiggling her bottom against him.

Dick Hazzard leaned forward, turning toward the two of them, and said, too loudly, "Well, this thing won't last all that long. Hour at the top, man."

"What?" said Philip. "I thought you said—"

Dick laughed. "Hell, it's not like I'm in charge of the thing!"

You *bastard*, Philip thought.

"I hope it doesn't take that long," said Lisa Wing. "I've got stuff to do."

"What?" said Philip.

"Oh, gosh—lots! We're having a party tonight, for one." She dug into her purse.

A man and a woman arrived and took the pew directly in front of them. The man was dressed in a gray suit, the woman in blue. She was sporting a shiny patent leather purse.

Lisa gestured at them with sleek fingers. And stuck her tongue out.

"We're throwing a hell of a party, aren't we, babe?"

She stuck a finger against her lips, and shushed him. "*Yes.*"

More people were filing in. An old man was working his way up the aisle on a walker. A woman was behind him, moving step by step. She placed a hand on the man's slumping shoulder.

The old man huffed by their pew. He was hooked up with oxygen.

"God, how'd you like to be that fucking *old*?" whispered Dick Hazzard.

"Will you shut up, stupid?" whispered Lisa Wing. She giggled.

The man in the gray suit turned slightly around. And then the woman in blue whispered something in his ear as she too turned slightly around.

The service began.

The minister spoke of Barnhart Bigfoot's great contribution to his family, his church, his community. He spoke of how Bigfoot's greatest contribution was the contribution of love—unconditional love. "He never, ever, gave expecting the slightest return."

"What the hell?" Lisa Wing whispered to him, too loudly, her mouth squarely in his ear. He felt a spray, an incipient tongue, and he felt compelled to turn squarely back at her, kiss her cheek, touch her, and take her right there. It wasn't something he or any man, he told himself, could not help but want. Regardless of where they were.

He turned to her. "What the—"

"Hell. That's right." She again turned and whispered, but this time not squarely against his ear. "The way he treated me." Her voice was way too loud.

The woman in blue turned around and said, "Please. Have some respect. Would you? Please be still."

"Well, I'm just sorry," said Lisa Wing. "I'm just *real* fucking sorry!"

The woman gave her an acerbic look, glanced over at Dick Hazzard, and then at Philip. She swung back around.

She leaned over and whispered at the man in gray.

"Bitch," said Lisa Wing.

The woman turned just slightly.

Lisa Wing laughed.

The minister said, "And now let us pray."

Soon, the family was filing up front to view the casket.

"Not me," said Lisa Wing. "I saw that man enough."

The woman in blue turned around and faced her squarely. "You should have respect for the dead. *Whatever* your feelings. One of these days you'll be old, and then dead. You think about that."

"Depends on the dead," said Lisa Wing. "Doesn't it now?"

She got up and Dick Hazzard stood up. The three of them filed out of the church.

"You hear what that bitch said to me?" said Lisa Wing.

Philip's eyes ran over her. He didn't want her to use bad language. She was too soft, sensuous. Oily. Was oily the right word? No. Indeed not. Wet. He thought of her tongue in his ear.

"Yeah, I heard," said Dick Hazzard. "But you had it coming. Ha! Didn't you, babe?"

"You think I had it coming, do you?" she said to Dick. She turned to Philip. "You think I had it coming?"

"No. No, no I don't." But he did. He thought it was terrible. The poor sap, no matter what his name, was up there in that casket. He didn't like that word. Coffin? He didn't like that word either. But anyway, what would that be like? Boxed up like that. And then they'd be lowering you down and closing the lid—forever. God, how horrible.

Lisa Wing smiled. She placed a hand on his wrist. Squeezed it. "You coming to my party?"

"Huh? Yes."

"Here's where it is," she said. And she took out her cell phone. "Address and number. Okay?" She winked.

"Yes. Sure."

He took a minute. He loaded it on his own.

God, that wink.

4

He hurried along. He had a couple of hours left to make his appointment at that sailboat magazine. He practiced to himself as he walked. He tried out questions, answers. He imagined gestures. How he would sit, feet firmly on the floor, shoulders straight—hands in lap. Or if the chair had an arm? Hands on arms? No that might look like he was nervous, clutching the arm rests for support, or strapped down for the electric chair.

His father had said: *Everything's in the posture, son. You can read a man right off based on his posture. Never forget that.*

Philip saw the tall building up the block. Twenty-first floor. *Don't show up early.* He said it out loud: "Don't show up early because then you look too interested. Makes you look needy. Don't do it."

Good thing he had his rubber boots on. His suit pants were slightly wet, but they'd dry out—eventually. He entered a coffee shop. It was only a few blocks away, and he could kill an hour or more here. He got coffee at the counter.

He sat down, pulled off his boots. Let the pants dry.

An elderly woman with a small white dog motioned at him.

"Yes?"

"How are you, young man?"

"Good." He hated to be talked at by some person he didn't even know. And he could tell: she'd be a talker.

"Now, then," said the elderly woman, "my name is Lucy Lucky. I know—that's a silly name. But that's my name."

"It's not silly," he said. It was a silly name all right, bound to spark laughter, but he was quick to say nice things to old people even if it meant lying.

"Of course it's silly. But what's your name?"

She was eating a huge pickle. She took a quick bite, a rather large one. Pickle juice dribbled down her chin. She took a napkin and carefully wiped herself dry.

"Philip Fellows."

"Oh, what a nice name! A very nice name. So many people would surely give their eyeteeth for a nice name like that. What do you do, Mr. Fellows?"

"Nothing. I'm looking for a job." He looked down at his coffee. Body language: *I'm not interested. No further conversation, please.*

"Doing what?"

He raised his coffee cup to his lips. He tried to be evasive, hard to hear. "Something that pays." When she studied him, he went on: "I've got an interview soon." And then he looked up at the clock.

"I see you noticing the time. When is that appointment, Mr. Fellows?"

"Soon."

"When?"

"About an hour." He thought, should have said *fifteen minutes.*

"Hour! Well, then, you need to be on your way. You should be early. Early bird, you know."

The small white dog was squirming in her lap. Suddenly it bared its teeth at him. It growled, snarled, snapped.

"Don't mind my Elmer," she said. She stuck her face up to the dog. "You straighten up. And I mean *now.*" The dog whimpered. "What job?"

"Job? Um . . . working for a magazine staff."

He sipped his coffee. One minute. He'd put up with this twenty questions another minute, and then he was out of here.

"Well, well, a magazine staff! Well. Editor, I'll bet—the way you're so nicely dressed."

"No. I'm afraid not."

He took a gulp of coffee. It was too large, and he burnt his tongue.

"What's the matter?"

"Hot."

"Well, I'll say! You know, sir, I am an inveterate coffee drinker. I must drink—why I'll bet I drink thirty to forty cups of coffee a day. My blood pressure is, of course, over the top. I'm a walking time bomb. Really, I am. Aren't I, Elmer?" She rubbed the dog's back and then nestled close to him. "He's my only pal, Mr. Fellows. When he goes . . . well, sir . . ."

He was struck by this. "That's good that . . . I mean—"

"Are you as bad in your coffee drinking as I?" She smiled, but there was a mischievous gleam in it. Her eyes had a golden glint to them. Her lips seemed too tight for her mouth.

"Well, I suppose."

"Well, don't be. As you get older, things change. There is that tendency to overdo, and that tendency to overdo puts a strain on things. Poor Elmer, he's afraid I'll fall flat on my face when I'm carrying him. Aren't you, Elmer?"

The dog whined a little. But then the old lady was pinching his neck—rather hard, Philip thought.

He looked again at the clock. It struck him that he must plan his time carefully, not get too loose. He must allow enough time for the walk, for finding the elevator, taking the elevator—and perhaps even the restroom for a quick brush down. A checking over of oneself in the mirror. A final touch kind of thing. But right now, he must get shut of this woman. Find another coffee shop—soon!

He stood. "I must go."

"Yes, you must—you absolutely must. Always be early. Never be late."

"Yes, ma'am."

"But I don't think you'll get it," she said. "I'm sorry to say that, but I just don't feel it in these old bones, Mr. Fellows."

"You what?"

He had been about to step toward the door, but that remark of hers had stopped him cold.

She smiled. Her lips looked dry. Her golden eyes seemed to bathe her face in a warm light. But it wasn't a light he could somehow trust.

"You've got to know yourself, Mr. Fellows. That's very important in this life. Do you know yourself?"

"Sure. Of course I do."

"Do you now? I'll bet you don't." Those eyes, and those lips that looked dry like paper. He imagined them peeling and falling off.

"You don't know a thing about me," he said. "What the hell?" He started to sit down. He felt defeated and weak.

"No reason to curse."

"Why not? You don't know a *thing* about me." He did sit down.

"Oh, I think I do. I do think I do, young man. Because, you see, I'm a psychic. I have been for years. And something told me to speak to you. As soon as I felt your aura—something impressed me. I felt the need to exchange energy with you, young man, and to try to get locked in on what was happening. And I'm sorry, but please, don't even go to that interview. It's not right for you—I can't say why, but I can only tell you it's not right."

He stared her down. "Why'd you say *editor*?"

"Oh, I knew you weren't going for editor, young man. I'm not totally silly, even at my age. It was a talking point. It gave me time. Time is what we all need. Time to get to know ourselves and others. Don't go to the interview. It won't be worth it. It won't be good. No, no, young man. It will not be good."

"Oh? Not good in what way?"

"Listen to me, or don't," she said. And then she turned to her dog. "Elmer, Elmer, they listen or they don't. Isn't that right?"

He rose, carried out his coffee, and bolted for the door.

Loony bin! Loony, crazy, wacky!

He found another coffee shop and doused himself but good.

5

Jeremy Buddrick was perhaps two or three years older than Philip, and here he was fully employed. A Human Resources man—long chin, long arms. Dressed in a blue suit with a maroon tie. When he rose from his desk, he had a half grin like he'd discovered something salacious, but he was holding back on it.

How much was this Buddrick pulling down?

"A monthly magazine for sailboat enthusiasts, Mr. Fellows. How does that work for you?"

"Sounds good."

"Do you mean that?"

"Yes, I do." God, compromise yourself—sure, go ahead.

"There are others, of course. What made you choose *Sail Away* magazine? What particularly appealed to you?"

Nothing. He hadn't been stirred up in the least. Well, maybe the cover of the last issue he'd scanned, that sailboat out on the blue water, its gentle lift as though it were about to cruise its way to the Great Beyond, that man and that curvaceous tanned woman . . . okay—perhaps that. He said, "Well, the look of it, for starters. I like the look of it. The presentation values."

"Presentation values."

"Yes. Isn't that what you call them?"

Buddrick eyed him. "I suppose you may if you want."

Philip hesitated. "I just mean that I like them."

"Well, it is true that the Art Department does have great presentation values. What else?"

"Uh. Well . . . the features. Very good features."

"Name one." Buddrick leaned back and worked a pencil against his upper lip. Then he stuck it in a pencil sharpener, and it made a loud grinding noise.

Notes—damn it, they were in his coat pocket in a small composition book. His mind had gone utterly blank. He hemmed, hawed, finally recalled. "The one about sailing after dark. Very interesting. That was, you know—pretty interesting."

"Uh-huh—and what was so interesting about it?"

Damn. He hemmed, hawed. And then finally: "Interesting? Well, the setting . . . principally."

"The dark?"

"Yes. And the water."

"Uh-huh. Are you a sailor, Philip?"

"No."

"You've never sailed a craft, have you?"

"No."

"Are you a reader on the subject, generally speaking?"

"No . . . not generally speaking. But . . . on occasion."

A lie. A vile lie.

"Then I don't get it. I really don't get it, Philip. Why in the world would you want to hook up with a magazine which specializes in something you have absolutely no experience with, or any demonstrated interest in—which you've read hardly a thing about?" He sat forward quickly. He looked upset. His eyebrows twitched.

Philip gathered his forces. He must rally. He must not take the duck head. "I majored in English, and I'd like to write for a magazine."

"Any magazine? Or *certain* magazines?"

"This magazine."

"Why?"

"Well. The magazine is quite professional looking. And—"

"Don't bullshit me, Philip. You don't know a thing about it."

He said nothing. A sudden weakness came over him. His hands seemed to dangle before him. Where to put them?

"And besides, you won't be *writing* anyway. You'll be doing all kinds of let's call them miscellaneous tasks." Buddrick waited as though dropping a pebble into a well and listening for its sound. "Are you a multitasker?"

"Multi . . . . Yes—yes I am."

"Example."

"Example?"

"That's what I asked for, Philip."

He searched his mind. Buddrick was staring at him. That half grin was working on his lips.

"I'm sorry—I can't think—I just can't—"

"Oh, surely," said Buddrick. "Surely. Come on, *everyone* has multitasked. But I need one, just one, example. Surely you can give me one example."

"I think I can. Sure. I think I will be able to."

"Then do so."

"I will." Philip searched. It was hard to think with Buddrick waiting on him, staring at him. "Well, I do it all the time actually. But just thinking of an example—that's kind of hard to do. One that might mean something here. I mean, okay—an ordinary example: I make toast while I'm writing an email. Or I make coffee while I'm making toast. I used to work on a paper in the middle of talking to my girlfriend."

"Yeah. Sure. Not all that applicable, is it? To an office situation."

"No. No, but you asked—"

"On the job, Philip. Multitasking on the job."

"Well, I carried a box of donuts on the way to picking up a file of some sort."

"Donuts? You carried donuts?"

"Yes."

"Don't women usually do that?"

"It wasn't all the time. It was just for a while."

"You wouldn't be carrying a box of donuts here, I can assure you."

"That's good."

"You didn't much care for it, I assume."

"It was okay."

"You wouldn't be making coffee either."

"Good. I really don't care for that."

"What you *would* do, *must* do, is be a team player. This is one thing that is extremely important at *Sail Away*. Being a team member. Are you a team member, Philip?"

"Team? Yes. I am. Definitely."

"Example."

God, *again*? "Well . . . I get along well with my co-workers. I don't make trouble."

"What co-workers? Where?"

"The last place I worked."

Buddrick held the application up and scrutinized it. "At Homey Seven?"

"Yes."

"Waiter."

"Yes."

Buddrick pulled out a sheet of paper which Philip recognized as his boss's highly favorable recommendation, though they hadn't gotten along all that well. His boss had said, "I don't screw a man over, Philip, just because he doesn't work out here. I'm just not that way." His boss had extended his hand for a shake, a warm one. Tears had sprung to Philip's eyes. God, it was embarrassing.

"Are you a conformist, Philip?"

"Huh? No."

"Is that right? Well, now, where do you draw the line between non-conformity and outright rebellion? Or *do* you draw the line?"

"No—oh, yes. Of course I do."

"Where?"

"Where? Well, I wouldn't follow just *any* instruction. Not just anything."

"You wouldn't? What wouldn't you follow? Let's think of your job here at *Sail Away*, assuming you worked here. What might be a command you *wouldn't* follow—a direct command from your superior. Example, please."

"I—I don't know. That's awfully hypothetical. I really can't say."

"Can't you? Use your imagination, Philip. Let's say you were told to write a story that went against your general moral principles."

"I thought I wouldn't be writing."

"Hypothetical, Philip." Buddrick toyed with his sharpened pencil.

"Well, then, I wouldn't go along with it—if it did that. Go against my moral principles. But what kind of assignment might that be?"

"I have no idea. Do you?"

"No."

"But you're telling me you wouldn't follow along. You would disobey your boss."

"Not normally. Just under the condition you spoke of."

"I see. Let us hope such a condition doesn't arise. Are you always so pious, Philip? Or do you see yourself as one who goes with the flow?"

"It depends."

"On what?"

"What the flow is."

"Ah! That's good to know." Buddrick fixed his eyes on him.

Philip searched for something else to say.

"I think I'd like it here," he said. He was thinking the very opposite.

"Nice."

Buddrick jabbed his sharpened pencil against the phone carriage.

"Well," said Philip after a moment.

"Deep subject," said Buddrick.

He hated that expression. It angered him, and he stood up. He hadn't planned on it, and he had no idea where he was going.

"Finished?" said Buddrick.

"Yes."

"Good. You have the job." Buddrick settled back in his swivel chair and grinned at him.

"What? I do?"

"*Certainement.* You're the kind of man we're looking for here at *Sail Away.*" Buddrick rose and extended his hand.

"Thank you!" Philip shook his hand. It was a dry, lifeless shake.

"You may well be wondering what kind of man that is."

"Uh—"

"Don't wonder. Now, Philip, I have your email address, and I will be sending you some employment papers, and so forth, plus we will run a background check. If all works out, if there's nothing dark in your past—any ghosts, sir, that is—you're on the team."

"Thanks." Philip felt his heart grow glad. "Thank you."

"It's a good team to be on," said Buddrick. "This is a company with advancement potential. You can rise in the ranks here—if you know what's what."

"Great!" He started to, but he didn't, ask for clarification of *what's what*.

"Be here next Monday. That's your start date. All should clear by then."

"Thanks."

"Welcome aboard. *Bienvenue.*"

Again the hand. Buddrick's grip was flabby. But it was unlikely there'd be more handshakes. The job would turn in other directions. As he made his way out of Buddrick's office, he glanced at the many cubicles, and he shuddered.

6

He exited the building. He could have and probably should have asked, *When do I get paid?* But then maybe that would come off as too inquisitive about money matters. It would lack professionalism, possibly. Yes, and how could you maintain an air of professionalism at *Sail Away* if on the very day you were hired, you asked about money and hadn't done a lick of work?

Still . . . my god, why hadn't he?

What a fool you are!

You should go back.

But he didn't.

Back to the library. His second job appointment was in an hour or so. Even though he'd been offered a job at the sailing magazine, he must, of a certainty, apply for the job as a research assistant in the Department of Panegyrics. He had never heard of such a department, but he knew the word referred to elaborate praise. How a whole university department could be centered on elaborate praise he couldn't quite imagine. And yet wouldn't working in such a department be better than being a general office boy at *Sail Away*? A gofer? He must, of course, try for it.

He looked about, got on a machine, spotted some books. He hurried to the stacks. No time for Adam Most. No time at all for that little weasel. Not twice in one day. He found what he wanted, a book by Bill Brightly: *Giving Praise.* He skimmed some of it, took a few notes.

And then a hand on his shoulder, resting, then gripping, a familiar one, as he was peering further into the stacks searching for something on paeans, eulogies, tributes. Please. God, no.

"Philip. God bless, I'm sure glad to see you."

He knew that voice. He'd know that voice *anywhere.*

He turned to face Adam Most. "Oh . . . hello."

"It's been a tough day, Philip. I'd like to share with you what's made it so tough—really intolerably tough. Would you listen?

Could you find it in you to listen?"

Adam Most called upon one's empathetic nature—one could not, if he had a bone of fellow feeling in him, resist the entreaty to take note. To bend one's ear. But there were limits. There had to be limits, didn't there?

"Well, Adam, I really don't have a lot of time. I have a job interview in about . . . an hour." Philip consulted his watch. Yes, that was correct, and so he wasn't lying. Besides, he wanted to finish up quickly here and have a little something in a coffee shop. It was a downtown campus, so he could manage the time thing, he thought.

"That'll do. Here it is, Philip. Please, please sit down. Please do." He pointed to a table nearby with four chairs.

"Torture?" asked Philip.

"It might as well be." Adam Most scooted a chair toward him. A heavy oak chair that rubbed and squeaked on the hardwood floor. Right near the stacks, in the way of traffic.

Philip sat down.

"Now, then, listen. Are you listening?"

"Yes."

"I told you about the torture."

"Yes. You did. Dear God. "

"Well, that *was* terrible—I know. But this . . . this is also terrible, Philip. It's simply awful."

"Yes. But please, no more of that."

"No. That was sufficient. Except I've got in mind a few more books on torture I do want you to read—but that can wait. This is terrible, but in a different, an altogether different way. It has to do with the soul. After reading what I've been reading, Philip— skimming six whole books in the last few hours!—I don't think we have a soul. I am seriously troubled to have to say this, but where's the proof that we do? I am convinced, Philip, even as I say this, and even as I am thinking what I'm about to say, that I don't have a soul. I am *nothing*, Philip. *Nothing*. Figure it out. How *could* I be something if I have no soul? Isn't that preposterous to believe that I *am* something? How could I be? There's no way. There's absolutely no way, Philip."

The little weasel was bent toward him, his hands gyrating about. It was the dancing monkey in him fully springing forth.

"Yes, there *is*," said Philip. "Look, we have a soul. I know we do."

"Who's the *we*?"

"What? You. Me. That's who."

"What do you *mean* by those things," said Adam Most. "*Me*? What's that mean? How am I, this creature with flesh, blood, and bones, a *me*?"

"You're a me," said Philip. "Count on it."

"I can't count on that," said Adam. "That's the problem. I'm a thing, and that's all. I'm like that chair you're sitting in."

"No—no, goddamn it, you're *not*." God, he'd gotten so tired of hearing that from about three dogmatic professors who dwelt insanely on it.

"Yes, I am," said Adam softly.

"There!" said Philip. "You just said *I*."

Adam Most smiled—knowingly. He had settled back, and he had laid both hands out on the table top.

"You could bleed me out, bit by bit, like a stuck pig, Philip, until there *wasn't* a *me*. There's your *me*."

"So, the me is in the blood?"

"No, it's in the brain."

"Then the bleeding—"

"Does the brain work without blood?"

"No. But damn it, I've heard it. I've heard it all before. And I don't want to hear it. Not anymore."

"Meat," said Adam. "We're meat. Meat, blood—with complex electrical circuitry. Isn't that awful. That's all we are, Philip. Meat and blood. Well, bones too."

"I don't want to talk about this," said Philip. "I've got to run. I really do."

"What's the rush, Philip, given what I've just told you? I don't see a reason for going on, Philip. Really, I don't."

The man looked slack-jawed. Philip imagined him mounting a chair, fixing a rope to the ceiling, and kicking the chair away. Hanging. Strangling.

Here was a man who was stifled by intellectual thought. Books were a danger to him.

Oh, god, *what if?*

"You've surely encountered stuff like that before, haven't you?" said Philip, trying to sound soothing, sympathetic.

"Yeah, maybe. But this book"—Adam held up a book with a glossy cover—"this book, brand new, Philip, it comes right at it. It makes you realize. It makes you think. What the hell am I? Why go on? Why take another step?"

"Animals," said Philip. "They go on."

"Yeah. You want to be an animal, Philip?"

"No. But they do go on. They look happy, don't they? Take a look at a dog, a cat, a rabbit—"

"Me? I feel such despair—maybe it's just me, but it makes me feel real despair."

"Hey," said Philip, whacking him on the shoulder. "How about going out for some coffee? I'm buying."

"Coffee."

"Yes."

"Yeah, well, I guess. I guess I could."

He left for a coffee shop, Adam Most in tow. He'd make that appointment. Yes, somehow.

7

Adam Most was back at it.

"The idea that I'm just meat—*meat*—that's what gets me. Meat. And ever since I read that stuff—"

"How much of that book have you read?"

"A good thirty pages, and I skimmed five others too. And for the last few hours I've been looking at everybody and thinking, 'You're meat. That's all you are. Meat sitting down, meat walking around, meat looking at other meat. Meat eating meat. Meat.' I mean, goddamn it, who wants to be meat?"

"You shouldn't think like that," said Philip. "It's not healthy."

"Maybe not. But it's true."

"Did you think it was true before you read those books?"

"No. Maybe."

"Which?"

"Try no."

"But now everything's suddenly changed?"

"Yes, everything is changed. Death, for instance."

"What about it?"

"Death."

"Maybe you should get off that subject," said Philip. "I've got an interview, and I need to practice. I can't just go in there cold, you know."

"Where is it? Who's it with?"

"The Department of Panegyrics at the university."

"Department of what?"

"Panegyrics. You know—praise—"

"I know what it means."

"I don't know a thing about panegyrics."

"Who does? I haven't read anything about it at all. I will, though. I'll read some stuff tomorrow. Oh, god."

"What?"

"Praise coming out of a meat machine."

"Will you quit it?"

Adam seemed to shrivel up. He was malnourished. Malnourished meat? There was something about him—Philip couldn't say exactly what.

"Maybe I ought to go back to the library."

"If you wish. You're not going to read more of that same stuff, are you?"

"No—panegyrics. I want to read all about it."

"Why? What do you hope to gain?"

"I can speak more authoritatively on the subject."

"But with whom?"

"You."

"I may not even get the job, Adam. Maybe I'll never have another thing to do with panegyrics. So wouldn't you be wasting your time?"

"I want a nap or something."

"You look sick."

"I *am* sick. I got up early, about four. I couldn't sleep. I read a bunch of stuff. I can't even remember what it was now. Oh, wait a minute. It was about race cars. I don't know why I read about race cars. I had some magazines the library was dumping, and I started reading about race cars. I could probably hold a conversation with some race car fan. But I'd have to get some sleep first."

"Don't kill yourself."

"Look out there." Adam pointed outside.

He did.

It was that same man he'd seen this morning outside his apartment. The man in the black topcoat.

"Who is that?"

"I don't know."

Another man came into the frame. He looked oddly like the first man—they could be twins. Suddenly they both left.

"They looked kind of dangerous," said Adam.

"I don't know who they are. It must be some mistake."

"They were staring fixedly at you."

Fixedly?

"I don't have the slightest," said Philip.

"Maybe they're FBI or CIA."

"I don't know why they'd want me. Besides, if they want me, why not come in and speak?"

"Maybe." Adam Most stood up. "I've got to go."

"See you."

"I feel better now," he said.

"That's good."

In five minutes, Philip left the coffee shop and looked both ways up and down the sidewalk. The two men were nowhere to be seen. The one was certainly the one he'd seen back at the apartment. The other his double. How could he go back to the apartment? Wouldn't that be dangerous?

8

His cell phone rang.

Woman's voice. Strident, raspy. He didn't catch the first words. But then she went on: "Oh, god, oh god, what am I going to do? What? Are you done? Are you coming home *finally*—finally coming home? You better be. You had *better* be coming home. Now. And I do mean *now*. Not ten minutes, fifteen, thirty, an hour, two hours—god, four hours, six. I'm tired of it. I'm just so . . . so tired of it! You know that? You probably don't know that, do you?"

"Who *is* this?"

"*What?* Who is *this*? You're not Duane. Where is Duane? Is he off spinning his wheels somewhere?   He gives you the phone? I can't believe it. He gives *you* the phone."

"You have the wrong number.   I'm sorry—but you have the wrong number."

He started to end the call, but he didn't want to be discourteous.

"So you don't even know Duane?"

"No."

"Well, I'm sorry. I'm really sorry. I can't believe. I just can't believe—okay, I'll go then. I'll call him back. If I can get the right number . . . I feel so bad."

"It's okay. Don't be embarrassed."

"I didn't mean *that*."

"Oh, because—"

"Of him, yes. I guess I shouldn't be talking to you about him, but now that I am, and have, well, all I can say is that he is one first rate bastard! What's your name?"

He started to say it, but then didn't. "I've got to go," he said. "I'm sorry, but I've really got to go now."

"Well, I don't blame you, but please, just please, let me ask you something. Would you, please, just let me?"

"Well. Okay. What?"

"Let's say *you* had a Duane in your life, a Duane-ess, we'll say,

45

what would you do?"

"I don't know Duane," said Philip. "At all. So really how can I answer a question like that?"

"Give me a minute, okay?"

"All right."

"Let me explain. Is that okay with you? Is it?"

"Yes."

"Okay. Here's Duane. Here's Duane on a daily basis. Here's Duane pulling me down in every which way:

"Number one: Duane coming home drunk.

"Number two: Duane gambling his entire paycheck away.

"Number three: Duane and his bevy of girlfriends.

"You there?"

"Yes."

"Well, do you have anything to say? Come on, you gotta have something to say. I'm tired of people just saying, 'Yeah, that's too bad. But that's life, babe. Maybe you should dump good old Duane.' Like I'm not smart enough to figure that out on my own!"

"I'm sorry," said Philip, "but really, I can't help you. And I've got an appointment. I've got to go. Really, I must." Because he thought: There *are* limits, aren't there? You have to know there are limits.

"Sure. That's fine. I understand. But thanks for listening."

"A pleasure," said Philip. He'd started using that particular expression, probably because of his recent job searches. Sometimes, employers would say that when he thanked them for a nice business lunch, as they called it—when he got one. *My pleasure*, and a business smile. It had a professional ring to it. But really he didn't like to say it. It made him feel like a fraud. And yet he had. He'd just said it.

"It was?"

"Yes. But I *must* go."

"You seem so nice. You listen to people. That's a good trait in a person."

"Thanks."

"I mean it. I don't say a thing like that unless I mean it."

"Thanks."

"Listen, my name is Charlotte Sanders. Why don't you stop by and see me?"

He drew a breath. "Stop by?"

"Sure. Why don't you stop by? That'd be nice. Sweet."

"I don't—know. Why would I do that?"

"Why *wouldn't* you do that?"

"I don't know you," said Philip. "At all."

"When did that stop a man? But go if you wish. My address is 405 Carleton. South city. I'm really a lot better than I sound. I was just so angry, so really angry with Duane. I'm nice, very nice, when I'm not angry."

Her voice was now plaintive, sweet, breathy if raspy. It reminded him, in a way, of Lisa's wet tongue in his ear. He began to feel weak, jittery.

"You are?"

"I am. I don't bite. Really."

"What about Duane?"

"Oh, don't even mention him. I'm locking him out. I mean it!"

He imagined fists banging on the door, broken windows, neighbors, the police.

"I'd better go," he said.

"I don't beg," she said. "It'd be up to you."

"Okay."

"I'm nice looking. I'm very pretty, I've got a nice figure, and I don't cuss. Except sometimes."

"I really—I can't talk any longer."

Silence.

And then: "You know what? I'll bet you'd be no better than Duane!"

And then the phone went dead.

He was right outside The Department of Panegyrics.

47

9

From where they sat you could see the busy street below, with the snarling traffic. Through the window cracked six inches above the roasting hot radiator, he could hear the cacophonous, unruly noise of motors growling, grumbling, racking off, screeches, whining of bad shocks, horns. The office was wall to wall bookshelves, cluttered, double-shelved, with books stacked on the shelves and on the floors.

Here, thought Philip, here is a learned man.

The professor whose desk he was sitting at had a name tag that read Professor Alejohn. His whole desk was cluttered with books and papers.

"The Department of Panegyrics," said Professor Alejohn, "is an unusual department. How many departments of Panegyrics are you familiar with? Think now before you answer."

His small black eyes narrowed in on Philip.

"None. Are there any—others?"

"That's right. None other than this one. We're quite unique. He grinned, revealing a mouthful of bright white teeth. His thick red lips tended to smack as he finished a burst of words. "That's why we're a leading exponent of panegyrics in the country—or should I say in the world? Yes, in the world, unless there are some other unheard of ones, perhaps in developing countries I'm not familiar with, but really I doubt that. Do you know why?"

"No."

"Because the formal study of Panegyrics is a highly cultivated, highly refined science. That's why."

He gave Philip a wink. His large ears twitched.

"Oh," said Philip. He nodded.

"Why Panegyrics? Because an encomium is one form of human communication that is universal and ongoing, but I do want to clarify. *Nota bene*, sir. While the word generally is used to mean published praise, or formal speech, we here at the University have extended the meaning to ordinary, normal praise, one person to another. For that's where most praise is to be found? Wouldn't you say?"

"I guess so."

"And indeed: what would life be without it? What it comes down to, though, is how we structure our praise. This is the discipline. Panegyrics here at the University is a serious discipline—extremely cutting edge."

Unique. Cutting edge. Redundant, wasn't he?

Philip tried to adjust himself in his chair so that he felt comfortable. He had a few things to say, things he'd caught in the library books, things he'd hoped to work in at a convenient spot.

"Any questions—so far?"

"Well . . . yes, possibly." Philip lifted a finger. "It does seem to be a form of address that has . . . a kind of structure."

"Yes, it does. Good." The professor seemed to expect more.

Philip couldn't remember his second point. He searched his memory.

"Good," said the professor. "Well, then, I have a form for you to fill out, a sort of professional baseline we might say." He handed Philip the form attached to a clipboard, with a blue pen dangling from a chain.

Philip scanned it. There were twenty questions.

"Go ahead. Begin."

Professor Alejohn smiled and remained seated, and Philip felt the man's eyes heavy on him as he peered down at the form. He looked up. Yes, the man was still staring at him. There was a look of profound expectation on the professor's part. Philip got the idea that Alejohn suspected at any given point that Philip would take issue with the nature of the questions. And a cursory look at them told him he would. But how could you land a job if you were so quick to quarrel?

He must fill out the form, so he looked more closely. Question #1: "How often on a normal day do you deliver praise?" The choices were: 0 – 5, 6 – 10, 11 or more

How often? How could he possibly know? He'd never *ever*

thought about it. He supposed if you complimented someone for doing something, or praised them for being nice, that would count. But what if you just said *thank you*? He had said a few *Thanks* to that woman Charlotte Sanders, but how about on a daily basis? He marked the 0 – 5 category.

Question #2: "Is your praise usually given for: A. the well-being of another, B. partly for your own well-being plus the well-being of another, C. totally for your own well-being?"

Probably B, which seemed like the safe thing to mark. He wasn't entirely other-directed, nor was he entirely self-directed.

He found himself marking most of the remaining questions in the median position. He didn't see himself as either extreme. If ever asked, he would have to admit: *I am a man who lacks certainty*.

He handed the completed form to the professor.

Professor Alejohn leaned back in his swivel chair, which let out a raucous screech, and held the form up to gaze at it in the sunlight coming through the blinds. He seemed marvelously relaxed. He reminded Philip somehow of his grandfather in his study scrutinizing a business deal. He'd make humming noises, clearings of throat, hacking coughs. But these noises didn't change the fact that he looked quite at ease, and pleasured, by his scrutiny. It was always that way. The man loved peering at forms. He could see that Alejohn was one such man himself.

"You're quite normal," the professor said, as he swiveled around and slid the form on his desk. "There's one question, though, that does bear some discussion."

"Oh," said Philip. "What?" His insides churned.

"You say you praise mostly when you're in a good mood. Then wouldn't you say that the praise you give, generally speaking, *is* about you? Not about the other? At all?"

"Well—maybe. Yes, I guess it is."

"It's a hard truth to swallow, isn't it? Because what, one might ask, would come out of your mouth if you *weren't* in a good mood? Just think of it."

"Yes, I know." Philip shifted in his seat. "I realize that."

"It's always about us, isn't it?"

"Yes. I guess so. Often it is. I suspect it is."

"But that just makes us human, doesn't it?"

"Yes." He suddenly recalled that second item from his research. Perhaps time to share it? "People who stumble in their speech," he said, "may be more concerned about themselves than others."

The professor smiled. "Brill Brightly. Yes—that could be true. Brightly is not one to pull punches, is he?"

"In trying to achieve an image of grandeur, they blow it," said Philip.

"True. That happens. Sometimes. But going on, beyond Brightly—where were we?" The professor's hands were folded before him. He seemed to be in an attitude of prayer. "How do we fashion the right praise in order to fashion the best we can for ourselves? Should we simply lie and say that we love a woman's new hairdo when in fact we loathe it?"

When Philip didn't answer immediately, Professor Alejohn said, "A standard ethical question—no?"

"No—I don't think so," said Philip.

"Or a boob job if we think it's . . . a bit too much?"

"No."

"Why not?"

"Because it would be a lie."

"And?"

"I don't like to lie," said Philip.

"Even so, how do we perfect the lie—if we see the need? How do we offer praise and do it well?"

"I don't know. I suppose—I suppose—"

"Of course you don't, but then you probably have a pretty good sense for it, at your age. Yet you don't have a text on it. A comprehensive, working knowledge of the primary principles and the fundamental premises. Do you?"

"No."

Professor Alejohn went for a box on his bookshelf. He lifted the box top off and pulled out a manuscript the thickness of a ream of paper. "Here's that comprehensive theoretical tome, sir. It's definitive." The professor whacked the manuscript hard against the desktop, the ends of pages making a discernibly loud clacking noise, then handed the thick manuscript to Philip. "Here, look at it. Feel it, sir."

Philip felt its thickness. This was thickness with ink. How ponderous. How weighty.

"Thumb through it. Fan it. Feast your eyes, as they say."

Philip turned pages, slowly at first, and then more quickly. He felt its papery texture. This was no cheap parchment. The print was professional, the formatting official. How in the world could someone produce this much? In college, he'd been daunted by a paper that ran fifteen pages. And here, a manuscript of . . . he quickly checked: five hundred and twenty-seven pages. God, what . . . what a mind to be able to crank out such a weighty work. He felt jealous. He had to admit it.

Perhaps, he thought, I could write a whole volume of poetry.

Two hundred or more pages.

In this book I would declare who I am. Me. Philip Fellows. Here I am, paraded before you. My thoughts. Wonderfully expressed thoughts. With fine sophistication of language. Elegant, yes. Not a cliché to be found. And abstract. Highly abstract!

"What I need, Mr. Fellows, is for an assistant to help me further my study—to conduct extensive field research to gather fine, specific detail. This will mean many phone calls and knocks on doors."

"Doors," said Philip.

"Yes—knocking. On doors. But I don't want to give you the impression that the research comes exclusively or even primarily from John Q. Public. We gather surveys nationwide from college students, professionals of all kinds, captains of industry. Panegyrics is a growing field. It's becoming a pandemic Encomium How-to."

"I thought," Philip hated to object, "I thought *yours* was the only university department."

"It is. But many scholars, from a bevy of different departments, countrywide, are engaged in serious study of this very provocative discipline. Provocative because it's so cutting edge, for one thing."

More redundancy. Somehow this disturbed Philip and made him skeptical. It was like finding typos on a flyer. The whole thing seemed somehow suspect.

The professor beckoned for the manuscript. With a curled finger.

Philip handed it to him.

The professor restacked the pages. He fanned them.

"Now, then, you would start next week after a few training sessions. You would cover Sectors 43 through 49. The zones highlighted in blue." He directed Philip's attention to a large map on the wall opposite the bookshelves. "You will have an electronic, hand-held device with which to enter information, with all this information sent to and stored in a central storage bank."

"That's quite an area—isn't it?"

"Sizeable—yes, sir."

"What would my starting salary be?" Not a mistake, he decided. Ask. It's professional to inquire.

"No salary. Commission."

"No salary?"

"That's not satisfactory?"

"What's the commission based on?"

The professor grinned knowingly. "A number of factors. And we're looking for the man who's got a positive, can-do attitude. He knows that commission only is quite fine because he—or she—will be data hungry. Ravenous." Professor Alejohn rose. "I've got some employment papers for you to go over and sign, and of course there will be a background check. You don't have a history, do you?"

"History?" Philip rose.

"Drug use, felonies, misdemeanors, infractions of any kind that would blemish your record?"

"No."

"Squeaky clean? Well, good, then." The professor extended his hand. His shake was quite firm compared to Buddrick's at *Sail Away*.

He pushed a button on his desk.

A woman appeared. Fiftyish, with bright green eyes, and quick, jerky movements.

"Phyllis will require more application materials of our

candidate—won't you, Phyllis?"

"So you're Philip?" Her green eyes leaned heavily on him.

"Yes, but I'm not ready—"

"For what?"

"To do any more."

Her eyes bounced. "Oh, really? No more?"

"No. I can't live on commission."

She grimaced. "Come. Come, come." She grabbed him by the hand. She walked him to a cubicle. "Sit." She pointed with a quick, bony finger.

It wasn't a suggestion. It was an order.

He noticed the chair. He sat down.

She took a seat at her messy desk, stacked with papers and files, swiveled around, and pulled a drawer out of a gray metal cabinet.

She grabbed a thick file and delivered it with a wham to her desk. It slid a little, and she caught it. She opened it.

"Look this way."

He leaned forward.

"I can't give you names, but notice the commissions."

He looked. One figure was $459.24, another $552.69. Third was $223.21. Then he saw $32.49.

He sat back.

"Um," he said.

"I guess you can see that if you show some effort, you can make some very fine money. Serious money."

"But what about *that* one? That $32.49?" He stabbed it with his index finger.

She leveled her green eyes on him. "No effort. That individual put in a couple of days and quit. You can't get your strategy in two days."

"Strategy?"

"Oh, I'm sorry. Your approach. That's all it is—an approach."

"Approach?"

"Your presentation. But we're getting ahead of ourselves. Let's get your application finalized, and then we can talk further."

She handed him a booklet with a score sheet, filled with tiny circles. And a black ballpoint pen.

He spent an hour filling in responses and grew weary of it. He also felt clueless.

Phyllis stood peering over his shoulder. He heard her wheezy breathing. "Are you stuck?"

"Yes."

"Let's read the question out loud. Sometimes that helps. How is that?" She didn't bother to wait for his response. She went right on: "All right, now listen, Philip: 'When you give praise, do you tend to: A. lower your voice? B. keep the same volume as with most utterances? C. increase your volume?' Well . . . how is it for you?"

"I don't know. I'd be guessing. In fact, I've been guessing through this whole thing."

"Guessing. Why?"

"I've never paid attention to this stuff—to any of it."

"Such as?"

He flipped through the booklet. He pointed at a question. "Like this one. 'Are you generally one to give praise: A. to those who do not deserve it? B. to those who deserve it somewhat? C. to those who deserve it greatly?' I can't decide. It varies."

"You give praise to those who don't deserve it?"

"Well . . . sometimes, I suppose."

"Flummery? Why ever for?"

"Well . . . to make them feel good, I guess."

"How dishonest." She shook her head.

"I don't mean all the time," he said. "Just sometimes—you know."

"I'm sure we all do it," she said. She laughed. Her red lips crinkled.

"I just don't think . . . . I just think this isn't quite, you know, my cup of tea."

"How original. Look, just think some more. Reflect a little more on your choices. All right? Are we agreed?"

"I need to go."

"Go?"

"Yes."

"I don't understand. Don't you realize that if you do not complete this questionnaire, that you cannot be hired for this position?"

"Yes. I know."

"You don't want the position."

"No. I don't feel . . . I don't feel that I would be right for it."

"You don't believe in panegyrics."

"Sure. I believe in it."

"But you don't want to work in this field."

"I didn't realize it was a field. Well, until now."

"Oh, yes—it's a field. A very special field." She leaned over and grabbed up the booklet, the score sheet, and the pen. "It's fine if you don't want the job, Mr. Fellows. But you're missing a great opportunity. Praise is one of the central functions of the human person. Giving praise helps us connect, one with another. If it's the right kind of praise—if it's well-deserved. Never lose a chance for giving well-deserved praise."

"Okay," he said. He wanted something to eat.

"But don't give it lightly."

"No." He rose. He nodded. And then he said, "I've got to leave now."

"This is an opportunity," said Phyllis. "I'm afraid you'll regret having missed it."

"I'm sorry," he said, and he left.

He had another interview in one hour, with Hunt and Hart, and he must think about it. He must prepare.

10

The building was a huge one, and it had a very large cafeteria and snack lounge. Philip sat with a sandwich and coffee. It was quite crowded here, and he felt lucky to have found a place to sit. He removed a pad and pencil from his satchel. He began writing.

A man in a white shirt and blue tie was looking around, and he spotted the empty chair at Philip's table.

"May I sit here?" he said, clutching his tray.

"Uh—well."

"May I, sir?"

Philip cringed. He didn't like sitting with strangers. But how say no? His hesitation made him uncomfortable. "Sure—go ahead."

"Well, then—good," said the man, and took a seat.

Philip went back to his sandwich and pad. He truly did not like sharing a table with a stranger. Let's say they were the talkative type. They'd try to engage you in conversation, and he wanted to think to himself. And besides, right now, he had work to attend to. He was jotting down things he wanted to be sure to say in the interview.

He felt eyes heavy on him. Why, why, did people always stare at him? He felt like asking.

"Busy, are you?"

He looked up. "Yes. I've got a job interview."

"So do I."

"You do?"

"Yes."

"Oh," said Philip. What else was there to say?

He went back to writing. He ate his sandwich, taking notes, and not looking up.

"What are you applying for?" said the man.

My god—again? Another oldster with prophetic talents?

"A job selling."

"Oh? Had any experience?"

"Not a bit."

"That's probably better." The man adjusted his tie.

"Why? Why is that?"

"Less jaded." He loosened his collar. "Man, it's hot in here. Isn't it?"

"I guess."

"Just because it's cold outside, they don't have to jack the heat up to this register. Do they?"

"No." He hadn't noticed that it was particularly hot, but he didn't want to sound argumentative, so he agreed.

"No reason to roast people, huh?"

"No. But doesn't it depend on the person's own system?"

"I suppose. Go on back to your writing. I don't want to interfere."

"Thanks." Philip bit into his sandwich and wrote. He looked up at the clock. His interview was in another twenty minutes.

"Philip Fellows, am I correct?"

"What?"

"You're Philip Fellows."

"Yes." Did he have on a name tag? He started to look—no, that was at that one interview where they had so many applicants that they handed out name tags. And then they would scan the bar code on them at various points in the process. God, what was your chance there?

"I'm your interviewer, Philip. Of course, how would you know? Anyway, that's the case. You have an interview—I have an interview."

The man extended his hand. It was a large, thick one.

"Mr. Morris?"

"That's right. Digby Morris. I used to go by D. H. Morris, but hell, face it—my name's Digby. Get used to your name, right? You're stuck with it. For all eternity." He removed his necktie. "Philip, I hate a necktie, but when you have an interview, you tend to think: 'Dress up for the occasion.' It's a matter of the dignity of the office— and all that. Right?"

"Right."

"Now, then. Let's scrub the idea of going upstairs. What do you say?"

"Okay—"

Digby Morris reached for Philip's pad. He spent a moment scanning it. He turned the page. "Good notes. I've seen them, Philip. I trust they're good—let's say enough for that. Let's move on, shall we?" He slid the pad back to Philip.

"Yes . . . sure."

"How about an excursion outside in the green field? Well, not exactly green, but it *was* green until the winter squelched it. Even so . . . let's pretend it *is* green, and pitch a few, bat a few. Do something other than the expected? What do you say?"

"Pitch a few?"

"And bat a few. Balls. Baseball. Huh?"

"Uh . . . well . . ."

"Not a baseball man?"

"No . . . but—"

"Come, come, Philip."

He rose. "Okay—I'm game."

Game? Damn but he hated that expression! But there it was—right out of his mouth.

"Good. I'll have to make one quick trip upstairs, and then I'll come back down with the requisite gear. For the occasion. That suit you?"

"Sure."

"You know what, Philip? I think you're going to be a very good addition to the team. I have this . . . well, this very good feeling about you. Give me a minute, okay?"

"Sure."

Digby Morris took off.

He had left his tie on the table.

Philip consulted his notes. He had identified three sales ideas:

Put the customer first

Don't pressure the customer

Don't blame the customer

These seemed like good principles to follow. He repeated them over and over in his mind just in case Digby Morris pumped him about his sales philosophy. He didn't want to stumble and make an idiot of himself.

It took the man twenty-five minutes to make it back.

"Damn! I'll tell you, Philip, sometimes I'd just rather not show up for work. I mean, fuck it . . . *sorry*, something I just dealt with upstairs . . . pardon my French, as they say. But it gets so . . . such an absolute pain in the ass. Ever felt that way?"

He paused a tad. "Yeah."

"You don't mind pitching, do you?"

"No."

"Kind of cold out there, but hell, it beats this place, don't you think?"

No—he liked it in here. He was an inside man. He liked sitting, sipping coffee. Reading. Thinking. Outside was good, but not to play ball. He was not a ball man.

But he said: "Yes."

"I'm not an office kind of guy, Philip. I'll be upfront about that. I hate being cooped up. I'm the kind of guy who likes to get out and about. Nervous energy, I guess. Go ahead, you first."

They were at the elevator.

"That field is just wonderful, Philip. I call it the Green Field. It's how I imagine eternal life—Heaven, you know. Right now it's under six to eight inches of snow, but in the summer? They laugh at me, but I get right out there and bat around the balls. A few of my salesmen like it, and we have a smashing good time—to put it in Brit lingo."

"Good." He couldn't think of anything else to say. He knew nothing about sports. And he worried he'd pitch the ball so that it went every which way. His arm was way out of shape. In fact, he hadn't thrown a ball since before college, at some sort of family reunion.

"Yeah, it is. It really is, Philip."

They took off, and Digby Morris began to run. The man was lankier than Philip had imagined. He ran like a scarecrow after a bird.

Philip ran too. He panted when he got there—a huge vacant lot between two gigantic buildings of glass and steel.

"This field's going to be bulldozed in the spring," said Digby Morris, giving it a general wave of the hand. "Better enjoy it while you can. Breaking ground for an eighty-story job."

He pointed up, and kept his finger at it. He seemed to be imagining that building in the overcast sky, where a spear of yellow sun flashed through.

Philip imagined it too. Just like the others, with dark, tinted windows. Another gray monolith rising out of the ground like a tombstone.

Then he imagined the sultry feel of summer, a breeze blowing through thick green mowed grass, the lushness of it, the clover smell of it.

He liked that part of it. He imagined lying with a new woman in the grass, a woman whose affections he had just conquered. She would have a strong scent of perfume, linking her to the perfume of the summer grass—heady. It would all be watermelon heady.

"Ball, Philip—you ready? You don't look ready."

"You want me to pitch?"

"That's right. And don't worry about me line-driving it and knocking off your head. I've got some control, Philip. Fine control—I've worked at it."

"Oh, no," said Philip. "I'm not." But he was. You're damned right he was. *You could die today*, he thought.

Digby pitched him the ball, and Philip headed a good distance away from the plate.

Sixty feet or something, wasn't it?

"Stop! Right there!"

He stopped.

"Lay it in there, Philip!"

He wound up. He threw. The ball went way to the right of Digby Morris, and the man stood there, confused. And then he went to retrieve the ball.

"Damn. Bad arm?"

"Yeah. Terrible."

"It's okay, Philip. Give it another try."

Digby Morris threw the ball hard, and it burned in, sizzling the pocket of Philip's glove. It might as well have been iron. His hand hurt, hurt bad.

But he got ready for the next pitch. God, how he hoped he didn't blow it.

He threw it hard this time, really hard, and it was sheer luck because it went straight, true, a beautiful, a gorgeous pitch. The bat connected, a harsh crack like a gunshot, and he looked. A line drive whistled right by him.

No time to react.

There—gone.

It couldn't have missed him more than a few inches.

"Whew!" shouted Digby Morris. "Whew!"

"I about . . ."

"Got good and creamed! Yes, you did!" He held up two fingers. "God, Philip, you were this close to being a *dead* man. If that ball had hit you . . . Jeez, but then it didn't. It didn't. Okay, that's enough. Let's pack up, but let's don't go up to the office—that's no place for this thing. How about a bar? I know a fine bar."

"A bar," said Philip.

"You a drinker?"

"Yeah."

"Then why not?"

They rode off in Digby Morris's car—a sleek white, well-upholstered Lincoln—and parked in a small lot behind a dark bar called Beef Eaters. Only a few people were in there, and Digby motioned at a booth.

"Two stouts."

The bartender nodded.

They sat there and Digby Morris stared at Philip until Philip thought he must say something or the man would burn a hole in his face.

Digby laid a hand on the table. "Now, then, some things you must know, and in this order, Philip: You've got to *sell* to keep this job. Two, don't give your whole life to it. Three, whatever time you do give to it, it's stolen from you. I assure you. Selling is a bitch, and who needs it, but we've got to eat, right? We want the material pleasures, right? We want stuff. All kinds of stuff. Still, I hate to break the news, but this job puts your life right on hold, buddy. Every minute you give to it. Every fucking *second*. Wasted, wasted, wasted."

Whew, thought Philip.

"You don't like your work, then."

"Hell, no. I hate it. Everybody hates it, if they're honest. Oh, they'll *tell* you they love it, but believe me, they don't, Philip. They're just not honest like I am. I'm brutally honest. That's what I am. You want a brutally honest man, you're looking at him."

"Oh. So you're discouraging me from taking it?"

"Hell, yes, I'd discourage any sane man from taking it. Especially a man like you, Philip, who looks like he just bid Mama goodbye this morning. Sorry, but you do have that look. You haven't let go, have you?"

"What? Of course I have—"

"You're no youngster wet behind the ears?"

"No. I make it entirely on my own."

"Don't get sore. Look, even so, you haven't found yourself yet, have you? Not really."

"Of course I have."

"Well—good. Good man. As to the job. Take it, Philip, unless you have a better alternative. Do you?"

"Yes, I was offered a job at a magazine."

"Oooh, well, now—what magazine?"

"*Sail Away.*"

"Never heard of it. And so why are you here?"

"It wasn't for editing. It was for other things—menial chores."

"Ha! Never settle for menial chores, sir. It diminishes you. Be the protagonist of your own life, sir." He seemed to hang on this thought. He took a moment or two. "Of course this job diminishes people even more. Take the other job, Philip. You'd probably feel better about yourself." The two stouts arrived. Digby raised his. He clanked his against Philip's, still resting on the table top before him. "That's what it's all about, isn't it? When you come down to it?

What's it profit a man, right?"

"Yeah—" Philip took a gulp. He took a second gulp. Two big gulps.

"That's it," said Digby. "Let it out. Let it out, buddy." He downed a third of his stout. "Let it out, Philip. Let it *all* out."

Philip did. He drank half his beer, and then he set the mug down too hard. He was feeling better. This Digby Morris made you feel better. He saluted with his stout. "I want the job!" The stout came down hard on the table. "I definitely do!"

"Up to you. Hope there's no buyer's regret, but if there is ... hell, just pack up and move on. Right?"

"Pack—"

"Pack up, sir, and move on. On, on, and on until you find the right spot. Make your living by loving, Philip. I firmly believe it."

Digby Morris had an incipient grin working on his lips.

"Would I get a company car?"

A stare, a long one. Too long.

And then finally. "Hell, yes. Of course you would. And an expense account. Plus free lunches three days a week at the Mayo Bend—ever eaten there?"

"No—I don't think."

"Pretty average, take it all around."

"And the salary?"

Digby Morris drew out his cell phone. "It's all here, stored up, Philip—go mobile, huh?" He fingered the screen. "Okay—there's your starting salary. Note the commissions. And . . . here's your expense account. All pretty fine, and I'm sure it looks pretty good to you, being unemployed as you are, with only that lowly, menial position in the offing. Huh? Isn't that right?"

He felt pressured. He didn't like to feel pressured. The stout was working, but it wasn't working enough. He took another gulp. He held the mug before him.

Think.

Think.

Do it.

"Uh, I do hate to ask," said Philip. "I don't mean to be pushy—"

"You don't? You mean unprofessional?"

"Yes. But I really do need to know. When would my first check be?"

"Easily stated, Philip. We pay at the end of each month. Direct deposit. If you started today, you'd get paid at the end of the month—pro rata. That's how it goes."

He felt good that he'd asked. And now he had more questions. He took a long, long pull on his stout. He was feeling good. He looked about, and about, and then his eyes rested on Digby's.

"Well, I—"

"More stout here!" shouted Digby Morris.

The bartender raised a finger.

Digby watched him. The bartender came with two more stouts.

"What's the company car like?"

Digby whipped his head around.

"You mean is it some trashy junker? No, it's a brand new car, Philip. It's a well-oiled, greased, cat-purring, slick machine. A salesman has to show up looking good. I'm sure you can appreciate that, and I'm sure you'll like it. Nice to take the girls out in."

"You mean—"

"Job use only, Philip. But then who pays attention? How are they—the guys in Accounts—really going to know if you took your girl out for a nighter or went to call on a possible client? Only if you *do* that, C-Y-A. We all do it, but we cover our asses. It only makes sense to do so, now doesn't it?"

"Oh. Yes."

"You don't like that, do you?"

"No. I don't think I'd want to do that. To risk that."

"You'd be surprised what you'd end up doing. Besides, just tell them you got confused. You got your cars confused. Happens all the time."

"Oh—yeah," said Philip.

Digby Morris raised a finger to his lips. "I'm not sure you're right for the place after all. Or maybe you're *just* right for the place. Me? I'm wrong. I know I'm wrong. I've been at it ten years now, and every day, every stinking day, I say to myself: 'I'm going to break out, get clear of it. Do something I really want to do.'"

"What's that?"

Digby swilled beer. He wiped off his lips and chin. "Play ball. I should have been in the majors, but here I am a goddamned salesman. You know what we sell, don't you?"

"No."

"I thought it odd you didn't ask. You asked about the salary, the expense account, the car, when you'd get paid—but not what you're selling. So now I've saved the best for last. You're selling hunting equipment. Guns, traps, bows, everything in between. You a hunter, Philip?"

"No." *I didn't ask about the expense account*, he wanted to say— but didn't.

"You might want to look into it a little before starting. Know what you're about to sell, right?"

"Yes. That makes sense."

"Seems to me it does."

"Are you offering me the job?"

"Sure. Why not? If you pan out, we'll keep you. If not, we'll dump you. Pull the lever on that trap door, and *wham*, down you go!"

This gave him a jolt. He didn't like the sly grin crinkling Digby Morris' lips. "But how soon would that happen?"

"Oh, well . . . in a few days, week, two weeks—it could be a month. You see, Philip, we'll have to judge whether or not you're worth the salary, the use of the car, the expense account. It comes down to numbers, Philip. Number crunching. And I'll bet you can appreciate that. Can't you?"

"Yes, of course."

"You've got to put it in high gear, Philip. Sell like you really believe the hell out of that hunting equipment. Like you *live* for it. Like there isn't a thing in the world that means more to you than that hunting equipment. Not a *thing*. Learn the lingo. Learn the walk, the talk, the dance, the prance. Read the mags."

"Oh—yeah."

"Still interested?"

He had drifted off. He was thinking about that company car. He was thinking about what it would be like to take Sophia Cross out in that car. Breezing down the road. Cranking up the music. Her up against him, smelling strongly of perfume. Rat juice, Dick Hazzard called it.

"Yes. Yes—I am," he said. Yes, he would read the magazines. Yes, he would do what it took. He didn't know a thing about hunting. He had never hunted, not really. He had shot a rifle. And a handgun. Once at a friend's place in the country. He could still recall the oily, smoky smell that hit his nostrils. It had a serious smell to it. A-man-that-knows-the-score smell. He didn't feel like he knew the score. But sure, he could do it. He would do it. If it took knowing the score, he'd know it. You're damned right.

"Good. Well, then."

"I'm your man," said Philip. He gulped some beer.

"There'll be a background check, of course," said Digby Morris. "Anything to hide?"

"Hide? No—"

"Hey, don't get excited." Digby reached out and whacked him on the shoulder. "If they'd checked me out, I'd have failed. No doubt about it. Hell, Philip, when you're a young stud, anything's possible, isn't it?"

"Uh—yeah, I guess. I guess so. But I don't have anything to hide. Really, I don't."

"A straight shooter?"

"I guess. Is that okay? I mean—"

"Sure, sure." Digby gave him another whack on the shoulder. "I'm just talking about myself, Philip. I sowed some wild oats. I really did, Philip. I'm not shitting you."

He didn't like this particular expression. It was nastily scatological—not to his taste at all. "You did? Like what?"

"You need another strong one, don't you? A couple of guys like us, we get to talking, and pretty soon, the old beer gut starts aching for a little suds, a little suds to wash the palate. Am I right?"

"Yes. But—"

"What?"

"I'm not done with this one yet."

"Hey. No problem. One in reserve."

"Yeah. Yeah." Something drifted around inside Philip, like the stout was seeking an exit.

"Two more!" yelled Digby Morris. He unbuttoned the top two buttons of his white shirt.

"Great!" said Philip.

"Man, oh man. Man. Feels good, doesn't it? Feels real good." Digby Morris fingered his unbuttoned shirt.

"Yeah!"

"Nothing better," said Digby. He was grinning, but it was like there wasn't anything behind the grin, like Digby had plastered the grin on his face and exited. He was elsewhere.

The bartender arrived with two more stouts. Philip downed his old one in one long gulp and grabbed the new one.

Digby Morris had laid a hand on his shoulder.

"Yeah," said Philip.

"What I did. Like to know? Would you?"

"Sure, tell me."

"Well, Philip . . . I will tell you. You look like the kind of man a guy can share a secret with. You are, aren't you?"

"Yes. I think so."

"A man a guy can trust."

"I am. I try to be."

"Well, hell, then. I'll spill the old beans."

"Okay."

"Okay. See it was like this: I was out drinking and driving. Plowed. Smashed. Fucked up royal. You get the drift."

"Yeah."

"You never did that, I take it."

"No—well, a little, I guess. Some."

"I'll bet. But look here, Philip, it was four o'clock in the fucking morning. Four, Philip. That's when old men have heart attacks, when boogie monsters come drifting in the window, when the thugs show up and take you away to dark places with their various instruments of pain and suffering. Four o'clock, Philip. The Hour of the Wolf. Dark as the devil, and I was drunk as the devil. Get it? You understand what I'm saying?"

"Yeah."

"I wonder if you do."

Was that a five o'clock shadow? And what was that glint in the man's eye? And was that saliva—or beer suds—slathered on his lips?

"I do," said Philip. "I certainly do understand." Hell, what *was* the man talking about? He had no idea in this alcoholic stout haze. He could hardly see a thing.

"I killed a young woman, Philip. I killed a young woman, and I killed her boyfriend. I wrapped my car around the tree, and the two of them—they died. Wham, bam, gone. My two best friends, Philip. My true love, she was—I'd had my designs on her, oh, yes, I'd had my designs on her forever. I mean sheer, unadulterated lust we're talking about here. I had my hand on her legs, drinking like a fool, when the tree sort of appeared. Right there, sort of just appeared. Like a wall might suddenly appear right before us. Picture that. Can you picture that?"

"Yeah."

"I've often thought of that. I was tooling along . . . just tooling along . . . and there it was: a tree. In my face. You know what, Philip?"

"What?"

"I wasn't hurt a bit. Not a scratch, sir. I know you don't believe me, you think I'm stretching things, but I'm not. I did not have *one fucking scratch*. When I say that, you must believe me because it's true. I got out of the car, with the front end crushed so bad that it was like there *wasn't* a front end. I got out and I walked away. You know where they were?"

"Who? Oh—"

"Thrown through the windshield, of course, because neither of them would wear a belt. Me, I always wore a belt—out of sheer fear, Philip. I've always been a fearful fellow. Fear and spontaneity. The one checks the other, you see—but not enough. Not enough, Philip. And the other, not as much as those two whose names, incidentally, were Brandy and Butch. Well, his name wasn't really Butch, but we'll call him Butch since that's what everybody called him. I called him that."

"They died," said Philip. His words slurred. His tongue didn't seem to belong to him. It was elsewhere, wrapped around his mouth someway or other.

"What?"

"Died. Dead."

"You got that right. They died. Dead."

"Terrible."

"What?"

"Terrible. T-e-r-r-i-b-l-e."

"Yeah, really." Digby tossed more stout.

"Sorry."

This came out better. He downed more stout.

"Sorry—yeah. Do you know what it's like to look down at two mangled bodies, two bloody, mangled bodies, and know it's your fault? And there you are, fit as a fiddle, your clothes not even rumpled, and peering down at two bloody bodies—the bloody bodies of a woman you love, or *did* love, should I put it that way? One you'd lusted to death for? And the other, a pretty damned good friend—most of the time, anyway. Oh, there were times when . . . you know. But anyway, you know what goes through your head?"

"What?"

"What do you think?"

"Well . . ." He did not want to say it exactly—no.

"The end of the world, Philip. The fucking end of the world. For you, anyway. Only, you still hope—in spite of it. I thought of what I might do to bring them back to life. I thought of what I might do if I could only maybe say a prayer or maybe call an ambulance. I had a cell phone—not everyone had one of those back then—but I was too petrified to call. How could I say anything over the phone? You tell me. How could I?"

"No. Of course. I mean . . . And so—"

"I ran, Philip. I ran and ran."

"Oh, god."

"I sure did run, but they caught up with me. You know that?"

"Oh."

More stout.

"They sure did. And how could they not? They caught up with me and nailed me pretty damn bad."

"What? What did they do?"

More stout.

"Fifteen years in the slammer, Philip. You know what that's like? Fifteen years in the big old slammer?"

"God, no."

"Bad, Philip, real, real bad. Very, very bad regardless of what they say. Only, get this, Philip, I didn't serve all of the fifteen. I served four years, eight months, twelve days, four hours, and twenty-nine minutes. And some seconds. And then they released my ass."

"Um."

"*What?*"

"That's a long, long time. What was it like? How bad was it? Did they—?"

More stout. Down the hatch.

"Rape me? No, I'm a pretty big guy, Philip, in case you haven't noticed. And I was pretty tough in those days. But it was the boredom, Philip, the absolute unrelenting boredom."

He imagined it. The endlessness of it, the eternity. Four years and—

"And it's the lack, Philip, of privacy. That's what gets you. Always being public. Always. There isn't a thing you do that isn't public. Everything about you, *in* you, it's all for public consumption. Maybe that's why I hate the office—it amounts to the same thing. Don't you think?"

"I don't know. Is it . . . because of that?"

"Who knows, Philip? Who knows?" He drank down two long gulps of stout, then raised his hand for more. "I'm actually a very private person, Philip. You wouldn't know that. Would you? You'd think being a salesman, well that would be for the extrovert, the people person, the crowd guy, the group man—but no, not me. I go home thirsting for a retreat from the public they. Know what the public they is, Philip?"

More stout came. Philip finished his old one off in a big quaff.

"Uh—"

"Read your Heidegger."

"Well, I did a little, some, but—"

"Well, you should. But see, here I am venting. Here I am spewing." Digby bent over and felt of the table. "I'd like to say this isn't me, Philip, but it is me. This is who I am. You are now confronting the real, the absolute, the genuine Digby Morris, unveiled. Fuck the world!"

"God, why?" He clutched his new stout.

"Why?" He studied Philip for a moment, and then turned away and coughed and laughed.

Philip got the strange sensation that the man was checking himself for a hernia.

"I'll tell you why. Because it wasn't the boredom so much as the guilt. You know what it's like to carry that around with you? Don't ever, Philip, do anything you'll regret. Don't ever do it." He tapped his forehead. "Think a little. Think first before acting. I do it all the time now." He whacked the table. "There isn't a moment, Philip, that I don't regret what happened. Not a goddamn moment I don't think of it. I don't see it. I don't feel blood on my paws."

"Sorry. Really, but you didn't mean—"

"Sure I did. Because if you don't *not* mean, you *do* mean. If you catch my drift. Don't tarnish your soul, sir." He checked his watch. "About time to report back. To the station. I call it the station, Philip. You're reporting to the station tomorrow morning, at eight sharp, aren't you?" He stood up and wobbled. And then he gripped the table top.

"Yes. I'll be there." Philip stood up. He wobbled too.

"Good for you. Fucking A."

"You're not driving back, are you?"

"Hell, no. *You're* driving back. You think I'd drive back like this?"

"No. But I can't drive either." Philip wobbled. Even so, he went for his stout.

"Hell no, I *wouldn't*. You think I didn't learn something—huh?" He tapped his forehead. "Think, Philip. Think."

"Call a cab."

"Cab. What about the car?"

"I don't know." He quaffed more stout.

Digby motioned at him. They both sat down.

"Finish our stout," said Digby. "Meanwhile, think on it. Figure out what's next."

They sat there an hour. Digby ordered more stout.

Eventually, they moseyed out to Digby's car. Digby got in— behind the wheel. The door was still open.

"You can't drive like that," said Philip. "You can't—no!"

"I'll be fine. Fine. Get in." He yanked the door shut.

"No—no. I'll see you tomorrow."

The window shot down. Digby stuck his head out. He signaled for Philip to approach. "Closer," he said.

Philip did as told.

They were face to face, Philip at the open car window, Digby poking his head out.

"Now don't be late tomorrow, sir. Make that good first impression. After that, hell, it'll depend on everything you do. Got it?"

"Yeah, but—"

"No buts. And it ain't easy, partner. It's a bitch, really. We'll keep you on if you produce. It's all about producing. That's what counts in this world. And why shouldn't it—fucked up as it is?"

He made out what Digby Morris was saying, but the man's words were slurred and had a bizarre Texas accent to them. His breath smelled like a cross between rotten peaches and kerosene.

"Right," said Philip.

"Fucking A," said Digby and pulled his head in. He gave Philip a wave and took off.

"Hey!" shouted Philip.

But Digby's car shot out of the lot and disappeared as it cornered onto a street.

Philip waited for the sound of a crash, but he heard nothing.

He was on foot.

11

Back at his apartment, the stink hit him. A combination of sewer gas, mold, and cigarette smoke, and some sort of Indian cooking down the hall. Or was it?

He collapsed on the bed, set his alarm for an hour later, and drifted off, went black. Dreamed. Bad dreams, dreams that dove in on him, stole his equanimity, left him filled with great dread.

He couldn't recall what he'd dreamed.

He sat up, thirsty. He went to his tiny, dented refrigerator and took out a bottle of water. He got dressed—jeans, sweat shirt, coat, jogging shoes.

He was on his way to the library.

It wasn't all that surprising to meet up with Adam Most a third time in one day. The man was resting at a table with his hands firmly gripping a book. When he spotted Philip, he put the book down.

"Oh, say, Philip, we *must* talk."

Here we go again.

"I don't have but a minute—and I'm serious. I really am."

"It won't take but a minute."

"Okay. But a minute—just that. One minute."

"Look." The little weasel shoved the book at Philip.

Dreams of Love.

"It's an important book," said Adam Most. "Very important study. Very important to understand these dreams of love we all have. All of us. Not some, not the majority. Every single one of us has such dreams of love." He picked up the book gently, then let it fall, the pages fanning. "There isn't one exception, Philip."

"That's interesting."

"But you don't think so."

"Yes, I do."

"I mean even your old lady rotting in the nursing home. She dreams of love, Philip."

"If she can dream."

74

"She can dream."

"Okay, that's good—but I've got work to do."

"Even in a coma, Philip."

"No. Come on."

"Even, and here's the one that's going to get you—even in the act of dying. In the very last throes of pain and the struggle just to stay sane, they dream of love, Philip."

"Well—maybe. Loneliness. Need. Sure, I can buy it."

"No, no. I mean, in their very last breaths, Philip, they look *forward*. They look forward to some sort of love. They don't give up with those last breaths. They're still looking ahead. We're always looking ahead, Philip. You know that? Don't you?"

"Well—"

"We're never right here. We're always out *there*."

The same intensity. There's a reason you avoid such types. There's a reason you give them a wide berth. "I know it. I believe it," said Philip. "But I've got to go. I mean it. I've got work to do. I really do have work to do."

"Okay. Sure." Adam Most went back to his book, smoothing out the pages.

Angry? Wounded? Or resolved not to be a pest—for once?

And now he must look further into this matter of hunting.

He gathered up magazines. He read a story of a deer hunt. He found one of a bear hunt. He looked at ads for guns, for ammo, for lures. For deer stands. For camouflage gear.

Proud, ruddy men standing tall with dead bucks, posed for the camera.

Proud, ruddy women, likewise. Women hunters?

Philip got a feeling. He felt it fluttering in his gut. He felt it in his neck.

And then he tried to sort it out.

A clerk for a sailboat magazine, a researcher for the Panegyrics Department, a salesman for hunting gear. Job-wise, who could say that one was better than the other, or worse than the other? Who wanted any of them? Who did?

Money. You need money. The more the—

He saw Adam Most on his way out.

He looked about. A rear entrance. He spotted a fire door.

But Adam was suddenly upon him.

"Done, huh?"

"Yes." He hurried by the little weasel.

"Wait a minute. Wait—please."

"What?"

"Something I didn't say."

"What?"

"Dreams of love, see, they're all the time with us. Waking *and* sleeping. Every dream you have, asleep, I mean—it's connected to wanting love."

Philip shook his head. "No, no. That's not true."

"It is true."

"No, no."

"It is certainly true."

"No."

"The author of this book, you see—"

"I suppose he's going to say that if I dream that I've failed an exam, let's say it's chemistry, that's dreaming of love?"

"Yes. Sure. *Whatever* the dream, nothing to the contrary, it's about love. In some way. This is what we are, Philip. This is all we are. We dream of love. That's it in a nutshell. It's beautiful, isn't it?"

Meat machines dreaming of love?

He didn't say it.

"No. Not if we don't find it."

"Even if we find it, you think it's satisfied? There's always that need, Philip. Need, need, need. A gigantic yearning. Just a minute." He flipped through the book. "I want to read you this one passage. Just hold on one minute—just one, please."

Philip's legs tightened. They must go. They must be advancing quickly out the door!

"Why do you think that book's the last word on the subject?"

"Because it is. Just a minute. Hold on just a minute. I won't take up any more of your time. I know you're busy. I know that, but just one minute." Adam continued flipping through the pages.

Philip thought of the party. He thought of Lisa Wing. That wet tongue in his ear. He didn't want to miss that party.

"Okay, here it is. Here. Let me read. Are you ready? Are you listening?"

"Yes."

"Good. Okay, then. Here it is: 'What seems unlikely, though the research has suggested otherwise, is that some activities, notwithstanding their apparent unlikelihood to support my thesis, do in fact suggest that the dream of love *always* troubles the soul—*always*, without exception, troubles the soul.'" Adam Most lay down the book. "There you have it. Fascinating, isn't it? Always to be dreaming, and being troubled, as the man says, about love. Aren't you fascinated? Or am I the only one? I hope that's not the case. I really hope I'm not the only one."

"I don't know," said Philip. "I don't know if I like that."

"Why not?"

"I don't want to be troubled by love."

"Oh, well. But you see, the principal meaning of 'troubled' is 'stirred.' Are you stirred by love?"

"Well," said Philip.

"No matter. Everyone is stirred by the dream of love. I must get back to it, Philip. I'm losing time." He looked up. He pointed at the clock. "This place closes at eleven. I wish it stayed open longer, but it doesn't. Eleven. That's it. And I've got so much to read yet."

"Why don't you check out the book?"

"Why do that? I like it here. I love it here."

"I don't get it."

Adam Most shrugged. "Well, I must be getting back to it." He looked up at the clock.

"Okay. Well, I must be going."

The man didn't look up. He was engrossed in the red covered book. It was a thick one.

12

The streets were dark, and it was beginning to rain, just drips at first, but cold, and it was turning to ice. He was in a part of the city where the buildings were mostly abandoned, slatternly. Noises: plastic bags, aluminum cans, newspapers flapping wildly, swept by the wind. And then he saw a man standing against a short, squat building with broken, boarded-up windows.

He hurried on.

When he looked back, the man was not there. The rain came down harder, and this time it was definitely ice.

Then it began to snow.

Hard snow. A wintry mix.

Blizzard, he thought.

He hadn't checked the weather.

"Get in, will you?" shouted Lisa Wing. "You walk? What happened?"

"I walked."

"You don't have a car?"

"No. But I will soon—"

"How far you walk?"

"Three miles. Or more."

"To come to my party. Well, what a hero! Isn't he a hero, Dick? In all that out there?"

"Oh, yes—oh, yes, Phil here is a flat-out hero. You keeping that coat on?"

"Maybe for a minute."

"He's cold. Don't you see he's cold?" Lisa Wing moved toward him and clasped her arms around him. "Come to Mama. I'll warm you up."

"I'm getting a beer," said Dick.

"You're the first one here," said Lisa Wing. "Maybe you'll be the *only* one here with that snowstorm coming."

"Coming?" said Philip.

"It's hardly started. They're calling for a foot or more. Maybe two. Didn't you hear?"

"No."

He thought of next morning. What would he do? Take a cab? He had no money.

"You'll have to stay here," said Lisa, still hugging him.

She wouldn't let go. In the other room, he could hear Dick whistling. He whistled a lot. Sometimes he was a non-stop whistler. It got on Philip's nerves.

Philip pulled loose. What if Dick? "I guess I ought to get this coat off. Is there a place—"

"I'll take it. You want some wine? Beer, chips, anything?"

"Sure."

She leaned in close to him. She whispered: "I'm in *love* with you. Dick doesn't *know* it." She smiled. Her lips were slightly wet.

"What?" he said. "What—"

"*Happened*? I don't know. Why question it? It's just the way things go. I'm in love . . . are you in love with someone?" She pulled him close, kissed his ear. She whispered with wet tongue: "*Are* you?"

"God," he said. "Yes. Yes." He was fastened, hard against her, as Dick waltzed in, whistling.

"Hey. Something going on here? Something I ought to know about?"

"No, no," sang Lisa. She hung his coat up in the closet, and then sort of danced her way through the living area into what he assumed was the kitchen.

"What is it?" said Dick, giving him a punch on the arm. "What's this about, Phil?"

"*Philip*, please."

"What's it about?"

"Nothing *I* started. I didn't start anything."

"Yeah? You saying she did? Maybe you'd better leave, bud-boy." His eyes were small ball bearings, with a steely glint.

"I guess so."

Lisa Wing danced her way back, holding two wine glasses.

"One for each of you, my dear sirs!" She thrust the glasses into their hands.

Philip's hand was still cold. But the cold wine glass felt good against it. Cold against cold was somehow good.

Lisa danced off.

"She's just that way," said Dick. "You can't trust her. Hell," he said, downing a half glass of wine in one gulp, sporting his beer in the other, then wiping his mouth on his shirt sleeve. "Tell you what, Phil, she really can't help it, I guess. Considering the family she was raised in."

"What family?"

"What?"

"I mean what kind of family?"

"Bad. Old lady's a drunk, old man's a thief, two brothers ran off somewhere, sister's a whore. You name it."

"She's really a whore?"

"Well, you know."

"You've got a nice place here," said Philip.

"She's the one that makes it a nice place. If I can keep her. But she's always threatening to run off. Here, there, meet up with her brothers, go the way of her sister, drink herself to death like her Ma. I can't keep up."

Lisa was dancing back with a glass of red wine. "Is *nobody* coming to my party?"

"Should have scheduled it when there wasn't a big snow," said Dick. He patted her bottom.

The doorbell rang.

"Well!" said Lisa. "Finally!"

"They're pretty much on time, really," said Dick. "Only fifteen minutes late."

Lisa pulled open the door. Three young people stood there— two men and one woman.

"Come in, come in, come in!" shouted Lisa.

They came in with a blast of frigid air. Their coats and hair were dusted with snow. They held forth several bags with glass bottles jingling. The young woman with long blond hair and pouty red lips had a large paper sack in her hand. Philip saw inside it: chips, crackers, dip. Green dip. He was hungry.

"A major nice place you have here, Dick—and Lisa," said a young man with a thick beard and large white teeth. He was eying Lisa with interest. He turned to Philip. "Sebastian Croner."

"Philip Fellows."

"Fellows. Any relation to the professor?"

"Professor? Which professor?"

"Professor Heinrich Fellows—of the Music Department."

"No."

"Plays string, wind, brass, piano, organ, and drum. A man of many instruments. A Renaissance man. He speaks of liaisons with the Panegyrics Department. Are you familiar?"

"Yes."

"Music, the professor says, is a form of praise."

They went over that for a spell.

Tina, the blond woman, had just returned with Lisa Wing, grasping a glass of red wine. "Is he boring you?" she asked. "I'm Tina." She smiled at Philip. She extended her hand. It was quite cold.

"No." He gripped her hand, perhaps too long. He thought to warm it up. He somehow couldn't release. He withdrew finally.

"My heavens," she said, and smiled.

The other young man was short, thin, and was looking about. His present occupation was the dining room ceiling. One hand was extended, palm up, toward it, as though trying to gauge something. "Ah!" he cried out. "Ah!"

"I see Boris is interested in the ceiling again," said Sebastian.

"Would you quit that? His name is *not* Boris," said Tina. She laid a hand on Lisa Wing's shoulder. "He won't quit calling him *Boris.*"

"Who wants to be called *Tommy*?" said Sebastian.

"Who wants to be called *Dick*," said Dick. "I do."

"Him," said Tina.

"I'd rather be called Boris. Do unto others." Sebastian stuck his tongue out.

"Do unto yourself, don't you mean?"

"He's so selfish, isn't he?" said Lisa Wing.

"Anyway," said Sebastian, turning to Philip, "it's a new department. And Professor Fellows doesn't want to leave anything out. No stone unturned, as they say."

"Your tribe, huh?" said Dick, giving Philip a quick gut punch.

"I don't know. I don't think so."

"Professor Fellows," said Sebastian. "Perhaps a relative of some order."

"I don't know of him."

Lisa Wing went to Tommy, who was now climbing on a chair, gaining a closer look at the ceiling. He was running his hand over it. "*Whatever* are you doing?"

"Nothing. Nothing at all."

"You're doing *something*."

"Observing. Just observing."

"He's a nutcase," said Sebastian. "Don't try to make any sense of it."

"Who's not a nutcase these days?" said Dick, moving toward Tommy.

"He's not a nutcase," said Tina. "You call everybody a nut case. Everybody but you, and you *are* a nutcase."

"How is that?"

"The way you carry on."

"Be specific."

Tina marched over to Lisa. "What do you say to a man who always demands that you be specific? What in the world do you say?"

"Be general?" said Dick.

"I say nothing," said Lisa Wing, now on a chair looking up at the ceiling along with Tommy.

"Well, good, that's what I'll start saying too. What *are* you all doing? Looking for bugs?"

"Perhaps there's something wrong with our ceiling," said Lisa Wing.

They all gathered around the two on chairs, peering up at the ceiling.

"I have a theory," said Tommy, placing a foot on the table, "that if your ceiling seems imposing—"

"Imposing," said Sebastian. "What do you mean by imposing? How can a ceiling be imposing?"

"Let him finish," said Tina.

"It can be imposing if and only if it comes between you and what you desire, and the other term is 'interposing.' Does it seem to block out, or is it simply a removable cap? There you have it. I wouldn't expect anybody to understand it, but there you have it."

"I think it's kind of nice," said Lisa Wing, and she patted Tommy's shoulder. And then she patted his leg.

"I kind of like it," said Tina. "Actually I like it a lot. It's . . . very mysterious."

"It's mystical," said Lisa. "I like the mystical."

"It's perhaps the truth," said Tommy.

"Scientific?" said Sebastian. "It wouldn't hold up to much in terms of empirical support, would it? Do you know?" he said to Philip, "that the structure of music is also the structure of praise, or at least this is what the empirical data suggests to Professor Fellows. This is what makes him want to create the liaison."

"Oh, cut it out," said Tina. "God, I get tired of that talk."

"What talk?"

"About . . . stuff like that. And then you put Tommy down."

"Tommy's her real boyfriend," said Sebastian.

"Of course he is," said Tina. "Why wouldn't he be?"

"You never know," said Dick. "Do you?"

"Care for a hard one?" asked Sebastian. "We brought along a quart of Old Kentucky."

"He'd rather remain on the chair, I guess," said Dick. He gave Tommy a whack on the back.

"Philip?" said Sebastian. "Coming?"

The three of them migrated toward the kitchen.

13

They were outside, gathered around Sebastian's car.

"You amaze me," said Sebastian. "What are you, fish or fowl? I suspect you're neither."

"I wouldn't know, and don't care," said Dick.

"You don't care. *Everyone* cares. They say they don't, but they do."

"Well, I don't."

The snow had covered the tops of cars, blanketed the yards, and filled the street. Against the street light, the snow had a blue radiance that struck some sort of chord in Philip, though he couldn't quite name it. He felt he wanted to say something about it, but he couldn't imagine what. Something was on his tongue. *You're no poet, Phil*, Dick had told him when back in college he'd shown him a poem. *Only it's not the worst thing I've seen.*

Sebastian lit a cigarette. "Seems to me you should."

"Maybe I should, but I don't."

"When's she due?"

"I don't know."

"You don't know the date."

"No."

"She didn't say."

"No."

"She'll say. You'll know all right. That's *all* she'll talk about."

"Yeah? How do you know?"

"Tina."

"Really? She's pregnant? No, she doesn't look pregnant."

"She *thought* she was pregnant. Actually wanted to be pregnant. All she could talk about. But she wasn't, sad to say—from her perspective, that is. Not mine."

Dick shoved Philip a manly one. "When are you getting a girlfriend, son?"

Philip shoved him one back. "I've got one."

"Yeah—who?"

"A waitress."

"Yeah, what's her name?"

Bad idea—this. Very bad. Dick was a blabbermouth. He'd better not say. If it got out—

"Come on, who? Who, Phil?"

"You wouldn't know her."

"That place you eat practically every morning?"

"What?"

"Oh, I know about it. I see you go in there."

"How? When?"

"I see—never mind. And that's Sophia Cross, is who you're referring to. Of course, you wouldn't be referring to that old hag in the back, now would you?"

God, what a mistake. This had to stop—and it had to stop right now.

"It's another waitress," said Philip. "I don't know any Sophia Cross."

"The hell you don't. *She's* the waitress, the *only* waitress, at the time you arrive."

"Yeah?"

"Yeah. Sophia Cross. Got one bad ass of a boyfriend, there, Phil fellow," said Dick. "Best watch thine p's and q's."

"Back to the subject at hand," said Sebastian. "Lisa."

"It's not a large matter," said Dick.

"Marrying her, are you?"

"Probably not."

"Things are brewing," said Sebastian, and scooped up a handful of snow. He rolled and pounded it into a ball. He lobbed it at a tree. "Things are changing."

"Maybe, but I'm not getting excited," said Dick.

"Taking it as it comes, huh? Live every day."

"Why wouldn't I?"

Philip scooped up snow, pounded it into a ball, and pitched it at a tree. It hit square. It splattered. He thought, *Maybe I do have an arm.* "She doesn't look pregnant," he said.

"Well, she is."

"I'm going to dump that girl eventually," said Sebastian. "But not for publication, all right?"

"Tina? Why?"

"We don't see eye to eye. And I'm getting real tired of her bullshit obsession with dear old S.K."

"S.K.?" said Dick.

"Kierkegaard, my boy. Ever read him?"

"No."

"Philip?"

"Uh—a little. Back in college. *Being and Time!*—yeah. I read some of that, I think."

"Don't think so, sir. Not our guy. *Either/Or, Fear and Trembling*—not exactly your garden variety nighttime reading, but get this—*The Sickness Unto Death.* Huh? How about that? *Death*, man."

"Oh, yeah," said Philip. "Whatever that means."

"That's right, amigo. *The Sickness Unto Death.* Get this, his name means churchyard, or graveyard. How about that for depressing? Well, I'm crapping out on it. I'm crapping out on *her.* Maybe she'll dump me. She will, and knowing that, I'd like to be the first to do the dumping."

"What'll you do when you've dumped her?" said Dick. "Who's next in line?"

"A woman at a bar—the Night Speak. Older, has passion like an acetylene torch. Tina caught me with her once, planting a kiss. We fought about it for days."

"She's a good looker, Tina is," said Dick.

"So is that woman at the Night Speak."

"Name?" said Dick.

"I have to supply the name? You don't believe me?"

"Come forth. No name, and I won't believe you."

Sebastian scooped up more snow. He lobbed it at the same tree. It was turning bitterly cold. The snow was coming even harder. The car had a good eight to ten inches covering the roof. Sebastian pulled a pint out of his pocket and took a long swallow. "Man, sure does warm the gizzard. Ah! Name, huh? Her name is Judy."

Dick laughed. "No one's name is Judy. Come on, what's her name?"

"Judy. Like I said."

Dick was scooping snow off the roof.

"Bullshit. Judy—yeah, right."

"I've been having some bad things happen to me," said Sebastian.

"Yeah? Like what?"

"Philip, you look like a bright guy. So let me ask: What is your take on this? You wake up one morning, and your toe feels strange. It feels numb. Your head feels weird. Your side quivers. Your leg aches. What is it? Dick here—he'll make light of it—but you seem to be a serious sort of man, an educated man, so you tell me. What would you make of such a thing?"

"I don't know—it sounds like a medical problem."

"Your mind's playing tricks," said Dick.

"No, sir. I'm not listening to that. Because here it is: It happens, say about five in the morning—I checked my alarm clock. These various things I mentioned started. In my toe, and spread so that in less than a minute, about a half minute, my sides were quivering. And then I was shaking, and scared, and fearful of some sort of apocalyptic event. Alien invasion, nuclear war, Armageddon. But.. . it was over in about a minute and a half. I lay back down, and I was sweating. I was shaking. I was really, really shaking. God, *scared*. Let me tell you, I was scared."

"When did this happen?"

"This morning, for one."

"All the drinking," said Dick. "It takes its toll."

"I don't drink that much."

"That and the smoking."

Sebastian flicked his cigarette. He once again removed his pint and took a long swallow. "I don't smoke that much, and I don't drink that much—sometimes, like right now, it feels good, especially if I've been scared by something. And, for the past month or so I've been scared. One thing or another, I've been scared. Very scared. You can't talk to a woman about a thing like that, so it's good to have a couple of men like you all to talk about it. You tell a woman, and—well it's perceived as a weakness. Or you scare her. That's not good. You know?"

Dick whacked Sebastian on the arm. "Tina thinking she was pregnant—that's got you going. Panic attack."

"What if it's cancer?"

"Doubt it," said Dick. "Though I guess it could be."

"Oh, thanks."

"Any time. But look it's *not* that, you idiot. It's something in your *head*. Something fucked up in *there*. Lay off the booze a little, and it'll get better."

"What if it's a brain tumor?"

"I hope not."

"Or what if I'm going mad?"

"No . . ."

"Philip, do you think I'm going mad?"

Dick laughed. "How the hell would he know that? He just met you."

"From what I've said," said Sebastian. "Really, do you think it's possible?"

"I don't think so," said Philip. "It really sounds more . . . medical."

"Yes. It does, doesn't it?"

"Damn but this snow is getting deep!" shouted Dick. "You all're going to have to stay the night!"

14

He was drunk, plowed, messed up. It was fifteen inches of snow out there, and he hadn't brought boots. He'd have to call in. He'd first have to decide which job to call in. He got to talking about it, asking advice.

Sebastian had him cornered. "You've got three you're looking at. That's it, right?"

"Yes."

"Three. So which do you want?"

"I don't know."

Dick gave him a punch. "He could never make up his mind. That's Phil."

"Philip. Please."

"Yeah." Dick took a long swallow from a bottle of scotch.

"It's three in the morning," said Sebastian. "Three in the fucking morning. I'm going to sleep here in a minute, so you've got to decide. Me, I'd take the Panegyrics one—maybe you could work with your namesake."

"I didn't fill out the whole thing."

"What?"

"The whole app."

"But you think they'd take you. They wanted you, you said."

"Yes."

"The other two—they suck, don't they? Of course they do."

"You coming to bed?" A womanly shout.

Tina.

"Yeah, in a minute!"

Dick laughed. "If you don't go, I will."

"Cut it," said Sebastian. "Help this man. Which is it: the sailboat magazine gofer, the research guy for the university department, or the sales rep—for guns, ammo, and so forth? You're not telling me you'd actually take a job selling guns, ammo, and so forth? You don't look the type."

"Gets a car—company car," said Dick.

Tommy stumbled up to them. He had a glass of whiskey with a straw in it. "Snow's still coming down."

"Yeah," said Sebastian. "We know, but help us decide—which job this man goes with. He needs a job, everyone needs a job, so help us decide. Which of the three?" He named them off. "And, most important, we must understand why the choice. Get at the root, you see."

Tommy looked at the door. He went over to it. He drew the curtain at the window and peered out.

"Did you hear what I asked?" said Sebastian.

"I heard. Sure, sure. Me? I'd say the sailboat one. That's me. Up to you, my friend," said Tommy and raised his glass. He stumbled but put his hand out and touched the wall. He started to fall but sat down on the floor.

"You okay?"

"Doubt it. Probably poisoned myself."

"You don't look so good," said Sebastian. "Don't drink anymore. Get that thing away from him," he said to Dick. "You want a dead man on your premises?"

Tommy drank quickly. "You know what," he said, letting the empty glass fall into his lap, "I'm going to say that the sailboat is a definite ringer for this man. He looks like a sailboat man."

"He doesn't know a single thing about them," said Sebastian. "Do you, Philip?"

"No—no, I don't."

"We went out in a canoe that one time," said Dick. "Maybe that counts."

"I don't really have to know anything about sailboats, I don't suppose," said Philip. "I'd be an all-around menial duty type. If you can imagine."

"Not good. Much better the official researcher for the university department—in my opinion." Sebastian winked at him.

"But no company car," said Dick.

"You don't drive, do you? You have your license?" asked Sebastian.

"Yes. Of course."

"No car, though."

"No."

"Well, it's true you'd have something for your labor—a company car. Nothing to sneeze at, but the hunting thing? You ever shot a gun? Eviscerated a deer? Cleaned a weapon?"

"No."

"But you say this guy—this, what the hell's his name?"

"Digby Morris."

"Yes, right. Strange name. He's cool, you say."

"I thought so."

"But there's the probationary period. You'll lose out. You'll have a car, and then you won't. I don't like loss myself. I'm not happy with loss. You have it—you don't. I don't like that." Sebastian shook his head. He continued to shake his head.

"Are you coming to bed? Or aren't you?" Tina shouting.

Sebastian waved. "I'm coming!"

"Like I said," said Dick. "I'd be happy."

"Shut your goddamned mouth." He whacked Dick on the shoulder. "I'd take the university department. More prestige, and not much chance of getting dumped. That's my take on it."

Tommy looked ready to swoon. He was leaning over and touching the carpeted floor. He popped up suddenly. "This snow, I predict, will be three feet deep. Four. Five. That's something, huh? But what if there was nothing, nothing at all? You ever thought of that? Nothing? Nothing at all—ever?"

"I've told you," said Sebastian. "You can't have nothing. How could there *be* nothing?"

"Ah, ah, ah!" shouted Tommy. "Well, let's see now—*ex nihilo.*"

"I'm going to bed," said Sebastian.

"Snow," said Tommy. "Even so—"

"Supposed to stop by noon," said Dick.

"Three feet deep. At least."

"Foot and a half tops," said Dick. "I'm going to bed."

"Take good care of her," said Tommy, and winked.

"What's that supposed to mean?" said Dick, and he went over

and slapped Tommy's head.

"Nothing."

"Better not."

Dick went off.

"He's a lucky guy, huh?" said Tommy. He was swaying back and forth.

"Yeah, he is."

And Philip remembered how Lisa Wing had said she was in love with him. Was that for real? Three times he'd noted signs of it during their siege of drinking and playing charades. Once, she had smiled, just an incipient sort of smile, and then placed a hand on her hip. And a second, she had laughed at him when he messed up on imitating Dick, but it wasn't a laugh *against* him—it was as though she were laughing with him. And Dick looked angry—and she didn't make apologies. She laughed, then smiled. And then the third: it was the clincher. He was topping off on some bourbon, and then he felt a hand on his shoulder. She lay it there, and then Sebastian arrived, and she removed it. But the way she removed it, it was just a gentle lifting, so that he felt it still there for a second after she'd taken it away. Maybe she did love him. But she was pregnant. *Damn! You just have to be, don't you!*

But being pregnant—that probably hopped up her hormones.

"I've got a theory about snow," said Tommy.

"Yeah?"

He looked drunkenly sober, and he studied Philip perhaps for an initial reaction. "Yes, I do. Would you like to hear?"

"Okay. But I've got to get to sleep in a minute. I'm dying for some sleep."

"It won't take long. Just this: It comes down, you see, when there's something wrong with things. When there's disjunction in things. When there's a missing harmony in the hereabouts. It's beautiful to behold, but it's cold and strange, and it's evil in its pure white sublimity."

"You could freeze in it."

"People do. Many people, some within a few feet of their house, as I'm sure you know. But that's just the surface, that's just what you read in some stupid magazine. I'm talking more metaphysical—I'm talking about some principle underlying everything. When things aren't quite right, it snows. When it snows big, like now, and keeps snowing, things are very, very wrong. White covering everything. You ever thought about that? Why white should cover everything? Cold, wet, and white? Doesn't that seem strange and odd to you?"

"Not really. I like it at Christmas."

"You like it. Do you like floods, droughts, and the like?"

"No—I've got to go to sleep. I really do!"

"Are you coming to bed?" A womanly shout, but not Tina.

"Who's that?"

Lisa Wing entered the room. "Are you? You going to stay up all night? You two?"

"Not me," said Philip.

"You come on to bed then," she said. She took Philip's hand. "In our room."

He gave her a look. "Your room?"

She smiled. "We won't bite. You'll freeze out here."

She guided him back to their room. She opened the door. He noticed the motionless bundle in the bed—Dick.

15

"You don't have to worry," she said. "He's asleep."

She was in the middle, and she'd patted the mattress for him to sleep on her other side. "Right next to little me," she said.

"But—"

"Go to sleep. It's okay."

"I could sleep on the floor," he said.

"Don't be such a prude. Go to sleep."

He lay there. He lay on his back. He turned on his side, away from her. After a moment, he felt her touching him.

He turned over. "What?"

"I can't go to sleep."

"I'm sorry," he said. "That's bad. I hate that."

"Would you get me something?"

"Sure."

"Get me a drink of water. Okay?"

"Sure."

"No—make it milk."

"Okay."

He got up and stumbled and ran into the bedpost.

"Watch out," she whispered. "Be careful."

"I will."

He struggled for the door. Which way was it? It was closed and let in no light, and besides, it was dark out there in the living room, and so how was he to find his way to the kitchen?

First the door.

"Are you okay?"

"Where's the door?" He whispered, but was he too loud?

She sat up. He saw her shining face in the darkness. Her eyes, like cat's eyes. It was strange. They were so luminous. "It's that way." He saw the white palm of her hand.

"Good." He headed that way. It was more to the right than where he'd headed before. He ran into something, then felt, and took hold of the doorknob. Yes, yes.

"Thank you so much. You're such a sweetie."

"It's okay. I'm happy to—"

She was shushing him. He saw her finger against her mouth. Those lips.

He got out the door. He moved on. Rounded a corner. He could see the stove's pilot lights. This directed him to a point, and he moved from there to where he recalled the refrigerator, found the handle, pulled open the door to the light. Milk. A gallon. He kept the door open, for light's sake, and reached up and pulled open a cabinet door. Glasses, cups, bowls. He took down a glass, half filled it with milk, put back the gallon jug, closed the refrigerator door, let the pilot lights guide him out of the kitchen, walking backwards, and came to the bedroom door. He carefully turned the doorknob, but it squeaked. The hinges screeched. He could see her sitting up in bed. He felt like her husband.

He handed the glass of milk to her. Dick was snoring.

He got back in bed.

She drank it down. She handed him the glass.

He leaned over and set it against the wall.

She pulled at him. She pulled him close. "We could, you know. If you want to?"

"What?"

"Don't be coy. We could. If you'd like."

He found his voice. "Here? Now? With *him*?"

"Oh, don't bother with him. He sleeps like the dead."

She was snuggling against him. She had him all riled up. She had begun to kiss his neck.

"I can't, like this," he said.

"Oh, don't be so silly. He'll never know."

He whispered in her ear: "Maybe he's awake right now."

She whispered back: "He's not awake. You needn't *worry*."

So tempting. Right here, right now, so available, but next to Dick? Next to Dick Hazzard, his old roommate? How could he? He couldn't do that. Could he?

"No," he whispered. "No, really, I can't."

"Have it your way," she said. "At least you can keep me warm."

She snuggled close to him and began to rub his stomach. He had this strong sense that soon she would be rubbing him elsewhere. She seemed on the verge. He kept waiting for it. Knew it would come any moment. He wouldn't have a chance if she did.

It's not fair, he thought. This isn't fair.

"I feel so lonely tonight," she said. "Don't you ever feel lonely?"

He wanted her. He desperately wanted her. He couldn't imagine wanting anything more. "Yes," he said. "I do."

"What makes you lonely? Tell me."

He tried to be quiet, to whisper.

"I don't know . . . living alone . . . living by myself . . . not having anyone to live with. You know—"

"You said the same thing three times," she said. "Basically. It was redundant."

"Oh."

"But that's okay. You're just tired. You want someone, huh?"

"Yes, yes I do."

"Like me?"

"Yes. I do."

"Then I'd think you'd show it a little more."

Pouty. He recognized pouty when he heard it, or saw it. Sometimes, Sophia Cross was pouty when she told him about her boyfriend, her lips puckering. She looked like a little girl. He felt sorry for her, but he also felt horny and stirred up. Pouty did that to him.

Dick moved in the bed. He rolled over, and there was a loud noise.

Dick had hit the floor.

Philip pulled away, went for the floor, and tried to crawl under the bed. The glass rattled against the wall. It rolled.

Lisa laughed. It was a tinkling laugh, then a snicker.

"What the hell?" cried Dick. "What the hell? Who threw me off the bed? I hurt my head. Damn!"

"Oh, god!" laughed Lisa. "Did you hear yourself? You rhymed!"

"Hey! You think it's funny? My head."

"Oh, come to Mama, I'm sorry."

"You better be."

"Let me feel." Silence, and then a soft singing, and then, "I don't feel a thing. You're perfectly okay. Go back to sleep."

"Yeah. Okay. Good night."

"Good night."

"What are you doing awake?"

"I can't sleep."

"Get a glass of milk."

"I did."

"Well, hell, I don't know."

"I'm going to sleep—you go to sleep."

Philip lay there on the floor. Under the bed. It was cold, and he was scared—scared of Dick waking up. The man could punch a bad one. He'd knocked that one guy who'd intimidated him back a good three or four feet with a punch that made a noise like you'd hit a sack of flour, only with something hard inside it. Bone. He'd connected hard with bone.

It was a good ten minutes, and then, a sweet whisper: "It's okay. Come on up."

"I don't know," he whispered.

"I'm coming down to get you," she said, all sing-songy.

He crawled out. Carefully. Where was that damn milk glass? *Don't make it roll.* He got on the bed. He moved to her, to whisper at her: "He'll *hear.*"

"I'm so lonely," she said. "You sleep here with me, or I'll never speak to you again."

No, he thought. *You can't let that happen.*

Only, he thought, nobody ever meant that, and she didn't either. Maybe she wouldn't speak to him tomorrow morning, or even the next time he saw her, but then the anger would melt away, and pretty soon she'd be speaking to him. And more.

Something propelled him: "I love you too."

Silence.

"What? What'd you say?"

"I love you," said Philip. "I'm falling in love with you—too."

He got pushed away. "Who said anything about love?"

"Huh? What? I thought you said, when I got here . . . you said, didn't you, that you'd . . ." He couldn't get it out.

"Oh, *that*," she said, laughing. Too loud—she was too loud. "You're still thinking about *that*. Forget it. I don't do things out of love, honey, only because I want to. Aren't you the same way? Isn't everyone? Dick is. I can tell you. Dick definitely is."

Too loud. Much too loud. He shushed her.

She giggled.

"Oh, well," he said. "I'm sorry."

"No doubt about it," she said. "We're all that way."

"He told me," said Philip. "About the baby."

"*What?*"

"The baby."

"*Baby*. What baby?"

"Huh? What? You and him. The baby. You being pregnant."

"He *what?*"

"Oh . . . I didn't know. Maybe I shouldn't have."

"I'm not *pregnant*! Dick!" She slapped his sleeping body. Philip went for the floor.

"What—what?" cried Dick. Philip hurriedly crawled under the bed. The top of his head scraped against the box springs.

"You said I was *pregnant?*"

Silence.

Slapping.

"Hey, what the . . ."

"Wake up!"

More slapping.

"What the . . ."

"Wake *up!*"

"*What?*"

"You said I was *pregnant*. Is that what you said?"

Sleepy voice, half there. "I was just . . . talking. Probably said . . . you'd like to *get* pregnant."

Silence.

"Oh? Is that a fact?"

"Or I'd like to get you pregnant. Loving you the way I do—you know. You know. Man talk. Crap like that."

"*No*. That's *not* man talk. Men do not talk that way. They don't talk about *like* on that one. They talk about *are*, the facts, and they commiserate together—don't they? Huh? Don't they? Get drunk and blame the woman, don't they? Huh, don't they!"

A loud slap.

"Ow!"

"Don't they?"

"God!" he yelled. "Hell, I was just drunk, honey. Hell, I don't even remember saying it."

"Yes, you do. You said I was pregnant. Now why in the world would you say a thing like that?"

"I don't know."

Stirring about in the bed. The box springs sinking.

He about let it out, a yelp, from the sharp springs scraping his forehead.

"You did say it, didn't you? Didn't you?"

"Yeah, I said it. Sorry."

"Dick!"

"Well, I won't do it again. I'm tired. I'm exhausted. Don't worry about it. Never happen again. Okay? I want to go back to sleep. *Please*."

"Why'd you do it? Why? Why ever?"

Back slaps. Back slaps sounded different than arm or head slaps. These were back slaps.

"Hey, hey, quit it!"

Rolling over. Sitting up.

Philip eased himself farther under the bed. He scraped his shoulder against a prominent spring.

"What if *I* said something like that?" said Lisa Wing. "What if *I* did? Huh?"

And then she started to cry.

"Hey, hey, now, now, it's okay . . . it's *okay*. Maybe I said it because I really would kind of like for you to get pregnant, you know?"

She still cried.

She sobbed hard.

"Really, maybe that's why I did it."

Noises outside the room. The door opened suddenly. "You all okay in here?"

Sounded like Tommy.

"Yeah. Go to bed. Everything's fine."

"All right. Okay. Fine and dandy. Night, folks."

"Night."

Tommy all right. Probably hadn't slept yet. Probably not the kind to sleep—much, if any. Probably on speed half the time.

Lisa Wing had stopped crying. She was now murmuring at him. "Did you really mean that? That you want a baby? Do you?"

"Sure. Sure I do."

"You want to get married too?"

"Oh, well, soon—sure. Soon."

"Well, I guess that's not necessary. And maybe the baby's not necessary. I don't know. I hate to think of all the pain and stuff. My sister had one. God! But . . . it's kind of sweet for you to say what you did. And I forgive you."

"Thanks, honey."

"Go to sleep."

"Yeah, night."

"Unless you want to . . . you know."

No. God. No.

"I don't know," said Dick, with a whine, a wheeze. "Doubt if I could perform exactly . . . after, you know, all that booze, and I'm so, so, you know—petered out."

Lisa laughed. "That's funny!"

"Didn't mean it to be," said Dick, and Philip heard instant snoring. Yes, Dick was one to fall immediately, suddenly, into sleep, and snore without a minute's hesitation. Didn't he know that from rooming with the guy for three years? He'd say "I'm going to just lie down here, Phil, for a minute," and then whammo, Dick was out.

"Philip?"

"Yes?"

"It's okay now. I *feel* you under the bed."

100

He didn't answer back. But he did try to crawl out.

He eventually crawled out, the spring scraping his scalp.

The damn milk glass rolled and rolled. He'd kicked it.

You're dead meat.

But he wasn't. He came up and faced her, and no Dick. Snoring, he was.

"Get in bed, honey. Sweetie. We've got room."

Honey? Sweetie?

He crawled back in bed with her. He moved right up next to her. She pulled him close, close.

"It wouldn't hurt," she said. "Really. If you want."

"I'd like to," he said.

"Of course you would."

She began to pull at his briefs, then got them down a little.

He panicked.

"No, no," he said. "I'm too tired—really."

"God," she said, "men! I thought women were the ones who got blamed for not being in the mood!"

Too loud! Way too loud!

"Maybe in the *morning*," he whispered.

"Oh, if you wish," she said.

He lay there and tried to avoid her.

"Night," he said.

"Night."

Her voice harsh—no question.

16

When he woke up, it was still dark, and he crept out of the room with his clothes in hand, and dressed in the bathroom. He stood in the living room and stared out at the snow-filled yard, deep, deep, up high on tree trunks, tree limbs weighted down with snow. The street and sidewalks were filled.

"Want some coffee or something?"

It was Tina standing there. Smiling. Really pretty. She was in a blue terry-cloth robe. Had she brought that with her? Or maybe a borrowed one?

"Yes, please."

He was reminded of his mother coming into the living room and calling his dad, engrossed in the paper.

"Sebastian is dead to this world," said Tina. "But I'll be glad to make coffee for you. Little woman that I am."

She made it. He stood at the window watching the snow. He felt her eyes on him. He turned around and she was smiling.

How pretty she was.

Sophia. Oh, god.

My scrumptious, delicious one.

They sat in the kitchen and sipped coffee. She talked about where she and Sebastian lived, how they'd probably have to stay here for the day until the streets were plowed, how she'd miss work, but it wasn't a big thing, and how Sebastian hated his job and would love to miss. In fact, he missed a lot, but somehow they kept him on.

"Where does he work?"

"He didn't tell you?"

"No."

"I thought he told everyone. That's funny. Well, he works as a pencil pusher for an insurance company. He hates it. Forms, files, piped-in music, break in the morning, break in the afternoon—fifteen minutes—and forty-five for lunch. Start at eight, end at five. What a grind. My job's the same. Grind. No other way to put it. I loathe it."

"How long have you two been married?"

"Oh, we're not married. We've been living together for . . . what is it, three years come March. It's kind of like marriage, but it isn't marriage. Know what I mean?"

"Yeah."

"You married?"

"No."

"Got a girl?"

"No."

"Looking around, huh?"

"Well, I have someone, but she's already taken."

"Oh. That's hard," said Tina. "But you'll find a way to get her. There's always a way to accomplish a thing like that. And I'll bet you do."

With brutal Rod Busby in the picture? He could end up in the hospital. He imagined punches to the gut, punches to the face. Broken nose, lips bloodied, teeth knocked out, jaw bone broken. Ribs. *No, no—no.*

But he said to Tina, "Sure. I'm hoping for it."

"Oh, no. You've got to do more than hope. You've got to give it every inch of your being."

She seemed surprisingly serious. What was up?

"Something wrong?"

"Not exactly." And then she turned away. "Yes." Her voice broke.

"What's wrong?"

She was looking out the window. "Sebastian is such a bastard. I'll bet you noticed."

What was he supposed to say? Agree? "Well," he said.

"Oh, come on, you noticed. Everyone does. A know-it-all. And yet I love him. Isn't that stupid? How stupid is that?" Her voice was breaking. She still had her back to him.

"I'm sorry. I'm really sorry."

"It's the most important thing in life. The very most important thing. To find someone you love, and who loves you back." She turned to face him. Tears were dribbling down her cheeks.

"I know," he said. "God, I'm sorry."

"Oh, *believe* me. There's something really spiritual about it. Don't you think? Don't you?" And then she said, "Well, I guess it's not the *highest* form of love, not according to S.K.—but really—"

Sebastian waltzed in.

"What's up?"

"You," said Tina. "You, always. You want something for breakfast? You want some coffee?"

"Sure." He sat down. He looked utterly at ease. But self-absorbed.

Tina got a cup and poured him a full one, leaving no room for cream. "What do you want to eat?"

"Eggs. Scrambled."

"Okay. When do you think we'll get out of here?"

"We won't be getting out of here today, that's for sure."

"I thought as much."

"I need to," said Philip. "I really do need to."

"You won't," said Sebastian. "Might as well hang here, play some poker, and drink the rest of the booze. Is there any?" He pointed up.

"How would I know?" said Tina, breaking eggs. "I don't keep track of that kind of thing."

"Look up in that cabinet, right above your head. Right there— that's where Dick stores the goodies."

Tina shook her head. She made a half turn and reached up. She grabbed two bottles of Jim Beam. "Looks like you're in luck."

"Beer? Any beer?"

"You want me to check the fridge, don't you?"

"It's okay. I'll do it." He got up and pulled open the door. "A six pack left. Not much, but a start. Where's the store around here?"

"I thought you said we're stuck here."

"We can always walk to the store—if it's not too far."

"You don't have any boots. How are you going to walk in that?" She made a wave at the backyard.

Tommy came into the room. "Dick's got boots."

"Is that right? Do Dick's boots fit Sebastian?"

"Doubt it."

"Which means Dick'll have to walk in his own boots, probably," said Tina, cracking another egg. She began to beat them.

"Who needs to go out?" asked Tommy leaning at the window sill, looking out.

"Nobody. Only he thinks he needs to," said Tina.

"Not all that important, unless you have a thirst for beer," said Sebastian.

"Drink your rotgut," said Tina, pointing at the cabinet above her.

"That's not rotgut. Well, I guess it is rotgut, but it'll serve."

"What?"

"It'll do the trick, won't it, Tommy?"

"You're an alcoholic, Tommy," said Tina.

"Me? No, I'm not—well, I might be." He danced a little at the window. "Man, what a sight out there!"

"It's pretty," said Tina. "Isn't it?"

"If I ever die, I'd like to die in the middle of that!" said Tommy and rushed toward Tina, picked her up, and swung her around.

"You fool!" She kissed him. "He's really okay," she said, as Tommy put her down. "He's like our little puppy dog, isn't he?" she said to Sebastian.

"I could use some toast," said Sebastian.

"He never listens to a thing I say," said Tina, looking at Philip. "You know that?"

"Wanting a piece of toast isn't exactly like ignoring," said Sebastian. "I just want, I need, a piece of toast."

"Hangover—again? Okay, you shall have your toast," said Tina, and grabbed the loaf of bread and stuck a piece of bread into the toaster. She drove the lever down.

"More coffee?" she said to Philip.

"Yes—please. Thanks."

She poured it. "At least somebody around here appreciates me."

"Don't you ever stop?" said Sebastian.

"I'll bet this snow lasts all winter," said Tina.

"I don't mind," said Tommy.

"Wait a minute," said Philip. "What about the—"

"Yeah, man!" said Tommy, fixing him with a grin.

"I'm going out to get some beer and chips," said Sebastian. "Want to go with me, Tommy?"

"In that? Don't know."

"Thought you loved it."

"Looking at it—whew!"

Dick and Lisa Wing waltzed in. "Wow, wow," said Dick. "You see all that?"

"You sleep okay?" asked Lisa.

"Like a mummy," said Tina.

"Oh—I want some coffee," said Lisa.

"I'll get you a cup."

"Me too," said Dick.

"Got some boots, Dick?" said Sebastian.

"Yeah—why?"

"I want to go out and get beer."

"They wouldn't fit you."

"Where's the nearest store?"

"No need to go. There's this delivery place."

"Beer? They deliver beer?"

"Practically anything. If you buy enough."

"Good. I've got some cash," said Sebastian. He plunged in his pocket.

"No, no, I've got it," said Dick.

Philip looked at him. He and Dick exchanged glances.

"I've got to go," said Philip.

"Now?" said Dick.

"I've got a job to get to."

"Oh? Now which is it?" said Sebastian, pointing a finger.

"That research job," said Philip. "I've decided on that research job."

"Good choice. Good man. But why? Know *why*. *Know* it."

"I don't want sales," said Philip. "I really don't want sales."

"Who'd want sales?"

"You pick that research job over a company car?" said Dick. "What the hell? You stupid? You crazy?"

"Hunting," said Philip. "I don't know a thing about it."

106

"Who the hell cares? Wing it."

"Hey, I take exception to that," said Lisa.

She gave Philip a look which he couldn't read as anything other than a come-on. A big come-on. He wanted her. He really *did* want her. Maybe even more than Sophia. He couldn't be sure.

She blew him a kiss.

Dick didn't see it. Philip smiled, and then for diversion said, "Well, if you don't need those boots—"

"Take them," said Dick. "Lisa, get him the boots, would you?"

"Am I your servant?"

"If you *would*," said Dick, and took a gulp of coffee.

"I suppose I don't mind," said Lisa.

He followed her to the bedroom. She closed the door.

She moved in close. "If you ever get lonely," she said, and stuck her wet tongue in his ear. They collapsed on the bed. They lay there for a little, her face snug against his, but then he heard noise outside the door, and he got up quickly.

"Jumpy!" she said, and laughed. She handed him the boots.

They went into the kitchen.

They were in some sort of conversation, Tina in the middle of it. "I find Kierkegaard interesting—in ways. Maybe I can't live up to him, but even so—"

"Dogmatist," said Sebastian.

"You haven't even read him."

"So? I've heard you read him. She charms me with reading him out loud," said Sebastian. "Wacko stuff. Out there in religious la-la land."

"That's real fun, huh?" said Dick.

Lisa jumped in: "Tina's always been that way. Real mystical. Right?"

"Oh quit it," said Tina. "Look, I can tell you a story. If you'll just listen."

"And what is it now?" said Sebastian. "About your uncle? He went off on his own to find the Lord. Found him in Timbuktu."

"In Indianapolis," said Tina. "Well, I guess he did."

"Tell us," said Lisa. "We like stories."

"Depends on the story," said Sebastian.

"I'd hear it," said Philip. "Tell it. Tell it."

Philip took a chair and Lisa landed on his lap, and then she moved quickly to the chair next to him when Dick gave them both an acid look.

"If you'll just bear with me, I will. All right?"

A hush fell, and Tina began: "My grandmother was standing in our yard. She was looking out toward a field. We lived in the country. And suddenly she said, 'Oh, my, here they come! Here they come!'

"'Who?' I asked. 'Who's coming?'

"'Oh, can't you see them?' she says. 'Can't you see them? It's my father and my mother and this angel—this white, absolutely alabaster white angel with enormous wings!'

"'Your parents,' I said. 'And an angel?'

"'Yes, this big, big angel, see? Such big, big wings!'"

"Please," said Sebastian. "Do spare us."

"Shut it. I want to hear," said Lisa.

Tina smiled, went on: "But I didn't see anything. I didn't. Yet it was right then, right on the spot that my grandmother sinks to her knees and falls dead. Right in front of me. Can you imagine?"

"Dead," said Lisa.

"Yes, just like that." She snapped her fingers.

"How do you figure?" asked Lisa.

Sickness, thought Philip.

"Well, I don't know if I *can* figure." Tina was cradling a cup of coffee in her hands, like she needed the warmth. Then she took a slow sip.

"You think she saw the angel, really?" asked Lisa.

"Oh, yes, she *saw* the angel. No question. Big and white, you know. How big? I don't know. But I guess with a good wing span. Maybe ten feet? Imagine a huge white angel, with a ten-foot wing span. That would undoubtedly get your attention. Wouldn't it? You'd probably keel over right there on the spot if you were eighty-eight, sickly, and a spiritualist of various kinds. Now wouldn't you?"

"You don't think there really *was* an angel, though, do you?" said Lisa.

"*Was* in what way?"

"Oh, you know! I mean actually *did* exist. Actually was there."

"Exist *how*? Was *where*?"

"Oh, Tina, you know what the hell I mean—please!"

"That's my Tina," said Sebastian. "Four sheets to the wind when it comes to nitpicking."

"Don't you mean three sheets?" said Dick.

"Four, three—who the hell cares?"

"Like this coffee cup here, you mean?" said Tina.

"Yes," said Lisa. "Like that."

"Or like me holding the coffee cup?"

"Yes."

"I don't really know," said Tina. "It existed for *her*—isn't that enough? She saw it. And what's that mean? If you saw it, it's there, isn't it? In some way?"

Philip put his finger up. "No. I really don't like that idea! I heard enough of that back in college, and I really don't like that idea. Really, I don't."

"I don't much either," said Tina, "but my grandmother saw all kinds of things that didn't exist. At least you would probably *say* they didn't exist."

"Like what?" asked Philip.

"Aliens, for one. And she didn't just see things, she heard things too."

Sebastian's lip was curling. He gave Tina a nasty, toothy grin.

"Such as?" said Philip.

"Trees singing, grass and weeds humming, birds talking, the wind repeating lines out of the Bible, the ground mumbling Shakespeare. She heard that too. She heard Shakespeare coming up from the ground. Down deep somewhere. She'd crawl around with her ear to the soil. You see she'd studied Shakespeare in college, and had been an actress when she was young, and she could repeat many lines, and she heard whole parts delivered below her feet. And she would sometimes bend over and say, 'That's right, that's right. That's how it goes. Like that.'"

"Hey!" shouted Sebastian. "And so the old gal was bonkers!"

"Off her meds," said Dick.

Sick, sick, thought Philip. Ripe for death.

"You might say," said Tina, nodding. "Or you might say she was just more in tune with things. More disembodied, I'd like to think. She sometimes spoke of flesh being a garb that she wanted to peel off. One time I saw her standing before the mirror muttering it: 'I remove this, yes . . . this part, yes, and this, and I peel it, see, I peel it down just like a banana peel. Ah! Yes.' And then a giggle, and a laugh. The woman was mad, no doubt, but I've got to thinking, maybe not so mad."

"She was mad—of a certain," said Sebastian. "I think we can close the book on that one."

"But I do like the story," said Lisa.

"She was perhaps a poet," said Philip. And he was thinking: *How beautiful Tina looks there with her large bosom and libidinous lips.* She suddenly reminded him of this buxom blond woman professor who'd given him no end of lascivious thoughts.

"She gave up on the flesh—entirely. It was sometime after her baptism in the river. It was a deep, deep river, outside of a tiny little burg, and she'd gone there swimming plenty of times, and picnicking with her family, and fishing, and so forth, but this young pastor, a wild-eyed young man with flaming red hair—I saw his picture, she'd kept it in an old album—he did the baptism, and he sunk her down, but she didn't come up. She didn't come up because somehow she'd gone under into the deep bowl of the river at that point, and she'd gotten entangled in a branch of an old log stuck down there. It was a fright."

"What happened?" asked Lisa.

Philip felt her leg brushing his own. An electric current ran through his gonads.

"Go on? Sure. See, what happened is that she drowned. They got her pulled out, maybe after an hour, and she was purplish and puffy, you know how they are when that happens. Purplish and puffy, and teeth yellow and brown with river bottom. Hair against a white scalp. Already, it seemed rigor mortis might be setting in. That's what they said, anyway."

"*And?*" said Lisa, bending forward.

"Go on?" said Tina. "Sure. See, what happened next was that they had her hauled out, her limp thirteen-year-old body spread out on the river bank, and these people hovering over her, and this young wild, red-haired pastor weeping, blaming himself, and then this girl, my grandmother, she opens her eyes. Wide."

"What?"

"Yes, she'd drowned, you see. She was *dead*. Totally dead. But now she's back!"

"Uh-huh," said Sebastian.

"May I?" asked Tina.

"Do charm us," said Dick. "I go for a good tale now and then."

"*What?*" said Lisa.

"All right. *Listen*, then. An hour under the water. A whole hour. She is of a *certain* dead. Only she's not. She opens her eyes. This alarms them, this greatly alarms them. They stand back as she begins to rise to her feet. They fear something, something nemesis-like is about to occur. They fear a demon's gotten in and is now about to destroy each and every one of them. But no . . . no, it doesn't happen. She stands before them, she spits out river water—and then she announces, 'I have seen the mystery of all things. I have seen down there, down at the bottom, the Mystery of All Being.' I think she capitalized that whole business—if you know what I mean. You think they could doubt her? You think they *would* doubt her?"

The way she asked this question—with such penetrating intensity. It made Philip wonder. Was Tina herself some sort of spiritualist? Would there be a chance with such a woman? Like if you popped the question—what then?

Sebastian raised a finger. "No they wouldn't, but then let's do consider the bunch of hicks we're talking about. Huh?"

"Garden variety nutcases," said Dick.

"I'll tell you what," said Lisa. "If my Uncle Barnhart Bigfoot rose from the dead, I'd be scooting. And fast."

111

"Not your real uncle," said Dick.

"What's your point?"

"Tommy?" said Dick.

"Huh?"

"Goddamn," said Dick, "are you with us?"

"With whom?"

"Isn't it with *who*?" said Lisa.

"No," said Sebastian. "It's with *whom—whom* is the object of the preposition *of.*"

"Okay," said Lisa. "Fine."

"Well, it is," said Sebastian.

"May I continue, please?" said Tina.

"If you must," said Sebastian.

"Thank you." Tina went on: "So . . . after this, she begins to hear things in the wind, the trees, the ground. The Mystery, she calls it. And she sees a spacecraft landing, and points to it, but nobody else sees it. Just her."

"Now that's pretty cool," said Lisa.

"It's damn poetic," said Philip.

"I think I need something to drink," said Dick.

"It was that Mystery she gave everything to," said Tina. "I couldn't do it myself. It's not for me. But anyway, once she tried to give away everything she owned—you've heard of a busk?"

"Yes," said Sebastian. "I'm sure we have."

"Well, she was bent on cleaning out everything—I mean every *single* thing— because she was told in a storm cloud to give absolutely everything away. It went something like this: *You must disrobe yourself and your house and belongings of every single thing.*"

"Her clothes too?" asked Lisa, biting her fingernail.

"Yep. She had to get rid of her clothes, her family's clothes, her house, her everything. *They* wouldn't strip naked, the rest of them, but she did. They locked her up for a while after that, for simply trying to do it. She got out, though. But it was a long time. Asylums back then—they weren't a pretty sight."

"Poor old granny," said Dick.

Suddenly, Philip was struck by this: Tina without clothes—not that thirteen-year-old, but Tina herself. Huh? Huh? God, but . . .

"Well," said Sebastian. "Are we enlightened?"

"But I sort of like it," said Lisa. "It's funny. In ways."

"Gotta admit," said Dick, "But the old gal would put a real damper on a party. Now wouldn't she?"

"She knew," said Tina, "something about S.K.'s sickness unto death. And you've got to give her that. It's a whole different world— you know?"

"*Sickness*," said Sebastian, "is right. Anybody drink to that?"

Dick got up and went for the cabinet. He came forth with a bottle of Jim Beam.

Sebastian held forth his cup.

Tommy held forth his.

"At this hour?" said Lisa.

Philip found Tina's eyes. They were sedate, powder blue. Was she about to speak the Mystery herself?

"You know what?" said Dick. "I got something for you, Tina."

"Don't encourage her," said Sebastian. "Nothing by S.K, please."

"Nope," said Dick. "Just a minute."

They sat and waited.

Dick returned with a book and handed it to Tina. "Here, you might find it useful."

She held it up before them. "Logic. What? You think I'm not logical?"

"Hey, I flunked the goddamn course, but I thought maybe you, you being the brainy type—you'd get it."

"Nothing brainy in what we heard here today," said Sebastian.

"Will you please just shut up?" said Tina. "Please?" She glared at him for a few moments, and then turned to gaze at the book, turned pages, making meditative noises, and then she looked up— at Dick. "I'll take it. It looks useful."

"Now you've done it," said Sebastian.

Philip watched the two of them. Tina caught his eye. Ah! Those powder blue eyes and that red lipstick. That silken blond hair!

17

It was cold, the snow drifting knee-deep, and he had so far to walk. It was good, he thought, not to have to show up at any particular time—all he had to do was restart that application. He could stop off and see Sophia Cross, have a cup of coffee—no pancakes because he was full after eating at Dick's, but he must see Sophia.

You're a bastard, aren't you, Phil?

A first-rate bastard the way you came on to that Lisa Wing.

No, no. She came on to you.

And you tell me how a man can resist that.

The snow was getting down into his boots. He'd tied them tight, but his socks were wet, and his feet were cold and hurting.

When he got to his apartment, he removed his boots first thing. He rubbed his feet. He sat on the hard bed, too tired to do anything. He lay down, took a nap, and then got into the shower. The shower head dangled down. If he didn't watch it, his head would brush up against it, or a vagrant hand would catch it—and it would come down hard and land on his foot, leaving water gushing from the pipe. The damned thing had fallen once before, barely missing his toes.

He got out of the shower, got dressed in his suit, his blue one. He put on a red tie. He pulled his boots on, his own boots, *dry*, which he'd been a total fool not to have worn (*What the hell's wrong with you, Phil?*) and got his pant legs into the boots.

By the time he arrived, it was lunch time. He spotted her from the plate glass window as he headed for the door. He stomped the snow off his boots on the narrow edge of sidewalk. Then he got in, sat down at his usual place, and she caught sight of him and headed to his table.

"Hi, how are you?"

"I'm fine. And you?"

"Good."

She looked extra special good. He'd hoped she would be a little distraught, worried about her abusive boyfriend, but she seemed just fine. Perky, even.

"I'd like a sandwich, I guess," he said.

"What kind?"

"Tuna fish."

"Your favorite dish?"

He smiled.

She was in some sort of mood.

"What's a matter?"

She looked around, gazed outside. A man stood out there, across the street. Immobile. Staring.

Him!

"I'm afraid for you."

He pointed. "Him? I don't know who he is, but I'm not worried."

"Not him," said Sophia. "Rod. He'll be here in a minute. And I'm afraid—"

"No reason to worry."

"You're not thinking."

"You don't want me to leave, do you? I'm not planning on leaving."

She stood there, apparently debating it. "Maybe you should. Really, maybe you should." She took him by the arm and started to pull him.

"No, no," said Philip. "No. I've got a right to be here. I don't have to leave just because the big *Rod Busby* is coming. Why would I do that?"

She got a look. She said nothing for a few moments. "He knows who you are. That's why."

"Huh? How would he know me? He's never seen me."

"Oh, he's seen you."

"When?"

"Oh, believe me, he's seen you. So you've got to be quick."

"I didn't see him."

"He saw you. Take my word. You've got to get out of here."

"No," he said. "No."

She looked put out. "Okay—well, okay. I tried to warn you. Just remember that—I did try." She headed quickly to the kitchen.

Angry at me. A first. You don't want a woman angry. No—no.

He sat there watching the man across the street. He was tall with a long black coat and Russian hat, and he wore tall black boots, up to his knees. He wore glasses, and his nose protruded down from them. He stood very still, just staring.

Rod Busby showed up.

Philip recognized him from a picture Sophia Cross had shown him. He was more built than he'd looked in that picture. He was five ten or so, had a bulldog face with short blond hair. His teeth were stubby looking but perfectly white. Philip caught all this when Busby stood at the entrance, eying him. "Well, now. Do I behold our very own Philip Fellows?"

"Yes."

Busby advanced on him, extending a hand. "Pleasure to meet you, Phil."

"It's Philip. Not Phil. Nice to meet you."

"Yeah, yeah. May I sit?"

"Uh—"

"Well?"

"Sure."

"You ain't, though, are you?"

"It's okay."

"Yeah, well, I'm hungry as hell. Where is she? I don't see her."

"In the kitchen, I guess."

"You'd know better than I would. Wouldn't you?"

"What do you mean?"

"You know what I mean."

"What?"

"Eating here practically every day."

"It's a nice place."

"Nice scenery too, huh?" Rod Busby whacked his arm. A devious grin formed on his lips.

"What?"

"Just kidding! Just kidding. So . . . Phil-o, what do you think of

Sophia, my sweet girl?"

"She's nice."

"And? That's all?"

"She's a very nice person."

"Ha! That's it, huh? A babe stacked like that, with meat in all the right places, and that's *all* you can say?"

"She's your girlfriend. What do you want me to say?"

Rod took up the salt and pepper shakers. He dinged them together.

"Really. So you *would* have more to say if she wasn't—that it?"

"No."

"I'll just bet." He whacked Philip on the arm.

Now Sophia was on her way, balancing a tray and a drink. She had a grim look on her face. She had her eyes on Rod Busby. They did not waver.

"Hey, honey, that for me?"

"No."

"Why not?'

"Were you here?"

"No."

"Well, then, it's for him. This is what he ordered."

"Yeah? Who'd have thought?"

"What?"

"I'll take what he has there—looks good."

"As you wish." Sophia took off.

"You know, sometimes," said Rod, "sometimes, I just don't know. Sometimes I just have to think that life's a bitch. Ain't she, Philly?"

"Philip."

"Yeah, yeah." He again whacked Philip on the arm.

It hurt. The man had large fists. Red knuckles. The word *brutal* came to mind.

Philip sat before his tuna sandwich. He did not want to eat with Rod Busby staring him down.

"You going to eat that thing?"

"Yes."

"Well, hell, eat. You didn't buy it to look at it, did you?"

117

"No." He bit into it. While he ate he watched the man in the black attire. What? What the hell?

"What's to look at, Phil-man?" said Rod.

"Nothing."

"Oh, yeah? Well, you were looking pretty hard—at that guy over there. You know him?"

"No."

"He must know you. Or want something. What's he want, Phil?"

"Philip!"

"Oh, goddamn. Well now, Philip, what's he want?"

"I don't know. I really don't know." The man shifted his weight to one foot.

"Well now, we'll just see," said Rod. "Won't we? We'll just see about that." He rose, moved quickly to the door, yanked it open, and made a beeline toward the man standing across the street.

Philip chewed. Chewed and watched.

Rod Busby shoved the man. Two quick shoves.

The man in the black coat backed away and then turned away, walking briskly.

Busby ambled back toward the restaurant, yanked open the door, and rejoined Philip at his table. "He won't be bothering you anytime soon, my friend. He's got religion now—I gave him a little taste of it."

"What'd you say?"

"Not much. Said, 'You got a problem there, buddy? You got some sorta problem, do you, something you need my particular help with? Is that what's going on here, buddy?' And then when he stared at me, I gave him a couple shoves. He took off. End of story, Phil. Some sort of pervert. Don't worry about him." He grabbed Philip by the shoulders. "Okay, buddy?"

"Pervert?"

"Your garden variety pervert, Phil."

Sophia was heading their way balancing a tray.

"Well, now, that's some fine service," said Rod Busby.

"Then treat me right."

"When don't I treat you right, babe?" Rod grabbed the tray.

"Hey, just like I like it, without the crusts." He turned to Philip. "She cuts them special for me. Isn't that nice? Isn't that just sweet?"

"Not always," said Sophia.

"Not always—what? When?"

"You don't always treat me nice."

"Oh? And when's the bad?"

"I think you know."

She stood there glaring at him.

Rod Busby grinned and then ripped a piece off his sandwich. His bite was quick and savage.

Sophia headed off. Philip made a point of not watching her. He glanced at Rod, and he saw he *was* watching her.

"Got a bee in her bonnet, Phil. Just a minute." Rod Busby got up. He made his way toward Sophia, who was hanging toward the kitchen.

Philip watched.

Busby was gone a few long moments.

He came back swaggering. He sat back down. He slammed a hand down on the table. "I don't know, Phil. I just don't know. They can be bitches, can't they? They can be utter bitches. But then what would we do without them? You tell me."

"What happened?" It was out of his mouth before he'd given it a second thought.

Busby grinned at him. "You're asking? You're wanting to know? That it?"

"No. Sorry."

"Yeah, you're wanting to know. I can tell, Phil-o. And so, you have a drink with me tonight at the bar of my choice, and I'll think about it. Maybe I'll tell you what we jawed it up about."

"Tonight?"

"That's what I said. Didn't I?"

"I don't know."

"Don't know what?"

"I don't see how."

"You turning me down for a drink?"

"No—"

"You'll show. You'd best do it, Philly."

"Okay."

"Good."

"I've got to go."

Rod Busby shot his hand out. "Pleasure, Phil. Pleasure to finally meet you. Why'd we wait so long, buddy?"

"I don't know."

Philip was on his way out.

"Hey, don't be a stranger!" yelled Busby. "Bar None—that's the bar. Be there! Ten o'clock!"

But he was already out the door and on the sidewalk heading to his next destination. Hunt and Hart.

18

"You're a bit late, aren't you, Philip? Tardy, dilatory, what's the deal?"

"I'm here—"

"I can see you're here. And so I'll show you around." Digby Morris put his hand on Philip's shoulder and squeezed. "Don't let it happen again. The worst thing—the very worst thing a sales guy can do—is be late. Got it?"

"Yes. But—"

"No buts on that one, sir." Digby moved ahead and said, "Todd, this is Philip. Philip—Todd."

Todd sprang up, in a slick gray suit. "Philip, nice to meet you." He stuck his hand out. "What's your pleasure?"

"Pardon?"

"What's your sales orientation, your whole manifesto of sales methods you're bringing to Hunt and Hart?"

"Oh, I . . . I don't have any. What's yours?"

"Ha! What's mine? What's mine, Dig?"

"A hell of a lot more than mine, I'm sure," said Digby Morris.

"Just name one," said Todd, turning to Philip. He fixed him with a stare.

"No—no," said Digby. "He's new. Philip, now we meet Al, the great Al."

"*One*," said Todd, moving to cut off Digby Morris. "Just name one. You don't get on here unless you deliver your spiel, and that spiel includes, doesn't it, Mr. Morris, a battery from the Manifesto."

"Manifesto," said Digby. "Ah, yes, the Manifesto."

"Name one."

"Okay," said Digby, "Philip, name one. Looks like you've got to name one sales hook from your toolkit to satisfy Todd here. To get by Todd. One sales hook, one lure, one feeler that sucks them right in. Sells ten thousand boxes of ammo to Vendor A, Vendor B, or Vendor C like you were *giving* them away. That it, Todd?"

"That's it, Dig, you nailed it."

"I don't know," said Philip. "I don't have the slightest. I came to say I'm not taking this job—after all."

"What?"

"I'm not taking the job."

"Not taking the job?"

"No—I just stopped by to say I'm not taking the job."

"Now that's a good one," said Todd. "I'll be damned."

"You really mean that?" said Digby. "You want a cup of coffee? Let's go down and get you a cup of coffee. What do you say?"

"Well, I've got to be moving. I've got appointments—I'm sorry."

"One cup."

"Oh, there he goes," said Todd. "Number one sales man, Hunt and Hart Ammo Man of the Year twice running."

"Oh!" said Philip.

"One cup."

They rode the elevator down, Digby speaking of baseball. "You know what, Philip? I play baseball year around. You know I'll probably hit a few in that snow out there!"

"Baseball now."

"A fanatic, sir—but you know, you really can't help if you're a fanatic. Can you?"

"No."

They went through the food line. "Here, get something to eat, Philip. It's on me. How about some dessert with that coffee?"

"No, thanks. I've already eaten."

"Well, then. Coffee then. That's fine—fine."

They sat. Digby Morris went on about baseball, how he was looking forward to spring training, how he'd had a huge collection of baseball cards from childhood, traded them, kept averages on his computer. "Look, Philip, I can't promise anything. You might not last a week, two days, a day, but I've got this good feeling about you. This very good feeling. I think you might be just right for our company. You see, we get these bullshitters like Todd—totally ripe with it, sodden, huh?—and you'd make for a nice balance around this place. Being the honest type. That doesn't work so well in sales, but I think I can trust you. I don't think you'd stab a man in the back. Take Todd back there, he's got his knife always poised and ready for action."

"Really? What do you mean?"

Digby laughed. "Use your imagination, Philip. There are a thousand ways to stab a man in the back, and most people know half of them, and they're working hard on the other half—playing catch-up. They go to bed with it on their mind, hatch up their little schemes, get up with it, waltz through the day with it, labor and wait—for a ripe opportunity. And it comes. It always comes."

"Damn."

"You don't see it that way—do you?"

"No. Well, maybe. I don't know. With some people, I guess. But all? Not everybody."

"You're an innocent man, Philip. Callow. Aren't you? Maybe it's your age. Maybe it's your background. Who knows what it is. But I like it. We could use a little innocence around here."

He didn't like the turn of this conversation. "Well, I've got to be going . . ."

"Right there," said Digby Morris. "That's what I'm talking about."

"Huh?"

"You know what a lot of men—men in my line of work—you know what they'd say back to me after I'd laid a thing like that on them? They'd say, 'Fuck off, Dig. You think I'm innocent? That's what you think? You better watch your back, and you best watch your windows, sir.'"

"Well" said Philip. "I've really got to go."

Digby grabbed his arm. "Don't be angry now. Don't get offended like a woman."

Philip rose from the table. "Well, really—"

"See, I like that. I'm not putting you on. You're a straight shooter, Philip, I can tell. I can read a man. After all, I've trained myself for years to do it. My whole life. Let me tell you something: A salesman knows people better than a psychologist ever could. A salesman reads a man like a cartographer reads a map."

"You read me, do you? I'm that transparent."

"Philip, Philip. Don't overreact now. Go ahead—sit down."

He remained standing. "I must—"

"Sit, sit. Do sit down. I don't mean to offend. My apologies if I have."

He sat down. Reluctantly.

"I don't know squat about you, really—I mean the particulars: about your life, your wants, needs, your fears, but I know character and personality. I can spot that in a minute—or less. I could sit down with anybody in this room"—he swept his hand at an area filled with tables—"and I could peg any one of them, Philip, and that's no lie, in one minute or less. It's a gift, partly, but it's also a long practice."

"I see."

"I see? That's all you've got to say? *I see*?"

"I don't know what else to say."

"I like that. What else is there to say?" He smiled and lifted his coffee cup to his lips. "Here's what I'm thinking. Try us out for one day, just one day, and then if you don't like us, give us the big kiss-off."

"I don't know. I'm not sure."

"Why not?"

"I don't want to be let loose after one week. It'd be a waste."

"You assume we'd can you."

"Well, yes. I'm not a salesman."

"How do you know? You ever sold?"

"No."

"Am I an electrician?"

"Are you?"

"Don't know a thing about it. But I *could* be an electrician. If I wanted to."

"I doubt I could be. And I'm not sure I want to be a salesman."

"Who is sure? Who can be? You want money, Philip?"

"Money? Yes."

"Every big sale is a ding on the bell, Philip, my fine feathered friend. A nice big ding. We've got one huge bell rigged up in our office. Every big ding on that bell means credit and cash. You need either of them?"

"Credit?"

"For a job well done."

"Oh."

"And cash to go with it?"

"Yes, of course . . . and I would get the company car—when?"

Digby grinned. He studied Philip for a long moment.

He held a finger up. "Today if you want it."

Philip sat there. His blood rushed.

"Come on upstairs. Let's get started."

The decision was being made for him. He followed along.

19

He left work at five after a ho-hum afternoon of reading company literature. It was quite unlike reading books for college classes, quite unlike studying for tests. It was dull, stupid, mindless drudgery this so-called "literature" was—there was nothing to connect to. It made him think of being in the presence of frat jocks with business careers in mind. He had nothing to say to them. He did not want to say anything to them.

To get the car, he signed some papers. He followed a uniformed man to a parking building a block off. "All yours," said the man, and gave him a salute.

How silly, he thought. But the man seemed friendly, and he didn't want to feel like a snob. He saluted back. The man gave him an odd look. Then he laughed. He had a loud, boisterous laugh. Not a business man, thought Philip. A working stiff of the lower order.

Philip drove off. The roadsides were piled high with snow. The radio was on classical music. He felt at ease; he felt alive. A real job, however dumb it was. And this fine, fine car. A car like this, it made it all worth it. One could put up with a dumb job with a car of this caliber. A sleek, shiny Lincoln, my god.

He found parking in a lot behind Sophia Cross's little restaurant. Getting into the lot, he had to manage a bulge of snow. Snow was piled up all around the periphery. Sophia would be here now, he knew it, because she was on from seven until seven. A long, long shift, and she had told him sometimes her feet hurt. Well, why wouldn't they? And my legs, she had said, they get so tired. He often thought about her tired legs and how he would rub them. Yes, wouldn't he like to? And then he'd imagine Rod Busby showing up in the very act of his rubbing them—all the way up to her panties.

Caught. Red-faced Rod.

A dead man, Phil. You wanta be a dead man?

He got out of the car, gave it a little pat, and made his way around to the front of the restaurant. He took his usual table at the window.

"You again," she said, but she smiled.

"I can't get enough of you," he said.

"Well, that's sweet. What do you want?"

"What was wrong?" he said. "Did he say something to you?"

She grimaced.

"I'm sorry," he said, "to poke my nose in where—"

"No. I'm glad you did. I really, really don't think there's much there," she said, resting her hands on a chair, "to continue anything. But I'm afraid—I'm afraid of stopping it."

Her lips trembled.

"Why—what? What do you think would happen?"

"He could be bad. He could be real bad. He has been. I don't know. I don't love him anymore, Philip. Not at all."

Music to his ears.

She scooted the chair over a little. It looked like she might take a seat. He noticed the old lady in the back watching. She had a massive head of black hair that stuck out on the sides. She peered over those beetle brown glasses. She didn't flinch a muscle as he stared her down. Maybe she was coming back here. If she did, he'd defend Sophia. He would tell the old lady it was all his doing. He'd started it. She was just doing her job.

"I'm going to tell you something," said Sophia. "But don't ever, ever say it to him. Okay?"

"No. I won't. You can count on it."

She hemmed and hawed. And then she said, biting her lip, "He told me he choked this guy. He choked him until he almost died. The guy ended up in the hospital. It happened last spring. They were just horsing around, and suddenly, because he thought the guy was making fun of him, he got him around the throat. And he wouldn't let go."

"My god."

"That's right. He came *this* close," she said, with two fingers spaced a hair's breadth apart, "to finishing that guy off. Some fellow frat jock. The guy should have nailed him, you know, called the cops, but Rod told him—right after he called 911—that if he opened his big trap about it, he'd finish the job later. That's what he said—'finish the job.' That scared me bad. Because he's gotten me around the throat before. Right here." She pointed, and then she grabbed his hand and put it on her throat.

Her soft throat.

This worked on him. He was ashamed of himself.

"Something's got to be done," he said. His hand fell away from her throat.

"He said 'big trap' to me too," said Sophia, her voice a whimper.

"Something's got to be done."

"What do you want to eat?" she asked. Her expression changed. She was half-smiling.

"Pizza. And a beer."

"Oh, that's good. I could use that about right now. When I get out of here, maybe I just will."

"Maybe I could join you," he said. It was jumping, but there it was—right out of the chute.

"But you'd be full," she said, smiling.

"For the beer part, anyway."

The old fat woman with the massive hair job was beginning to march their way. Her legs were fat and wobbly, but she moved surprisingly fast.

"You've got to go," he said. "That old lady."

"Oh? Well, hell with her. Just hell with her! I get so tired of it! I really do!" She turned and hurried back toward the kitchen. She was moving fast when the old lady grabbed her arm and swung her around.

The old lady sternly shook her finger at Sophia. Twice, three times. Four. But Sophia ignored this, pulled loose, and hurried into the kitchen. The old lady watched her, one hand on her large hip, and then she turned toward Philip and stared at him. It was a hateful one, but he thought, *I'm your customer, you idiot.* How dare you treat a customer like this?

Sophia came back, empty-handed. "Guess what? I'm quitting. That's what I'm doing. That old hog won't be bossing me around after this. I gave her two weeks, but you know what she said? 'As soon as you serve that young man back there, I'll have your check out of petty cash, and you're on your way out, honey.' How's that? I'm on 'my way out.'"

"Good! Good! Let's go catch a pizza and a beer somewhere else. Some place that appreciates you!"

Catch a pizza? Damn it, Phil!

"Oh, I can't. I ordered it already."

"Let'em eat it then," said Philip. "Let'em pick up the pieces. You and me, we'll go get a pizza on our own. We'll show'em." Why, he wondered, have you suddenly fallen into this particular dialect? But there it was. He had.

"You think so?" she asked. "Really?"

"Really. I do."

"Well," she said, and took his hand. Her hand was soft and warm. He squeezed it.

He rose.

"You go tell her," she said. "I don't want anything further with that old hog."

"What?"

"*Please*. You tell her."

She was pleading with him.

"Me? I don't know—"

"If you want to be my knight in shining armor, you'll do just that."

He stood there.

"Well."

He patted Sophia's arm, and he headed quickly for the old lady.

"Philip," he heard her say. "Oh, *Philip*."

He'd never seen the old lady up this close, and something slowed him down. Was it her mottled cheeks, her beady black eyes, those glasses, or was it those pasty dry lips? Or, her elephantine ears jutting out from that whacked-out hairdo? It was all of these— surely. *Old* came to him. Frazzled. Fizzled out, and inhospitable to anything smacking of youth. Look at that mole on her chin. All this struck him face on. Like a hardball square in the forehead.

"Yeah," she said. "And what is it you want?"

He cleared his throat and coughed. It wasn't something he

wanted to do, but the old lady had made his throat tickle. He worked to speak. He couldn't seem to. He couldn't formulate a phrase. *Yeah, yeah, Prufrock. Sure.* When he'd heard about Prufrock, Dick had said, "That's you, amigo." But he went ahead now. He blurted it out: "She's not *serving* me. She's *going* with me. We're leaving here together. So make out her check now. Right now."

The old lady studied him. "You've got some nerve is what I think," she said. "To take that tone with me. I don't know you from Adam, but I do know one thing. And I can see it plainly. You think you're something special, but you're not. There's nothing special at all about you, young man, only the same old stuff I've seen all my life. You ought to go inspect yourself in the mirror from time to time, and you'll see what I'm talking about. Go on—there's one back there in that room marked Employees Only. Go on, and see, and you'll see what I'm saying. Nothing special about you, only you *think* there is. But it's all in your head." She trotted off, a bounce in her step. Her legs looked like enlarged plastic pinions of some sort.

He started to yell at her. But he didn't.

The old woman was more formidable than he'd imagined. What tongue! She'd been around the block.

"Don't you think so?" he said to Sophia when they were at the Swank Pizza joint over a Bigger than Average Pizza and a Bigger than Average pitcher of cola.

"Yeah, she's been around the block all right. But what block? Or, should I say: Which *blocks*?"

She seemed different here in the half-darkness of the pizza joint, with her hands holding his. *His* girl, just as Tina had proclaimed. Yes, he had latched onto her in a propitious moment. You didn't miss a trick, he thought.

Miss a trick?

Damn!

It's what his father was always saying.

"I got the idea," said Philip, "that she fancies herself some sort of psychologist. Like she thinks she can peer right inside you."

"Well, she does fancy herself that way. She was some sort of lady cop, and then juvenile correctional officer—all that, and she's got this very restrictive way of thinking about people. She sees me as some sort of juvenile offender—and you too, now!" She laughed, and tightened her grip on his hands.

His girl.

His lover.

A woman.

My god, and what a woman.

It was over now, that terrible struggle to get her. He'd been at it for months, and now—here now was the payoff.

She withdrew her hands. She stared at him.

"What?"

"Maybe you could do me a favor. It's kind of a big one, and I'd understand why you wouldn't want to do it."

"Sure," he said. "I'd do it. I'd do anything for you."

"How sweet."

"Anything."

"You *would*?"

"Anything. Anything."

His face grew hot.

Coming on too strong. Way too strong.

She smiled. A knowing smile. "Hadn't you better find out what it is first?"

"Okay—sure."

"You do care for me?" She took his hand. "You would do anything?"

"Yes, yes," he said. "Yes, I would."

"Oh, god, thank you for saying that. Some men won't say that, but I kind of figured you would. Maybe that's why I like you so much. You're so nice."

She gripped his hands again, and now he realized he'd spoken better than he'd known. He'd said the exact thing he should say.

"Thanks," he said.

"Well, here it is . . . I'll just tell you. I guess I'll just say it—"

The pizza arrived. It was thick, with several toppings. The waitress had very large breasts, and she was leaning over, exhibiting cleavage of a kind that Philip found hard not to look at, and he tried desperately not to be aware of them, but well, what to do? He wanted to make sure that Sophia didn't realize he was aware of them. But wouldn't it look odd if he wasn't? How could a man not be? Somehow it seemed wrong, or rather odd, if he *didn't* look at them.

"You all enjoy your food," said the waitress, and one hand went down on his arm, then his hand, and rested there, while she scooped up two pieces of pizza and delivered them to their plates. Her breasts bounced as she did this, but he kept his attention on the pizza as much as he could—and on Sophia, who looked on soberly.

And then she said to the waitress: "Thanks so much. It looks good. Really good."

"It's very good," said the waitress. "Enjoy!"

He didn't watch the waitress heading back.

"God, so big," said Sophia.

"Oh—yeah," he said.

"She cut them so big," she said. Raising the pizza slice to her mouth.

Oh, the pizza.

"They *are* big," he said.

"It's a hard job she has," said Sophia, "and you should tip her."

"I will."

"Very hard."

"I know."

"Harder than a lot of people know."

"I'm sure it is, and who would know better than you?"

She nodded, and took the pizza off her plate, and said, "Well, once again, here it is."

"Yes?"

"I need," she said, biting into the pizza, cheese coating her lips, "for you to do me this huge favor. And if you would, I'd be so, ever so thankful. And grateful."

"Of course."

"It's hard. It's very, very hard."

"Okay—that's okay."

"It may not be. But I'll say it anyway. Here it is—I'm just so unwilling . . . I want you to . . . tell Rod . . . Rod Busby that I'm breaking it off with him. And if you do, really Philip, I can't tell you how much that would mean to me. I'm just afraid, I'm just really afraid to tell him. I *am*."

He gathered himself up. "Okay. Okay, I will."

She was staring at him. She wiped off a smear of cheese on her lips and took a drink of her cola. "You sure?"

"Yes. I'll do it. I will. I'll be seeing him at that bar tonight, and I'll tell him."

"Bar? What bar?"

"Bar None."

"You're meeting him at the Bar None."

"Yes."

"Why?"

"He wanted me to."

"So . . . he got you to go there." She shook her head. "I'm surprised you'd agree. Why ever?"

"He was . . . kind of persuasive."

"Don't let him be . . . you'll make a big mistake. Believe me."

"What mistake?"

"He's not to be trusted. Rod is not to be trusted. He's going to end up in prison one of these days. Assault and battery. Murder. Torture. Genocide. I didn't know all this when I took up with him, and I've been working the last year to try to dump him. But he doesn't let loose. He latches on. He burrows his way in—you know?"

He didn't like the way she put that. He got an image. But he said, "I'll get rid of him for you. I promise."

"Don't get hurt. Oh, please. I'd never forgive myself."

And yet she'd asked him. What did she expect?

"I won't."

"A bar's not the best place to handle it. Especially Bar None. Have you been to that place?"

"No."

"Well, it's kind of . . . wild. I don't know what other word to choose, but it's not decent, I guess you'd say. There's decent places—some of the college hangouts, some of the more upscale places on the Walk, but that one—that one's pretty downscale, and it attracts some of the worst. I wouldn't go, Philip, no matter what you told him. I wouldn't. Please—don't."

He plowed into his pizza. Nerve, he thought. Don't flag. Resolve.

"I'll be okay."

"You're not Clint Eastwood. So don't feel like you have to be. I was thinking of something more . . . official. Genteel, even. You know, you give him a call—I've got his number in my purse—you call him, or maybe you could email him, and just pass on what I said. Just say you're the messenger with the bad news. You don't have a stake in it. I was just too much of a coward. Feel free to say that."

He deliberated. Well, it *would* be easier.

She was staring at him.

"Maybe I could do what you—"

"But you don't want him to get the idea you're afraid. You don't want that. That's the worst you could do."

She stared at him.

What the hell?

"Well—"

"When's he want you to show up at that bar? I'm not saying go, but when's he want you to?"

"Ten o'clock."

"Ten. That's better than twelve."

"I'm meeting him."

"Oh, you," she said, and he saw tears in her eyes. She wiped them away. "You're the kind of man I could fall in love with."

20

You're definitely dead meat, Phil.
Dead meat, palsy walsy.
Look at it this way, fella. You are one hunk of dead meat, boy.

21

Bar None was loud with tattooed, grisly looking men. Noisy, riled up. A loud argument was going on in the back. And then a fight suddenly broke out, punches flying hard.

A man's nose was dripping blood.

A man's eyes were swelling up, blackening.

A loud cry.

A loud groan.

Fists, more fists.

"What're you drinking? I'm buying."

"Beer."

"Two beers, Pete."

They waited. Rod was working on some peanuts. "You want some?" He pulled Philip's hand over and poured some in. "Don't say I never did nothing for you, pard."

Philip ran his hand up to his mouth and dumped them in.

The fight was getting worse. It was spreading.

The beers arrived. Rod Busby tipped his back. "Drink up, buddy."

"Thanks." He sipped.

"So . . . you want to know what she said."

"Sure—okay."

Rod Busby poked Philip's arm, and then his chest. "What need to know do you have, Philly?" He poked again—harder. It hurt. "That's what I asked myself. I asked myself over and over, Philly boy. 'How the hell's it this guy's business what she and I flapped our yaps about?'"

"None of my business," said Philip. "You're right."

"You're fucking A. It's between me and her, buddy." He poked again. His thrusts were even harder, more painful.

Philip made ready to go.

"Sit."

"I've got to go."

"Sit."

Something made him do it. Pure fear. Adrenaline rush in his chest like an electric current surging.

"Now, then," said Rod Busby. "You're a real bastard, aren't you? I don't think I like you. In fact, I think I hate your guts, buddy." He gulped beer. He bunched his shirt up and wiped off his lips. "You don't want to get on my bad side, Phil-o. Not wise."

"I wasn't intending to."

Loud cries. Curses. Tables being turned over.

The bartender seemed oblivious to it all.

"Let me tell you something." Rod Busby now had his thick hand clenched around Philip's wrist. "I don't want anybody—*anybody*, you hear?—horning in on my girl. Who's my girl, Philly? You tell me who that girl is."

"Hey!" He stood up and tore his wrist loose. It felt like a rope burn.

"Hey what?"

"That hurt."

"Sit down."

"No. I must go."

He looked around. How to escape?

The barbarians were, of a certain, at the gate. Get out now—now.

"Fine. Have it your way. I was going to tell you what she said—and what I said back. But fine, go on. No big deal. What's it to me? I don't care if you hear it. Only I thought that's why you trotted down here—so you *could* hear it. But now, just like a fickle little girlie, you change your little mind."

"She wants me to pass something on to you."

"Yeah? What?"

Philip hesitated. And then he rushed to say it: "She's afraid of you, Rod."

"Yeah?"

"That's right. She's afraid."

"Well, now, I hate to bust your bubble, Philly boy, but it's a good thing for a woman to be afraid of a man. Keeps them in line. There's things women don't have any say in, son, and they need to know their boundaries. Word to the wise."

"Sorry. I don't think that way."

"What're you, some kind of pussy?"

"No."

"I hope not, Phil."

"She wants out."

"Yeah?"

"I'm just passing it on."

Loud noises.

A few tables away, men were punching, kicking, pulling hair.

Loud cries. Oaths.

"Put her there," said Rod Busby, and he extended his hand. "I don't hold anything against you, buddy boy. Women—it's all we can do. It's all a man can do. Naturally you'd want that girl. Who wouldn't? She's a real beauty, ain't she? Hey, shake on it."

No. He knew better. He saw what was up.

He went quickly for the door. He grabbed it and was out of there.

The wind was cold and raw and burned his face.

And then he saw him, standing under a street light. Watching. Yes, it was that same man, tall, thin, black coat, black Russian hat, with his hands shoved in his pockets.

"What's he want?" It was Rod Busby taking him by the arm. "You want me to put him out of his misery, Phil?" He put his arm around him. "Because if you want that, that's just what I'll do. One buddy for another."

"Oh, no. That's okay."

"You take it easy, old buddy. Don't let the bed bugs bite. Let your old Rod man handle this one." He hurried off. Philip watched him get in a truck. He watched the truck dig out, roar down the street, whip around in the middle of the street, and tear right by the store where the man in the long coat had his hands jammed into his pockets.

The truck wheels rammed over the sidewalk.

Rod Busby let out a raucous yell.

The man backed away a little, against the side of the building, but still stood there.

The truck snorted off the sidewalk, whammed the road, gunning it, racking off.

22

Well, that was over. He'd done it, and it was over. He would tell her.

She'd like this. She'd go for this.

But first he must get back to his apartment.

It was so cold, bitterly cold, and a freezing mix was burning his face. He bent over and walked deliberately against the wind with his hands against his face, blowing hot breath to keep his nose warm. He had a good mile or more to go.

Why, why, why in the hell didn't you take that car? But then you'd have to break that rule. Find excuses. Well, you just might have to.

When he came to the apartment, he got inside the lobby and leaned against a wall. Ugly, bare, and stinky in here but a refuge at least. Cold, cruel out there. He rubbed his numb cheeks.

I'm taking the car, he thought. If I had a face mask or something, well, that would be one thing, but I have none. I'm taking the car. I'll fill the tank.

He hurried up to his room, got inside, flicked on the light, and looked about. Whoever it was watching him, no sign of him here. Nothing had changed. Everything as usual in this rundown, noxious hole.

He took a hot shower and got dressed. He packed some clothes and toilet articles. He packed those torture books Adam Most had insisted he read. He packed his suit.

He set his suitcase next to the door—all ready now.

You're life's about to begin, Philly fellow.

He checked his cell phone. Twelve o'clock. Too late to call? Probably. But why not? If you want anything at all in this world, you've got to take risks.

Don't you?

But be smart about it, son.

All right, Dad.

He called.

Her voice: "Hello. I'm so sorry I'm not available. Please leave a message. Thank you."

Formal.

"Sophia, this is Philip. I did it . . . I told him. I just wanted you to know." He sent the message.

Stupid. Why had he blurted it out? No composure. No cool. But no changing it now. No erasing it.

He slumped in his overstuffed chair, with the springs leaking out, digging against his backside. Some odor he couldn't name wafted its way from somewhere in the room, probably where a dog had peed. Pets weren't permitted, but who would worry about that in a place like this?

He had beer and rested, leaning his head way back, trying to relax.

You screwed up. Screwed up.

Because it now struck him what had happened.

Rod Busby had left the bar. He'd made a beeline for her apartment. He had knocked her around. Oh, god, no. Yes, that is what had happened. Why had he let that happen? He should have called earlier, much earlier. Warned her. Right off, as soon as Busby's truck tore off down that street, he should have called her and told her that Busby was on his way, straight to her place. My god, why hadn't he called her right then and told her?

Hurt—Sophia Cross hurt. Hurt bad. He could visualize her in the hospital, in intensive care. He could see her swollen eyes, her cut, swollen lips—a broken arm in the sling. Traction. Maybe in traction.

Now you've really, really done it. You and your fucked-up ways.

Phone ringing.

He went for it.

"Hi, this is Sophia."

"Oh, god, Sophia! Sophia!"

"Yes?" She sounded suspicious.

"I was worried, is all. Rod Busby—is everything okay?"

"Sure. Why wouldn't it be? Did you tell him?"

"Yes—yes, I told him. I did. And he acted . . . sort of crazy."

"Oh?"

Philip described the way Rod had torn out in that truck of his, did a U-turn, and really snorted off down that road.

"Typical. That's the way he drives."

Was Rod Busby there? Was that something in the background? A hum of voices? A snicker? A snort? But what business of it was his? Her place, her doings.

"I was afraid . . . I was really, really afraid . . ." He forced a laugh. "I was afraid he was coming for you—out of anger, you know."

"What? Oh, no, he's not like that. That's not Rod. No, not at all."

"Really? He's not—"

"No, no. No."

Oh, so he *was* there. She wasn't free to talk. That bastard's fists were ready to brutalize her.

"He wouldn't do that, huh?" said Philip.

"Oh, no. No . . . it's more like it happens when you least expect it. You say something, tick him off—you know. It's an anger management thing. Really, Philip. That's what it is. A sudden burst. An explosion. He goes off. God, I'm so tired. I'm going to have to go now and get some sleep. Okay?"

"Sure."

"Bye."

"Wait . . . wait just a minute. Look . . . could I come over? Would that be okay?"

"What?"

"I'd just like to come over."

"No. It's too late, Philip. It's way too late. I've got to get some sleep. Got to find a job tomorrow. I quit, you know."

"Sorry."

"I've got to go. I've got to get to bed."

Bed.

"I wish I was there. I wish I was right there with you. In that bed."

Something wouldn't let him restrain himself. Perhaps it was love—true love. Dizzy, he thought, dizzy in love.

She laughed. It was a sweet, jingly laugh. "I know you do."

"I love you," he said.

"What?"

"I do."

"Well."

"Where can I meet you? And when?"

"You've got my cell phone number," she said. "I'm really tired. I've got to get to bed."

"Without me?" said Philip.

"What?"

Was that irritation? Was it?

"Please. May I come sleep with you? May I?"

Mother may I?

It was out there now, his great want, his great need.

But cool? There was no cool in it.

"Oh," she said, and laughed.

"Well?" he said.

"Not if you're thinking of something serious. Because I'm going to be dead to the world by the time you get here."

"You mean—"

"I'll leave the key in the mailbox." And she gave him the address.

"Really," he said.

"You remind me of Rod, in ways," she said. "Only he's so crude about it."

Rod? Ah!

"I'll be there."

"I'll be asleep. But you can get in bed with me."

"Okay," he said.

She giggled. "You're such a case," she said. "Aren't you?"

"Yes," he said.

"Boy, I do pick them," she said. "Don't I?"

"Well."

"Goodbye."

"Goodbye."

Such pleasure ahead, he thought. Such bliss soon to come.

But hadn't he crawled?

Damn it, you fool, you crawled!

Oh, well, he thought.

23

He parked in the lot in back of her old brown-brick, three-story apartment house. Walls of snow were piled several feet high around the small lot.

In the lobby he found the key in her mailbox—Box 51. Area 51? It made him laugh.

Stealthily he padded down the hall. Late, and he didn't want to be asked questions. *Do you live here? What are you doing here? May I see some sort of identification?*

Questions like that.

He came to Apartment 51. It was at the very end of the first floor hall.

He turned the key in the door. He got in. Dark in here, and he stumbled on something. Light? *Where's the light?* He could flick on a light, but it wasn't his place. It wouldn't be right, would it? He might disturb her.

"Is that you, Philip?"

Her voice. It sounded high-pitched and strained.

"Yes. It's me."

"I'm back here. Just turn on the light at the door. You can switch it off right inside my door. Be sure to lock the outside door."

Dangerous? Break-ins?

He did. He made his way to the bedroom. It was just off the living room.

He flicked on the light.

She put a hand up, dazed.

He flicked the light back off and went toward her bed. "Right there," she said. "Your side." He heard her hands patting it.

He got his clothes off, down to his briefs, and got under the covers.

She immediately moved for him.

He moved for her.

"Just hold me," she said. "Nothing else right now, okay?"

"Sure."

"I've been afraid all night. So afraid. I'm so glad you came."

"You are? Afraid of Rod coming?"

"No—not of him. I told you." She held onto him harder. He felt her face, her hair, her warm body tight against his. She was now kissing him.

No Dick Hazzard in this bed, he thought.

"I'm glad," he said. "I'm so glad." Yes, glad, he thought. So, so glad.

"He's got his own key," said Sophia.

"What?"

"Oh, it's okay. It's late."

"You don't think he'll show."

"No. I don't think so."

"I hope not—not like this," he said, and laughed.

"It's not him," Sophia said. And then she began to cry. "It's not him. It's worse—it's a whole lot worse than Rod Busby ever was."

"What?"

"Oh, I can't even talk about it. It's so stupid."

"What?" He held her tight. He held her tighter. "I can't. It's just silly and stupid. So silly and stupid."

"No, it's not. I'm sure it's not."

"Yes, it is, but you wouldn't laugh, would you?"

"No, of course not."

"You promise?"

"Yes. I would never laugh—never—"

"I don't know."

"Please do talk about it," he urged. "I'm here. I'm okay. Maybe I can help."

"You?"

"Maybe. Go ahead," he said.

Silence. Trembling against him. Her body tighter and tighter. Hard. Harder than he'd ever been. Like iron, he thought.

"Okay . . . if you won't laugh. If you won't say I'm silly and stupid."

"I won't. Believe me, I won't. I never would."

"Okay . . . well—"

"Go ahead. Please."

"Okay. Well, it's these premonitions—I get these premonitions. Do you know what I mean?"

"Yes—I think." He held her hands and they were cold and trembling.

"They're just . . . awful." She began to sob.

Yeah, like iron. And not right, not right—wrong to be like that, given the fact that— *you bastard, you frigging bastard.*

"I'm sorry. I'm so sorry. I'm glad I'm here—with you," he said.

"I wish you *could* help. You are helping, though, just holding me."

"What premonitions?" he asked.

She sobbed, and then sniffled, and then seemed to get better. "Oh, I hate to say. They're so insane. I hate to lay a thing like that on you, being so insane."

"Please do," he said. "I want to know everything. I'm in love . . . I'm deeply in love with you."

"You say that."

"But I mean it."

"Oh, I'm so glad," she said. "I've always wanted someone, just someone, to be deeply in love with me. Rod's not, you know."

"No," he said. "He can't be. He definitely can't."

"Why do you say that?"

"What?"

"Why?" she said.

"Because of the way treats you."

"Well, he's had his moments. But he likes me, I know that. I guess you're right, though—he doesn't love me. Not really. Does he?"

"No. I don't think so."

"You think you know, huh?" she said.

"You can't be that way toward someone you love," he said. "Like saying a woman needs to be afraid of a man."

"Huh? What?"

"Well . . . that's what he said." He cringed.

"He said that?"

"Yes. He did."

"I do think a man should be manly," she said.

"But that doesn't mean—"

"No, of course not."

She was quiet, really quiet. He heard moaning. Oh, god, he thought . . . oh, god. He felt her hair against his ear. But then it struck him: "You still thinking about those premonitions?"

"Huh?"

"Those premonitions you spoke of."

"Oh, jeez, Philip, they're just terrible. Horrible. And *dreams*. When I have premonitions, I dream a lot. I've been afraid to go to sleep. What if I dream this or that? What if I dream this or that *again*?"

"I thought you said you'd be dead to the world?"

"I guess I wished," she said, clutching him harder. "Are you afraid of death, Philip?"

"What? Death? Sometimes. But I don't think about it very much." He paused. "Maybe old people do. You don't, do you?"

"All the time. Practically every minute. And I'm not old."

"No," he said. How young, how luscious. "Every minute?"

"Practically. Of late, anyway."

"That's not good," he said.

"Sleeping really scares me. All that blackness every single night! What if I don't dream? Then maybe I'm gone. Oh, god! Erased! But if I dream, then I'm alive. I've got to be. That's *me* dreaming. See?" She laughed. "Silly, aren't I?"

"But if they're really bad dreams—"

"At least I'm dreaming!"

"Oh."

"You see?"

Odd, he thought. But he searched for something to say—something to put her at ease. To get things going.

"It's not silly," he said. "Don't think it's silly. It isn't. It's part of life, death is, and all the worry about it."

"God, what a cliché!"

"Oh. Sorry."

147

He stroked her leg.

She moved a little.

He stopped.

"I liked that," she said. "Why'd you quit?"

"Oh," he said.

He stroked her leg again. He ran his hands all over her. He couldn't stop.

"Take me," she said. "Now!"

"Yes!" he cried. And then it suddenly occurred to him. No condom. *Why didn't you bring a condom, you idiot? You idiot!*

"I don't have—"

"In the night table," she said. "Right there beside you."

"Oh." He reached, felt. There it was.

He got a sick feeling. He felt it run all over him, his gut, his legs, his hands.

"Don't get any ideas," she said. "Like I stock those or something."

"No," he said. "No, of course not."

"Were you thinking that?"

"No."

"I'll bet you were. I would be."

"No, really. I wasn't."

"They were *his*," she said. "His, not mine."

"Of course."

His. Rod Busby's. He did it to her right in this bed. On this side of the bed.

She stroked his hand.

He got it on.

"I just think about it," she said. "I can't seem to help myself. But you don't?"

"What?" he said.

"Death. I think about death."

"No." He moved toward her, took her in his arms.

"It's such a ... formidable thing. Isn't it?"

"Yes—"

"Like you rot—you actually *rot*. All your insides. Your whole body. How yucky! And worms! You're left with bones—finally. Just bones. Think of that. Bones—that's it."

He went flaccid.

"Like I say," he said. "I don't . . . I don't normally think about it."

"But how couldn't you? Especially when it's so cold like this. And did you know it's supposed to snow another whole foot by noon tomorrow? A whole fucking foot! Like the foot we got already—like that's not fucking enough!"

He wished she wouldn't curse like that.

"A foot?"

"Yes, a foot! Isn't that horrible? Isn't that just terrible? You feel like you're buried to death! Things are happening, Philip. Bad things."

"I know."

"Will spring ever come? Will it?"

"Yes," he said. "Because if winter comes, can spring be far behind?"

"Yes, it can," she said.

"It's from a romantic poet."

"I don't feel very romantic."

He pulled her as close as he could. He still had the condom on. It hadn't come off. But he worried it would.

"It'll all be okay," he said. "Everything will be." And then it struck him. How would he get to work in that car? Well, he wouldn't. He'd have to call in. *The roads are too snow-covered*, he'd say. He'd stay in bed with her all morning. Could it get better than that? Could it?

"You see," her voice came at him, "I think of the cold snow, and I think of graves covered with all this cold, deep snow, and I think of those people down there in their . . . I hate to say it . . . I really do hate to say it . . . but their coffins, or caskets—which is worse, do you think, coffins or caskets? I hate them both, and notice: They both start with 'c'. Isn't that horrible? It's just horrible, isn't it?"

"Right," he said.

"Down there, deep. *Deep, deep, deep.* Six feet under the cold, hard ground, under the heavy blanket of snow, so cold, so utterly cold!" She let out a whimper, and he grabbed her.

"They don't know it," he said. "They're dead. They don't know anything. They're totally dead."

"Of course they don't. Of course, but I *feel* like they do. See, I feel like down there, they're lying there, looking up, and being so, so cold. I tend to imagine them with their eyes open, and sometimes reaching up to rap the top of their coffins or caskets. I just hate those two words, don't you? But anyway, how would you like to be down there, in that ground, so, so cold?"

"I wouldn't," he said. "If I was alive. But if I was dead, I wouldn't know it. And so it wouldn't make a lot of difference, would it?"

"I know. I know that. I know it in my head. But see, I think of them knowing it. And then I think of *me* knowing it whenever— whenever it happens, and how I'll be. *Me.*"

"Blackness," he said. "Utter blackness. Or maybe you'd be in the afterlife."

"I can't think about things like that!" she cried.

"Oh."

Silence.

"But I do."

"You won't be like that for a long, long time," he said.

"Like what?"

"Like—" Did he have to *say* it? He waited a moment, and then he said it softly. "*Dead.*"

"Age isn't everything," she said. "There's things that get you. There's things that cut you down in your prime. Bad things. And you don't know when or where they'll be, Philip. You could be waltzing along on the sidewalk, and a car could lose control and run right over you. Wham, you're history. You're smashed all over the cement. You're mangled. Your blood and bones and flesh. It's awful to think of. Really, isn't it? How fragile you are. So, so fragile. I don't want to be fragile like that! Why was I even *born* if I have to be fragile like that?"

She hugged him even harder, and he felt fingernails digging into his back. He winced a little, but held his tongue.

"I don't know why either," he said. "It seems so stupid."

"But you don't think *I* am," she said. "Do you?"

"No, no. Because I've felt it. I know it's true. You can't dispute it."

"From a child, I knew it. I've always worried about it. Dogs smashed, cats smashed, birds hitting windshields. Why'd my dad always have to have a bird hitting his windshield? Why?" Her voice broke.

"I don't know."

"How could you know?"

"Maybe you're just tired," he said. "When you're tired, things . . . have a way, you know."

"But you understand," she said. "Don't you?"

"Yes," he said. The condom was off now. Where was it?

"Most people, they act like they'll live forever," said Sophia. "Haven't you noticed?"

"You mean because they're . . . happy?"

"There's nothing wrong with being happy. I didn't mean that. I want to be so, so, so incredibly happy."

"I do too," he said. "I really do."

"Oh, let's quit talking," she said, "and get to it." She took him in her arms.

"Just a minute," he said. "I've got to . . . get another one."

"Oh, I'm sorry," she said, laughing.

He liked her laugh. It was high and tinkly.

But when he felt in the night table drawer, there weren't any more.

"Maybe the one I . . . if I can find it," said Philip.

"I doubt it. Let's go to sleep. You can get some in the morning. If you can get out—which I doubt!"

He heard her giggling.

He had trouble sleeping.

Once he woke her and said, "Would it be okay . . . would it be okay if—"

"No. No. Absolutely not. And it's not safe—not with me."

"Why's that?"

"It's not safe. Just accept that."

He didn't sleep until near morning. She woke him. "Want some breakfast?"

"I want you," he said.

"Oh, you're so sweet. Are you sure about the contents of that drawer? Take another look."

He plunged his hand in there, the light of the morning illuminating the drawer. And then he ran into something curled up like a thick, dead worm. He removed it, dangling from two fingers.

"Oh, my, oh, my," said Sophia. "Here, I'll get something."

She returned with a wastebasket.

He let go of it.

24

"I'm not frigid or anything," said Sophia, "so don't get that idea. It's just that I'm not taking any chances. And I've got a kind of ... medical thing."

"Oh, what ..."

"No need to explain," she said. "And I won't."

He looked out the window. The snow was coming down hard. It wasn't letting up at all. "I could walk it," he said, "if there was a store nearby."

"Say, you've got a real need," she said. "You're pretty desperate. Aren't you?"

"Men get that way," he said.

"I know they do. I think it's great. Where would we be if men didn't get that way? What would happen to the human race?"

What a cliché.

But he put his objection to this aside. "I know," he said, and took her into his arms.

She held him tightly. "Me—I don't care about that ... as much. I care about it a lot ... but not *just* that. I want *us*. Do you understand? I must have *us*."

"Yes," he said. "Yes."

"And that means that you understand me. What I want, what I need. What I *feel*."

"What is that?" he asked.

"I mean generally. Not right this minute."

"Of course."

She led him into the kitchen and began pulling out pots and pans.

"What I need ... I have great needs. Really great ones. I hate work. That's one thing. When I have a man, I want him to work. Unless it's work I like. And there isn't much work I do like. You know what, though?"

"What?"

"I liked serving you those pancakes. I hated that restaurant, but I liked serving you those pancakes."

"Good," he said. "I'm glad. I really liked eating them."

"I hated the job itself. That old bitchy, witchy woman. As you saw."

"Yes—I saw it all right."

"I'll never take a job like that. Ever again. It's got to be a job I feel good about, or I won't take it."

"Oh," he said, "but what about this apartment? How can you live—doing that?"

She grinned. "He's got it paid for, for the next three months. So that's covered."

"Him? Rod? Three months?"

"Yes—he got a deal. Three months in advance, and discount—twenty percent. Good, huh?"

"Then it's his apartment," said Philip.

"Sure it is. But he's locked out. If I have anything to say about it."

"But you don't, do you? He could throw you out."

"Oh, god. Well, you're just full of good news this morning, aren't you?"

He saw his error. He shouldn't have pointed this out. She knew it, of course. How could she not?

"I'm sorry."

"Don't be. It's true, but it'll never happen. Because I have my own power. I have great power, Philip."

He didn't ask. He imagined she would tell him. But he said, "You're very strong—in ways. I noticed that."

"Stronger than most people would imagine. Like that old witch. Old bitch. Like Rod Busby—even you."

"Me?"

"Yes, you. But I don't mean this in a critical spirit. I simply mean that there's a lot you don't know about me. I'm fragile, on one end of it all, but very strong and resilient on the other. I have spirit, Philip. Great spirit! You respect that, don't you?"

"Yes. Of course I do. I believe in spirit." And he thought he did because above all he was a romantic. If there was one thing, there was spirit, and it had to soar, and soar high.

"If you don't have spirit, you have nothing. Nothing counts. Only spirit counts. The only thing is, I can imagine so much, oh god, that can damage my spirit. For instance, those dead bodies buried under the snow. That damages me, Philip. I'm so close . . . so close to the pulse and heartbeat of others and their lives. Even that old bitch, even Rod Busby. I'm . . . I think I'm psychic or something. I truly do."

She was putting on coffee, and she'd dropped four slices of bread into the toaster. He watched her, with his eyes taking in her sweeping curves under the loosely fitting robe. He was dying for her. He swore to himself that once breakfast was done, dishes done, he'd be out there looking for a store that sold what he needed now more than anything—a box of condoms. Two boxes. Three. He swore to it.

"And if I am psychic," she said, "that would be good for us, wouldn't it?"

"Yes, it would be," he said.

"But you don't know how, do you?"

"Well, I'm not sure."

"I can foresee things," said Sophia. "Isn't that good? Don't you see that as good?"

"I think it would be, or could be," he said.

"But what about the dead bodies?" she said.

"Oh."

"Like if I saw someone, and then saw them like *that*, that would be horribly disturbing, wouldn't it?"

"Yes. It would. It would be . . . terrible."

"That's what I saw. That's why I was crying."

"Oh, god. Who? Who'd you see?"

"I don't know. I just saw him, or her—vaguely. I couldn't make out who it was. I couldn't make out the face. I didn't want to. I couldn't say if it was male or female. But so alive, dancing about, and then—the next frame: the coffin being lowered down. It was winter. The snow was deep. Very, very deep." She grabbed a cup, her hand trembling. "I need some coffee. I really need some coffee.

155

Just desperately."

"I do too."

"Good. Here's a cup for you."

They sat together with coffee and toast.

"This is nice," said Philip. "Very pleasant."

"My mother and father—they're both dead. And they're in a graveyard right in the center of town. You probably think it has to do with them, right?"

He cogitated. "Yes, I suspect it does. After all, both parents . . . dead."

"Not really my parents, though," said Sophia. "So I don't know."

"Oh, so you were—adopted?"

"No—they were just people that looked after me."

"Oh."

"I called them Dad and Mom, but they weren't."

"Oh."

"I try to feel something, but I don't—that's bad, isn't it?"

"You weren't close."

"No, not really."

"Sad."

"Sometimes I think so."

They were quiet, and ate.

Condoms, he thought. You'll get those condoms all right. More than one pack, too.

25

"If that's what you want," she said.

"I do," he said, putting his arm around her. "Why wouldn't I?"

"Well . . . there's a store about a mile from here. Shoppers Paradise. Out on Grand—at the strip mall."

"I'll walk it."

And then he felt a quivering in his gut. *Money.* He stood there, temporizing.

"What?"

"I don't think I have . . . enough money."

"You need some money?" she said.

He felt his face flush. Cheeks warming, gut quivering. "I guess it shouldn't fall to you . . . you know."

"Oh, don't be silly. Let me get some money," she said.

Her paying. What, what did that mean? How feel about that? How?

In a minute she came back with a twenty. She whispered in his ear: "I guess it takes two to tango, doesn't it?"

"Um," he said. And he began running his hands over her.

He wished he could take her right there on the spot.

"Wait just a minute," she said, pulling away. She left the room and hurried back with a scarf, a pair of thick socks, and some tall rubber boots, taller than his. She placed the scarf around his neck. "Wrap it around your face. It's cold as hell out there."

He did it.

"Now," she said. "Put these on. Here, sit down. Put your feet out."

He did it.

She removed his shoes. She pulled the thermal socks on his socked feet.

He got his shoes on.

And then she pushed his right foot into one of the rubber boots. "Fits nicely. Good."

"They're—"

"Rod's."

"Oh," he said.

She smiled.

The street outside was filled with snow. A car was stuck, squealing its wheels. It was cross-wise, and oncoming traffic was stopped, waiting.

He went around to the back—to the lot. He spotted his big Lincoln. Or thought he did.

That would take some serious digging out.

26

The snow was deep, deep, and still coming down. He jammed his hands in his pocket. The wind bit against his face in spite of the scarf. He blew hot air into it. His feet were cold in spite of the thermal socks and the boots.

A mile she'd said. A whole mile.

Except for her old apartment building, it was mostly a residential neighborhood of old bungalows. At least there was a sidewalk. But in most places the sidewalk was so blanketed with snow that he couldn't make out what was sidewalk and what was yard.

He trudged on.

His cell phone went off.

He struggled for it, and he got it in time.

"You doing okay?"

Sophia.

He said he was.

"You're so brave to go out in all that," she said. "To get—you know what."

Was she afraid to say it? He said it for her. "Condoms."

"Yes. And I'll bet you buy a gross," she said, and laughed.

He imagined the two of them in that apartment of hers, no jobs, just time to themselves. He'd stay in bed with her all day, naked, and into the night. Now and then they'd get up and fix snacks and go right back there. That was life, wasn't it? Life as it was meant to be? Why work? Where'd that fit? Genesis, he thought. Ushered out of the Garden. But I want the Garden, he thought. What if you *could* have the Garden? Why not go for it? Some had it, didn't they? Rich people, like the ones his father knew. Huge homes, swimming pools, country club memberships, serious money stashed away in offshore accounts, and in Swiss banks. Why should they have it and others not?

And then he thought of Digby Morris. He didn't want to call him. He didn't want to say the car was half buried in snow. Worse than half buried.

Freezing. That's what he was. But he finally came to the four-lane Grand, heavy with traffic. A car slid about and then righted itself. Another car somehow got slowed down just enough that it didn't T-bone the sliding car.

There was a traffic light, where he could cross.

He took a step and fell.

Straight down.

His hands went up, his body wrenched.

Down into the abyss.

Am I? Am I still . . . ?

Snow up to his face. He could barely move.

He got his right foot positioned to put his weight on his right leg, and eventually he pushed ahead with the weight of snow against his chest.

Stuck. Stuck.

He yelled out. The traffic boomed on, motors racing, engines racking off, snarling.

He could hear it—he couldn't see it.

He worked at freeing himself.

It took him a good fifteen minutes to climb out and to get to the road. He swept the wet snow off his coat and jeans. He checked his cell phone, but it was okay, dry somehow in his tight jeans pocket. He'd have to sit somewhere and dry off the rest of him. He couldn't buy any clothes because he didn't have any money to speak of, not more than a few dollars over that twenty Sophia had given him.

No money going for clothes. No, no. *You won't need clothes where you're going.*

In ten minutes he was entering Shoppers Paradise, snow stomped off his boots, tracking. But who wasn't tracking? He saw others tracking.

He sat in a large food bar with coffee.

Get warm.

Buy those condoms.

Don't fall in that ditch.

Hot shower at Sophia's.

Hot shower *with* Sophia.

He began to warm up, but his wet jeans bothered him. Perhaps he could remove them in the restroom. He removed his boots. His socks were so wet.

Tired. Exhausted.

He put his head on the table, with his coffee cup before him.

Ah!

Nice, nice. Gray images flashing.

Gone, gone.

Dreams.

Odd dreams.

Bizarre, but blissful. Then not so blissful. Belligerent, some figure, muscled up, with shiny bald head and savage teeth.

A jarring.

Blackness to light.

A tapping.

On his shoulder.

He rubbed his eyes.

Tapping.

He looked to see.

He tried to focus.

Cop?

No.

Security officer.

In blue, standing there. He wore a look of displeasure, a look of judgment, of scorn.

"You can't sleep here, sir. If you need to sleep, it will have to be elsewhere. Have you been drinking?"

"No."

"Are you sure?"

"Yes."

"Just coffee, huh?" The security officer was a man of about forty, Philip judged, a man with an attitude. His face was red. His fat lips rubbery. Brownish.

"Yes."

"Well, wake up now. Drink some more. But don't sleep here. Understand?"

"I had trouble sleeping. Probably the . . . weather, all that snow."

"You had to get out in it, did you?"

"I fell in it."

"What?"

"I fell in a ditch."

"Oh—unfortunate. Well, just keep your head up, sir. This isn't a motel."

"Okay—sorry."

"I'm not asking you to be sorry." The security officer eyed him, and then moved on.

He drank down his coffee. He went for more.

27

There he was, that man in the black coat, standing in the very place Philip would soon be—at the traffic light. Philip stopped.

The man spotted him, raised his hand.

Then he hurried off. In the same direction Philip was going.

Philip hurried after him.

He came to where the man had raised his hand. He could see straight up the sidewalk—but no man.

Why should that concern him? Some sort of menace, that's what he was. And he did not like a pest. Someone who had no manners. Someone who didn't get it. *No one wants you standing around staring at them! Okay?*

He felt in his coat pocket. There they were—those condoms. He gripped the box.

His cell phone went off.

"Hello, hello, hello!"

"Yes?"

"This is Charlotte. Charlotte *Sanders*."

"Charlotte—"

"*Sanders*. I told you."

"Oh."

"Are you coming or *not*? I throw out an invite like that, and you don't even take me up on it? I can't believe it."

That woman—that Charlotte, of a few days ago.

"That was a wrong number," said Philip. "You know it was."

"So? Lots of wrong numbers, but maybe it was a right one—so don't be a fool, honey."

"I'm sorry. I don't think I'd better."

"You don't think you'd better."

"No."

"And why not? Don't you want a little fun?"

"Huh? You mean—"

"Oh, boy! I suppose you've pegged me for a whore now, haven't you?"

"No. No, of course not."

"Well, good. Then you come over, like I said."

Her voice was scratchy, raspy, a smoker's voice.

"I don't think I can. Work."

"Work? You at work?"

"No."

"What are you doing?"

"Walking."

"You're funny. Is walking working?"

"No. But I'm just busy."

"Busy at walking. Well, why don't you just make yourself busier and walk over to my little place?"

"Uh, well—"

"Indecisive, aren't you? Well, I'll tell you something, smarty boy. Pretty soon, one of these days, you'll be calling. But maybe I won't be available then. So maybe it's best that you take advantage right now. Life's a bitch, you know. You think you can count on something, but no—whoops, you can't. It's gone, gone, gone. And that's when you regret it. *R-e-g-r-e-t.*"

"I'm sorry."

"Don't be sorry. Just be smart. You got something here, a woman who wants you. Take advantage."

"You mean if I come over—"

"What?"

"You know—"

"Boy, what do you take me for?"

The phone went dead.

It's not me, he thought. I'm not the one.

He hurried along.

He was there, almost. Trudging toward the apartment house with the orange glare of sunlight on the windows. He opened the front door, then made his way down the hall, fingering the condoms in his pocket.

He entered her apartment.

164

And then he had to focus. He had to see clearly what was there before him.

Rod Busby.

Right at the door.

Meeting him, facing him.

"Well, now, come on in, Philly fella. Sit down. Sophia's been waiting for you. I've been waiting for you. We're about to have a little talk—aren't we, Sophie?"

"Don't call me that!"

"Well, all right. Soph*ia*. Is that better?"

"Please, Rod. Would you just please, please leave?"

"Leave? You know when I got here, Phil?"

"Philip."

"Yeah, Philip. You know when?"

"No—when?"

"About thirty minutes ago. Wouldn't you say, Soph-*i-a*?"

She sat on the sofa looking bored. No, worried. He saw her chin trembling. Her face was creased looking, her eyes teary.

"Please, please, please, Rod."

"Seems to me that you'd want your boyfriend to be here, and you wouldn't want to be asking him to go with the *please, please, please* crap."

"There's no reason for you to be here. It's over. You and me—we are over."

"Is that right? Just because *he* says?" Rod Busby circled a finger in the air and then pointed directly at Philip.

"He didn't have anything to do with it. It was me. That was *my* message."

"Your message, huh? It's over, huh? That's what you're telling me?"

"Yes! How many times must I say it!"

"Don't get uppity." He advanced toward her and laid a hand on her shoulder. She jerked away. "And *you* . . ." He swung around to Philip. "So . . . you're just the messenger fella, huh? You don't have a thing to do with our little sweetheart here. Our little Soph-*i-a*. Isn't she just a little tigress? Isn't she?"

"Quit it! Don't call me that!"

"I always call her my little tigress. And she never shows the least little appreciation. Don't you think that's just downright bad, Phil?"

"I guess she ought to be in charge of that. What she wants to be called."

Rod moved swiftly, grabbed Philip's arm hard, and swung him around. His head hit the wall.

"No!" shouted Sophia.

"Called *walling* in my profession," said Rod, and he laughed. Philip was seeing double.

Two Sophias advanced on two Rods. They slugged him on the chest, went at his face, but both double arms were now being gripped by Busby's thick double hands, and he was slinging her around like a rag doll. And then he was slapping her, back and forth across the face.

Anger management?

Philip's eyes cleared. He rushed Busby. He shot a fist out at his face and connected. He shot another fist, and didn't.

Busby got him straight in the mouth, and a second on the jaw. Philip fell, and a hand caught him, a rough, wrecking ball hand. Another fist drove right into his gut, and he couldn't catch his breath. He lay on the floor gasping, wheezing.

"God, you've killed him, you bastard!"

A snort. A snort of a laugh.

"He'll be all right. Just a few good ones, darling. Well deserved, weren't they, Philly?"

"No," he got out.

Philip looked up and saw them. Busby stood with his arm around a squirming Sophia.

Busby was grinning down at him. "Look at him. He looks like he could be taking a nap. Ain't he sweet?"

Philip wasn't getting his breath back.

Rod Busby let loose of Sophia quickly, and she spun around. She hit at him, and he backed away, laughing.

"I've got to go, you two. Hey, Philly boy, you take it easy down there. Ooh . . . ooh, well . . . *well*, what do we have here? Now what do we *have*?"

He bent down and jammed it against Philip's face. "My, my. Fell right out, didn't it? Right out of the old pocket, didn't it? Plan on using these, son?"

That box of condoms—they were flashing in his face. Hard box corners were rubbing hard against his lips and nose.

And then scraping across his chin.

He yelped out.

"Have a use for them, do you? Let me guess, just let me guess with *whom*?"

"Quit it!" shouted Sophia. "You quit that."

Busby laughed. "You know what, Phil-o? She never, ever, let her old Rod do it just naturally because, see, she didn't want anything permanent. Maybe old Rod, maybe he wouldn't have minded. Another little Rod running around. That'd been okay. Maybe. Maybe it would have been just fine—from Rod's point of view. Huh?"

She shoved him. "You never, ever, wanted a baby. You said it'd make you puke."

"Well, I'll have to admit," said Rod. "With the shitty diapers and so forth—"

"Quit it! Just leave us alone. Please, just leave us alone."

It was a side of Sophia he'd come to know: this desperate pleading—a needy need for another human being to take notice.

He wasn't sure how to feel about it. He only wanted this moment to pass. For Rod Busby to be gone. For the time of bliss to arrive.

"Okay. If it means that much to you. But I'm taking these—okay, Phil, sir? Is that okay with you?" He pushed the box of condoms against Philip's lips. "You know why?"

Philip squirmed to free himself.

"You leave him alone," yelled Sophia, and again went at him.

Busby hardly moved an inch.

"Okay," said Rod. "Okey doke." He grabbed the condoms, pitched them up, caught them, and stuck them in his pocket. "You won't be needing the little buggers, will you, Phil?"

"You won't *either*," said Sophia, and she gave him a hard shove.

And this time he landed hard against the wall.

"Hey! Walling me! Son-o-bitch!" Busby shook his finger. "Tell you what, honey, you do that, ever again, just once, and I'm going to put you six feet under. Got me, babe?"

"You heard him!" cried Sophia. "You heard what he said. So if something happens to me—"

"Oh, hell, don't be a fucking drama queen. What am I going to do? Dig it myself?"

"You're going to kill me. That's what you said. And you know what? I think you meant it."

"I'm going to kill *him*," said Rod. "You best leave, Philly-o."

He reached down and yanked Philip up.

"No," said Sophia. "No. He stays. This is my place, and you have nothing to say about who comes or leaves. Nothing."

"Your place, is it? Who rented the little bugger?"

"You throwing me out?"

"If I have to, yeah."

"Look," said Philip. *"Look, you—"*

"Look, what?" Rod Busby got him by the neck.

A choke hold, tightening.

He couldn't think. He couldn't see.

And then the choke hold relaxed.

Knife in the picture.

Sophia. With a knife. A long kitchen knife. Aimed at Rod Busby's throat.

"You leaving—or not?"

"Whew! Baby. If you're going to get that way."

"You leave, and you leave that box here."

"You want the box."

"Yes. You leave it."

Still wielding the knife right at his throat.

"Okay, okay. The knife, baby."

She withdrew it from his neck.

"Whew. Okay. Okay."

"Now."

"Ho, ho, hee, hee! My little Sophie, a murderess! Can you

168

imagine!"

"I'll use it, Rod. I *will*. Don't think I won't." Her voice gravely. He wouldn't have imagined it. It sounded like Charlotte Sanders' cigarette voice.

"Well, if you have to be that way about it. Jeez."

"I am that way about it."

"Got to go then," said Rod, handing the condoms to Sophia. He turned to Philip. "Don't use them all in one afternoon, hey."

Sophia shook her head. "Go away!"

Rod Busby gave it a grin, then exited. Sophia slammed the door. She locked it.

"Well," she said, and put the condoms on a small lamp table. "You need to get out of those clothes. You need to take a hot shower or something." She took his hand and led him toward the bathroom. "I've got some clothes here—a few things Rod left behind. You can put them on. I'll have them ready for you. I'm going to go fix us something."

He stopped outside the bathroom. He touched her on the shoulder. "You want to get in with me?"

He was shaking from what had just transpired, but he couldn't help but move on—to ask. Chemicals, he thought. The chemicals making things happen. Fear, lust—lust now.

Her eyes grew large. She laughed. "No . . . you go ahead. I'm going to fix something. You want a beer? Or something hot?"

The way she said that—*hot*.

"*Hot*."

"You know what I mean."

"Yeah."

"I'll fix some hot chocolate then. That's nice on snowy days like this, isn't it?" She left.

He got in the shower and tried to hatch up a plan.

Damn. Was she interested or not?

She opened the door and dropped the clothes in. She didn't even look at him. "Here you go!" she said. And she was gone It couldn't have been more than a second

Afterwards, he got into them. They were a bit big on him, but

169

then Rod Busby was a bit bigger. He hoped he didn't look too foolish.

On the way into the kitchen, he noticed the condoms were gone from the small lamp table. But of course you wouldn't leave them there, now would you? Because somebody might come by, and then how would that look? It'd be material for a joke, and Sophia wasn't the crude type. She wouldn't joke about a thing like that.

"Oh, hi," she said when he came into the kitchen. "I'll bet you feel better. And I've got a little something for you. She came up to him, took his hands, and kissed him. "Here, sit down. Take a seat right there." She pointed at the place where she'd set plates and silverware for two. With tall white mugs of hot chocolate. And a platter—yes, a platter stacked with pancakes.

She waited expectantly.

"Nice," he said.

It's like I've got a wife.

He took a seat.

"Good," he said. "Pancakes."

"I know it's kind of late, but we didn't really have anything before, so . . . I know you like them, and so . . . here they are!"

"I love them." He turned toward her. "I love *you.*"

"Oh, quit that." She turned her attention to her pancakes. She began cutting them up in small squares.

"That's nice," he said. "What're you doing there?"

"Oh, it's just me. I cut everything up like this."

"Not your pizza."

"Of course not—not *pizza.*" She forked a small square into her mouth. He watched.

"No, that makes sense," he said.

"A lot of things *don't* make sense," she said.

"Like what?"

"Oh, I don't know. I don't want to talk about it."

"What? Something wrong?"

A strained sense here. Something afoot. He took a sip of hot chocolate.

She looked engrossed in her pancakes, and it was exclusive of him. It could be a nice little thing here with her, eating, drinking, and then off to bed, but he felt a strain. Maybe she was second-thinking the sex. Maybe the love too.

"What?" he said again.

"I . . . I don't know how to explain it. I really don't."

"What?"

"Well . . . I guess . . . well, I guess I expected . . . a little bit more. I don't know."

"More. More what?"

She gave him a look. The look lasted longer than he'd want it to.

"Maybe I shouldn't have."

"What?"

"Well, with . . . *him*. I expected a little more with him," she said, setting her fork down. She raised her cup of hot chocolate. He thought he saw tears forming.

"What? What'd you expect? What did I . . . what didn't I—"

"Oh, don't ask that. Please don't ask that."

"Okay. Okay, I guess I know."

She set her hot chocolate down. "What do you know, Philip?"

He gave her a long look. "That you expected me to handle it better—physically. Take him down. I ended up on the floor. *He* should have."

"No. Of course not. He's stronger. You'd never be able to handle him. Don't you think I know that?"

"No question about that. But I did try. You saw me try. Didn't you? Huh?"

"That's not it. You *tried*. So? I know that. I'm not discounting that. But I tried too. And it was me. *I* was the one that had to get the knife out. Did *you* get the knife? No, *I* got it. It was me. That's who got it."

Angry—god. But why?

"You expected me to get the knife?"

She shook her head. "I don't know what I expected. I guess I just expected more."

"I'm sorry."

"Don't be."

They ate their pancakes in silence.

171

After a while she said. "I'll bet you wonder where your condoms are."

Her mood had changed. Light, bouncy.

"Oh—where are they?"

She took his hand. "They're in my bedroom, of course. What'd you think? I'd leave them in the living room in plain sight?"

"No—definitely not."

"I hate him. I absolutely, completely, hate that man. Do you know that? I don't know why I ever hooked up with him. I really don't."

She leaned over toward him and kissed him. "Eat, but really I want to get back to the bed soon. I'm kind of . . . well, I don't want to say it out loud, but I *am*." She whispered: "If you know what I *mean*."

"Yes," he said, "yes," and squeezed her hand.

"Not too hard," she said. "That was Rod. Always hard. Everything he did. Hard, hard, hard. I didn't like that, one bit."

She kept her hand in his, and he held it tightly but not hard.

"I think I could love you," she said.

"Oh, god," he said.

"Yes," she said.

28

Afternoon into the night. My god.

Such a siege. Every possible coital position. Every possible love-word used. Every imaginable feeling experienced.

"I feel sick," she said.

They were lying abed. It was the next morning. The sky through the window was a bleak gray with cuts of pale white light that splintered the light blue of the wall. It made him think of that one Emily Dickinson poem.

"Where do you feel sick—where at?"

"You just ended a sentence with a preposition."

"Oh . . . well." He felt his face growing hot.

"It's no matter. I can't tell."

"You can't tell?"

"No. It's just a funny feeling. An odd, weird feeling. Maybe I'm not sick—not exactly."

"Maybe you need some breakfast."

"Maybe, but we don't have much here, so I guess we should go out."

He liked the "we." She was now speaking of them as one. One unit—no longer were they "me" and "you."

"I could go get us something."

"No, no. I don't want you to leave me. I'd feel sad and lonely." She moved against him.

She was still naked from the night before. He worried about the condoms leaking. What if they had?

"Something wrong?"

"No."

"You don't have to worry about me. I'm okay."

"Good."

"You still sound funny."

He wanted it again. And he turned toward her and took her in his arms.

"What's this?" she said, and laughed.

"I'd like to," he said, "if you would."

"Yes," she said, "of course. But first do something for me."

"What?"

"You won't want to do it."

"What is it?"

"I do wish you'd do it."

"What?"

"Make a call."

"A call?"

"Yes—oh, if you just would, please."

That element of pleading. But different. A needy need, but a different kind of needy need.

"Sure. What is it?"

"To a friend of mine. I need some money. And she'll loan it to me. If you would. Just would."

"Call her—for money?"

"Say I'm sick or something. She'll loan it to us, I promise."

She had now said *us*. He desperately wanted to take her right now, but first the phone call—apparently.

"She's really nice, but I just can't speak to her right now. I just don't have it in me." She took his hand and held it, and he remembered not to squeeze too hard. "Could you?"

"I think so. What's her name?"

"Gina."

"Gina what?"

She smiled. "Does it make any difference, honey? She's just Gina to me, most of the time. And her name is hard to pronounce. But she's really, really nice. It'll be easy to talk to her—I guarantee."

It struck him how needless, then, that he speak to her—this Gina person. But he had this strong impression that were he to flinch, she'd hold off on a sexual need he was now feeling a very powerful urge to satisfy. And so he grabbed the phone. "What's the number?"

"Oh, she's long distance. You'll have to use my cell phone."

"Where does she live?"

"More like, where is she *presently*? I don't think she lives anywhere. She's loaded, totally loaded, loaded. She's all over the place. But if you call a particular number, she's got some sort of forwarding service—I don't know how it works exactly, but it'll get her anywhere in the whole world. So . . . it's kind of fun really."

Fun?

No, he thought. It's *not* fun. How in the world *could* it be?

"You'd like to do it first," she said, "and then call, I suppose."

He nodded. "If you don't mind," he said.

"I guess that's okay. If you promise."

"I'll do it."

"God," she said. "Get the condom out, but be sure you put it on good. I really, really don't want offspring at this time in my life. As broke as I am."

And that was why she'd bought the condoms? He guessed so. It was good of her. And it told him this too: her need was as fierce as his.

Or was it?

"I don't really feel sick now," she said.

And they went at it. It was better this morning than the night before. It was . . . god, what was it? It was like he was completely hers, and she was completely his. Where did he end, and she begin? He didn't want to imagine there was a point of separation. He wanted to think they were like two circles, the same size, conjoining, and then making one circle. One circle of absolute, unadulterated pleasure and joy.

Such pleasure, pleasure, pleasure—and forever, he thought, as he was getting his briefs on.

"You don't really have to call her," said Sophia, pulling on her panties. "Not if you really don't want to."

She was sitting on the edge of the bed, and she turned to smile at him.

He was in love with her now in a way he hadn't been before. Or was it just lust? He couldn't be sure. Anyway, before, he had seen her from the outside, now from the inside—in that circle. "If you don't feel comfortable with it, I'll do it," he said.

"You're a real sweetheart," she said. "But what will she think?"

"Yeah, I don't know."

"She might not trust you," said Sophia. "But I just get so tired, tired, of always asking her for money. Still . . . okay, there's something you don't know. Something you do need to know." She pulled on her top, her breasts bouncing, and then brushed her hair back. "Gina has been my friend for years and years—ever since eighth grade. We always loaned each other money, gave each other money, did things for each other. We were best friends—BFF!—and that was that. We lied for each other. We shared boyfriends. You know?"

"Huh?"

"Don't look so funny. It's not so weird. We were really, really good friends—and still are. My boyfriend wanted her, and I told him, sure, sure, if you really, really *do*—but don't fall in love with her. Do it, but don't take it any further. 'Okay? Don't.' And he promised me. He did."

"Um. Did it work out?"

"I don't know. I guess it didn't because he was a little funny after that. Not really himself anymore, but maybe he was just feeling guilty. You can feel real guilty over a thing like that. I don't know why—it's hard to know why a thing like that is so, so important, but it is. It's like it's *you,* you know. You don't just screw, see? It's *you*—you get what I'm saying?"

"Yes," he said because he was feeling the same thing.

"So," she said, and it looked like she might cry, "he gave her his *you*, or his *I*, if you want to put it that way. It was a mistake. That's what it was. I tried to put it out of my mind. But it wasn't the same afterwards . . . it wasn't. But anyway, getting back to Gina. She finally met this man who was really, vastly, immensely rich. Or, could get at a huge amount of money—I suppose I should put it that way. Could get his hands on lots of it. *Big* money. Big, big, big. Okay? You get where I'm going with this?"

"Yes. Money," he said. "Loads of it."

"That's right. And it's nothing to Gina. She asks for ten thousand bucks, and the man hands it over. It's like somebody handing you a dime. Who makes a federal case out of a dime?"

"Nobody."

"So . . . if you call her, you can just leave a message if she's not there, and say your girlfriend, Sophia, she needs a bit of money—and say the amount. And she'll wire it like within an hour if she can or at least as soon as she gets the phone call."

"How much," he asked, "have you asked for . . . in the past?"

She smiled. She took a moment.

"Not that much. I asked for a thousand once. When I was behind on my rent, and didn't think I'd ever catch up."

He knew what his next question was, and she did too.

"I guess then I ought to—"

"I need fifteen hundred, honey. I really do. And we're going to be living together, aren't we?"

"Yes, yes," he said. "Sure. Of course."

"Don't worry about Rod either. I can handle him."

"No," he said. "*I* can handle him." Of course he couldn't, but he said it.

"God, I know we'll be *so* good together," said Sophia. "I just know it. Call, and then we'll go out for breakfast. If she's there, we'll pick up the cash on the way."

So now he was going to have to call that Gina woman.

"How old is she, by the way?"

She looked at him funny. "Gosh. What difference does it make? Could it make?"

"Your age?"

"Yes." She seemed mystified, and even a little sullen.

"I'm sorry," he said. "I was just trying to get a fix on her."

"Oh? But really, if she was my friend back since eighth grade, you think she's some woman age thirty or forty or fifty?"

"No. No."

"Well?"

"Sorry."

"Hell, no. She's my age. And you know how old I am, don't you?"

Twenty-one, she'd told him. He reminded her.

"I just turned twenty-two yesterday," she said, with an incipient smile.

177

"Yesterday? You didn't tell me."

"So?"

"Why didn't you tell me?"

"Because I hate birthdays. That's why. I utterly loathe birthdays."

"Really? *Why*?"

"I don't like cake, I don't like candles, and I don't like ice cream. And I don't like aging. So there you have it."

What a litany! "Aging?"

"Yes, aging."

"But you're so young."

"Well—I don't like celebrating a day such as that. Just because some sperm—microscopic—fertilizes some egg—microscopic—I'm supposed to make a huge deal over this little *me* with my microscopic origins? What's that birthday but a big ballooning of that hugely tiny zygote?"

Hugely tiny?

"But it's an important day. Like—you were born that day. Saw the first light of day. Like—you came into this world. That needs some recognition, doesn't it? Some attention paid—a party or something?"

"It's a sad, sad world, Philip. And you've got too many people out there celebrating their grand fucking entrance. You think about it. About a hundred million people are probably celebrating their grand fucking entrance into this hell hole this very day. Doesn't that seem a bit stupid? Laughable even? Risible?"

Risible? And did she have to curse?

"No—I don't think so. No," he said.

"Are you going to call her, or not?"

"Yes."

She pinched his arm. And then she did something to her phone and handed it to him. "Press right there, and you'll be talking to her. Fifteen hundred. Do ask for fifteen hundred. She won't mind."

"Then why don't you call her?"

"Because like I told you—I don't feel like it."

"Okay," he said. Besides he did want more later, so he thought this a small price to pay. If you thought about it even for a second.

He pressed the key. The phone rang three times, and then a female voice came on. It sounded surprisingly like Sophia. It could have *been* Sophia.

"Hello? My name is Philip. I'm a friend of Sophia Cross's. And—"

"Sophia! God, how *is* Sophia?"

"Fine. She's fine. Doing . . . really well."

Sophia was shaking her head. "No," she whispered.

"Good! Is she there?"

He looked at her and pointed at the phone.

"*No*," whispered Sophia.

"Well, not right now," said Philip.

"Well, what's up, then? Why are you calling me?"

"Oh—well. I'm calling on behalf of Sophia."

"Yes?"

"She . . . she needs some money. She's really in need of money right now, and she's otherwise indisposed, or she'd be—"

Sophia bent over laughing. She had her hand up to her mouth.

"She's *indisposed*? Pray tell, how?"

"Sick, I guess, kind of sick."

"Sick of what now?"

"Oh, well . . . flu? I don't know."

"Oh, you'd know the flu. How much does she need? And let me ask Sophia herself, if you please. SOPHIA! SOPHIA! Quit the FUCKING DISAPPEARING ACT!"

Sophia still had her hand up to her mouth. She grabbed the phone. "Hi, Gina. How is it? How is life, life, *life*? . . . Um, really? Oh, no, I'm not sick. Isn't he a silly boy?" She grabbed Philip's hand and held it. "So, so, so silly. But I love him. I've got a lover now, Gina, a *real* lover. Not like that other horrible, terrible, sicko—you know. I don't even want to mention his name. You know it all too well."

She stuck the phone up to Philip's ear.

That same voice, identical somehow to Sophia's, said, "Yes, yes, yes, the one that put you in the hospital." And suddenly her voice dropped to a lower pitch, and kind of snarled even, and she said, "I'd like to kill the big bastard. The bastard fucker. Want me to put a hit out on him?"

179

Sophia had her face against Philip's, listening.

Why doesn't she put it on speaker?

She took the phone. "No, not yet. Well, my new boyfriend, this wonderful Philip, whom you just spoke to, and who asked for money, but not the *amount*—he's going to protect me from all such things, aren't you, honey?"

Philip smiled and nodded.

The phone went smack up against his ear.

"Well, goodie, goodie," said Gina. "For him."

Sophia grabbed the phone.

"Including money problems. But for now, could you, would you, loan me a little? Just a tad?" She directed Philip to lean close to her.

"Sure. How much? Ten million fucking dollars?"

Sophia laughed loud—an unfamiliar laugh, harsh, bristly. "No— though I could use it, I could!"

Philip could hear Gina's voice, again a kind of snarl, "Well, he makes more than that in a week. Sometimes in a day—as I've told you. Repeatedly? So if you need it, *ask* for it. I'm serious. *I am.*"

"I don't want to be that much of a leach," said Sophia. "Really. How about fifteen hundred?"

Philip's face was close to her cheeks, and they felt warm, soft, satiny. Was her face ... wet? Slightly wet. Was that a tear?

"Okay, fifteen hundred. And don't tell me you'll pay me back later because that is pure bullshit and you know it."

"I know."

"So don't say it anymore."

"I won't."

Philip's lips were close to hers, but because of the phone—not square on. Yes, her face felt wet, slightly wet.

"I hope you don't. Shall I wire it the same place?"

"Sure."

"I might send more than that."

"Oh, don't. Don't do that. You'll make me feel guilty. And you know I don't like feeling guilty."

"Your call."

"Thanks, Gina."

"Love ya, kid. Do take it easy?"

"I will. I definitely will."

"And tell that new hombre of yours that if he ever, I mean *ever*, is mean to you, to watch his windows, okay?"

"I will."

Sophia put the phone down. Tears were streaking down her face.

"You want to go back to bed again?" he said.

"Yes," she said. "Yes, I do."

29

They spent the rest of the morning and the whole afternoon in bed, and finally he was tired of it. She was tired of it. They lay holding each other, heavy with covers, watching TV.

It was some sort of thriller. But he couldn't say what it was exactly. Or follow it.

"Sometimes," Sophia said, "you just can't do it anymore. Wonder why that is?"

"I don't know. Funny, isn't it?"

"Well, yeah, because there's the urge, urge, urge, see—and then it's all gone. Gone, gone, gone. Where in hell does it go? It's like eating and drinking. You know, like with a big, big meal, you think you'll die if you eat another bite? Only, well, I guess it's not quite like that. It's more like the yearning just goes dry. But then it eventually comes back. Other yearnings," she said, "other yearnings. What *are* they? Oh, yearnings like for good movies—like that one I saw, about the man and the woman who were artists and had the little cottage on the beach. I was thinking, I could see that all day, don't let it *ever* go away, ever quit, but then I got to thinking: No, I'd tire of it. Yes, I would. It'd get stale. Everything in this goddamned world gets stale, doesn't it?"

"Yeah—I guess so." There was that word. He hated that word coming out of her pretty mouth. Such pretty, supple, sensuous, moist lips.

"I think the whole world is just so stale, don't you? I mean, it gets that way so fast."

"Yeah."

"Maybe we ought to do it again just to prove that it doesn't *have* to be stale. I mean check it out. Do it once more, and study it. Is there an ounce of pleasure in it? Is there an ounce of excitement, of looking forward to the next move, the next coital position, the next surprise, and so forth?"

Coital?

"You *want* to?" Because how would he perform? After all, six times since the previous evening? *Six times.*

"I'm okay with it," she said.

"Okay."

"You're not, though."

"Yes—sure. I am."

"Well, then."

There were no clothes to remove. They were still naked from the last go-round.

She lay there naked before him, wanting to, or at least wanting to experiment, and he knew he should feel something, but he didn't. He wanted to feel something. He moved toward her. He couldn't get it going. He couldn't get it doing anything. He was limp and lacking.

"Don't you love me?" she said.

"Yes. Yes!" he said. Was he shouting?

She sat up in all her gorgeous beauty and sensuality. She laid a hand on his shoulder. "Are you *sure*?"

"I love you. I love you," he said. "More than you can *imagine*!"

She gave him a look. "What's that mean?"

"Huh?"

"Imagine. What does 'more than you can imagine' mean?"

"Well," he said, "I don't know. I hadn't really thought—it just came out. It means *a lot*. That's what it means."

"I guess I can imagine plenty on my own," she said.

She seemed to go into some sort of funk. He'd have to dig his way out.

"I meant a whole, an awful lot," he said.

"I don't know," she said.

"Don't know what?"

"I don't know—about a lot of things."

"Neither do I."

"I don't think you can know," she said.

"Maybe you can't."

"Do you think?"

"I'm not sure. Think about what?"

"Oh, god, it's all so confusing!"

"What is?"

"Don't ask me a question! I want answers. I need a man with answers."

"Oh."

"Aren't you ready?" she asked. Her voice sounded rather sneering.

"I'm . . . drained out. Literally, I mean," he said.

"For me?"

"No, it's physical. That's all it is—physical. A physical draining out."

"Oh," she said, "I guess I can understand that. Later, then."

She turned over in bed, with her back to him. He wanted her, but his body didn't. He wanted her as *them,* but his body didn't. He lay there helplessly as he heard her snoring slightly. He fell asleep after a while, but didn't know when.

It was dark when they awoke. And they had something to eat and watched TV. And then they fell asleep again.

The next morning he got up and looked out the bedroom window onto the snow. It was coming down hard, hard, and cars parked on the street outside were covered up entirely. He needed to get out in back to the lot to clean off his car. If he didn't call the office soon, they'd send a cop out to find it. But then how would they find it? You probably couldn't even see it. Why didn't he want to call in? Speak to Digby Morris? He had no idea. He just couldn't talk to the man. There was nothing in him to talk to the man.

"How bad is it?" she said.

"Oh," he said, "you're awake."

"Yep."

"It's deep, really deep."

"That surprise you?"

"No. It just keeps coming."

"We ought to build a snow fort. It's wet and you can make things with it."

"Well, yeah."

"You sound really interested."

"No, I am."

"Come to me."

He came to the bed.

"Now," she said, "if you want."

He did. They made love twice, tight together, flesh to flesh. The more fused the flesh, he thought, the more one body. And then he thought, *one mind*. Yes. More than anything *that*. One mind, one mind, one mind. One heart, please. A fusion of the spirit, the psyche—an *us*, two separate beings becoming one. One soul. Was it love? Did it make any difference? Maybe it was only lust. Maybe it was. But such pleasure in the bonding. Was it two meat machines fusing? He shook his head—no. No, no.

No, he would not let Adam Most confuse him. He would not let Adam Most depress him. Poor Adam Most. He couldn't imagine him with a woman. Books only—that's all he had: books. Library books, not even his. But the ideas—they were his, or at least he was trying to make them his. But they were a jumble, and he was lost in the clutter and fog of them.

They had breakfast, and he drank several cups of coffee.

"You'll get high blood pressure. Drinking that much caffeine."

"I need it, though."

"Well, you don't have to worry about it all that much while you're young. It's just later you have to worry about it."

"What makes you think about that?"

"Because I was in nurse training for a spell."

A spell?

"What was that like?"

"Okay, I guess. I liked it some, but other times, I hated it. I hated being so close to other people's flesh. It was . . . hard. Hard to take. I have a problem with others having . . . flesh. Isn't that silly?"

"How could they *not* have flesh?"

"I don't know. It doesn't make sense, I know. It's just other people's flesh—it can be so icky. You know?"

Icky?

He thought of his own flesh. Did she—on occasion, at least— ever see it as *icky*?

"But what if they didn't have flesh?"

"Then they'd be spirits. And maybe that would be okay." She waved her arms about. "Just spirits. Sprits flying here and there, flying all about, high, low, all around! Flying, flying, flying. Up and down, and all around. Just pure being. That's all. Being, being, *being*."

Her voice had grown singsongy.

"Or they'd be skeletons," he said.

But she didn't hear him. She flitted about the room with her arms airplane wings, gliding.

It was like she'd been drinking. "My," he said. "I don't know about that."

She stopped suddenly. "What's wrong with it? That's how I envision the afterlife. Flying, flying, flying. Up, down, and all around! Don't you?"

She poured herself more coffee, and then him too.

"Hey," he said, "aren't you worried about me overindulging?"

"You're going to anyway, and so why not face it?" She kissed him. "Besides, you've got years and years before you have to worry about blood pressure."

"I hope."

"Blood pressure. Just think about it. It's like water in pipes, and it's got to have all this pressure, see, but not too much, because then—wham, you go . . . kaput!"

She *had* been drinking. Or pills? Or maybe . . . maybe all that sex had given her a big high. He tried to remember if he'd read anything about that. Yes, endorphins. Big boosters, they were.

"What are you so all keyed up about?" he asked, and smiled to show he wasn't criticizing.

"I want to make a snow fort! And I hope you do too." She took a sip of coffee. "I'm not sure I actually *believe* in spirits—or an afterlife. But I'd like to." She looked away, out the kitchen window onto the bungalow next door, where a woman was sitting at a breakfast table, glancing toward them, a white cup raised before her. Eavesdropping on each other?

"Yes," he said. "Me too."

"I think a snow fort is what we need," she said. "Because it's kind of a protection from the world. I think of it that way." She continued to gaze out the kitchen window. A car was making its way through the narrow alley back to the parking lot. "It's made of snow, it's enclosed, and nothing comes in. It's just you and your special other. That's all there is, you and the other. I want that. And I want a snow fort."

"Me too," he said. "And we'll live in it. Fix it up with—" It was the wrong thing to say, maybe. He felt it hanging out there—in the air.

But after a moment, she jumped up, clapping:

"We will, and we will never, ever, get jobs again, and we will do it five times a day, or a dozen, and we will beg, borrow, and steal what we need. And that's it, in a nutshell."

Nutshell?

"I like it," he said. "I like it a lot. That plan of yours."

"I'll get some warm clothes for both of us. Yours are in the washroom hung up. You just wait here."

He thought about calling the office. Damn, he didn't *want* to call the office. But he didn't want a cop car showing up for that company car either. Still, he *was* meaning to go back, he'd emphasize that, but all that deluge of snow, it had simply kept him from it. *You could have called*, the cop would say. No, no cop would say that. Digby Morris might say that, but not some cop. Or would he?

Perhaps, though, he would be shackled.

Shackled?

Sophia came out with her arms loaded with coats, hats, scarves, and boots.

"Let's get in these, and then we'll make the fort, and we'll fix some hot chocolate, and we'll have us a wonderful, wonderful day!"

She sounded a bit strained. What was it? And why?

"Yes!" he came back.

"Wonderful," she said. "Wonderful!"

"Yes!" he said, but his heart wasn't in it. He was scared for Sophia. Maybe she was worried about Rod Busby, but he didn't dare mention the name.

30

Snowing. They stood looking out the bedroom window onto the street.

Snow plows working away. Cars being towed off.

"They'll pay a bunch for that," said Sophia.

"Good thing mine's in the lot."

He liked the sound of that—*mine*.

"I've never seen it like this," said Sophia. "It could completely bury us. If it keeps this up. We'll have no power, you just watch. There's no power on the south side right now. Those outages make their way in waves. They will move north bit by bit. Maybe in a day or two, they'll be here. It's like a pandemic."

"Really? Are you sure? It doesn't work that way, does it?"

"How do you know? I think it does."

"I've got to call the office," said Philip.

"Just don't bother with them. Just don't give them another thought. Oh, besides, we've got to go pick up that money—from our dear little friend."

"Oh, yeah."

"We're running short on food, as you've probably noticed."

"Yeah."

"Fifteen hundred bucks. That's nice, isn't it? We could . . . stay in a hotel. Just for fun, couldn't we?"

"In a hotel—why?"

"Just for fun. For a change of scenery."

On borrowed money? From her friend?

"There's nice hotel a couple miles out Grand. The Hotel Horatio. Once you get that car dug out—or we could take mine. You'd have to dig it out. But when it's cold, it doesn't start a lot of the time. So . . . yours would be better, I'll bet."

"Where's yours?"

"On the lot, of course. It's a little green thing. But you wouldn't know it now, would you? It would mean snow off a dozen hoods before I could find it."

"You don't know where you parked it?"

"No—not really. Let's take yours. If you'll just start digging it out—"

A hotel on borrowed money from a friend, and conveyed out there in a stolen car? It might as well be stolen. Why in hell couldn't he call Digby Morris? Why in bloody hell not? Something held him back. He felt paralyzed. He had no idea why.

"We could dig it out together," he said, "if you want."

"No. That's a man's job."

"Yeah."

"But first that snow fort."

They spent an hour building it. It was so easy with the wet, heavy snow.

"I'm cold. I'm so cold I'm just dying!" she cried. But she stood, gazing at it.

"I am too."

"Isn't our fort so beautiful, ever so beautiful?" Sophia said, taking his hand. She squeezed it tightly.

It looked a bit like a plain old wall to him, a rounded one with a deep depression in the middle. And situated up close to the rear of the apartment house, on the edge of the parking lot—if this *was* the edge. Who could tell with all this snow?

"Beautiful."

"We need to build an igloo and just kiss the whole world goodbye. Know what I mean?"

"Really?"

"Yes. Like an Eskimo. Damn right!"

"I'd better get that thing dug out," he said, pointing at the car. Or *was* that the car? It was a heap of snow in the approximate area where he'd parked.

"Okay."

She held his hand tightly as they made their way around to the front of the apartment house, then on into the lobby.

Then she held a finger up.

"What?"

"Wait here."

"Okay."

He stood there, waiting. In minutes she came back with a broom, a shovel, and a scraper.

"There, that ought to do it."

"Good," he said. "I'll do it."

He went for the door.

"Be careful."

"Of what?"

"Overexertion. Exhaustion. Heart attack."

"Oh."

He went out to the car. He plunged his hand in the snow for the door handle. He couldn't open it.

Frozen shut.

Of course it was, sure, let the cops come. Let them open the door. Let them go ahead and try.

Fucking A.

He swept off some snow with the broom, and then gave it up. *What's the point if the damned thing won't open?* He tried all four doors. No—wouldn't open. None of them.

He went back inside. He stomped off snow in the lobby.

"Well?" she said.

"The doors are frozen shut."

"Hmm. I could use a hair dryer, but where'd I plug it in?"

"I don't know. You got a long, heavy-duty wire?"

"No." She seemed to think. "Probably Rod would."

"No."

"We could try my car," she said, "but it won't start. I can *guarantee* you that."

"There has to be a way to open the goddamn car door," he said.

"You don't need to cuss like that," she said.

"I'm sorry."

"Don't be sorry. Things aren't going good for you. How long has it been since you've been to that job?"

"God, I've lost track of time," he said. He tried to recall.

"It's not a deal really, is it? Who cares if they sell more guns and ammo to kill poor deer, rabbits, bears, and other helpless creatures?"

"A bear's not exactly helpless. Is it?"

She frowned. "Don't be picky."

"Oh."

"But here you're not harming anything. I'll tell you what. We could take a cab. Why *not* take a cab?"

"Really? What'd that cost?"

"I don't know. It couldn't be more than ten dollars. Twenty. Or so."

"But we've got your place—"

"No! I want something special. Some place where we haven't already done it a thousand times. Some place nice. With a nice big TV and a nice bar and lounge."

"Hmm."

"It would be a vacation. I need a vacation. Don't you?"

"Yes." And he thought he did. He definitely did. Junk jobs, no girlfriend, at least not until now, no money, bad apartment, and before that, all that unending work to get his degree—and how was that paying off? Yes, he needed a vacation.

"We deserve a vacation. Don't we?" She took his hand.

"Yes!" he said. "Yes, we do."

Why call Digby Morris? He couldn't just yet. But he would find a way to get to the office the next day. Or maybe at least call.

31

Booted up, wrapped in heavy coats, scarves, gloves, with backpacks stuffed with clothes, toilet articles, three torture books, and various odds and ends, they hoofed it out to the mall to pick up Gina's money at Shoppers Paradise.

While Sophia went to Customer Service, he milled about in the store.

When she reappeared, looking a bit grim, he said, "What's the problem?"

"Nothing. You'd better buy more condoms, hadn't you?"

He nodded. "Yes."

She reached into her purse and pulled out a hundred and wadded it into his open hand.

"Get plenty."

"I will."

"You do that," she whispered at him, grinning.

He got a forty-count pack and paid for it at the pharmacy, and they were on their way.

"You get a bunch?"

"I sure did." He started to show her, then didn't.

"She's so, so nice, isn't she? To send that money just like that. Oh, there's stuff about her, of course, that I'd hate to say—"

"Like what?"

She shook her head. "Forget it. Call a cab."

He didn't have the number.

"Here. Let me check on it." And she got on her cell and gave it to him.

He called the cab company.

"Where to?" he asked, turning to Sophia. He'd forgotten the name of that hotel.

"The Hotel Horatio."

He liked the way her mouth pronounced it in a brisk, self-assured fashion. She took his free arm. He liked that too.

He told the dispatcher.

"They'll send a cab in five minutes or so," Philip told her.

"Good. We'll wait in here. Not stand out there and freeze."

"No point in that."

They stood in the vestibule, close to the doors, just far enough away that they didn't cause them to open. A blast of cold air hit them every time someone came in.

"I hope that cab gets here fast," said Philip.

"Yes, please! I'm freezing, and I'm getting hungry. Aren't you?"

"Yes—real hungry."

"Let's order something special. Forget the cost, forget the stupid cost—for once. I'm so tired of thinking money, money, money. Doesn't that get to you? It does to me."

"Me too—for sure," he said. And why not feel good about that money? It was Gina's bastard of a husband's money, as Sophia had emphasized on their hike out here to the mall. So, well, okay why should money be a big object, things being what they were?

He asked her about Gina. About that stuff about her—that she'd hate to say.

"Oh, forget it. It's not important."

"I am hungry," he said.

"A shrimp basket. That's not all that expensive. Is it? And there's a liquor store right next to the Horatio, where you can get some pretty good wine. How about that?"

"Yes," he said.

She twirled around. "I'm feeling giddy, giddy, *oh so* giddy. And you?"

The doors opened. She'd gotten too close to them.

More people hurrying in. Snow-covered coats. Rubbing hands.

"Yes, I am," he said, but he wasn't, and he couldn't imagine why. How could this not be the best day of his entire life? Yet he was hesitating.

But she didn't seem to pick up on his hesitation.

"When we get there, the first thing when we get there, let's take a shower together. A long, hot shower and do it right in there. And not worry about the condom," she said, and whispered in his ear.

He felt the wet tongue, and for a moment he confused her with Lisa Wing, and even, when he looked at her, she looked like Lisa Wing, just momentarily, and he froze. He froze.

This, she caught. "What's wrong?"

"Nothing. Nothing at all."

"Oh, I get it. You're all worried about me *getting with child*," she whispered, giggling. It was a half sneer. "Well, ever heard of the rhythm method?"

"Oh. Yes. Of course."

"Well—"

"God, yes," he said.

"I knew that'd cheer you up."

"I'm cheered up."

He took her hand, but he was careful not to squeeze too hard.

When the cab arrived, he saw the man in the black suit standing not fifty yards away, behind a long green car, half covered with snow. The man was watching him, hand on his hat.

"See that?" Philip said. "You see that? You see that fucking bastard?"

She was in the cab, and she slid over. "What bastard? Where?"

"Standing right over there—by that car."

"Yes—so?"

"He's following me—everywhere. Everywhere I go."

The cab took off. "Oh, come on," said Sophia. "Since when?"

"For days and days."

"Well, maybe you've won something big! Like a prize!"

"Sure. Maybe so," he said.

The cab roared down Grand, switching lanes.

He didn't want to mention how twice Rod Busby had intervened. How even that wasn't apparently going to stop the bastard from spying on him. What the hell?

"Isn't this just the best thing we've done so far?" said Sophia.

He smiled, and he squeezed her hand, softly.

"Yes."

"I like a squeeze like that," she said.

He saw that the cab driver was looking in the rearview mirror.

But he didn't let go of her hand.

The man winked in the mirror. He had thick red lips and a stubby growth of black whiskers. But Sophia didn't see it. She was looking away, out the side window, at the strip mall.

The Hotel Horatio was a large motor hotel, five stories high. He'd not been in this part of town before, or at least this stretch of road, and he was surprised at its vastness. They got a room on the top floor, and they went up the elevator, with their bags flopped on the elevator floor at their sides. She'd wanted to rent the place for a whole week, and he'd gone along with it, but it had surprised him.

When they were up in their room, she spilled the beans.

"You know how much money we *actually* got?"

"How much?"

"Ten thousand big ones. Gina gave us ten thousand fucking big ones. Can you believe it?"

"God, but are you going to have to—"

"No. No, Philip. I *never* do. I call it a loan, but Gina wants me to have it. You heard her."

"What's her husband *do* anyway? I mean *really*?"

She shook her head and smiled. "Oh, let's don't ask. Hey, let's have us one fine time, huh? Okay? Don't you think?"

"Yes. I do."

"A whole week! It's a nice place, isn't it? I always thought it was."

Always thought?

She caught his look. Her voice lowered: "Yes—I've been here, Philip, once or twice. Well, three times. And it is nice, isn't it?"

She waved her hands at the king size bed, the huge TV, the hotel furniture, everything. She flopped down on the king size bed.

"Nice, yes."

"I didn't stay out here with *him*, if you're worried about that."

"Oh, no, I'm not worried."

"It was with other boys, or men, if you have to know."

"No—that's okay."

"Well, I hope it is. I hope I don't have to confess everything."

"No, no, you don't."

"Because I'm not going to." She grinned. "You'd never drag it out of me."

"I don't want to know," he said.

"Like I don't want to know who *you've* been with," she said.

He thought. Yeah, who? Once, well, twice, if you counted that one time, which he wouldn't count, and that was it. Sophia Cross was pretty much it. Other than those two times. Which, really, amounted to just one legitimate time.

"We don't have to grill each other," he said.

"Who said anything about grilling? You still hungry?"

She got up off the bed.

"I am," he said.

"Well, then, let's go down to the bar and grill. I want to drink, drink, drink! Half the goddamned night, and come up here so entirely drunk out of my mind that I won't recall a thing. How about you?"

Not recall a thing?

She twirled around. She twirled around several times. She was a twirling top.

"No, no," he said. "I *want* to recall everything. Everything." He put his arms around her and began to dance. It was not typical of him. But suddenly he felt *alive*. There wasn't an ounce of hesitation in him now. He wanted to romp and roar.

"Gosh, don't be so intense," she said, pulling loose of him. "I just want to have a good time, is all. I feel like I've been going at it, going, going at it, day in, day out with that stupid goddamn restaurant job, getting up at five, serving one creep after another—" She stopped and blushed. "I don't mean *you*. You were the high point of my day. But others. They could be so awful, and then that witch watching my every goddamn move."

Two *goddamns*.

"You need a good break," he said.

"Yes. Now you get it."

"I do too," he said, and then thought, *I've got to call that damned office, and I will tomorrow first thing.*

"First I want to freshen up, though," said Sophia. She pressed herself against him and whispered in his ear. "I won't get drunk. Don't worry. Okay?"

"I'm not worried," he said.

"Well, don't." She went into the bathroom, and soon he heard the shower running.

He stripped and joined her.

"Oh, not now, honey. I just want to be left alone, okay? For a minute?"

"Sure." He started to leave.

"Don't be angry."

"I'm not."

"I'll see you pretty soon." She pulled him to her and kissed him.

He got back into his clothes. What was all that about in the shower, and the rhythm method?

He looked out on the parking lot where the snow was piled high in frozen white walls. Snow plows were working one end of the lot, with cars entering and exiting on the other end. Across the way was a large liquor store. Also called the Horatio. Hotel-owned. Perhaps the largest liquor store he'd ever seen. It occurred to him that if he wanted money, he'd have to ask Sophia for it. Back at her house, it was different somehow, but here, in more neutral territory, he felt a little uneasy at the prospect.

And then he got to thinking further. He should definitely go into work tomorrow, and yet would she want to be left here in the hotel without him? Well, probably best just to call in and tell Digby Morris about the buried car, and how soon—it might be a week, it really *could* be—he'd have it dug out and he'd be back to work. Right now, he couldn't do it. Of course, he'd get fired, and that would be that. Maybe, though, it was best that way.

He turned on the TV, and he still heard the shower running.

He got the weather channel.

More snow. Twelve to fifteen more inches coming. And, said the weather woman, they could be getting *even more*, and no chance of the snow melting because the temps would be sticking to around twenty degrees. Or less.

"The snow of the century," said the weather woman. "This siege is going to affect the economy, of course. It's already affecting local businesses. And now, our on-the-site Weather Guy . . ."

"Ah, this weather . . . . Aren't you tired of this weather?" the Weather Guy said to the weather woman.

"Indeed I am. Is there anyone who isn't? But what can we do?"

"They've put on five hundred more snow plows!"

"Well, that's a start!" cried the weather woman.

"We can thank our fine city for that!" yelled the Weather Guy.

"We're here . . . forever, aren't we?" said Sophia, emerging from the shower naked, her full breasts bouncing, and snuggling next to him, her panties dangling from one hand. "Just forever. Aren't we?"

He moved in. "I guess so. It looks that way. Umm."

He wanted her, but she was moving away, already getting on her panties.

"Let's go down to the Lounge. Doesn't it feel good to be here forever? *I* think it does. It feels like . . . it really does feel like those cute little Eskimos in their nice little ice houses, snug and warm, and protected from the world. See, Philip, the world's out *there*. All that snow. *Our* world's in here. In this place here. This is ours, ours, ours!"

She clutched him and kissed him hard, and then he felt his face get wet. She was crying, softly.

"Hey! What, what?" he asked. "What's wrong? What's wrong, honey?" He'd never called her honey. But if felt good, felt right.

"I don't know. I don't have the vaguest. Let's go on down now, huh? Okay?"

"Yes, let's do," he said.

She got dressed. She held her purse at her side as though it contained vast riches, and he guessed it did. She had that ten thousand bucks in it, or close to it. That cab had been twenty-five bucks. She'd shelled out thirty-five. God, that was something. It was running through her fingers, but then ten thousand? Why worry? It would take a while to go through that. Wouldn't it?

"Oh, I am *so* hungry," said Sophia.

They approached the elevator.

"You know what?" he said. "I'd like a pitcher of beer."

"No—wine," she said. "A bottle of their finest."

"Okay," he said, but he did worry. The room cost $259 a night. Add tax to that. Add food and drink to that, and they could certainly go through the whole thing in a month. That was less than forever. Wasn't it?

She'd made *him* register—of course. She'd whispered on the way in that *she* wasn't registering. How would *that* look?

"Wine's great," he said. He could have a beer later, back in the room. For some reason, he wanted a beer.

"Oh, oh, oh, let's just enjoy, enjoy, enjoy!" she squealed, grabbing his hand, and it concerned him. A man entered the elevator wearing a tan business suit. He was bent over the front page of a newspaper.

"Any big news?" asked Sophia.

"Hmm?" He looked up.

"Anything in that paper worth reading?"

"Is there ever?" He smiled, then went back to the paper, with raised eyebrows. Was it at Sophia's intrusion, or at something in the paper?

"Never," said Sophia. "There never is, *is* there?"

"Depends on what you mean," said the man crinkling the paper.

The elevator door whooshed open.

They headed on out, and Sophia burst out: "It's not in touch with who we are. It's a gigantic pack of lies! That's what I mean!"

The man shook his paper and folded it. "Oh, well, that's one viewpoint. You all have a nice day. Hear?"

"Wow," said Philip.

"Wow what?"

"Oh, I don't know. That took courage." He was thinking abandon, but he didn't say it.

"I'm totally down on newspapers," said Sophia.

They headed into Ye Ole Grill.

"Welcome," said a waitress. "Table or booth?"

Philip was taken by her stunning beauty. Classic face with smooth, fine features, supple lips, raven-black hair, small, cute ears, and curves that came close to shocking him.

Alluring.

Exceedingly alluring.

Ignore her. Don't be aware of her.

No, no, no.

"Booth?" he said.

"Whatever you think," said Sophia.

"Booth."

"Okay," said the waitress, and led them to a booth at the far end of the bar where they could look onto a street behind the Hotel Horatio, a narrow street lined with small houses, and some sort of small metal shop with snow piled high on the low-pitched roof.

"Drinks?"

"Wine," said Philip.

"Red," said Sophia.

The waitress made a few suggestions, and Sophia ordered.

When the waitress was gone, Sophia took him by the hands. "Put it on a tab. Guests can get a tab running here. For both food and drink."

"Oh. Good."

"You think she's pretty?"

He knew she'd ask.

"I guess."

"No, you *know* she's pretty. I could see it in you. It registered. It always does in a man. Even if they try not to show it, it's like a calculator spitting out numbers: Face, 10; Breasts, 9; Tummy, 8; Hips, 9. Crunching the numbers, spitting them out. And then there's the Intelligence Quotient. Is she smart, or is she some Big Dummy? All that. Women, I don't know about men, but women can read that like you'd pull a spread sheet out of the printer." She laughed. "Hey, tell me it isn't true. You thought she was about as good as they get. Didn't you?"

His stomach danced a little. "I don't even know her."

"Oh, boy! You don't have to. Not a man. He starts with the flesh, and he might get to the spirit, real doubtful, but you can bet he starts with the flesh."

"Well," said Philip.

"Oh, it's okay." And she squeezed his hands. "I don't mind. I mean how can you argue with basic biology?"

"Yeah."

"Do you want to sleep with her?"

The waitress arrived with the wine bottle and glasses. He couldn't help but note the supple flesh of her hands, a ring—friendship ring?—the delicate movement of each finger as she set forth bottle and glasses.

Sensual. Every single thing about her sensual.

"And now for your menu," said the waitress. "I'll be back in a jiffy."

Jiffy?

"Do you?" asked Sophia smiling.

"What?"

"Want to sleep with her?"

"No. Of course not."

"Yes, you do. Try to dispute that. Go ahead."

"No," he said.

"Yes. Of course you do. You want *intercourse* with her, don't you?" Her voice fell an octave.

He said nothing. Philip did not watch her walk away. He wouldn't be caught watching her walk away.

"You're not looking at her," said Sophia. "You can't fool me. Go ahead and watch. I don't mind."

He took her hand. "No, I want you. Only you. That's all I'll ever want."

"I'll bet."

"What?"

"I'm only kidding, silly. Can't you take a joke?"

"Oh, sure."

"I do like to tease a little. Haven't you noticed?"

"I like it," said Philip.

"You like everything about me, don't you?" she said, and this time she looked dead serious. There was an edge to her voice.

"Yes," he said.

"Open the wine," she said, pointing at the corkscrew. "That's your job, not mine."

He did it.

"It's so good to have someone who likes everything about you," she said.

32

The snow continued to fall. Snow not predicted, more snow than predicted, continual snow. From their room window, Philip watched a snow plow working the hotel parking lot and the Horatio Liquor store lot. The snow was piled up ten to fifteen feet high at the perimeter of the lot. Could they pile it up higher than that? If it snowed more, they'd just have to thicken the walls of snow, wouldn't they? A car trying to leave a hotel parking space was slipping and sliding and letting out a screeching pavement complaint. Finally, it got going and took off.

"We'll never *ever* leave here," said Sophia. "But then, I don't really care if we do. Do you?"

"No." But he did. What about the money? He was reading one of his torture books. He was beginning to see why Adam Most was so disturbed by this . . . by this bloody work of mangled bodies. And for what? Regicide. Attempted regicide. The wrong faith. The wrong political party. Terror. Or just diabolical amusement?

"I wish you wouldn't read that book," said Sophia. "How can you?"

"How can I not?" He put it down. "I hate it," he said.

"Well then? I *want* something," she said. She was looking out the window now onto the lot. "I want something."

"Like what?"

"Something to do. Something different. Want to make love?"

"Sure."

They did so for a few hours. And then they watched TV shows. Five in a row.

"I'm *so* bored," said Sophia. "I'm just really, really bored. Let's make love again."

"Okay."

"You know what?"

"What?"

"I don't worry about that one thing when I'm so bored."

"What one thing?"

"Do I have to spell it out?"

"Oh," he said. "Yeah."

"It's like I'm impervious to it."

Impervious?

They did it some more, and then they watched more TV shows, and then they fell asleep. They woke up in the dark.

He looked at the clock.

What time was it? 9:21.

How many days had passed? He couldn't recall. He hadn't phoned in to work yet. Somehow he just couldn't.

He lay still, wondering.

"Let's get something to eat," said Sophia.

"This late?"

"Yes."

"Okay."

They ended up down in the bar and lounge with food and drink. That booth with the view of the metal shop.

Philip got a buzz on. So did Sophia. Her hands were shaky.

Philip's cell phone went off.

Dick Hazzard. God, what'd he want? "Hey, buddy, what's going on?"

"What?"

"With Lisa. She's acting funny, man. Talking. About shit. Of one kind and another. Huh, what's going on there, Phil?"

"Philip! Nothing. Nothing at all. What do you mean?"

"Yeah, I'll bet. We talked about this, didn't we?"

"What?"

"Better heed me, my young man. Oh . . . Tommy's here. He wants to talk to you. Man, I'll tell you—"

Suddenly Tommy's voice came on the phone. It had the striking resemblance to a whiny, out-of-tune violin. "Hello, Philip, remember me?"

"Yes. Hi, Tommy."

"I told you about the snow. Didn't I tell you about the snow? Do you recall? About the snow? Do you?"

"Yes. I remember."

"These guys, they don't believe it. Tell them there's something to it. Tell them you agree—okay? Would you? Huh?"

Philip sat back. Somehow in his fog and haze, two more drinks had appeared. He shook his head. But he noticed his hand taking hold anyway. "Agree with what?"

"With *what*? You *don't* recall. The snow's not our friend, Philip. Remember me saying that?"

A loud yell in the background. "Tommy, you fucking idiot!"

Dick.

And then another voice on the phone. A woman's voice. "Just tell Tommy you don't agree. Snow is snow. *Okay*? That will quiet him down a little. If you don't mind. Please. If you just would, *please*."

That wasn't Lisa. It was Tina . . . wasn't it? Yes, that's who it was. "Is this Tina?"

"Yes."

"Hi, Tina."

"Hello, Philip."

Sophia was looking at him. She pointed at the phone. She had her drink raised to her nose, sniffing.

"Friends of my old roommate," he whispered.

Sophia nodded. But she still had a look.

"Philip—just tell Tommy you don't agree because things aren't *that* crazy. Will you? Will you, *please*?"

So where was Tommy?

"Hey, buddy. Listen, Phil, we're all snowed in over here, our little continued party-hearty, and they're all going great guns, and pretty soon, old Tommy, he unloads his message of doom, and it's got the women all worried—"

The sound of swallowing.

Phone noise. Now, a deeper voice, a lecturing voice. Sebastian. "Philip, there's something to what Tommy's saying." Noises. "That's what's . . . *I know, I know, but let me speak, please, will you*? Jeez. Okay, Philip, you there?"

"Yes."

"Well, there *is* something, sir, that makes sense about what Tommy is saying. There's something *wrong* here. The ladies don't want to think that way for one reason or another, but I think Tommy may have struck on something. That Professor Fellows I spoke of . . . did you meet him yet?"

"No."

"Meet him. Make sure you do meet him."

"Okay."

Phone noises.

"Hey, Phil, I'm going to give the phone back to Tommy now, and I want you to say to him that this is all a bunch of bullshit. Okay? Because the kid is driving us totally nuts." Then a whisper: "The women are coming undone. Got it? And Lisa," he whispered. "She's *gone frigid on me, boy.*"

Phone noises. "Philip?"

That was Tina.

"Yes?"

"I am *not* coming undone, nor is Lisa. It's just that things are kind of stressful here, hardly any food in the house, no way to get out of here—god, we made such a mistake not leaving earlier!— and having some loony kid spouting that stuff, right now, just right now, I can't . . . believe me, no one—"

Phone noises.

"This is Tommy. It's true, Philip. You think about it. It's true. The snow is coming and coming because something bad has happened. Something's died. Something's died in this world. It tells you that— it's a gauge, see—"

Phone dead.

Philip set it on the table to his side.

"What was *that* all about?"

Her look had sharpened. It was downright irascible.

He drank his drink. He was going to be sick if he finished it. But it was in his hand, and he couldn't leave it undrunk.

"About the snow."

"Oh. And so what *about* the snow?"

"Oh, well . . . silly stuff, really. That it's some kind of . . . I don't

206

know. Nemesis or something."

"Well, it is. Take a look! You feast your eyes on that out there!" Hyped up, this woman.

But maybe she should be: Street lights revealing cars buried. Snow piled up high in yards, against windows.

"Those roofs," said Philip. "That metal shop." A security light showed it in a splash of yellow—there had to be three feet of snow on that metal shop roof.

"They'll collapse. Those housetops. You just wait and see if they don't."

"What about *this* roof?"

"Yeah. And we're on the top floor," said Sophia. "Why'd we get the top floor? Why ever did we get the top floor? Can you tell me? Huh?"

He liked top floors. "I don't know."

"You don't know. What was in our heads?" She sipped her drink.

"We have to move," said Philip. "Right away."

"Your mind was on other stuff," said Sophia and took his hand.

That dark mood was melting. But he hoped he could get another room.

They sat there for a long while, and then he got really tired. He wanted to go up and sleep. He wanted to sleep a long, long time. He told her so.

"Me, I'm staying down here," she said.

"Okay. But I'd rather be up there with you."

"I'm not that sleepy. And I don't want to do it."

Somehow, even if he didn't want to, he didn't want her to say she didn't. He wanted her to be always ready to do it. That was, of course, unfair. But he couldn't seem to help himself. He got up. He staggered.

"You're as drunk as they get," she said.

"I'm heading up," he said.

"I hope you find the room."

"I will. I'll call about another room."

"You do that. I'll be down here," she said. "I'm so, so bored."

"And we can't go anywhere," he said. "Can we?"

"What do you think?"

"No."

"Well, then."

He got the elevator. He rode it up alone. It was always good to ride it alone. That way you didn't have to make conversation with someone or feel unfriendly if you didn't. You didn't have to punch buttons for people. You didn't have to smile.

In the room he called about changing rooms, but they didn't have any more rooms—all booked up. He asked about the roof. Wouldn't it collapse?

"No, sir. We're on that one."

"Are you sure?"

"Yes, sir. You needn't worry."

He stood at the window. What else could they say? They wouldn't be likely to say: *Yeah, we're looking for that to happen about any minute now.*

And then he saw him, that guy, that man, down in the parking lot, lighted up by a pole lamp. That man in black on snowshoes. Padding on snowshoes and stopping. And looking up at him. Staring. Same man. A black figure in the thick blanket of white. A man who had singled him out. Of all the people in this city, him. Why him? Their eyes met. That man down in the snow under a pole lamp, in a halo of yellow light, him up here in the lighted room. They stared long and hard at each other. Philip wanted to open the window and yell, but of course this sort of window didn't open.

Still, he yelled. He shook his fist. He banged the window.

The man was undisturbed. He stood in his snowshoes undisturbed. He continued to look up.

And then Philip noticed something he hadn't noticed before. There was something about the man's head. It seemed elongated. It seemed flat and elongated. Or maybe that was just the perspective, looking down like that. He couldn't tell.

He felt sick. He shook his fist again, and he pulled the drapes closed. And then he lay down. *I ought to call the cops. Now shouldn't I? Now why wouldn't I?*

33

More and more snow. No let up, days or nights, white against the dark. They tired of the hotel, the room, the bar and lounge. They grew tired of each other. Philip read his torture books. Sophia picked at him over it. She read other things—on her notebook. But then the power went out. It went out on a Wednesday, and today it was Saturday.

Her notebook was out. Their cells were out. Couldn't charge them up.

No hot water. "We can't do it without hot water," said Sophia. "I have to take a bath afterwards. No sex, no lights, no power, and it's cold. I'm tired of it being so goddamned cold!" She stayed in bed.

It made him want her.

No sex.

The sun was bright outside. He sat at the table next to the window and read. He was about to finish his third torture book. Adam Most would be pleased. He recoiled at the imagery worming its way in his brain, but something made him keep reading.

"I've never, *ever*, in my whole life, been so bored," said Sophia. She was propped up against a pillow. "I can't sleep anymore because I slept fifteen hours in a row. I can't have sex. I can't drink anything hot because there's no way to heat it. I can't watch TV, listen to music, read anything. *Some* people have something to read—if you like to read stuff like that, if you think you *ought* to read stuff like that. If you're weird or demented enough to read stuff like that. But me? I have nothing to read. And outside the goddamn snow won't quit. The goddamn snow is six fucking feet high!"

Two *goddamns* and one *fucking*. It was definitely getting worse.

"That was the other day," said Philip. "Six feet high—seven or eight now, and drifts up to ten, according to the news."

"What're you, a parrot?" she said.

"Huh? No, just affirming what you said. And adding the update. And that was before the power went out. When we could see the

209

weather, and the news. What's it like out there now?"

"Look," she said. "And you tell me."

"There's no telling," he said, "unless you had a ten foot stick and could insert it down and see where it rose."

"I'm tired of talking about it," said Sophia. "Get us something down in the bar, would you?" She seemed to brighten.

"Okay."

"Beer and chips. I'd go for that, wouldn't you?"

"Yes," he said, only he really wanted hot coffee.

"Good—but we'll have to watch the money a little. Just a tad."

"Huh?"

"As in watch the budget?"

They'd been here about ten days, and he was thinking, okay, maybe three to four thousand bucks. But not *ten*. Watch the money?

"How's that? You must have plenty left."

"Really? Why do you think that?"

"Huh? Why do I think that? Because you started with ten thousand. Didn't you?"

She laughed. It was a blistering guffaw. "You *really* believed that? That's funny."

"What? That's what you said."

"You'd believe anything, wouldn't you?"

"That's what you said."

"Mr. Parrot," she said.

"Huh?"

She smiled. "Well . . . just so you know, we don't have all that much, if the truth be told." She pointed a finger at him.

"*How* much?"

"You'll be disappointed."

"How much?"

"Well . . . a few hundred—and a pittance beyond that. That's what we're contemplating here," said Sophia.

Contemplating?

"Okay. How much did we start with—actually?"

"*We* didn't start with anything. *I* started with."

"How much?"

"You are so silly. You think she actually gave me ten thousand dollars. I can't believe it."

"Why'd you say it, then?"

"Why'd I say it? Gee whiz, Philip, why do you *think* I said it?"

Gee whiz?

"I don't know. Why did you?"

"Because, stupid, I just wanted to feel good. I wanted to feel upbeat. For once, okay? That satisfy you? And ten thousand dollars sure sounded a whole lot better than five hundred."

"Five hundred!"

"Yes—five hundred, Mr. Parrot."

"What happened?"

"Well, how's this? Try this on for size. My dearest little Gina says to herself. 'How am I going to make this little bitch squirm?'" She laughed. Her laugh spewed venom. "Don't you think she said that? I think she did."

"What about the other times?"

"She gave me a couple hundred a few times and a *thousand* one little time. And she spends that practically every minute of every day. That and more. In fact, that wouldn't even begin to *start* what she spends. She told me she spent twenty-five thousand dollars in a single day on some shopping spree, and I don't mean diamonds either. And then she went and told him, the big bastard, and you know what he said? He said, 'Is that all, my sweet little darling?' Because the bastard's three sheets to the wind half the time, coked up, cracked, all that crap."

"What're we going to do? What about the hotel bill!"

"You're a man. Figure it out."

"I don't have *that* kind of money." He felt his gut sliding to the floor.

"Correction. You don't have *any*."

"No."

"If you had a job," she said.

"Even if I had a job, how would I get in?" he shouted.

"Have you ever, even once, called in?"

"No."

"Well, you'd better—hadn't you?"

"Yeah." And he thought: yeah, probably I could swing it with Digby Morris. The man's pretty whacked out, anyway. "I'll call," he said.

She laughed, a raspy, sneering laugh. "Sure you will. You really think you have a job now—after dumping on them like that? You really think for one minute you still have a job when you didn't make even one single little phone call to check in, and left that car where it stood? I'll bet the roof's caved in. I'll just bet it is."

A cold, clammy feeling came over him.

"God, he said. Oh, god." It hadn't occurred to him. Maybe it was. Maybe it was totally caved in. Maybe the hood too.

"I'm so sick and tired of it all," said Sophia yawning. "Snow. You know what? If it ever, ever snows again in this world, you know what I'm going to do?"

"What?"

"I'm going to strip down naked and run outside screaming. That's what I'm going to do. And I mean if it snows even one teensy bit more, that's what I'm going to do. Watch me. Watch and see if I don't."

"You mean this year," he said.

"Yes, idiot, yes I mean this year!"

"Don't call me an *idiot*," said Philip. And he said it sternly.

"I'm sorry."

"And don't call me stupid, either."

"I said I'm sorry."

He looked outside. "What about the hotel bill?"

"Forgive me?" she beckoned him over.

He went to her. He couldn't help it.

"Want me?"

"Yes."

"Well, when the warm water comes, you can have me all you want."

He wanted her now. He told her. He pleaded.

"It's not like I wouldn't be using—"

She caught what he was saying. "No!"

He didn't want to plead. But damn it, he couldn't seem to help himself. *"Please . . ."*

"Absolutely not," she said. "But I could sure use that beer and chips."

"Okay," he said. "What about the hotel bill?"

"I don't know." She looked at him, and then smiled. "I'll call Gina. She'll cover it."

"How do you know?"

"I don't."

"Well, what are we going to do? We must owe five thousand bucks, or will."

"We're stranded, Philip."

"Yeah."

"Don't get all glum on me. You have no reason to do it. Maybe I do, but you don't."

"Why not?"

"Because a man is supposed to be a protector, and not a whiner. That's why."

That stung.

But he shook it off. "I'll get the beers," he said.

"Good—and chips. There's money in my purse. But see if you can put it on the tab down there."

"Okay . . ."

She drew him closer to her. She whispered: "If you absolutely have to have it, I guess I could."

"Really?"

"You need it, don't you? Men always do."

"It'd sure be nice," he said.

She nodded.

He went for the beers and chips. I'll call Gina myself if I have to, he thought. Damn right I will.

Two beers at the bar, $5.71. No, sir, no tab on this. No, sir, have to pay up front. Two bags of chips at the snack machine, $3. He carried them up the elevator.

Sex in a minute or two.

She smiled brightly at him. "That's what I need."

213

He brought them to her. "And if you really just have to screw me," she said.

"Screw?"

She saw his look. "Well, don't be an absolute prig. There's nothing wrong with that word. How about male and female fittings? Is a screw driver male or female?"

"Male."

"There you have it."

She gurgled some beer down. "Maybe when I get put out about practically everything in the whole fucking universe, I get a little crude. Okay? Go ahead and blame me if you wish. I was just trying to be nice. For a change. Being such an outraged bitch for the past day or two or however long it's been." Her voice broke.

"Oh, I'm sorry," he said. "I'm sorry." And he went to her.

"Don't be sorry. It's okay," she said. And she put her beer down and pulled him to her.

It was good.

What they did then was real good. Maybe the best, he thought. A new start, it felt like. A whole new world ahead of them.

She said it was good. Even without the bath.

"I needed that too," she said. "But now it's over."

He felt a gloom suddenly, irresistibly come over him. He sat at the table and looked out onto the snow. Maybe something bad *had* happened to the world. Maybe something *had* died. But what?

She'd changed. His Sophia had changed. He knew it. But he couldn't face it.

34

The snow had ended. The power was back on. More snow on the way, but they agreed: Philip needed to get out. Bring back things. Books to read, things to do. Good things before the next onslaught. She was scribbling things down.

The roads were being plowed. But that was hardly unusual. They'd been continuously plowed for days on end. The snow was banked up fifteen or twenty feet high. They saw it on the TV. They saw Grand from the fifth floor corridor window. With the walls of snow on both sides, it was like the cars, the few traveling on it, were bobsledding.

People off to work. Rush hour. But in that?

Sophia gave him the apartment key, gave him some money, and kissed him. "Be safe," she said. And so he set out for the buried company car and the job, three torture books in his backpack, and that scribbled list of Sophia's tucked away with them.

You couldn't walk on the shoulder. It wasn't there. There was only the four-lane Grand, and the mighty snow bank. Like a dike, he thought, against an imminent flood. He walked along the snow bank, now and then turning to look back at the traffic. He was walking on the wrong side, the traffic coming up behind him, but he wasn't crossing that road. If a car started to slide, he'd have to go hard for the snow bank. Make a big bad dive for it. A deep dent in it. "Make an impression in the world, son." *Ha, ha. That's right, Dad.*

He came to an intersection. The traffic light was out. He got across the road somehow. A street sign for the off-road was knocked down into the snow bank.

His cell phone rang.

"Hello?"

"She's done it! Both bills paid for and hotel's covered till the end of the month, and an open tab tripled down in the bar! So how about all that?"

"That's good! God, man—"

"Good? How could it be better?"

"It's great!"

"Yes—that five hundred? She just got confused—had a bad day. But she's sending us another thousand. So pick it up. I'll call on it."

"Great!" he shouted. He had to shout over the noise of the traffic on his heels.

"It *is* great," she said. "So great." Her voice sounded funny.

"We're back in business," he said.

Back in business? Frigging cliché!

"Oh, you bet we are," she said. And then, "I love you. You hunk of a man."

My god.

"I love you too!" he shouted. "End of the month, huh?"

"Yes. If we can make it that long. I'm still fucking *bored*. But at least I've got TV, my notebook, and my cell."

"I'm bringing back stuff, you know."

"I do need something to read, for sure."

"Like what?"

"Anything. As long as it's not *torture* books. Heavens to Betsy."

Heavens to—

"I'll get something," he said, softly. He heard an edge to his voice. "But what?"

"Surprise me."

He hedged. "What if you don't like it?"

"Well, that's okay—I guess."

The noise of the traffic building. His cell phone hard against his ear.

"You sure?"

"Yes! Yes! Just bring me something to read."

"Can't you read stuff on your notebook—or your cell?"

"I want paperbacks, Philip!"

"Oh."

"I want a little *delight*, okay?"

"Sure." He looked back. A car going into a slide. Something clicking in him: *I am going to die.* He went hard for the snow bank, scrambling, climbing up, up, digging hard, his cell phone clutched in his hand like a dead bird. Below him he heard growling, snarling motors, and then a long *whoosh*. He got situated in a dug-out place in the snow bank and heard Sophia's voice, still on the line.

"Hey! Did you *hear* me?"

"I about got hit!"

"What? Hit? Hit where?"

"I'm okay. But it was close. Car—I about got run over."

"Oh, my god—"

He looked down below. He looked at the snow-packed road. "Just a minute."

"Huh?"

"Just a minute."

He got down, edged along the snow bank, then back on the road. The very edge of the road.

He heard her voice, but he couldn't make out the words.

Then she was saying: "Are you *okay*?"

"I about got run over! Just about got run—"

"I heard *that*. Well. You shouldn't have left. Now I'm going to worry, worry, worry. Where are you?"

"I don't know."

"Honey. Where are you?"

Honey. Nice, very nice. So much in words, so much.

He looked about. Walls of snow. Snow plows working away. Walls of snow against windows of buildings in the strip mall directly across Grand.

What if a plow came along with that large blade? He looked back. No . . .

"I don't know. Not really."

"You don't know where you are?"

He tried to explain. "See, it's snow. Everything is snow!"

"You'll never get there," she said. "How will you ever recognize my road?"

It was a question. An important one.

"The street sign," he said. "If it's *there*."

"What?"

"If it's not knocked down." He mentioned the one knocked down.

"You poor thing. I'm sorry. Do be careful. Okay?"

He swore he would, but now he was wondering if he *could* tell where that road was. Too much white, he thought. There's just too much white out here.

"Get condoms," she said. "Don't forget."

"I won't."

"I doubt you will."

"I won't—for sure."

"I'll just bet," she said.

They ended the call.

Where was he? He'd have to find the street sign. There'd probably be the street sign. Once he saw the street sign, he'd make it just fine. If it was a major road, it'd be marked up high over Grand, but not her road—Queenie Street. It wasn't major.

Yet he did spot the Queenie Street sign and hoofed it down Queenie all the way to her apartment. He called Sophia and said how he'd finally made it, how the long hoof had exhausted him, but he was here, power off, though, and it was cold. Ice cold. He was having a beer, though, relaxing, and was planning on going out pretty soon to clean off that company car. If he could find it.

"You think you can?"

"I know where it is."

"You think the roof's caved in?"

"I hope not."

"More's coming," she said. "Like they said."

"I know."

"But it's coming sooner. I just saw it on TV. You'd better get out here soon. Or we'll be separated from each other."

"When?"

"This evening. A foot or more. Up to two feet. No reason to clean that car off at all."

"I *have* to get it back. I've got to get it turned in. They're liable to arrest me or, who knows—"

"We're going to be cut off from each other if you do," she said. "And then what?"

He panicked.

Stuck here, no power, no food, no sex. Nothing.

"Well," he said. "Look—"

"Get the essentials," she said, her voice half strident, "the money, the condoms, paperbacks, something to snack on, drinks, a few surprises for little me, and then get right back out here. Forget that stupid car! Take a cab!"

She had a point.

Still, he couldn't help it. He had to get that car back.

"I'll get out there fast," he said.

"Okay," she said. "I hope you do."

And so he grabbed the shovel and the broom, and found some gloves, and headed on out—to the lot. He started sweeping the top of the car off.

This had to be the right car.

He worked away.

He got down to the metal, and oh, good, no roof caved in.

If this was the right car.

He swept off more and more and even took the shovel and carried away huge plates of snow, slamming the shovel on the parking lot.

It took him a full hour to get all the snow off—yes, yes, and it was the right car.

Good car. Luxury. Lincoln.

Now those frozen doors.

He turned the key in the lock—driver's side. Nothing. He pulled hard. Nothing. He went around from door to door, sticking the key in the lock, and gripping the door handle, and pulling as hard as he could.

Nothing.

"The hell I'm leaving you here!"

He kept pulling and pulling. Yanking and yanking.

Nothing.

Truck pulling in the lot. Huge truck tires. Rod Busby stepping out.

Advancing on him.

"Phil-o . . . having trouble, are you, my fine feathered friend?"

"Yes. That's *right*. I can't get the goddamned thing open." Not in the mood to deal with this criminal. Not making excuses. Not apologizing.

"Maybe I can be of service, my dear little fellow." Rod Busby coming up to the car, giving Philip a little shove to one side, motioning for the key. Inserting it with a quick, hard turn of the wrist. And then turning and leaning way back with both thick hands, pulling. Giving it a yank and a yell.

Suddenly the door flying open, and Rod flying back. A good three to four feet into the lot, landing on his ass in the snow. Laughing, getting up and approaching Philip.

"Glad I came along, honcho?"

"Yes!"

"What've you been up to, Phil-boy?"

"Killing time."

"Porking my girl, are you?"

He hesitated. "I wouldn't put it that way."

"How would you put it?"

"We've got a thing. I guess you know what that is."

"A thing, huh? Well, you know what, Philly? I've been all morning working on applying for the CIA. You ever thought about the CIA?"

"No."

"Know how much paperwork's required?"

"Probably a lot."

"You got that right. A lot. You staying out at the Horatio, are you?"

"What?"

"You heard me."

"Well."

"The Hotel Horatio. That *was* a thing. You know that, Philly? A real thing in ways that other such places aren't. Correcto?"

"What do you mean?"

"What do I mean? It's a thing, my son, that gets Sophia all hot and going. Her and her friend Gina, and her fun trips down to the bar and the hot showers, and the time to lie around and fuck and

220

eat snacks, and watch the old tube, and whatever else you can imagine—because it's not having to do anything. Sophia, you see, she doesn't like to do *anything*, Phil. Non-doing, that's her specialty. Except for the pleasures of the flesh. You know about the pleasures of the flesh, Phil, sir?"

"Yes."

"Me, I need more a-doing. And that's why I'm joining up with the CIA, hombre. There's several things you need in hand, prereqs, and I've met them all. Each and every one of those little prereqs I've more than met."

"That's good."

"You don't know what it is, prereq-wise, do you, so how would you know if it's good?"

"I can guess. I suppose."

"You can?"

"I suppose."

"Okay."

"But I've got to go."

"Not till you guess."

Pinned, screwed. "Brains and brawn, I take it."

Rod Busby whacked him on the shoulder—a fellow feeling whack. "Yep, that's me. Both."

"Look, I've got to go."

"Take her, Phil—she's yours. I've got my eyes on another little gal anyway. She's yours, take her." Busby headed for his truck.

Philip got in the car, and he turned the key, and it started right up.

A salesman's car's got to start, doesn't it? You damn betcha.

Busby got his truck going over the lot. And then he backed up. And then he went forward. And then he backed up.

He motioned out the truck window.

Rod Busby was doing him a favor. *What's next, hombre?*

Philip followed. The car ate the snow.

Damn fine car. Damn fine car!

He got on the road and headed back for Grand. He hoped he could get over the roads. *Were* there roads?

Back to Hunt and Hart.
But first drop off those torture books.
And that meant Adam Most. God, no.

35

The little weasel spotted him at the circulation desk. "Philip—where have you been? Where? Where have you been, sir?"

"Trying to stay out of the weather. And you?"

"Here, mostly. Only the library was closed for a few days when the snow was so high they couldn't open the doors. You see it out there. It's, it's—"

"Deep."

"Scary in its deepness. Isn't it?"

Tommy. No, he didn't want to dig into that.

Adam Most motioned at the torture books. The librarian was now gathering them up.

"You read those, did you? I certainly hope you did read them. Tell me you did."

"Yes."

"What did you think—what do you think—now that you know?"

"Know what?"

"Well, what it's all about. That's what it's all about, Philip." He jabbed his index finger against the circulation desk. "Contained in those three books on the big T is the real history of the world." He spoke more softly, almost a whisper, with a whine. You might think he was about to weep. "Call it what you want, but that's core stuff, right there. That's what it all comes down to, slice it how you might. Huh? Don't you think? What do you think?"

"Well—"

"*What?*"

"Grim. Depressing. Very depressing. It's hard to sleep." But that was a lie because he slept pretty damn well after sex with Sophia. The release of endorphins, huh? It was only the nights without sex that inhibited his ability to fall asleep, not those torture books, although he had to admit the grimness did take its toll on him, lingering somewhere back in his mind, and he did what he could to think other thoughts—to keep it right there: in the back of his mind.

"You bet they're depressing. You bet they are, Philip, but I've got something even more depressing—would that were possible. *A Pictorial History of the Slaughter of War.* It comes in a three-volume set, Philip, and it's not one of those books—or sets of books, to be accurate—that you must read in the library. Not reference, that is. But it's a boxed set, and that makes it easy to carry it out. Got a car?"

"Yes."

"Well, then, you're going to want to take this book, or this *set* of books, Philip."

"Why? Why would I want such a thing? Or things?"

"Because it's the real thing. It is, and they are. If they don't get you in their vice grips, burn you alive, or electrocute your gonads, then you can bet they'll cut you off in some grand gesture of war. It's what man was made for, Philip. War, war, and more of it."

"Why?"

"Why? Hey, it's not *my* doing? I don't know *why*. The nature of man—I take it. Or just the way things are. The nature of *something*. Here—just one minute. Hang on, just one minute, Philip. No—you come with me. Please, don't run off. You come with me."

He followed Adam's gyrating form to his table, where several books were spread out, haphazardly, along with composition notebooks and a yellow plastic pouch filled with pencils.

"Now then, sir." The little weasel held up a large, thick book. It was quite handsome, with a gold cover and gilt-edged pages. "Here it is. Volume One. But of course you must also read Volume Two *and* Volume Three. These are crucial. Quite so."

"What about you—aren't you—"

"Done. Read them—twice. So, you take. You take, Philip."

"Okay . . ."

Adam boxed up the set for him. "Now, then, how's that? Hey, how is *that*?" He handed Philip the large gold-colored box, embossed, with the three volumes fitting snugly inside it. "Nice, isn't it? Very nice. Very, very nice. A lovely looking boxed set, isn't it? Don't you just love boxed sets, Philip?"

"Yes—I do." And he did—he loved boxed sets. That was a fact he couldn't dispute.

"It sort of . . . well, it masks the . . . pain of what's inside—in a way. I mean you take a look at that box, and it's quite handsome. Very much so. Handsome is the word."

"Yes, it is." And then Philip extended his hand. "Thanks. I've got to go to work. I must—right now, this minute."

Adam nodded. "I've got to get back to work myself." He looked down, then briefly looked up, and then smiled, and went back to his reading.

But when Philip was only five or six paces on his way out, he heard a yell, a raucous, bristly one:

"Reading about happiness now, Philip. Marvelous, marvelous books. Just marvelous. Have them to you soon!"

"Thanks!" whispered Philip.

He stopped at the circulation desk and checked out the boxed set.

"You take care of these, sir," said the librarian.

"I will."

"They are, after all, a beautiful set of books. Understood?"

"Yes, ma'am."

"And in the snow?" She shook her head.

"I'll be careful. Very careful."

"All right. See that you do." She turned to look in Adam Most's direction, and she scowled and shook her head.

He hurried out to his car. He placed the boxed set on the passenger's seat beside him and drove off. He found a parking spot in a parking building two blocks from the office building, and he had to hoof it back. It was 1:10 when he entered the lobby and 1:15 when he entered the offices of Hunt and Hart.

The receptionist wanted to know.

"I'm Philip Fellows. Sales."

"Oh . . . oh! Gosh, that's right. Go see Digby Morris—right away. Immediately! Well . . . I didn't mean to put it *that* way. But go see Digby Morris. He's been trying to reach you."

No—not true. Not once had Digby Morris called him on his cell phone.

"Thanks."

"Go ahead," she said, and smiled. There was an air of pink plasticity about her eye lids and lips. He wondered if they were real.

He went ahead. He spotted Digby Morris standing next to a tall, well-built man with a pony tail flopping down his back against his light brown suit. The man had a kind of mischievous grin on his face. And now he was leaning over laughing. Digby Morris was laughing too, and then he spotted Philip.

"Hey, hey, hey, here's our man, Philip Fellows! Come, Philip. Come. Come meet the guru of ammo sales, Arnie Butchler, District Three General Manager. "Arnie—Philip. Philip Fellows. Salesman of the ... what rank, Philip?"

"Pardon?"

"Rank. You know. No sales yet, Arnie, but he'll do. I'm sure he'll do. Won't you, Philip?"

"Yes. I think."

"He *thinks*." Arnie Butchler, thick rubbery smile, extended his hand. A hard shaker. His smile was large, welcoming, but there seemed to be a question in it. What question was it?

Arnie continued to smile, to look.

What question?

He still continued to look.

"What?" said Philip.

"Philip," he said, and laid a fatherly hand on Philip's wrist. He parked it there, and then gently squeezed it. "Philip Fellows."

"Yes, sir."

"Philip, you're new to the game. New. Newness shows. Newness always shows. You can tell a new man. He radiates *new*— 'I'm new.' It's written all over him. Do you know what I mean? Are you clicking with me, Philip?"

"Yes. I think."

"Because you're new." Arnie Butchler exchanged smiles with Digby Morris. "I like new. New is fine. New is new. And ... it's quite fine. Don't you think, Dig?"

"Nothing better than new," said Digby, "as long as it yields performance. Am I right?"

"Oh, you're right. Isn't he right, Mr. Philip?" said Arnie Butchler.

"Yes. Performance—of course."

"Good. Very good." Arnie Butchler took a long, deep breath. His eyes were fixed on Philip. "Do you know when you can trust a man, sir?"

"Oh . . . yes—I think so."

"You can trust a man when he's got the itch. We've talked about the itch, haven't we, Dig? We *know* the itch around here, and I'm thinking, Dig, this man standing before us has got the itch."

"Ah! Yes."

"The itch?"

"That's right, Mr. Fellows. You know what? I need some coffee? You want some coffee, Dig?"

"Yes, I most assuredly want some coffee."

"Coffee?" said Arnie Butchler.

Butchler's hand gripped his wrist. Philip squirmed. "Yes."

"Well, then, gentlemen." The District Three General Manager pointed.

They headed out, all three of them, past the secretary, who gave them a tomato-red smile with her sweet red lips, how shapely, and gave her blond hair, fully fluffed, a sensual toss of the head.

"Well now," said Arnie. "Did you see that?"

"Forget it," said Digby Morris.

"Oh, I don't think I can forget that," said Arnie Butchler.

They got on the elevator and rode on down. Arnie Butchler spoke not a word as the floors shot by, and Digby Morris now and then gave Philip a sly smile. Or wasn't it a grin? But wasn't there some barb in it? A measure of anger, hatred, resentment—or even sheer bile?

You should have called the man. Why in hell didn't you call the man?

Down below, in the Blunder Bus Bar, blue walls spidery with trails of wispy white clouds, Arnie said, "Both of you. Now then, both of you! Order what you want. On me—or, rather, on the company. And—excuse me—but f-u-c-k the coffee. Okay?"

"You're right—absolutely right," said Digby Morris. "Philip? What do you want?"

He wanted a sandwich. Chips. Beer. He expressed this wish. He spoke with confidence, assurance, in the presence of his boss, and this hotshot District Three General Manager.

One couldn't help but feel a bit important. After all, who else was down here with the likes of these two? The rest of them on the phone up there in the office, shuffling papers. Ha!

"Beer—yes, beer," said Arnie Butchler. "Beer it is. I'll take a beer. And you, Dig?"

"Yes. I'll take one, and then I'll take a second one."

"Ha! Well, don't float yourself away, my dear Dig—but then that's always the risk, isn't it?" Arnie snapped a finger at the bartender. "This way, please. This way."

There was the distinct air of the tyrant in the man. In the snap of that finger. Definitely in the snap of that finger.

The bartender was busy with another order. Anybody could see that.

Arnie exchanged glances with Digby Morris. He again snapped his finger. "Service, please—you, sir!"

Malice.

Arnie Butchler snapped his fingers a third time.

The bartender noticed. He motioned at another bartender, who moseyed over. The man fingered his beard. He leaned toward them. "Yes, gents, and what for you?"

Arnie gave them each the nod.

Digby ordered a beer.

Philip ordered a beer.

Arnie said, "And I will also quaff a beer, sir."

The bartender moseyed back.

"Now *there's* a man with a problem," said Arnie. "You all catch that?"

"Most assuredly," said Digby Morris. "Written all over his face."

"Written all over his whole body. A man with a problem."

"What problem?" said Philip.

Arnie exchanged looks with Digby. They both grinned. The beers arrived. Draft beers in big mugs with big sudsy heads.

"Tab," said Arnie.

"Yes, sir," said the bartender.

Arnie turned to Philip. "What problem? I'm working on that. This raises questions which could take a bit of time to answer. Don't you agree, Dig?"

"Indeed I do. It would take a while."

"Not to ignore your question, but to give it its absolute, unqualified due, let me ask *you* a question."

"Okay."

"Have you taken any psychology courses?"

"No—well, one."

"And what was that one?"

"It wasn't *really* psychology, but the professor made it *into* psychology. It was actually philosophy. Listed in the catalog as philosophy, and also in the course schedule, and the syllabus, and all that. But the professor . . . well, see, he said that philosophers are moving more and more into psychological studies for this and that, and physiological ones too, brain studies, you know, and so—"

"Enough. Goddamn it!" shouted Arnie Butchler.

"Huh?"

"Don't give me a history of your whole frigging life. *Was* it psychology? Or not?"

"Yes—in a way."

"No. *Was* it psychology?"

"Well, as I said, it became—"

"*Was* it, or not?"

"I—I tried to explain. It was and it wasn't—"

"I'm waiting, Mr. Fellows. A salesman does not like to wait, sir."

"It was psychology. De facto. If not de jure."

His wrist got grabbed. A brutal, twisting grab. "All right, Fellows. I ask you once again, *was* it psychology? I want a direct, a goddamn direct answer to my question. I do not want to be led around like a goddamn slave to your circuitous hedging. Tell me, and don't stall me. Was it, or was it *not*?" He whopped his pony tail with a free arm and gripped Philip's wrist even tighter. Philip yelped out.

Arnie grinned, just slightly. Then his thick hand dropped and landed on the bar.

"Psychology," said Philip.

"Good. Glad we got that one straight."

Philip took a long sip of his sudsy head. And he thought, well, hell, in a way it *was* psychology because if that's what it was de facto, who in the hell cared what it was supposed to be—originally?

"Yes, I'm glad we got that one straightened out, Philip," said Digby. "He's a good man, really, Arnie. We've got a good man here. If and *when* he gets his ass to work. Correct, Philip?"

A look, downright venomous.

But then, a sly grin.

Philip felt a quick fellow-feeling with Digby Morris.

"I'll do my best. I'm sure . . . I'm quite sure I'll score a few good ones here and there." He raised his beer and added: "Once I get a good start."

They were studying him closely, clutching their beers tight in their fists.

"Now, now, *now*—that is fine stuff, sir," said Arnie Butchler. "That is mighty fine stuff, and I applaud you for it." He clapped his hands hard several times. "Confidence, passion, sincerity, heartfelt enthusiasm—I love it. Don't you love it, Dig?"

"You can't help but love it."

"What we want, though, sir, is actual, *measurable* results. I haven't looked in your H and H Human Resources file yet, but I'll bet you've got the stuff to back up what you just said. I'll lay odds you do. That *start* business. Umm. If you would, could you fill me in with a stat here or there to substantiate that *good start* notion of yours?"

"Stat—"

"I'm waiting," said Arnie Butchler, "and one thing a salesman doesn't like to do—he simply *won't* do—is wait."

"Don't you mean customer?"

Arnie Butchler placed a finger to his lips. "If I had meant

customer, wouldn't I have *said* customer?" He drained his beer and held up his thick mug. "More, gents?"

"Sure," said Digby Morris. He finished his off in one long swallow. Philip gulped.

They waited. Now and then Arnie Butchler yelled out, "Bartender, please!"

Philip had a huge buzz going.

A man in a fog. White wisps of clouds on blue. Like beer suds trailing up? Something about this fine, fine beer quelled even the slightest anxiety. He grabbed Arnie Butchler's arm. "What's the percent alcohol in this thing, anyway?"

Arnie Butchler let out a long guffaw. His pony tail swung. "Your first time at the Blunder Bus, Philip?"

Philip kept his hand on Arnie's arm. He felt his fingernails dig in. "Yes."

"Not a veteran? Up in my neighborhood, the Blunder Bus is a hangout for . . . so many of us. So many of us, Philip. Well, you *asked*. And so I will tell you. It's got a real wham to it. *As* you may have noticed. Eighteen percent, Philip. Eighteen goddamn percent! Asian extraction, Scandinavian preparation, marketed by a Dutch firm, and drunk by nearly every man in the world who loves his beer and doesn't want some goddamn pansy juice. He wants a bear of a grip on his innards." He glanced down at his arm, with Philip's buried fingernails.

Philip let loose.

Arnie brushed his arm.

"Sorry."

"Don't be sorry. Is a man to be sorry when he gains his manhood?"

Digby let out a howl of a laugh.

"No!" shouted Arnie.

"No, No!" shouted Philip. "No, he is not!"

He wanted to shout. He wanted to shout as loud as he could. He wanted to shout all day long!

"A man wants to know who he *is*," said Arnie, and his pony tail swung and swished. "You think your average brew can tell you who you *are*—I mean when it comes down to measuring the experience of being a man in this goddamned fucked-up world? You think it can get right at the center of your guts and do that? I can tell you, without equivocation, Philip, that it can't. It *cannot*."

"Now that's one I can agree with," said Digby Morris, raising his mug in the air before him. "Old Arnie here knows his beer."

"More! Three more!" Arnie thwacked his beer.

The bartender arrived. He was two bartenders. He was three. Clinking mugs. Wet, cold to the touch. Nice, nice.

Ah!

He was guzzling. In his mouth. Down his throat it went.

"You're goddamned right I know my beer," said Arnie. "If there's one thing I do know in this world, it's my beer. You don't know your beer, you're going to be an unhappy man, son. Sir."

A whack at Philip's shoulder.

Fellow feeling. He liked it. He loved it.

"Yes!" he cried.

"Now, here it is, Mr. Fellows. Do *you* know *your* beer? Do you know it now?"

"Yes, yes," said Philip. "I do, I do, I most assuredly do."

"He most assuredly does," said Digby, and he saluted him.

"Well, then, if you know your beer—and it's Blunder Bus Eighteen—which is my own name for what we have here—"

"Yes?"

"Note—see?"

He pointed at the bartender.

Their bearded bartender was drawing drafts. He was delivering two to a table. He was standing by. He was working a toe of his right foot on the floor and his head bobbed as he did so. He might be about to display his talent for the jig. Or the tango? His arm suddenly outstretched, a crescendo in the music, a fanfare, and the man streaking across the floor in some sort of epiphany? Ah!

"A man with a problem," said Arnie Butchler. "No direction."

"Doesn't love his work enough."

"I'd say. Alienated worker who lacks what Mr. Marx called species-life. Wouldn't you say, Dig?"

"Indeed."

"Dances to their tune, right?"

"Right!" said Digby.

Philip worked at his beer. He felt the nurturing of the Blunder Bus Eighteen. Ah, so fine, so *intimate*. Seeking out each and every interstice of one's very being. That head. That sudsy head.

"But now, Philip, let us return to the question. *The* Question. That start you spoke of. Give me just one stat. Just one."

"One stat?"

"You heard me. One stat. Measurable results, son."

"One stat."

"Memory, memory, memory! Memory is vital to the salesman, Philip, sir."

"Yes—yes, I know."

"Memory. I'm waiting."

"I just started—I haven't sold a thing. Not one damned thing."

"He just started. One day in the office." Digby sneering.

"And?"

"One day in the office," said Philip, raising his mug. "And so you see, in one day it's not like I could accomplish a whole lot. Could I now?"

"Um," said Arnie Butchler. "But you see we need to distinguish here between a start and a *good* start. Don't we?"

"As you wish."

"Oh, I *do* wish. The matter must be parsed out, you see."

The man's eyes were on him. Pony tail bunching at his neck. Philip saluted him with his mug. "Shoot, then."

"Oh, well. Oh, my. Well, then, what after all *is* a good start? What is *good*? A meta-question, sir. And . . . what outcomes? What is your rubric, sir?"

"When the gong rings."

"Gong? Of course. Evidence of what? The itch—I do think you've got it, Philip. I do. And Digby here thinks so too."

Digby nodded. Suds covered his lips. He might be a rabid dog.

"But do you know what it *is*?" said Arnie Butchler.

"No—not exactly. I don't know, and I'm not sure I care."

"Who does? Not if they've got it. If they've got it, they've got it. No need to question, or care, is there?"

"Not at all." He was guzzling, and his whole body felt warm, blissfully radiant.

"But just so you know, it's fucking fundamental at H and H. Bottom-line, Philip. If you don't have the itch, or don't *appear* to have the itch, you don't get hired in the first place. *You* have the itch, Philip. I see it right now. I see it—I see it before me. Ever heard of aura?"

"Um-huh."

"Well, it's detectable to some, not to others. The same with the itch. Some can't detect it. But you better goddamn well have it in *this* business or you'll never hear that gong, never watch that gong get gonged. Hear?"

"Yes."

Arnie held up a finger. "Okay—now what *is* it? What is this thing we call the itch, Philip?"

The Eighteen fueled him. He leapt right at it. "The itch to succeed. Of course." And he had it. He certainly did have it. He was tired of being poor. He wanted more. A lot more! He definitely wanted *a lot*. A lot of money!

"The predictable reply. And if I were your professor, which I am in a way, I'd say that's a C-minus answer, at best. Blah, blah. And blah. But shall we get at the critical core of the thing, sir? What *is* the nature of the itch?"

Again, that pony tail swinging.

"The itch to scratch!" said Philip, and he laughed, and thought hell this beer could fuel anything. He was up for it.

"Ha! Yeah, in a way. In a way. I'd raise you to a B-minus, Philip."

"Really?"

"But go further. Go further, Mr. Fellows."

"Scratch every goddamned thing in sight!" He downed his Eighteen in one quick swallow. Something blew out in his gut.

He bent over.

He felt a hand on his. A quiet, gentle hand. A hand that intends to instruct, but in a gentle way. A hand that understands. "The itch, sir, that hunger in a man. That hunger that will not, can *never*, be satisfied. It gets ten, wants twenty. It gets twenty, wants thirty. It gets fifty, wants a hundred. And so on, and so forth. Hunger, Philip. I saw it in you right off. I saw it in your eyes, your mouth, your body movements. You're a hungry man, Philip. For the things of this earth. You'll never, ever, be satisfied. You'll go through life thinking you've just got to be, but no—it won't happen."

A slap on the face.

"Ow!"

"Look at me. You, Mr. Fellows, want it all. Am I correct? Everything of this earth, you want. The pleasures of the flesh, am I right? The pleasures of food, drink, sex, shiny material objects, glistening gold that a crow or squirrel would love to stow away for its winter delight—you want it all. Woman, you want her. You want to bed her down, down, down, and bring home the haul, impress her—am I right?"

"Yes!"

That Eighteen!

Another slap—right on the kisser.

"Ow!"

"I *am* right. I saw it, Mr. Fellows. I am right."

"Yes," said Philip. "Yes, you are right, Arn."

"Goddamn if I'm not!"

"He doesn't want to die," said Digby. "He wants to live."

"But . . . it's the lot man is born for," said Philip.

"Not you," said Digby.

"*Hunger*," said Arnie, his pony tail swishing against the bar as he zeroed in on Philip and grabbed him by the neck. "Hunger. It's a grisly fact to deal with, but sedateness is worse. Hunger, you see, is terrible and sublime." He let loose of Philip's neck and turned to Digby Morris and held up a finger. "Am I right?"

"Yes, you are. By my troth!"

"We've got a pack of hanger-ons up there, don't we, Dig? But how many hungry men do we have up there? Actual, real hungry men?"

Digby Morris worked his fingers. "Oh—maybe four or five tops."

"Kind of you to say so. But I'll bet we have not *one* hungry man up there. And yet . . . I grant you, every man is hungry in a way. It's part and parcel of what we call the human condition. You've got to be hungry, or you starve. But we're looking for a man with the itch—let me capitalize that: The Itch. A man who is incapable of ever being satisfied—he'll sell and sell and sell, and when that gong goes off, he'll squeal with delight like a big pig at the trough, and then *have* to have another fix. We're looking for a man needing that fix, Philip. You're that man. Basic Man before the humdrum of conformity ruined him. The man whose itch seeks power! Self-power. Ever read Nietzsche?"

"Uh. Yes—a little."

"Read your Nietzsche. Study your itch, Philip. Study The Itch. It's your enemy, but it's your friend too."

Arnie's finger was hard against Philip's lips.

And then they snapped.

The bartender arrived.

Three more.

"You're a good man," Arnie Butchler told the man. "Seek your inward power. Slough off the oppression, sir."

The bartender eyed them. "How many does that make? There *is* a dram shop law, you know."

"What does the Eighteen know about that?" said Arnie Butchler.

The bartender did a little dance step. And then he let out a long laugh, and he leaped up. "That'll be the end, sirs, of that particular drink. Coffee, though. Want some?"

"Know your beer," said Arnie. "Know your beer. And your itch."

36

Cell phone rang. In the Orientation Room. Digby Morris about to show some sort of film.

"Go ahead. Answer it. But then shut it off—okay?"

"Yeah."

Sophia.

"Where are you? It's coming. Falling and falling. Supposed to be the biggest snow on record! Where *are* you?"

"At the office. I'm at the office."

"Oh, Philip! No!"

Digby Morris grinning. Shaking his head, inserting a film. The TV screen coming on now, radiant blue. Digby Morris making a motion with his index finger, a punching-down motion.

"I've got to go. I've got to . . . watch this film thing."

"Watch a film? Are you entirely out of your mind? It's coming big, big, big—huge white splotches . . . oh, god, they're predicting *three* feet, Philip. Three fucking feet! Or even four! Get here. Get here now. Once you get the condoms. Did you get those yet?"

It was on speaker phone. How in hell did it get on speaker phone?

Digby Morris laughing. Bending over laughing. Or did he only appear to be bending over laughing?

Oh, hell. Philip punched the button. He got it off speaker.

Digby Morris still laughing. Snorting. He was now snorting.

"No," Philip whispered.

"You didn't get the condoms?"

"No. But I will. I'll get them. For sure!"

"You best get the condoms. You best—you pay attention, now."

Digby Morris again made a downward punching motion with his finger. "*Play,*" his lips said.

"I've got to go. I'll get there really fast," whispered Philip. "I promise. And with the . . . you know what."

"You'd better, or it's going to be high and dry."

Why didn't she use the pill? He'd never asked.

"*Play*," whispered Digby Morris. But he didn't look upset. Beer . . . it was all that Blunder Bus Eighteen. How fine it all was. How so very, very fine.

"You get here in an hour, or you may not get here at all," Sophia was shouting. "I mean it. Just take a look outside. You take a look!"

"Okay," he said. "I've got to go. I'll be there really, really fast."

"Yes, yes," she said. "You must. But do get the condoms. You must get the condoms."

"Oh, I *will*," he said.

Of course he would. Was there any reason for her to emphasize a thing like that? Of course he would get the condoms. That extra money from Gina, and then the condoms. Two essentials. Grab some paperbacks for Sophia and that other stuff on the scribbled list—and run.

"I'm so, so bored. I'm so absolutely out of my mind bored. Frigging bleak! Bring some delightful diversions! Or I shall go out of my tree!"

Shall?

"I've got to go."

"Okay. But do you love me?"

"Yes, yes—of course! Of course I do!"

Digby Morris was punching his finger down. An insistent, poking punching. "*Play*," he whispered. That same smile, undisturbed. Blunder Bus.

"I'm so glad. Because I love you more than I've ever, ever loved any man. Ever. And that's why I want the condoms. Because I want you to be inside me for hours at a time. Hours and hours. Whole, whole hours!"

Oh, my god. Hours? Whole hours?

"Uh—well. Yes!"

"Why does it always have to be over so fast? Just so fast!"

"No—no, it *doesn't*."

He looked at Digby Morris. He didn't want to watch this film. Now—leave *now*.

"Yes, hours. Oh, Philip, hours and hours."

She was just bored. When she got bored, she wanted sex.

"Play," whispered Digby Morris. "*Play.*"

"I must go," whispered Philip. "But I'll bring them. Lots of them!"

"Oh, please. Yes, please."

"Bye," he said. "See you soon."

"I hope so." It was a forlorn voice. Could he trust it?

Now, he thought. You get out of here *now*.

Hours. Whole hours.

He ended the call and Digby clapped. The man was wheeling about.

"Now, Philip, sir. We must consider certain orientation features which are standard Op P here at Hunt and Hart. Orientation is central to our purposes here at H and H."

"I've got only—"

"*Play!*" cried Digby Morris.

He made that pushing motion again with his finger, but still he hadn't pushed the button.

"Okay," said Philip, "but I can watch it only a few minutes because of . . . just a second!" And he got up in a flash and rushed toward the open office environment where sales personnel sat in enclosures of various kinds and were on phones, or muttering agreeably to themselves. And he could see out the large plate glass window the snow coming down in huge wet, white blossoms.

Snow plows clearing off the road. Roads and parking lots. Cars being towed off.

Always, always.

Five hundred extra snow plows. That was good.

Oh, my, oh my.

He rushed back to Orientation. That Eighteen was still fueling him. He could run. He could dance. He could prance. "I can watch . . . only a few minutes. And then I've got to . . . go. Did you see that snow?"

"You rhymed," said Digby. "*Go* and *snow*. Do you realize that?"

"No—not at the time I . . . said it, but now that you point it out."

Was he slurring his words? It was hard to tell.

"*Go* and *snow*," said Digby. "Now, Philip, this fine Orientation Prequel—"

"Prequel?"

"It's the beginning, Philip. Just the beginning."

"Oh. But I can't because of the snow. I must get out of here."

"That's better. Or worse. *Get out*? I sort of liked *snow* with *go*, sir."

"Okay. But only a few moments. Really. Because . . . even though I've got obligations here . . . I know I have responsibilities and obligations . . . important ones. But the snow . . . I don't drive so well in the snow!"

He *was* slurring his words.

"And I suppose you'll be driving the company car."

"Yes . . . unless I can get a cab."

"No cab in this city today. Use your head, sir."

"Well, then."

"Take the company car. Do yourself a favor. It's insured. You're insured. Do yourself a favor. Hell, if it slides all over the road and kills somebody, it's not like you intended it, is it? It's not like you aimed it at some unsuspecting poor sap. It's life, Philip. Life. People get wiped out every single day. Every single hour. Every goddamn single minute, or second. Somebody's number is about to be up right now. They're out there in their car, right now, and their number's up. Or they're in their bathroom getting ready to go out and shovel their sidewalk off. Their number's up. You see?"

"Yeah, but—"

"Or they're sitting at their computer writing an email, and wham, lights out. There she is, you can't argue with it, just live your life as well as you can. And then, Philip, give it all the finger—"

"Finger—"

"Whenever you can. You can't always be giving it the finger, though, because sometimes if you do give it the finger, you feel . . . well, kind of bad. It sort of corrupts you if you know what I mean. To constantly give life the finger is to become a man who is nothing more than this: a Man Who Gives Life the Finger. I wouldn't advise it. I really wouldn't. On the other hand, I wouldn't go with the Eastern way, which is to submit, or the Stoic's, which is also to submit and accept detachment and serenity as the greatest value—but enough of that . . ."

Digby took out a handkerchief and wiped his forehead. "I'm getting hot. Very hot—hot, hot."

"That beer—"

"Do be careful, Philip, sir, going in the snow."

"Oh, I'll be as careful as I can," said Philip. "But I must leave. I just have to leave in a minute."

"Go in the snow, I *know*," said Digby.

"Yes."

"Okay, then, we're going to have to speed the film up a bit. I don't want to give the impression that I'm . . . well, Philip, that I'm attempting to engineer subliminal messages in you the viewer, but I'm going to simply shoot through this Orientation Prequel, and actually, maybe it will work subliminally. And that's okay. That's perfectly okay. As long as one makes full disclosure, which I'm now doing. I'm going to put this thing on Play *and* FF and shoot right through it in approximately two minutes. And then you're free to go. In the snow."

"Good. Good."

The film began.

High speed. Smooth to his listless eyes, smooth and seamless—a lyrical, tale-telling of a life. Like Judgment Day? A life begun in the cradle and then the toddler stage, the adolescent, pictures with sister and brother, proud father and mother, dressed to the nines in their Sunday finery, the school, a fight on the playground, a Halloween costume, a birthday party, Christmas around the tree, presents opened, chocolate fudge stuffed in mouth, dribbling down chins, smiles, laughter, snow, sledding down long hills, Valentine's Day, a girl kissed, kissed back, Easter baskets, the hunt for Easter eggs, chocolate bunnies, spring sunshine, summer baseball, a ball whammed out of the stadium, a July Fourth picnic with fireworks, graduation ceremony, proudly displaying the diploma, dorm room, girl snuck inside, rapidly stripping each other of their clothes, insertion of a ring on girl's finger, wedding cake, baby being changed, the office, the computer, an angry boss, angry wife, angry child, child sick, grown children, a retirement party, a senior center, nursing home, hall filled with wheel chairs, old men drooling, nurses wiping their chins, grave markers.

The hell, the hell is this? What the fuck!

He gave it the finger. He gave it the finger twice.

Three times. Ten.

"Sobering, isn't it?" said Digby. "Sometimes, I like to run it fast like that. Snow, go, know—don't you just love it? But you see, what's it say, Philip? What's it say? What?"

"I don't like it! It pisses me off!"

"You're fucking A it pisses you off. It pisses everybody off and that's why we show it. Because, see, Philip, sir, you must, as they say, make hay while the sun shines. You must fucking A, do it *now* while you can do it. Later, you can't. Can you sell a fucking thing drooling in your goddamned wheel chair?"

"No!"

"You bet you can't. You bet, Philip, sir. You can't. Hell no, you can't. And we try to foster that realization as much as we can in our beginning salesmen—or rather sales *personnel*. In our Prequel Orientation film. Cradle to grave in one hell of a rush! Here's the dingdong truth of it, Philip, you've got to have three things in mind if you want to succeed at Hunt and Hart. Think of them as bulleted items in your toolkit.

"One, Be a Hungry Man, or Woman—that is have the Itch.

"Two, Know Your Life Span—hey, she's short. Or *he's* short.

"Three, Don't stab other Sales Personnel in the Back, unless you can get away with it. If you can, more power to you, Philip, sir.

"You see what I'm getting at here?"

"Yes, I do."

"Laid out plain and simple, isn't it?"

"Yes."

"Do it while you *can*. Do all you can *while* you *can*. One of life's precious lessons, isn't it?"

"Yes. But I've got to go."

Digby was wiping his forehead again. Then he was stuffing his handkerchief in his trousers pocket.

"Next step, Philip. Orientation Camp."

"Huh? What?"

"Orientation, sir. Knew you'd balk on that one. Who doesn't? But use your head, Philip, do you know a single thing about making a sale—in guns and ammo?"

"No, and I said—"

"I know what you said, but the point is, you don't. *Right?*"

"No."

"No. And so we've got to get you shaped up before we ship you out. Well, before you set sail. We've got to get you the best toolkit we can. Don't you agree?"

"I suppose."

"Okay, then. Take off. Go in the snow, I know, and then come back first thing in the morning. Be here about five because you'll need to get to the airport for a flight out. We'll put you on the Business Seven, and you'll get there at the Orientation Center around eleven. And you'll be ready for your ten-week course in Gonging Your Way to Success. That's what we call it."

"Ten week—"

"Can it be done in less than that?"

"Five o'clock—I can't—"

"Business Seven, Philip. No other way. Best time to arrive. Eleven is. Get checked in, get your bunk—"

"Bunk?"

"Sort of a boot camp atmosphere about it. But subterranean. A thousand feet below the surface of the earth, I'd venture, in that the elevator makes a dozen or two stops down. Ours is Sub Floor Six."

"Look. I don't think I much care—"

"Oh, no one does, but let me tell you, each and every one of our Hunt and Harters has been through the program, Philip. Each and every one of them. They didn't like it much, but then there were certain benefits that they didn't much mind. Hunt and Hart has a heart, Philip. They're not going to stick a man down in the cave and expect . . . well, do I have to spell it out?"

"You mean—"

243

"I do indeed. I mean exactly that."

"My god."

"Yes, it's sort of hard, actually, to return from the Orientation Center. In your head anyway. Many never do. Most don't. Okay, they sort of beat you around on a daily basis, but then . . . do consider those benefits, Philip."

"Beat you—"

"Philip. Come on. *Metaphorically*. Okay? A guy's got to man up to sell this stuff. I hate it, but I accept it. I hate most everything about this disgusting, wretched place, as I've explained before— patiently, haven't I? But I do what I do because . . . I've invested my life in it. I've invested way too much. And the Gong—I really hate that, I hate the frigging ringing bells! But I like the dough and the respect you get for it, with that little brass plaque that comes down from Arnie—our mutual friend had to go, incidentally, after puking his guts up in the toilet. But he's on his way to his next stop, and he'll be okay as long as he stays off the Blunder Bus Eighteen for a bit. But he won't. If I know Arnie Butchler. Man, I'd sure like to hit a few out there . . . but that snow. You *don't* go in that snow, Philip."

"No—but I've *got* to go. I must."

"Woman friend. *Sure* you do. And so go. In the *snow*."

He waved at Philip and attended to the film.

"But I can't make it here at five. The snow—it's supposed to lay down three or four more feet. Nobody's going anywhere in it, I don't think."

"No, probably not. Three or four feet, you say?"

"Yes, that's what my girlfriend said."

"Oh, of course. Women know, don't they?"

"Yes. I guess."

And then he laughed. "Oh . . . yeah."

"Yes."

"Then I wouldn't advise that Orientation Center. Or well, if you do go, don't tell her. Women don't like that. They don't like that at all. Stuff like that—manly stuff. Masculine. Testosterone stuff, Philip. Or would you be under the opinion that they do?"

"No. But then—"

"No buts, Philip."

"But what about the women salespersons? Don't they have to go—"

"To an Orientation Center? Sure."

"Where?"

"Don't know. Don't know the first thing about it. It's run by others, don't even know who. But now, Philip, if you can't make the Business Seven, or even go in the next few weeks, take care of that car, and do get it back. Because as you say, you've got obligations— serious ones.   I probably won't be in myself, to check on you, but others will—and have, I'm sure, and they may be drumming up a case of some kind against you as we speak. The wheels turn slowly around here, but they do turn. You know?"

"What?"

"Yes, they do turn. Those wheels. The building of the case. You're not here, you've got the car checked out, no weekly log filled out on mileage, gas, trips made, times, etc. Not here, but out *there*, with that dazzling Lincoln. The wheels are surely turning. Ha! A pun! Wasn't it?"

"But I told *you*—"

"Me? I count very little around here, Philip. There are others— they handle that kind of thing."

"Who?"

"Oh, who knows? You might start with Accounts. But then, they answer to others. I don't know—can't tell you anything very helpful because I've always been here. I've never missed. But take *you*, you've had that car out for, how long is it?"

"Well, I can't really say, or remember exactly, but—"

"Two weeks, or more—a month? Hell, you lose time with all that snow, don't you? I do. I have no memory—of practically anything."

"It wasn't a month—I know that!"

"Get with it," said Digby. "Get it going, and watch thine p's and q's. Easy to get the job, but as I said earlier, hard to hold on to it. And watch the little legal stuff. They'd love to can a guy and then even bring criminal charges, but only if you really piss them off. Don't ever piss them off. Bad to do that—very bad."

"Criminal charges?"

"Pardon?"

"Criminal charges?"

"What about them?"

Philip dug in his pockets for his car key.

"Here. I'm surrendering this. Right here. Right now."

"Oh, well, not to *me*. I can't take it."

"To Accounts, then."

"No, no, they don't want it."

"Who *does*?"

Digby Morris shrugged. "Can't say—"

Philip kicked something. A trash can, it was. It rolled around and emptied out half its contents.

"I've got to go. Now! I *must* go."

"Okay. But do be careful."

He hurried off. Besides, he couldn't leave his keys here. He'd left that three-volume boxed set of *A Pictorial History of the Slaughter of War* in the car.

37

He raged through the heavy snowfall to the parking garage, shielding his face from the harsh, stinging cold. He was soon on the road. It took him an hour through blizzard conditions to get to Grand. Snow plows ahead, two or three of them. Slow, but at least you got there. Thank you, city! He slowed, stopped at the red light. Snow laying down before him. The Lincoln didn't want to go. And suddenly a loud thud, bumping him hard, and he looked back and saw the huge black truck. Damage? Oh, god. He sat still, and then he got out. The light changed. The truck raced its motor, the man in the truck with a black ball cap flicking out a cigarette butt. Philip advanced toward him as the man was lighting up, baring his teeth. Dark, unkempt beard. Racing his motor, raising his middle finger. He thrust it up and up. Philip stopped, then hurried back to the Lincoln, got in, buckled up, and drove off, turning right at the light. He glanced back, and then increased his speed.

At Shoppers Paradise he checked the rear end. There it was, big dent. Horrible. Disfiguring. There it was, and what was he supposed to do about it? Report it to the company, of course. Describe the man in the truck, the cigarette butt flicked out, the lighting of another as he approached the man, the bared teeth, the motor racing, a growl to it—that finger thrust up and up. Was he making anything up?

Okay—that's for later. Right now: the essentials.

Money first.

An inquiring, heavy-set woman in Customer Service. A face that registered sympathy and understanding. An incipient smile through thick red lipstick.

"Sophia Cross, you say?"

"Yes."

The woman pulled open a drawer. "Yes. Here it is, but do you have identification of some kind? Are you married to Sophia Cross?"

"No."

"Well, I can't give you this money unless you can show a legal connection with the payee."

"She can call you," said Philip.

The woman shook her head. "No. I'm afraid that won't do. Anyone could call—don't you see?"

"We need that money. We really need it."

The woman glanced at it. "It's for one hundred dollars, and I know that's not a lot of money, but I'm sure every little bit helps. But I'm sorry. The payee will need to present herself and pick up the money."

"One hundred dollars? I thought—"

"Yes, sir—that's what it is."

"One hundred dollars."

"You were expecting more?"

"She can't get here in this snow," he said.

"I know. It's hard—very hard. And I'm very sorry."

She did have a sympathetic look on her face. She could be his mother. Perhaps his aunt. "Thanks," he said.

He did at least have some money Sophia had given him. He went about the store.

He picked up five boxes of condoms, two bottles of red wine, several paperback thrillers, and snacks. He was a half hour getting this stuff, three bags full, and he worried about the road. What if he couldn't get over it? How could he? Laying it down, laying it down. Well, he'd walked it once, and he could walk it again. He'd walked all the way from the Hotel Horatio to Sophia's apartment. He could certainly walk out to that damned hotel if he had to.

But with three bags?

He got right behind a snow plow, *ah*, and turned into the lot of the Hotel Horatio as the snow plow went on, laying down sand, chemical mixture, scraping a path which would be covered over in another minute or two. Why not wait? Because it was always snowing, always, and what if you waited until it stopped? It wouldn't stop—that's the point. It would never stop.

He pulled into a place between two other cars. He got out with his three bags full and took another good look at that dent.

Big.

Bad.

What a wham. Yes, disfiguring. One couldn't help but notice and glower at it.

Have to be reported. No question.

What did this driver look like? The guy in the truck?

Well, tough guy, you know, cigarette dangling out of his mouth, and then flicking it out with a long, dirty finger. Right out the open window. Almost got me with it. Ball cap. He wore a black ball cap. Gave me the finger. He did.

What else did you notice?

Thick hair. Beard. Scraggly kind—you know.

What kind of ball cap?

I didn't catch that.

No insignia on it?

I didn't see one.

The hair. The beard. Long or short?

About normal. Not long, not short. But scraggly—it was unkempt, working class type.

How old?

About thirty-five maybe. If that. Brutal looking guy.

Did you go up and speak to the man?

Hell, no, looked like he'd be the type . . . you know.

To what?

To get out of that truck and bust you in the mouth.

Did he give any indication—

Look, he would. Trust me. Bust you in the mouth, and put out your lights. We're talking black eyes, broken bones. We're talking hospitalization.

Really.

You're damned right. You think I had any chance at all with that guy in that truck? Fix the goddamn dent, and just let me alone! Will you?

No need to curse. No use for language like that.

Yeah? Well, I'm upset. Really upset. Why in the hell did that have to happen? You tell me.

Who knows? Who knows the answer to that one, sir. If you know, you tell us, okay?

I will. You damn betcha I will.

He shook his head at the dent. He studied it and studied it.

And then he headed for the lobby of the Horatio, sharp wind against his face.

Because now, yes, now. Soon you will. All fixed up. Laid in for the duration.

You're no Don Juan, Phil. That from Dick.

Well, I can try to be, can't I?

Hey, if you can manage it, more power to you. Makes the world go round, you know.

Good old Dick.

He entered the lobby. He marched straight for the elevator.

He came to the elevator, waited a moment, got in, and punched the button for five. All by himself. Up we go. Three bags with five boxes of condoms, a pile of snacks, wine, the whole works. Time to party. Party hearty. More snow, but settled in, hotel lodging and bar covered, no money, but who needs it?

Job? No, not going to show up at five tomorrow morning! Benefits. But beatings? Now what exactly *does* that mean?

Benefits are up on Floor Five, my fine feathered friend.

Yes, yes.

He got off on Floor Five.

He came to their room.

He got out his key card.

Inserted it.

Door opens.

Stands there, staring. Staring.

What the—

What *the*—

Rod Busby?

Rod Busby in bed?

Staring at him.

Sophia in bed. Half smile, but . . . rattled. Yes, rattled.

Busby's arms around her.

Their heads on one pillow, Rod Busby sneering at him. Rod going for a beer on the night table. A sneer of a grin as he takes a slow sip, then salutes him with that beer can.

"Phil-boy. My dearest Phil-boy."

"What are you doing here?"

"What's in the bags?"

"What are you doing here?"

"I repeat," said Rod Busby.

"Leave him alone," said Sophia.

"I repeat," said Rod.

"Things. Things I bought."

"Could you be more specific, Philly?"

"Snacks. A few books."

"And . . ."

"Oh, you're such a sweetheart," cried Sophia. "Could you bring the books—over here? And let me see?" She patted her side of the bed.

He studied her. He drew out the five paperback books. Thrillers, all. He held them up.

"Bring them over here," said Sophia. "Please? If you would."

"Yeah, let's have a look," said Rod. "If you don't mind, son."

He left the bags on the floor and carried the paperbacks over to Sophia's side of the bed.

"Oh, gosh, these look good!" yelled Sophia. "You're such a sweetheart!"

"Let me see," said Rod, going for one of them.

"No—you just wait."

"Hey . . . women!" said Rod. "Cute, huh, Phil-boy?"

Sophia gripped Philip's hand. She gave him an affectionate look, and then sadly shrugged.

He went back to where he'd been before, just steps from the door.

"What else you got there?" said Rod.

"Snacks."

"Mind?" said Rod, putting out his hands.

"No." He went for them, and pushed the condoms to one side.

"Just give me the bags. That'd be best, Phil-boy. Or otherwise I'm going to think—"

"Just quit it!" Sophia slapped at him.

Rod Busby caught her wrist and laughed.

"Okay—sure."

"You can take the rest," said Sophia. "We don't need it. But thanks for the books. I do appreciate that." Again, a sad shrug.

"Sure," said Philip.

Rod whispered in her ear. She shook her head. But he whispered again.

She looked up. "Leave a couple boxes, okay? Just two?"

"Two, Phil-boy."

He went for them. He took out two. He lobbed them at the bed.

"Three, Phil-boy, assuming you've got three, and I expect you do. Three."

"No," said Sophia. "*Two*. Two is enough."

Rod Busby pulled her next to him and whispered in her ear.

She came away from that and said, "Okay, three, but that's it, Philip. If you have more than that, you keep them. Did you get Gina's money?"

"No. They wouldn't give it to me."

"What? Why?"

"It'd have to be you."

"But that's a thousand bucks!"

"One hundred."

"One hundred?"

"Yes. That's it."

"Damn! That bitch is getting more stingy by the minute," said Rod Busby. "Is that wine I see bulging that bag there?"

Philip nodded

"How much?"

"Three bottles."

"We'll take it," said Rod.

"You go ahead. I sure don't want it," said Philip. He stuck two boxes of condoms in his pocket, dropped the bags with the wine and assorted goodies on Rod's side of the bed, and said to Sophia, "I'd hoped for more—than this."

"I know. I know. I did too."

She was about to cry.

"I'd hoped," he said, "for a lot more. I'd thought—"

"Yeah, yeah," said Rod. "You leaving, Phil-o?"

Philip nodded. He made his way out. He shut the door—quietly.

Down at Registration, he found out that no one, *not* Gina, had covered the bill. He was into it for over five thousand dollars. "I'm checking out, then! Now," he said.

"You'll have to pay the bill first," said the woman, eyeing him.

"I don't have that kind of money. I don't have any money."

"Well, I guess you'd better find a way to manage this account," said the woman. "I strongly suggest it."

He sat in the car and called Sophia.

"Why'd you lie? About Gina. About the room, about the bar?"

"I didn't lie! She said she'd do it. You call her. You'll see."

He told her about the bill, how high it was.

"Oh, my god," she said. And then she said, "Honey, I've got to go."

He heard Rod laughing. It was more of a snort than a laugh.

"What's her number?"

She spouted it out.

"She'd better pay," he said. "Or you can't stay in that room! I'm not paying for—"

"I know, I know," she said. "What kind of woman do you take me for, Philip? Jeez."

"I'm sorry. I just—"

"It'll be all right," she said. "It'll get straightened up. You'll see. She'll pay it."

"Why him?" he asked.

Silence.

Then she cleared her throat. "Philip—"

"Why *him*?"

"I don't know. I can't tell you." And she did start to cry.

"Sophia," he said. "My Sophia.'"

"Oh, Philip."

And then the phone went dead.

He sat in the car. And then he got on the road, slipping and sliding. Lisa Wing, he thought. No. Dick Hazzard. But it made no difference, she wanted him. He could tell.

He was sure of it.

Dick Hazzard had had her long enough.

"Mine," said Philip. "Mine. You're mine, babe."

38

The snow plow was working Lisa Wing's street. Ah, twice lucky! He followed it. Where park? Dick's car there, half covered in snow. He got parked right by Dick's.

He headed for the door.

He knocked. He listened. Inside came the voices of women. Lisa and Tina.

Dick Hazzard at the door. "Well, well, well, if it isn't Phil. We weren't expecting you, Phil."

"Oh, Philip!" Lisa Wing moved quickly for him, embraced him, and pulled herself back and kissed him straight on the lips. "My god, you . . . why are *you* here?"

"To see you. I missed you." He gave Dick a look.

Dick coated his lower lip with his tongue. "Well, what demonstrative behavior do we have here, Phil? Huh?"

Tina stood by. "You sound like Sebastian." She shook her head and gave Philip a knowing look. "I get rid of one Sebastian, and now here's another."

"Only he's mine," said Lisa. "You're mine, aren't you, Dick?"

"You didn't get rid of him," said Dick. "He dumped you—or that's what you said."

"I know. I know. And please don't remind me of it."

"Want something to drink?" asked Lisa and pulled Philip with her toward the kitchen. And in there, she took him and began kissing him furiously on the lips.

He responded. He kissed her furiously on the lips.

"I've wanted you," said Philip. "There's never been anyone else since you—after that night. Not anyone that special. I mean—" He looked. No Dick—still in the living area, with Tina. This one was his. His now.

"Well, don't get any ideas, baby doll," said Lisa, pulling loose. "I'm Dick's. All the way."

"What? Then why? Why this?"

"Can't I like you too? And if you want . . ." she whispered in his ear.

He went hard as a rock. "I do. It's true!"

"Oh! Ha, ha! You rhymed!"

"Please," he said.

And then she spoke of sheer bliss, late night bliss, bliss he'd been too foolish to take that one night—recall?

"No more," he said. "No more."

"Nevermore?"

"No."

"Quoth the Raven?"

"That's right."

"You ready, then?" she said.

"Now?" He took hold of her. He whispered at her: "But how? Here? Now? Really, I mean, with Dick—"

"Unless you're just too chicken," she whispered back. Her fingers worked at his sides, tickling, teasing.

And then she moved away quickly and went about her business, into the refrigerator, grabbing a six pack of beer. Plus snacks of various kinds, a candy bar, a bag of potato chips, a banana.

"Before he left, Sebastian did at least go out in that car of his and get us a pile of stuff. A nice man. But . . . he left poor, poor Tina. She's all alone. All by her little selfie. Sebastian is such a bastard, no?"

"Maybe." He was thinking about Sebastian's telling him about the job. About Professor Fellows. A favor, it was. Rather intense guy, but okay—and he didn't write poor Tommy off as a complete nut. Shouldn't one respect him for that?

"Maybe?"

"I'd like a beer," he said.

"Here, then." She handed it to him. "Tina is only, lonely, wanting, wanting, wanting—you can tell, can't you? Being a man, you can surely tell a thing like that." She fell to whispering. "She wants somebody, Philip. *Somebody.*"

"Really?"

"God, how obtuse, men can be. How utterly obtuse." She took

off, dancing her way out of the kitchen.

He stood there. And then it occurred to him. No Tommy. Where was he?

He gravitated toward the living room. And he asked.

"With Sebastian," said Tina. "Holing up with Sebastian. Measuring the snow. Checking out Sebastian's ceiling. In Sebastian's little house. And Sebastian with that awful girl. I suppose he told you."

"Yes."

"I suppose they're quite happy. And I wish him happiness. If it can't be with me, I do wish him happiness nonetheless."

Nonetheless?

"We've got something cooking here," said Dick.

"What?"

"He wants to get rid of me," said Tina.

"No, I don't!"

"I'll be so lonely in that little house of mine. Still, I will go back. I was planning on going back yesterday, but then we started that game."

"Charades," said Dick.

"Yes—and it was so stupid. I do not like that game."

"Showed too," said Lisa Wing. "She's just way too serious about everything. Always has been."

"Maybe I'm just sad."

"We do need a bit of privacy, you know," said Lisa. "For this and that."

"Can you believe she just said that?" said Dick. "But then, she's on these meds, you know. So—"

"I am *not!*"

"Yes, you are."

"One. *One* med. Not *meds.*"

"If you haven't noticed, Phil, every little thought that pops up in her head, wham, she's right out there with it. The kind of thing you might hatch up in your little brain, you know, but never say—not out loud! For instance—"

"Oh, shut up."

"Mostly sexual—"

"Well, maybe if I had—"

"What? Had what?"

Lisa Wing started to cry.

Tina shook her head and was moving toward the two of them. "This isn't the right way. You don't discuss that sort of thing in public."

"Who asked you?" said Lisa, whimpering.

"No one. I'm just telling you. The two of you. It's not good."

"She had her last one . . . when was it, about an hour ago? And the closer to the event, the stronger the impulse. Odd, isn't it? Right, Lisa?"

"Will you please shut up?"

"She doesn't mean a thing she says," said Dick. He whacked Philip on the shoulder. "So don't get any ideas, son. In an hour from now, you'll see. Just give it an hour."

"You know what? I hate you," said Lisa. "You get out. You get out of my house."

"*Your* house."

"Yes—my house."

"I paid the last two rents," said Dick.

"It's still my house. Whose name's on the lease?"

Tina came up to Philip. "Leave them to their quarrel. Let's go." She took his arm and led him to the door. They opened it into the evening. Dark was falling fast. And then he saw him—the man in the black coat. He was standing behind a car on the opposite side of the street. He waved. Philip started to wave back, but he caught himself.

He opened the door and yelled. "Dick!"

"Yeah!"

Dick came out with a beer.

"That guy over there. In the black. Punch that bastard out. Would you?"

"What?"

"He's been spying on me."

"Hmm. Looks pretty harmless, Phil. Why waste a punch?"

258

"Because I don't like it," said Philip. "Not one bit."

They watched. The man didn't move. Just stared. He waved once, and then dropped his hand.

"Friendly bastard. Isn't he?"

"I want you to get rid of him. I want you to put the fucker in pain!"

Dick studied him. "You all right there, Phil?"

"Yes—I just want that bastard to leave me alone."

"Staring doesn't hurt, does it? Probably doesn't know anything else to do. Some people don't have social skills, you know. Poor bastard's probably just lonely."

"We must go," said Tina.

"Okay."

They headed to the car, her carrying some things in a bag, him opening the car door for her.

Maybe, he thought. Yes, maybe.

When they drove off, he caught a glimpse of her. Pretty. Single. As good as Lisa Wing. As good as Sophia. Why hadn't he realized it? He'd make a play. He'd Don Juan it right up. You bet he would. Soon, he thought. *Soon.*

39

His old life began again. Back to his apartment, engulfed by the stink, the mold, the mildew. Late that night, he called Gina and spoke to her about that hotel bill at the Horatio. How could he pay that? He couldn't! No way. Five thousand dollars. He didn't have that kind of money.

"You want me to pay it? Is that what you're saying?"

"Well."

"Why should I?"

"Because they're out there on my dime."

Damn. What a dumb . . .

"She just uses me," said Gina. "How would that make you feel? And you used me too."

"I'm sorry."

"No you're not."

"It wasn't that good anyway," he said.

"Oh, well, poor Philip! And poor Sophia!"

He expected her to end the call any second.

"I'll pay it back to you. Somehow. But the meter's running!"

What the hell fuck! The meter—

But funny, she seemed to like it. It struck a chord somehow. "Well," she said, "that *is* a bitch, isn't it?"

"Yes. Him and her. That criminal and Sophia."

"How'd he get in that room? Why'd you let him in?"

"I didn't! I was gone, and when I got back, he was there."

"Why didn't you throw him out?"

Philip laughed. "*Him*? You know how big he is?"

"Yes, yes. Sophia told me. Sophia told me all about him."

"Please," he said. "If you could just see your way to doing it." He wanted to say that for her, it would be so little to shell out.

Shell out?

But the point was: it would be *so little* for her to pay out, but for him, it was just impossible.

But he waited to hear what she'd say.

"Hmm."

A long silence.

"You still there?"

"Yes."

"Well, you see—you see what I mean, don't you?"

"I suppose I could pay the bill, and then say any future days are on their dime."

There—again. But this time, from her at least.

"Good!" he said. "And the bar tab?"

"Bar tab, bar tab—that too? What freeloaders you two are! My, my."

"I know—"

"I shouldn't, you know."

"Please."

"Really, I shouldn't."

"*Please.*"

Crawling. You scum, you!

"You know, I should never have gotten into it, bailing her out. What a fool I am."

"Sorry."

"This once. No more."

"Thanks," he said. "Thanks more than you can imagine—ever."

It was a mistake to say this, and he expected a thunderous, accusatory voice blasting out of his cell.

But she softened. "Well . . ."

"Thanks," he said. "So much."

"It's nothing," she said. "Only she should know, I'm not funding any future flings. Tell her that."

"I will."

"Call her now."

"I will."

"Oh, okay, I'll do it!" she said.

"You're a friend—forever," he said. And hated himself more than ever.

"Just this once I am," she said.

"Right."

He called Sophia, and she sounded relieved. But then her voice grew morose. "I feel like I'm anchored to a rock."

"Where *is* he?"

"Somewhere doing CIA crap. I guess."

"Yeah?"

"I wish it hadn't turned out this way, dearest."

"Why then? Why did it?"

"I'm weak. That's why. That's all there is to it. I'm a very weak person."

"I wish," he said. "I wish you weren't."

"Oh? Well, it's not like you're so strong yourself. Are you?"

He started to object, but then he said. "No. I want to be. I try."

"I'm so bored. Really I am, and I hate it. And it makes me so unhappy."

"I'm sorry."

"At least we'll be leaving here pretty soon. I bet I'll have to get some dumbass job. But once Rod's with the CIA, I don't know. Maybe I won't have to work."

"You'll go with him—"

"I'll have to. He would kill me if I didn't."

"No. You can't."

"You want me killed?"

"No."

"Well, then."

"Okay," he said.

"See you." Her voice broke.

And his cell phone went dead in his hands.

40

And so now it was time to change his life. He gave up on Hunt and Hart, turned in the Lincoln, a long and involved process, and finally showed up at the university to finish his application for the position of researcher for the Panegyrics Department.

After a half day of it, he was finished with all the application questions, but then he said he must meet his namesake, Professor Fellows, of the Music Department.

"Take the hall there," said Professor Alejohn. "He's in Eighty-one."

And so he met with Professor Fellows.

He was a stringy sort of man with gray hair whipped to one side, and a long nose that he peered down over. He sometimes fingered a large ear.

"Sebastian Croner spoke of you," said the professor. "And perhaps you know of a young man named Tommy?"

"Yes, I know of him, though I don't—"

"A young man whose theories are quite intriguing. His graduate studies, if you're aware of this, were not only in math and physics but also in music. A triple masters, you see. The young man is sheer genius. His view, for instance, of ceilings. Rare—and bearing further study."

"What about snow?"

"Snow?" The professor pointed out the office window. "Keeps coming, doesn't it? Yes, snow. In terms of physics, it doesn't make much sense. Or perhaps it does. Perhaps it makes a lot of sense. But even so, one must note that this Tommy—his thinking, his theories, they're not bound by natural laws. See, his are actually . . . well, they're more metaphysical. Snow, as I've heard him explain it, in the presence of his intellectual sidekick, Sebastian, is a sign of disturbances in the moral universe. Not just the natural. The moral. The white we see out there is sign and symbol of our imminent demise. Exciting, isn't it? I wish they had doctoral degrees and hefty manuscripts ready for the publisher . . . not so Tommy, and Sebastian's bachelor's—that's all he has—it's in accounting. And so . . ." He got a look. "Well, it's all very exciting, nonetheless, those ideas of theirs, especially Tommy's, from a purely theoretical viewpoint, I mean, not from the actual—because who wants doom? Do you? Do I? Of course not; the answer is always no. No one wants doom."

"Not me," said Philip.

The professor didn't hear this. He said, "Music is the means to everything. Perhaps you were told of my role here in the Department of Panegyrics. Were you?"

"The structure of music is—"

"The structure of praise—exactly. And praise is central, you see, to any being's existence. We all function by praise. It's the oil that keeps the parts moving. It's the fuel that makes the machine go. Without praise . . . well, I hope we do not need to even imagine a society where praise is not given on a fairly consistent basis. Such a society is dead. It's full of dead people. Without praise, what we have is death."

"But—"

"Praise is the nurturing of the soul. The soul, you see, functions on it. Dies without it."

"Oh."

"The soul *lives*, you see, with it. It strokes the ego. It gets at the core, you see. And all of humanity! Ah! We must penetrate. We must probe—we who live with the continual prospect of utter doom! We who—"

The professor seemed worn out. Was he going to expire?

But no, suddenly he was recharged, re-enlivened. He was looking at Philip with great intent.

"But," said Philip, "I don't understand my role here. I mean the filling out of questionnaires. I don't see why—"

"Vital—utterly vital. We must keep our fingers on the pulse. We must, with constant vigilance, keep our fingers precisely there." The professor swiveled around and inserted a CD in a player. "Now, listen. Please listen."

Philip did. He listened for a good ten minutes. Classical music.

Strings. Winds. Mostly strings.

"What do you hear?"

The professor smiled broadly, cupping one ear. He waited expectantly.

"Classical music. Strings and winds."

"Yes, but what do you *hear*?"

He watched it. The snow was coming down in a deluge of large, blossomy flakes. Weighty, those flakes—wet and weighty. The music seemed to go with it. It seemed to speak of the snow and the way it was so delightfully falling. Beautiful white, mysterious, especially as evening was falling, sundown a line of red coals through large, erect buildings, like an incipient conflagration.

"I, I—" said Philip. "I—"

"What?" said the professor. "What do you *hear*?"

"The snow," said Philip. "The sundown."

"Ah! But . . . no. I certainly hope not. Oh, dear no. Though . . . but yes, of course, it *is* involved—I beg your pardon. It is. Fundamentally, yes. Who can deny it? What we all *endure*. That which we struggle against! Our spirits! And therefore, the ceiling, you see—ah, that Tommy!"

Professor Fellows seemed lost in that. A look of great satisfaction worked at his lips.

"Snow," said Philip.

"Music," said the professor. "What you hear, sir, is a musical plotting of panegyrics. Each piece of orchestral music—it must be orchestral—plots the music of praise somewhat differently. Each measure is a different plotting. We are now beginning to plot, graphically, the answers to most of our questionnaires so that they are musical equivalents—my role, Philip, this is my role, and I will need an assistant. Fellows and Fellows. What do you say?"

"You mean I wouldn't have to—"

"What, sir?"

"Do the surveys. Collect the data?"

"Oh, yes, door to door, Philip, absolutely. But some of the time, some of it, you would be here with me doing the plotting, and then . . . ah, we'll listen to the results. Ah, yes! The fine, sweet music. For you see, if music is the structure of praise, the structure of praise is also music. Isn't it quite delightful?" His hands hit the desk. "Don't you agree?"

"But what about sad music?"

"Sad? The same—it's all praise. And happiness. The sadness speaks of the absence of happiness. Everything is about happiness, Philip, and praise is a key cog, a fundamental mechanism of happiness. Indeed it is. All complex, very complex, but you'll see, you'll see."

The professor's white teeth glistened. They could light up a dark room.

"Yes," said Philip, and he hoped so. Quite beautiful. The plotting, and then the music. He could long for that. It's the poet in me, he thought.

"There will be some discordant notes," said Professor Fellows, "but then those will end up in a minor key, and, I surely don't need to inform you that there is great beauty in the minor key. Do you not love Mozart's *Symphony Forty in G Minor*?"

He wasn't sure of it. Had he listened to it in his Music Appreciation course? It was hard to recall. Hard to recall any of the pieces he'd listened to, in fact.

"And now, Mr. Fellows," said Professor Fellows, "we'll have a bit of brandy, and then you'll plan on your first voyage out tomorrow morning—I think of it as a voyage because it is, in fact, a journey to otherness. Don't you think so? And we must know otherness. Mustn't we?"

The professor poured the brandy. He offered Philip a flute.

They drank. They were quiet.

A drink in a campus office. It delighted Philip to think so. It made him reflective. It made him feel oddly professorial.

Truly a moment of reflection. He felt it in the absence of sound.

And then Philip said it was late, and he'd need to be on his way.

"Behold the snow—the other," said the professor. "Perhaps we'll understand it if we try. Perhaps we'll understand it, and our connection to it. It's here for a reason, Philip, and so we must understand it while we can. Yes, we do plot the snow. A good point you've made. Yes."

"Math and physics," said Philip. "Tommy—"

"His bachelor's in Greek," said the professor.

"Uh. Really? Tommy studied Greek. Does that—"

"I imagine," said the professor. "A link surely. We must, after all, keep Pythagoras in mind. Must we not?"

"Yes," said Philip, and bid the professor goodbye. On his way out of the Department of Panegyrics, he thought about it. Yes, one must understand it. Yes, it was continually snowing. One must contemplate what was behind it—or what? Perish?

And then he saw the man in black standing in his very way. Positioning himself.

Ah! Well, now!

A confrontation, is it?

He came up to him. He did not flinch.

The man in black did not move.

"What?" said Philip. "What is it you want?"

"Sir," said the man in black.

"Yes? What do you want? What!"

"A word with you," said the man in black.

"What? What word? Why do you follow—why do you follow and follow?"

"You are in despair, sir," said the man in black. His face bore no expression. No sadness, a sort of blankness.

"What? Despair? What do you mean?"

"You are in despair," said the man in black, and he turned to go. He headed off at a quick trot.

41

Three hard knocks on his door. It was pitch black early, but he was about to get up anyway, yet three hard knocks? Who?

He got up, walked to the door, and slowly opened it.

An old whiskered man stood there with blood-shot eyes. Drool on his lips. "Your rent, son. Rent's past due. I'm going to need that rent in twenty-four hours, or this place here gets locked down."

"Rent—yeah. Yeah, I know."

"You pay it," said the whiskered man, scratching an ear. "Pay it or this place here gets locked down."

"Yeah, I'm sorry. But I don't have it, or I would pay it."

"You don't have it. When can you get it?"

"As soon as I get paid."

The whiskered man scratched the other ear. "When's that?"

"Well . . . I don't know. I'm on commission. So if I can make a few good commissions—which should be soon, I expect. I'm expecting a few good commissions soon."

"Not good enough, son. You got twenty-four hours, and this place here, it gets locked down."

Philip went off early that morning with that rent business weighing heavily on his mind. The snow was coming down at a steady pace. Deepening. The sidewalks hadn't been shoveled in places. In stretches, he was hip deep in it. Good boots he had. Yes.

But how long would it take to walk to the university in this?

Twenty-four hours. A place to sleep, and that was it. Where was he to bunk in? Not at Dick's, not with Sophia.

Sebastian.

Only he had no idea where the man lived.

Tina?

He had some money left over from his Sophia days. Not much, but a little, and so he looked for a coffee shop. Yes, some hot coffee with cream, about three or four cups, and then off to Panegyrics.

Off to his first day on foot, if you could get there on foot, to start conducting field studies.

He entered a coffee shop.

Ah, what a fine place. The relaxing aura of the shop. He wished he had a book with him. A sophisticated piece of literature, polished language to savor. Something fit for a man of taste.

He still had an hour to go before showing up to see Professor Fellows. To go out on the route. On foot he couldn't have brought any of those huge tomes dealing with the slaughter of war, but he might have brought something else. Perhaps a narrow volume of poetry. A volume of poetry in a coffee house. Yes, that could be very pleasant, very civilized. Elegant and sophisticated.

And then it struck him. He didn't like the way it popped right into his mind, but there it was. As he was about halfway done consuming his coffee, it came straight at him: *Charlotte Sanders.* He could call that woman with the smoker's voice, with the strident air, but perhaps very sexy when she wasn't angry. After all, she'd invited him to have a little fun, hadn't she? And wouldn't he be missing an opportunity—just as she'd said—if he didn't take her up on it?

And soon?

Wouldn't he?

He searched his cell phone.

Yes, there was that number.

Well, it might be worth trying.

It might be.

A place for the night—and possibly more.

But what if? What if that Duane—wasn't that his name?—what if he showed? Showed? He probably lived there. So that was out. Now wasn't it? *Had an opportunity and you blew it big time, didn't you, Philly?*

He drank his coffee, and considered.

Yes, that could be very nice—assuming he *hadn't* blown it.

Yes, it could be—assuming no big risk.

A couple cups of coffee, letting the idea brew right with the coffee. Give it a little time.

Speaking of time.

Time, time, time—it had gone by, and it was all, as they said, a blur. Snow. All that snow. It made you forget time. He watched it coming down now, a curtain of it out there, pelting the window.

It was the language of snow.

Talking to you, constantly talking at you.

Yes, yes, yes, snow. That's what had happened. And sex. Sex and snow. Snow and sex. With Sophia, but hints of it too with Lisa Wing—strong hints—and then that Charlotte Sanders inviting him time and time again—and then, nothing. Gone, surely. But then she'd *said* you'd better take the opportunity while you had it because after a while, that's what it would be—*gone, gone.*

Tina.

Tina, how pretty, how smart.   But how—what was she? Motherly? No, she wasn't motherly. He didn't want to think of her as motherly.

Womanly.

Not girlish, womanly.

She'd smiled when he'd dropped her off a few days ago. Smiled and patted his hand.   And then given him a bit of a hug when he'd walked her to her door. He'd helped her make her way through the deep drifts so she wouldn't fall into some hole. He'd told her about his own falling into some hole—a deep hole. Not fun. Not fun at all. You'd get buried, that was the thing; you'd never come up.

Don't focus on gloom and doom, son. Look on the bright side. You won't land in the next ditch, right?

Yes, Dad.

"Well, that would be just terrible," Tina had said, and then they were at the door of her small house.

She didn't invite him in. She gave him that hug and said she'd really appreciated the ride.

That was when he had that car. But now he was a man on foot. It meant a cab. He could sleep on her couch, maybe. But what about all his stuff?

Work up your courage, Phil.

Don't be a pansy ass.

He touched in her number.
He did it fast so he wouldn't chicken out.
The phone rang and rang.
He got a message.
It sound rather formal, brittle.
It worried him.
It depressed him.

42

It was a day of it, out on the route for the first time, slinging those questions. "How important is praise? What kind of praise is best? Is praise always good? Are there some occasions when praise isn't good—even destructive? Are there some occasions when praise must be given to save self-esteem, even to save life?"

Encouraging respondents to respond—that was difficult. But worth it because the more survey data delivered from the electronic handheld device into Panegyric's electronic bank, the better. Quantity equals points. Points equal commission.

The survey form contained twenty questions, which fetched some malicious grins. "Twenty questions, huh? That's your job, is it? You have twenty questions for me, do you?"

Well, that was one response he got, sometimes directly spoken, sometimes strongly hinted at. Why couldn't they have made it eighteen, nineteen, twenty-one? A survey man got the butt end of the mockery.

His handheld recorder kept a running tally: six hundred questions at the end of the day. Sixty bucks. Sixty a day, three hundred a week. Based on a five-day work week, that is.

Professor Fellows had him in his office for a debriefing.

Then he opened the floor to questions.

Philip had a question: Could he try multiple participants at a given place?

"Stick to the list, Mr. Fellows," said the professor.

"I'm losing time walking, though."

"Some places do, in fact, call for multiple participants. Those are the juicy ones, economically speaking. For instance, one of your targets is MISHMASH—NO!" He gave Philip a knowing wink.

"That's the name—"

"Indeed it is. They do protest. Ah! One can't help but wonder."

"Oh." And then Philip wondered. He looked on his list of targets and found MISHMASH—NO! Multiple participants—and what was that about a Special List?

"Special List? Well," said the professor, "not only do you have multiple targets within the target itself, but the survey itself contains double the number of questions. Which is quite lucrative for you the interviewer—as you can well imagine. Only, our preliminary judgments of this particular target suggest that it's not exactly hospitable to questions at all."

"Oh, no," said Philip.

"Oh, yes," said the professor. "But turn on the charm. Engage in panegyrics yourself. If this doesn't work, you can always back off—or try a different strategy."

"Such as—"

"Perhaps intimidation?"

"Really?"

"I jest," said the professor. "I leave the matter to your judgment."

And so they concluded their meeting. But before they parted, Professor Fellows said: "Oh, a point of fact: You will find your commission for the day direct deposited in your account."

They parted. Philip was ecstatic. Money to spend.

He had no lodging, but at least he had food money.

Lodging.

I do not wish to lodge alone.

43

And so.
Sitting in a coffee shop, contemplating the matter.

Charlotte Sanders. An opportunity. An opportunity indeed. How often did one get a call from a woman who wanted you to come over and have fun? What kind of fun could that be if it wasn't *that* kind of fun? It had to be, didn't it?

He held the phone up. He studied the number.

She might be pretty; she might be ugly.

But look at the alternative: Tomorrow morning, the old whiskered guy arrives in the pitch dark—you're kicked out, your stuff confiscated. Gone.

He made the call.

The phone buzzed six or seven times. And then the voice. "Yeah? Hello."

Smoker's voice, raspy, and somewhat—irascible?

Charlotte Sanders.

"Hello. This is Philip . . . Fellows. I don't know if you remember me—you got my number by mistake."

Phone noises.

"Huh? Look, just a minute here—there's some damn noise out there. Damn jackhammering. Just a minute."

Jackhammering?

He waited. It was at least two minutes—maybe three.

Her voice came back on—raspy.

"Yeah. Okay, I'm in my bathroom. Away from all that. That jackhammering. Man, you talk about noise. Sewer backed up or something—they had to plow out the road with all this goddamned snow! You say Philip—Philip who?"

"Fellows. Philip Fellows. You know, you called me and I—"

"Oh, yeah. You."

"Yes, it's me."

"Yeah. I remember. You stiffed me. You stiffed me all the way to

Christmas. Didn't you?"

It wasn't exactly an angry voice, though somewhat abrasive, but maybe that was the smoker's voice part.

"I know . . . I got busy, and then with all the snow. You know."

"Snow? I know? I don't know anything. What's the snow got to do with it?"

"Well, getting around. You know."

It was snowing as hard as ever right now, so was this a good argument? Probably not, but it was all he had.

"Where are you?"

"Where?"

"Yes—do I stutter? I asked where you are."

"I'm in a coffee shop."

"Coffee shop. What the hell? But you could be here—here with my lovely self, is that not true?"

"Yes. And here's the thing—"

"What now?"

"Well—"

"Damn! I can't stand those *jackhammers*." Her voice snarled. "Really. What's your take on jackhammers?"

"My take?"

"Yes, goddamn it, your take? Do you: Check a box—like them or hate them?"

"I don't think I really—I don't really have an opinion."

"So . . . you're wanting to feast your eyes on your poor little Charlotte Sanders finally. That it?"

"Well, yes. I mean, I'm sorry I didn't contact you before, but with everything—"

"I'm not interested in your excuses. You're wanting to meet your poor little Charlotte. Is it true or not? Check a box."

"It's true."

"Why?"

"Why?"

"Yes—*why*? Do I stutter? Because you know you'd like me? Is that it? You just can't hold back any longer? Is that it?"

"Well—maybe."

275

"I can understand that. And if you want, you can come see poor little Charlotte. You've got my address, I guess. Didn't I give that to you?"

"Yes—but I've—"

"You've lost it."

"Yes."

"I'm not surprised. Men! Okay—here it is again. Are you ready?"

"Yes."

She gave it to him. Yes, now he remembered. That was a good ways from here, though.

"Well, you coming? Or you going to let down poor, sweet Charlotte like before?"

"I'm coming."

"Goddamn those jackhammers!"

"Sorry—sorry."

"What're you sorry about? You have nothing to do with it, do you?"

"No."

"Just come over. There's nothing you or I can do about them."

The snow was coming down harder, still harder. God, was it coming down!

"I'll get there. Somehow."

"In this snow? You must be pretty desperate."

"I've got to . . . move my stuff," he said.

"What stuff?"

"My stuff—in my apartment."

"What? Oh . . . *I* get it. You want to move in. That's it, isn't it?"

"No—not exactly."

"How not exactly?"

"I just need a place for a night. Or two. That's all, not long." He was thinking Tina, beautiful Tina, when she answered her phone, he'd be able to sleep on her couch—if he was half lucky. If he was all the way lucky, he'd get a much better arrangement than that. Of course, he would. You bet he would.

"Moving in with poor old Charlotte. What about Duane?"

"Duane."

"Don't act like you've never heard the name Duane."

"No—I know. Does he still live there?"

"Yeah. He lives here."

Silence. He had to cogitate on this.

"Well, then, I can't—"

"Sure you can."

"I can?"

"Yes—because right now he's not here. Look, I gotta get off the phone. Come or don't come. Those fucking jackhammers are driving me nuts! And god, the snow—will it never end?"

The phone went dead.

Only now it was ringing—incoming: *Sophia*.

"Sophia," he said.

"Philip."

"Yes?"

"Rod," she said.

"Rod?"

"He's cut out on me. He's cut out on me, can you believe?"

"Well. Yes," he said. "I can."

"You can?"

"Well, yes. He's not exactly the type—"

"Type to what?"

"Stick with a woman. Is he?"

"Not this time. And it's not fair!"

"Why'd he cut out?"

"Because. The apartment rent . . . and then there's this other woman—this CIA type. Oh, god."

"So she—"

"Look, it's not like I'm desperate, Philip!"

"No, of course not."

"But I do want something. I want something of you. I want a promise."

"Oh?"

"Well, you'd better. Because you do owe me, honey. It's not like you didn't screw the living daylights out of me—"

"Huh? Screw—"

"What would you call it?"

"*Screw—*"

"Oh, come on. Don't bother me with that! When I get upset, you know how I get crude and curse."

"You're upset."

"Hell, yes, because Rod—oh, god, I don't even want to talk about *him*. Just promise me. Will you?"

"What?"

"If Rod goes, you come. That simple."

"Sure. And I could come right now," he said. Yes: *Forget Charlotte Sanders and her jackhammers. And Duane and all the rest.*

"Don't get jumpy. I can't guarantee a thing. But just promise. I need that right now."

Back-up plan, huh?

But he said, "Sure." He tried not to sound desperate. He tried to sound bright and brilliant.

"Oh, Philip," she said. Her voice grew soft, satiny.

"Yes?"

"Oh, Philip. Oh, my dearest Philip."

"Yes?"

"I feel better. Bye for now."

"Bye," he said. He tried to say it matter-of-factly. He tried not to care.

"Bye, bye," she said.

44

Good to move out of this creepy hell-hole. God, what a stinky, slimy cavern this truly was. Where exactly was that smell coming from? For some reason, it seemed important to know. Before one left. A sort of postmortem on one's old life: the essence of stink.

You enter the bathroom—yep, there it is. You stand in the living room. Yep, there it is. You go into the kitchen. Yep, there it is.

Gas smell? What? Open the door into the hall. Yep, there it is—worse! Something sick, spoiled, rotted, a mix of garbage, oil, and human mortality—you expected to see a corpse lying about, rotting.

Maybe there was one—in the walls.

Probably dead rats.

Other vermin.

Time to clear out.

Finally, finally.

But what about all the books?

So much to take:

His laptop.

His sheets of printed-out poetry, his pencils, pens, legal pads, notebooks, paper clips, and so forth.

And the other things: covers, sheets, pillow, pillow cases, towels, washcloths, toilet articles, toilet paper. Necessary. All necessary.

Clothes! Two suits. Casual clothes, underwear, socks, ties. All required.

He began packing.

Books first.

Good thing he had a half dozen empty boxes piled in the closet.

Heavy boxes, they'd sure be. Cumbersome to carry.

Philip went to the window. Wondering.

He saw the man in black standing on the opposite side of the street looking up at him. He banged the window. "You bastard!"

279

He went back to it.

Suitcase, shirts, and suits in his arms. He laid them on the bed.

He made his way down the stairs to the lobby, box by heavy box. He piled the boxes in a corner. He returned to his room, and he carried down his suits. He carried down his suitcase. He carried down shirts, trousers, jeans. He went down with his last item—the boxed set of *A Pictorial History of the Slaughter of War*.

And he stood in the smelly lobby and called a cab.

Philly, my boy, this place is history.

45

I t was dark.

The cab pulled around a big hole in the road guarded by orange barrels.

Jackhammers.

Philip stepped out of the cab, and the driver did too. The man started hefting the boxes out of the trunk, setting them on the snow-packed road. And the clothes, laying them on the boxes. Then more from the back seat. Philip assisted him. And then he paid the cabbie fifteen bucks and thought, *about forty-five left*, and the cab drove off.

He couldn't see the house itself, only a vague suggestion of it, topping the wall of snow along the road. But suddenly a lantern appeared through a crevice, wide enough to walk through, and he saw her standing there on the front porch, partly illuminated in a yellowish glow.

She was a trim woman, but she was built. He could see that. Narrow in the waist, curvy hips. She'd be something to fasten your eyes on—and more.

He hoisted a box of books and made his way through that cleft in the snow wall, over a cleared path toward the door, where she stood swinging that lantern.

"Jeez, will you look at you. Books," she said.

She opened the front door, and he set the box in the front room filled with lighted candles glowing.

He went back for more boxes. He hoisted them all in and then carried the clothes in, and his suitcase, and it was a couple of piles against the living room wall. He suddenly felt odd—like he was returning home from a semester at college, and here was his mother. But this woman wasn't anything like his mother; she was some nice looking woman with a hank of dirty blond hair. She'd said she was nice looking. She was. Only that abrasive smoker's voice. Eliminate that and—

She stood there shaking her head, lighting a cigarette.

It was cold. But she wasn't dressed like it. Sweat shirt, jeans, white socks, and jogging shoes. That was the extent of it. Like it was a cool, breezy fall day.

"Aren't you cold?" he asked.

"Cold? No. I'm not cold-natured. Besides, days I leave all the curtains open, and that brings the sun in, what there is of it, and like I say, I'm not the cold type. Hell, I can barely make it through the summer. I blast the air cons, all ten of them, all day."

"Yeah," he said.

"Well, come on—follow me. Take a box there. To the basement."

"Okay," he said.

He got a box cradled in his arms and followed her.

She stopped in the kitchen, with several lighted candles on the table. "That's the basement door." She rapped it with her knuckles.

"Okay."

"Get your boxes down there."

"Sure."

"The clothes—I'll take all that and hang it up. Oh, suits. I'll bet you look like a snazzy young beast in those threads. Don't you now?"

He liked a certain skeptical smile she got on her face. Her lips trembled slightly. There was a sensuousness to them. They looked wet. Moist, yes moist. He could see that in the candlelight.

"I guess so." But he knew so. He did look sharp in those suits. He could land a good job in them if there were any good jobs to land. You didn't need to wear a suit to do the Panegyrics work. Business casual—that was the best. Don't look overdressed was his thought.

"I'll just bet." She yanked open the basement door. "Dark down there."

"Power's out," he said.

"Why hell yes. Been that way forever."

"How do you manage?"

"Not easy. No hot water, no heat, no nothing. It comes in waves, you know. First, I thought, 'I'm hearing all these reports, but it's not me. I'm going to be okay, okay,' but then, it hit. Like a shadow creeping, only I wouldn't call it creeping. It moved real fast when it started that creeping."

"Too bad," he said.

"Yeah, too bad. Here," she said, and went for a kitchen cabinet. She came back with a flashlight and thrust it at him. "You'll need this."

She took off. He watched her hips wiggling.

He went for more boxes and piled them next to the basement door. And then he carried the boxes down to the basement, one by one, cradled in his arms, the flashlight gripped in his right hand, his left arm grazing the wooden handrail.

Step by step. Cautious now. Cautious.

You could fall. You could fall. All the way down.

Like some dark abyss.

Back upstairs, done with the boxes, he saw all of the clothes were now gone. She was in the living room, sitting, smiling. He approached her, and she stood and pointed toward the kitchen. "You want something? To eat?"

"Sure."

"I cook stuff outside. Set a fire under it. Right out there in my backyard. What do you want? Hot dogs, burgers, chips—you name it."

"I don't know—any of that, I guess."

"Yeah, sure. I know that look. I know what you want."

He couldn't help it. She was a luscious looking one, once you got past that voice, and besides, she'd called *him*, wanting him to come over. She spoke of fun. Spoke of get it now, or it might be too late. And he was horny. He hadn't been getting it at all.

"Well, I could use something to eat," he said.

"Don't think I'm a pushover," she said, wagging a finger. "I'm no whore. If that's what you think. Got it?"

"Yes."

"Good. Then let's go out and I'll fix us some burgers, if that's what you want. And chips to go with it? And beer?"

"Yeah."

"Refrigerator stuff's in the snow. Keeps it cold that way. Bring that flashlight with you."

He was still clutching it.

"Right," he said.

In the kitchen, she motioned at the newspapers, a small sack of firewood, kindling, and kitchen matches. "Come on," she said. "Let's get this stuff out there." She grabbed a frying pan.

They both loaded down.

She swung the storm door on its hinges, but it took a few tries to get it to stay shut. Out in the backyard, she grabbed his flashlight and played it about—against milk jugs, plastic bottles, two-liter bottles of pop, butter, blocks of cheese, jars of pickles, mayonnaise, frozen vegetables, twelve packs of beer, bundles covered in tinfoil, and so forth.

"Wow," he said.

"Wow yourself. You gotta live, you know. Don't you?"

"Yes. You do."

"You think I'll ever get power again? Maybe sometime next year. But you watch: When the snow starts to melt we'll have rivers. I'll need a boat. And until then—you know it's supposed to snow another twelve inches tomorrow? That's right, another goddamn twelve inches. Like we don't have enough. But what can we do about it? You tell me. What? Just survive it, is what I say."

"Why is it?" he said. "Why more snow? I just don't get it."

"You're asking me?"

"Well, yes, I guess so."

"You don't watch the weather?"

"No—I don't have a TV."

"You have power?"

"Yes. Where I was."

"No TV."

"No."

"Funny."

"What's funny?"

"Never mind."

"How do you know the weather—without power?"

284

"Me? I keep my ear to the ground."

"Oh."

"Here. Help me get a fire going."

She cleared snow away, and he saw a pit. She assembled her newspapers, kindling, and firewood. She struck a kitchen match.

He saw a grill close by.

Like a Boy Scout, he thought.

It took a little while to get it going. And then he could see her body in the glow of it.

"That's good," he said, warming his hands. "All fired up."

She warmed her hands too.

"It's going to snow, snow, snow, and so you keep that in mind." Then she shot him a nasty grin. "You might be stuck here when good old Duane gets back. You want that?" She stoked the fire in her pit. She set the grill over it.

"No."

"He's got a good left, I'll tell you. And a good right too."

"Oh."

"I'm just kidding. Duane's a real pushover. He'll probably try to convince you to stay. That's Duane."

"Really?"

"Probably wouldn't even care if you slept with me. That's Duane."

"Oh—but no, I don't think—"

"I'm just kidding. No, Duane would never go with that. That's not Duane. What Duane would like is a fellow poker player. Blackjack. Duane loves blackjack. And sports. Of course you can't watch sports with the power off, but he'll whip out the paper and he'll want to talk, talk, talk sports. You into sports?"

"No—not really."

"Bad for Duane, I guess."

He watched her in the light of the dancing fire. She was leaning over, and she was looking good.

"I'll have to be leaving soon," he said.

"You bet you better."

"Really?"

"You bet you'd better."

She was crouched down, unwrapping a bundle of tinfoil. Hamburger. Making patties, laying them out in the frying pan, setting it on the grill.

Then she stood up.

"Well," he said, and he came up to her and put his arm around her waist. God, she was beautiful. Her body, that is. That scratch pad of a voice, that was too bad, but you couldn't help but get beyond that.

"What're you doing?"

But she didn't move his hand away.

"I don't know—just touching," he said.

"Well, my, my, and my."

"You're Duane's, huh?" he said.

"Oh, well, I might be, and I might not be."

"When's he coming?"

"Oh, any time, practically any time."

"When?"

"My, my, and my. You *are* something."

"Please," he said. "When?"

She swung his hand away and confronted him, eyes piercing blue. "I liked you better before."

Her eyes danced in the flickering light of the fire.

"Before?"

"Get tough," she said.

"Tough?"

"I stutter?"

"Let's go to bed."

"Oh, that's original."

"I'm serious."

"Oh, I expect you are serious. I wouldn't doubt that—not one bit." She bent over again, and took a spatula to the patties.

"Now," he said. "I want you now."

She looked up at him and laughed. "Not working. Was working, not working now."

It did feel uncomfortable. He wasn't one to boss women around.

"I'm sorry," he said.

"What? You're sorry?"

"Yes, I'm sorry. I'll go."

"Right after you dumped all that stuff in my house? You're ready to trot?"

"In the morning."

"Suit yourself."

They had hamburgers and chips and cold beer. They sat in the living room on a couch with a dozen lighted candles. He tried to get his arms around her, but she wouldn't have it.

"Duane's coming," she crooned. "Duane's coming."

"Soon?"

"You can never tell."

He got up, went into the kitchen. He was bored. Really, why shouldn't he be? He whipped out his cell phone and called Tina.

No answer. Where in the hell was she?

He returned to the living room. He took a chair, across the room from her.

"I wish," he said, "we could do something. Isn't there something to do around here?"

"Like what? Screw?"

He recoiled at the language. If she'd just put it another way. "Well," he said.

"Give it up."

"I just wish we could do more than sit here."

"I suppose, if you act right, you could sit next to me," she said.

"You don't mind?"

"The question is," she said, "does Duane mind?"

"Does he?"

"Hell, no."

"Then if you don't mind, I think I'll come over there."

She patted the place next to her.

He went right over.

"You, you, you," she said.

"Me." Again he tried to get his arms around her.

"No," she said. "No."

"Okay."

"You know, most people don't have the slightest idea about keeping a house," she said. "Do they?"

"House? Keeping a house?"

"I'm not repeating myself."

"Keeping a house."

"That's what I said. I mean, really, you probably think I don't know squat about keeping a house, but then what can you do when some guy comes and dumps a pile of stuff on you?"

"I'm sorry. I won't live here forever."

"No, you won't. Duane, he doesn't know the first thing about keeping a house. Beer cans here, beer cans there—your garden variety junk food wrappers here and there, and then cigarettes stamped out. Here and there. I do hope you're not like that. If you are, you might as well take off right now because one Duane is enough in the Duane department."

"I'm not like that," said Philip.

"I'll bet. I'll just bet. Men are so tremendously sloppy! I can't believe how sloppy men are."

He noticed some sort of paper bag on the floor, up against a wall. The light of the candle threw a distorted shadow on the wall. "What's that?" he said, pointing. "Duane's work?"

"You think it's mine?"

"No."

"I'll assure you, it's not mine. You know what? I left it there just where it landed. Good old Duane wanted a sandwich and apple for lunch. He comes home with the bag I fixed him up with, and he drops it on the coffee table there. And leaves it. And then pretty soon, the dog, she carries it over there—and that's where it will remain. Right there, and I'm not picking it up. I've had it with picking up, picking up—get this, get that. I've had it."

"Where's the dog?"

"It was the neighbor's dog."

"In here?"

"That you can credit Duane with. Okay?"

"Yeah."

"You bet *yeah*."

"You two married?"

"Duane and me married? No. We're not, and never will be. Unless we make a big mistake. Or me, if I make a big mistake."

He had to know: "How long have you been living together?"

"Ages and ages—too long, I'll say that. Whatever it is, it's too long."

"How long, though?"

"You have to know. You're a curious sort of fella, aren't you?"

"I don't need to know."

"Four years if you have to know. Four years longer than we should've been."

"Then why—"

"Why still together? Hell, that's the way it is sometimes, unless you live on a different planet than me. Or Duane. That's what happens. Two people get together and they don't get apart. Who can explain it? You ever had a bad stomach ache?"

"Yeah."

"You go and cut your stomach out?"

"No."

"You waited till it got better, I expect. And that's what people do, only it don't get better. And that's me and Duane. We don't get better."

"I'm sorry."

"No, you're not." She moved up closer to him and stuck her arm around him. "But thanks for saying it."

He moved closer to her.

"Don't get any ideas. Sitting like this doesn't mean any more than sitting like this."

It was nice, though, and he could use his imagination.

"Wonder what time it is," he said.

"You always do that?"

"What?"

"Wonder what time it is?"

"Not always."

"Well, quit it. Time's a flying. Enjoy each minute. It may be your last."

He sat still with his hand migrating finally to her knee. She didn't say anything, or at least she didn't do anything.

"I hear him," said Charlotte.

He listened. "I don't hear anything."

"You don't hear *that*?"

He listened. "No . . ."

"You don't hear that."

"No." *Thunk.* "Yeah, yeah. I hear it."

"That's Duane's car. It goes like that thunkety, thunkety down the road. He's about two houses away now. That's the Badgers. He's at the Badgers."

Thunk.

"Who're the Badgers?"

"What the hell difference does it make? Could it make? You going to hook up with the Badgers?"

"No."

"Wouldn't do it. They got a meth lab. The damn thing's going to blow any day."

Thunk!

"I better—" He got up.

"Oh, sit down. He don't care. That's one thing about Duane. He don't care. Just generally, that'd be one true thing I'd say about Duane. *He don't care.*"

She went to the door. He went to the window.

Outside he could hear a car motor, and then he saw the flash of headlights through that crevice in the snow wall. "Where's he going to park?"

"On the road probably. That's where he usually parks."

"Really?"

"That's what I said."

They waited.

There was Duane now, shovel in hand, on the top of the snow wall.

"Maybe he needs some help."

"Going to take on that wall again. Yeah, probably does. I got a second shovel in the garage."

"Okay." He started to go.

"Take your flashlight," she said.

He grabbed it.

He went back through the kitchen and opened the door into the garage. There was a snow shovel right there, just past the entrance. He found the garage door with the aid of his flashlight, and when he yanked it up, he saw Duane up there on the wall of snow, like the king of the mountain.

46

"Howdy!"

"Hello. You need help?" He had his shovel ready for action, and he made his way out to Duane. He cast his flashlight up.

There he stood, a tall skinny man with a cowboy hat parked on his head, cowboy boots, a red bristly looking beard, and huge orange sunglasses. Or at least they looked orange.

He approached the snow pile, flashing his light.

"Hey, what's with the light?"

"Sorry. I'm Philip."

"Duane. I'd shake your hand, only you're way the hell down *there*." He lit a cigarette. "You going to help, are you?"

"Right."

"Come on up."

"Come up there?"

"Yeah. Start at the top—see?"

"Why at the top?"

"You want to start at the bottom?"

"Well. No—"

"How'd you like all this to fall straight on you?"

"No—"

"Like the sky falling. That's the way they are, I've said half my life. The sky's always a-falling. And you know, sometimes I just up and do a thing or two to *keep* it from falling. I use the old head I've got, right here."

"Start at the top, then."

"That's the way," said Duane. "Come on up."

"Okay." Philip dug a foot in and started mounting the snow wall, flashlight jammed in his jeans, shovel in his right hand. It took him a half minute or so, slipping, sliding, but he was eventually there, shaking Duane's hand. Duane was big on hand-shaking. He could see that.

"You keeping Charlotte company?"

"Yeah."

"Didn't try anything, did you?"

"No—no. Of course not." He hoped his voice wasn't shaky. But it sounded a little shaky.

"Well, I'm glad to hear it. I don't know if I can believe it, but I'll take your word for it, and I'm happy to hear it."

They still shook hands. Is he going to *release*? Philip wondered.

"Time we got to the task," said Duane. "Hey!" He was waving, and Philip saw Charlotte standing outside now, in front of the door with that lantern. He wanted her. So bad he wanted her. But now with Duane here—what was the chance?

Philip began to shovel, and then it occurred to him. Where? Where pitch the snow? "We can't shovel this into the street."

"No, buddy," said Duane. "We shovel it into the yard."

Duane's car was illegally parked. But he guessed that was business as usual.

"Aren't you worried about your car?"

"Nope."

"Why not?" He began shoveling heaps toward the yard.

"Because if it gets smacked, that's up to them. Up to them," said Duane shoveling and pitching snow heaps.

"Up to . . . whom?"

"Who?"

"Yes."

"Them. You know . . . whomever smacks the damn thing. You know?"

"Oh, right. But it's not . . . *whomever*, is it?"

"They want to hit it? Well, go ahead—hit it."

Philip turned and looked. He cast his flashlight over it. Well, it wouldn't be too big of a loss—not really. Several big dents in that black dog of a machine, and a bashed-in hood. How did that happen?

"We'd better hurry," said Philip.

"Why's that?"

Why answer that?

"This could take all day," said Philip.

"Why's that?"

"Why's what?"

"Why the big hurry? You want a heart attack, buddy?"

"Me? A heart attack?"

"How old're you? Twenty, thirty? What're you there, buddy?"

"Twenty-four."

"Twenty-four. Well . . . you could have one. You bet you could. Just drop dead in a flash. Hey, you gonna help out, or just stand there and gawk?"

"Sorry." He went back to shoveling.

"Yeah, you could have one. I seen one guy that was even younger drop dead just like that." Duane snapped his fingers. "Just like *that*. Whammo."

"Really?"

"Here one minute, gone the next. You tell me."

"What?"

"What?"

"Tell you what?"

"Hey, don't give me a hard time there, buddy. I don't take to a hard time."

"I didn't mean to."

"I'll tell you *what*." Duane shoveled snow hard, and pitched a boulder of it into the yard. "You got but one chance to make it big in this world, and you don't wanta miss that chance. That's why *her* in there"—he stopped shoveling, and jabbed the shovel into the snow pile. He leaned on his shovel, groaning. Car lights flashed by his black dog.

"Yes?"

"Yes, what?"

"About *her* in there."

"What about her?"

"You were saying—"

"Oh, yeah. She's the one for me, buddy boy, the very one, and I'd take and shoot my head off, don't think I wouldn't, if she ever give up on me. Just like that. Take and shoot my goddamned head off."

"You really would?"

"That surprise you?"

"I wouldn't do that," said Philip. "That would be . . . a bad thing to do. Very bad."

"You think so, huh? Well, see, I don't. It'd be the only thing I could see doing if that woman left me, and you can bet she's threatened to do it, too. Scares me bad, buddy boy, I'll tell you. Hey, get to shoveling, willya? I got one car, and one car only, and pretty soon I might not have even that. Jeez."

"I thought you said—"

"What?" Duane was shoveling hard. That shovel was going, going.

"Nothing."

"Well, spit it out."

"I thought you said you didn't care about that car."

"I don't."

"But you don't want it hit."

"Hell, no, I don't want it hit. What'd give you the idea I want it hit?"

"Because what you said was—"

"You know what? You run at the mouth, buddy boy. You might oughta give me more of a hand here. You ever heard of diarrhea of the mouth?"

"Yeah."

"Bad thing, that is. Some's got it, and it's bad. How do you clear it up? You can't take nothing for it."

"I don't like what you're saying—or suggesting," said Philip. He thought, you don't have to take this. Not from the likes of Duane whoever he was. You don't have to.

"You like beer?"

"Beer?"

"I stutter?"

"No—yes, I like beer. Of course I like beer."

"Like it with ice cream?"

"No!"

"Hell, who does? You ask practically anybody, and they'll tell you. It's no good with ice cream."

He had to ask: "Did somebody, was there somebody who thought it *was* good with ice cream?"

Duane thrust the shovel into the snow and pitched another boulder of snow into the yard. He stopped. "No. Did I say there was?"

"No."

"Well, hell, Philip."

They shoveled for another hour, got the pile down pretty good, not much of a hump, and then Duane yelled out, "Okay, buddy boy, it's time!"

"Okay," said Philip.

"Stand clear."

"Okay."

Duane was stomping toward his car, then climbing in.

He watched the car lights go on and then the car backing into the bare spot they'd created in the wall of snow. It was a wider cleft than the one with the path to the front door. He was curious. Why didn't Duane do this more often? Why park in the frigging road? He had to ask. Duane stepped out of the car, flicking his cigarette.

"Hell, I don't know, Philip. Sometimes I just do that. Okay with you?"

"Yeah, sure. The cops don't get you?"

"A citation or two," said Duane.

"Oh. Well—"

"Well, about time to eat," said Duane, his cigarette glowing. "You're gonna have to go to the store for the beer, buddy boy, at least the kind I like."

"Go to the store." He looked around. "Where's the store?"

"Gimme your flashlight."

Philip handed it to him.

"Maybe a quarter mile or less over thataway."

"In the dark."

"She's on that service road. You can't miss her."

"Oh, I don't know. No—"

"Take your flashlight. You can walk it. And get some chips when you go. And my favorite of all time—gummy snakes."

47

Duane shoved some money at him, a wad, and Philip hoofed it down the service road, flashlight in hand. Most of it had been plowed recently, so it wasn't too much trouble. He saw the lights of a store up ahead. By auxiliary power source, surely. It felt good to step in out of the cold. Warm. Lighted. Civilization, he thought. He bought a six pack and a couple bags of chips, some candy bars— and Duane's favorite: gummy snakes. It was the last package. After that, it was gunny rhinos, gummy hyenas, and gummy rabbits.

"That's odd, what you're selling in the gummy line," said Philip.

"What's odd about it?" said the cashier.

He trekked back with a couple of bags, and he was exhausted by the time he was knocking on Charlotte and Duane's door. It had been a long day. And all that snow shoveling.

"Hell, if it's you, come on in!" That was Duane.

He stepped in and half dropped the bag.

"You don't need to knock, son," said Duane.

He still had his cowboy hat parked on his head, his boots planted on the coffee table, but he'd removed his large, round sunglasses. Why that orange? His eyes looked bright, piercing. There was a pertness to them, the way they fixed on you, then sort of danced about.

"Okay."

"When you leaving?"

"Pardon?"

"When're you packing up that stuff down there and getting the hell out of Dodge?" said Duane, only he grinned.

"Soon."

"Yeah—have you some beer and chips first, hey?"

"Yeah."

"Take a load off. You look like a dead man there, son."

"I feel like a dead man."

Charlotte lit a cigarette and cackled. "He's not dead. I'll bet if you gave him half a chance he'd be all over little me."

"The way it is," said Duane. "You don't change a thing no matter the regulations, no matter the stuff they say, no matter what they come up with. You don't change a thing. A man's gotta do what a man's gotta do."

"What the hell are you talking about?" said Charlotte.

"Huh?"

"What regulations?"

Duane had the six pack in hand, and he was passing out beers. And then he ripped into a sack of chips and grabbed a handful. "Well, whatever they come up with when they do. I guess you'd know, wouldn't you. Same as me."

"You're full of it. You don't know a thing you're talking about."

"She's always a-saying that," said Duane.

"Because it's true."

"I've got to leave pretty soon," said Philip.

"Hell, you say. You sure bet your ass you do. We're running out of food around this place," said Duane. He looked at Charlotte. "Ain't that right?"

"Last time I checked. But then if you didn't eat like a total hog, maybe we wouldn't be."

"A man's a hog, a hog's a man," said Duane.

"Where do you come up with such crap?" said Charlotte. She looked at Philip. "Where? Where does he?"

"Huh?"

Duane's eyes flickered. "Me, I could use a bit of hog meat about now."

"You and your hog meat."

"Where you going?" said Duane. "And when?"

"First, let me check on something."

"Sure, you go ahead and check."

He went into the kitchen, and then stepped into the garage. Here he could make a private phone call. He touched in Tina's number.

"Hello?"

"Hello."

"Oh, *hello*, Philip. How are you? I see that you tried to call—I would have called back, but, well, it's been one thing and another.

I've been having to hold Sebastian's hand. This thing with his new woman isn't working out, and so he comes to me. Can you imagine?"

"Well."

"You probably can. I suspect most men are like that to a degree. Aren't they? No offense."

"I don't know—maybe."

"But he's back with her now. Nothing I said or did, I'm sure. Or maybe it was, but anyway he's back with her. Only my ceiling. Tommy stopped by and fixed it."

"Fixed it?"

"It needed a hole, Tommy said. You should see it. He's rigged something up there. Quite odd. Quite strange."

"I need a place to stay—for a while. I was evicted."

"Evicted? Oh, how awful. And you want to stay here?"

"Yes—if I can." He got a mournful tone. First his girl crapped out on him, then that.

"That awful girl. When it rains, huh?"

"I guess so."

"I guess I can give you a couch," said Tina.

"Thanks." He paused. "I do have several boxes to bring. Clothes, and so forth. Do you have a place—for storage?"

Silence. "Well, I suppose."

"That'd be good, really good."

"When are you coming?"

"Soon—if that would be okay."

"Yes—I guess. You come on over. The couch is yours—that's fine."

He got the directions.

They ended the call.

Philip went into the living room. Duane was downing a beer and had a hand stuck in the chips bag.

"Well, if it ain't."

"I've got a place. Can you give me a lift?"

"A place! Why, sure, buddy. Why, sure. Right now, right? You haul that stuff up from the basement—okay?" He motioned at

299

Charlotte. "She told me about it, chief. Your deal there—so you haul it all up, got it?"

"Sure."

"Because I ain't hauling it. Not me. You're the one doing the hauling. Got it, chief?"

"Yes," said Philip.

"He understands, he understands, he *understands*," said Charlotte. "Jeez."

"It's okay," said Philip. "I don't mind."

"Good there, buddy," said Duane. "Because my own ass is just plain tired." He stretched out more, banging his boots on the coffee table.

"You give him a hand," said Charlotte. "And I mean it."

"I told you—"

"You didn't tell me a thing. Nothing I'm listening to."

"Okay, okay."

"Get on down there and give him a hand."

"Okay, okay."

Flashlight in hand, Philip went on down the stairs to the basement, and behind him he could hear the thunderous boots of Duane gaining on him.

They began to haul up the boxes. It took three trips each. He took the boxed set of *A Pictorial History of the Slaughter of War* last. Charlotte was bringing the clothes on hangers. It took another twenty minutes to load up the car. He bid goodbye to Charlotte, and she hugged him. She hugged him for too long, he thought, suspiciously long, and then she kissed his neck, and then she planted a long one on his lips.

"What the hell's this about?" said Duane.

"You pay attention to your own business," said Charlotte.

"That *is* my business."

"It's your business if I say so."

"Can't reason with a woman like that," said Duane. "You ready?"

"Ready."

They headed out to the car.

"Where to, chief?"

"The library first. I have to drop off something."

"Where to then?"

He gave him the directions.

"Be a miracle if we get out of this here," said Duane.

The car spun and spun and went into a snow drift. But Duane got it backed out somehow, and they were on their way.

"You know what?" said Duane.

"What?"

"We oughta get some donuts is what we oughta do. You like donuts?"

"Yeah, I like donuts."

"Seems to me it's been a whole year since I had some donuts. Well, I had some maybe a couple months ago, but were they good? No, they were not. But see I want good donuts, not just your average. You see what I'm saying?"

"Sure."

They drove for fifteen minutes, with Duane looking for a donut shop. "You don't find good donuts just anyplace. It's got to be certain places. See what I mean?"

"Yeah."

"Not just anyplace."

"I know," said Philip.

"Hey," said Duane, "I just thought of the real place. The real donut place."

He made a sharp turn at a corner and sped up, sliding on the snow-packed street.

"Where?"

"The damn finest place in town as far as donuts go. You know what, buddy?"

"What?"

"It all comes down to food. That's what it all comes down to. There isn't anything, and I mean anything, in this world more important than food. Okay, junk food. Okay, chips, donuts, beer— what have you—but you tell me, what if there wasn't them things? What kind of world would we be looking at here? Huh? Africa? Some goddamned place without civilization and its rewards?"

"Its rewards?"

"Picked that up, buddy, right on the old radio here," said Duane. He thwacked it with a finger.

"Oh."

"But before you stuck your shovel in, what I was saying was this here: If you don't have those little pleasures, what's life worth, buddy? Nothing, nothing, nothing—like you're not even *alive*. Huh? Huh? You tell me I'm wrong. Go ahead."

The car made a sharp turn and rammed into a lot in front of Donut Castle. It was lighted up like a huge sparkling diamond.

"Wow," said Philip. "I'm hungry too."

"You see," said Duane. "You see? What if this place, a place like this, didn't exist, buddy? You might as well go cut your throat because I'm telling you, there'd be no reason to go on." He grew serious looking, and was that a tear in his eye dripping down?

"What—what's wrong?"

"She hates me, buddy. Damn it, but it's true. She hates me."

"No, no," said Philip. "She doesn't hate you."

He adjusted his cowboy hat. "Well, I hope not. I sure do hope not. But I'm telling you, and I say it again: This, right there, that's the kind of thing that keeps me a-going, buddy. You need your fill-up now and then. We're creatures with our regular animal needs."

"Radio?" said Philip.

"Huh?"

"Did that come from the radio?"

"What?"

"That bit about 'regular animal needs'?"

"Oh, hell, I don't . . . yeah, guess it did. From one of them things I heard. We all have'm, you know. Regular animal needs. I like the ring of it, don't you?"

"Yeah, I guess."

"Let's go get some donuts."

In Donut Castle, they sat eating one after another—cream-filled, cake, glazed—and drinking a pot of coffee. Donuts at night. It was good.

"Nothing like this stuff to meet those regular animal needs," said Duane.

"Do you think?" said Philip, "that people are just meat machines?"

"Do I think *what*?"

"Meat machines. You know, that's all they are is meat, bone, and blood."

"Hell, what else is there—you wanta try making it without them parts, buddy boy!"

"What about an immaterial soul?"

Duane chewed a glazed donut. "If you're asking if I'm like *religious*, I'd have to say no. We was brought up Catholic and Southern Baptist, but neither of us, hell, we ain't been to a church in . . ." He held up fingers and counted. "I'll bet it's going on five years, and that was a funeral."

"No. I don't mean that. Do you think people have minds? Or just *brains*?"

"You ain't got a brain, you ain't got a mind. You got a brain, you got one. Simple as that. Hell, Philip, don't be stupid."

"So all we are is meat machines."

"Jeez! You some goddamned butcher?"

Philip stuffed a cake donut in his mouth, and drank coffee.

"No."

"Can't watch the game tonight. Could go to a sports bar and watch it, but then, she'd be a bitching and a moaning."

"Sorry."

"At least I got the paper. You think they'll win?"

"I don't know."

"Well, hell, Philip. You got on opinion on it? Or not?"

"No."

"Well, hell."

Cards next, he thought.

But suddenly Duane was rising from the table. They took off.

Duane stopped off at the public library. He pulled into the parking lot, which was surrounded by a wall of snow, with only a few cars parked in the bladed spaces. Of course it was growing late. It had started to snow, and Duane mentioned getting back fast.

"I got plans back there," said Duane.

"I don't want to hear of them," said Philip.

"Jealous?"

"I just don't want to hear of them."

"Suit yourself."

Philip stepped into the library with his boxed set of *A Pictorial History of the Slaughter of War.* He hoped to drop it off, make haste, leave, get in Duane's car, and start his new life.

But there he was: Adam Most.

"Philip, Philip, Philip, where have you *been*?"

"Here and there. Everywhere."

"Well, sit down."

"I can't. Somebody's waiting for me. Out in his car."

"Oh—well, how was *A Pictorial History*?" He pointed at it as the librarian checked it back in.

"It was okay—actually, I didn't get to it."

"Yeah—typical. Who wants to, huh? We need stuff on the lighter side, don't we? But I've got just the thing, Philip. I've been reading savagely, reading, skimming, reading savagely, skimming, skimming, skimming. And please, if you don't mind, if you just *would*—"

He turned and darted off, only he swung around a few times, apparently to make sure that Philip was, in fact, still waiting. He hurried back with an armload of books.

"Here, here, here—these. Books on happiness, Philip. Remember—I spoke of them? The nature of happiness. It's all the rage. We are creatures, you see, who need, who want, a full measure of happiness. It's the secret of life. It's the meaning of life. You must be happy or—"

"You're sad?"

"Yes, and who wants to be sad?"

"Not me."

"Then check these out. Do check these out."

There must have been twenty books in that pile.

"You haven't read all of these."

"Skimming, Philip. We must learn to skim. And read savagely in key spots."

"I could check out a few. But not—"

"Please," pleaded Adam. "All of them. You must read them all to understand, to comprehend, any of them. Please, then, check each and every one out."

The librarian had a wry grin on her face.

The best thing was not to make a scene. Check them all out. Bring them all back. Don't make a scene. It's always best not to make a scene.

"Okay," he said.

Adam worked the books into three piles.

Philip handed the librarian his card.

Soon, he had an armful. He feared them sliding into a snow bank.

"You won't be sorry," said Adam. "I'm a happy man, believe me. Awesome! How awesome it all is!"

"I hope so," said Philip.

"Well, you bet it is!" Adam Most backed away. "I'm back to reading. And I've asked the librarian—haven't I, ma'am?—to order more. Haven't I?"

"Indeed he has," said the librarian, but she didn't look up.

Philip got out of there.

"More?" said Duane. "Damn!"

"Don't you want to be happy?" said Philip.

Duane lit up a cigarette. "Yeah? You going to make me happy, buddy? I'll be happy when I get this carload of crap over to . . . where'd you say it was?"

He gave him the directions again.

The snow was coming harder.

"Hope I don't get stranded," said Duane, blowing smoke. "You think that'll make me happy?"

They pulled up in front of Tina's place. The house was lighted. Power!

Duane got the trunk opened.

"I'm not lugging in that stuff," said Duane. "You brought it, you lug it."

"It'll take longer, then."

"Take all the time you want. Piss on old Duane."

"I don't feel that way," said Philip, grabbing a box of books.

"Sure you do. Everybody does. Duane—there's your man to piss on."

But he hefted up a box, and Philip could hear him crunching the snow-packed sidewalk behind him.

Philip got to the porch and almost slipped. "Watch out, it's slippery!"

Too late.

Duane slid. He fell on the steps. "Goddamn!"

"Hey! You okay? You okay?"

"My goddamn knees. My—I'm going to sue the hell out of you, Philip."

Worth ignoring.

"You peckerwood, I'm not bringing another box." He picked up his cowboy hat and pushed it down over his forehead. "Go ahead, take all day, let poor old Duane sit in the car and freeze and face the blizzard and the snowy roads all the way back in the pitch dark to the other end of town. What's Duane expect? That's just what he does expect. Has always expected." And then he turned and trudged toward the car. He started to slide in those boots, but he righted himself and let out a raucous curse.

Philip hurried back to get things out of the car. There was no reason to make poor old Duane wait while he carried stuff up. Leave it on the sidewalk. Well, if this *was* the sidewalk. But with this snow . . . ?

He pulled out boxes while Duane sat in the car, red embers of his cigarette glowing in the dark. He lay his suits over the boxes of books. Out here away from the lighted house, it was hard to see.

And then when he had everything out of the trunk of the car, and the backseat too, everything spread out on the snow-covered sidewalk, he came around to Duane. He rapped on the window, and the window slid down. "I'm done. Thanks for the ride, Duane."

"Yeah, yeah. Hey, they was some good donuts, though, wasn't they? Think I'll stop off at the Castle and get a dozen before going back. Now that'd be nice, and the woman, she'd like it too. Old Charlotte does like her donuts." He raced the motor. He flicked his cigarette.

"You do that," said Philip. He went around to the back of the car and patted it the way you'd pat the flank of a horse.

He got on the sidewalk and stood watching.

The car took off, and slid all over the road. But there wasn't anybody coming.

Good for Duane.

Probably never see the man again. Never see Charlotte again. History. Both of them.

48

He started hefting the boxes up to the porch. Pretty soon the porch light came on.

There stood Tina on the porch, waving.

My, she was a lovely looking woman. She bent over and grabbed up a box and then turned and carried it into the house.

Now he'd be living with Tina. Better, much better than anything before. Better than Sophia, Lisa, Charlotte—the best, really.

How could it ever be better?

He hoisted more boxes on the porch, and then he went back and got more. Tina was again leaning over grabbing up a box. She disappeared inside.

He knocked on the door.

"Come in!"

He went in, stood in the living room.

"You sure brought a lot. How long do you expect to stay? I had no idea that you'd bring this much!"

"I'm sorry."

"Don't be. But do carry it to my bedroom and let's get it piled up in one corner."

"Okay."

And so he lifted and carried, lifted and carried. She meanwhile sat on the sofa with a lamp lighted above her and read a magazine. Which magazine? He wondered, but he didn't want to appear rude—or too bold.

When he finally had everything piled up in one corner of her bedroom, including his clothes and odds and ends, this and that, he entered the living room and stood there momentarily, waiting.

"Oh, sit down," she said. "Would you like something?"

Step two.

"Well, yes, that would be nice."

"Tea?"

"That would be wonderful."

"Good. I'll make it. I'll be right back."

"Good."

"You can help."

"Oh—sure. Of course."

Step three.

And so there they were, the two of them, her putting on the tea, her gathering the cups and saucers, the sound of dishes rattling, her asking about sugar, or cream, him answering sugar and cream both, thank you, him standing there watching her, studying each body movement, sizing her up, her body, her hair, face, her perfectly white, straight teeth, him imagining the two of them, later, together, her moving toward him, him moving toward her—and then more fruits of the imagination: a continual cycle of love and sex, sex and love.

A real Don Juan, my fine feathered Philly boy?

But for now, just tea, cups, saucers—that was all. That's all there was, nothing more, and the teapot squealing, her pouring the tea, him saying, hey, thanks, thanks—great.

"And now we sit ourselves down to drink," she said.

"That we do," he said. And smiled.

And they did.

My, my, but she was a luscious treat. Why Sophia? Why Lisa?

Perfect, perfect, in all ways. But wasn't it all the shaping of one's own mind? How much was perceived, how much created?

"Do you like your tea?"

"I love it." He sipped.

"Do you think it will ever stop—all that?" She pointed at the kitchen window, partially covered with lacy white curtains. The snow was halfway up the window.

"I don't think so." He looked out onto the deep backyard. A security pole light made it glow. The snow was coming down, as always, in heavy, wet flakes.

"I'm afraid that Tommy is right," said Tina. "I got to thinking further about what he said. I was so angry with him the way he was so, so depressing—and, I thought, overly imaginative. Overly, well, over the top. Mystical, I guess, is the word I'm looking for. Or is it that?"

"Otherworldly?"

"Cosmic?"

"Supernatural?"

"Or is it preternatural?"

"It was alarming."

"And depressing."

"But you saw some sense finally?"

She rose. "Take a look at my ceiling in the living room. I tried to go along with Tommy—just in case he was onto something, just in case there *was* something, the slightest bit of truth, in what he was saying." She left the kitchen, beckoning for him to follow.

He liked the way her finger, very prettily curled. He liked the way her legs moved, the way her whole body moved.

"See, notice what I did. The owner won't like it, but if I move, or when I move, I'll have to cover it up—somehow. See."

He looked up. He hadn't seen it before. But then he hadn't looked up. Now as he looked up, he was somewhat alarmed to see a hole the diameter of at least six inches. It looked like a man's fist had punched through it. The edges were wrapped in aluminum foil.

"Why?"

"Because Tommy swore that the house has to breathe. It just has to. Things must go up. Everything about us, says Tommy, is spiritual, and spiritual emanations rise in the air. Rise! Go up. Always up. Up, up, up. How he dwelt on that. How he said it over, over, and over. My goodness." Her eyes were fixed on him. Was that a tear? "They don't stay put or fall to the ground, or floor, but rise in the air. Constantly, spiritual emanations rising in the air from a place in the center of our heads. Did you know that? The center of our heads?"

She looked exhausted.

"No—where's that coming from?"

"Tommy, as I said."

"But where's Tommy getting it?"

"I don't know. But he seems so certain. So absolutely certain."

"But it might be total bullshit," said Philip, and was immediately sorry. What had gotten into him?

"Bullshit? No, I don't think so. No."

"Well, I didn't mean to . . . say such a thing."

"I'm glad you did. I've had it with bullshit. I've had it with men like Sebastian. If you want to know my opinion, Sebastian was bullshit. Running off with that bar whore."

"Well."

"But I think Tommy knows—he knows something. He's so absolutely convinced about spiritual emanations. He's read a ton of things about this. Whoosh. Whoosh. Whoosh. Our spirits have to let off steam, out of our bodies—our heads, as it were—and where are those emanations to go? Upward, like hot air. And so, what if you don't have an opening, they push up against the ceiling. But if you have an opening, a release opening, then things go well—and you and everyone in your house is happy."

"Happy," he said. "I just checked out twenty books on happiness from the public library—at the behest of a friend."

Behest?

"Indeed. Happiness is oh *so* important. This is what we live for, Philip—to be happy."

"Yes—I know."

"Oh, dear god!"

"What?"

"What S.K. says about happiness—jeez."

"What?"

"Oh, never mind. It's too depressing. Come." She beckoned.

Tina headed for the kitchen.

Philip started to follow, but he got sidetracked looking at her living room bookcase. Books, books, books, and one whole shelf full of large three-ring binders in several colors with neatly printed labels.

"Are you coming?" she asked.

"Oh, yes."

Suddenly his cell phone went off.

"A call," said Tina, her voice rising a pitch.

"Just a minute," he said.

"Oh, take your time." He saw the number—Sophia *again*? He

311

rubbed the screen just slightly. He opened the bedroom door, where all his stuff was piled up.

"Hi, Sophia."

"Oh, god, Philip. Oh, god!"

"What?"

"Oh, if you just *would.*"

"What?"

"I'm having them again, honey. I keep having these horrible, horrible dreams—I can't get them out of my head! I just can't!"

"Dreams—"

"I told you about them. They're not really dreams."

"Oh. Obsessions."

"Dead bodies. Cold. Buried."

"Under the snow."

"Yeah. Where else?"

"And Rod's not there?"

"Nope."

"Maybe I should come over—"

"No. I told you. No."

"What then—"

"You can talk me through it. You can do that for me, can't you, honey?"

"They're just dead bodies," said Philip. "That's all they are."

"Oh, boy. That's a lot of help."

"Try to put them out of your mind."

"Oh, wow! You ought to be a shrink. I need help, actual *help,* Philip!"

"I don't know what to say, exactly."

"Tell me you love me."

He lowered his voice to a whisper. "I *love* you."

"I can't hardly hear you," said Sophia. "Speak *up.*"

"I've got to go," he whispered. "But I'll call you soon."

"Go?"

"I'm kind of . . . in the middle of something."

"You leave me like this?"

"Sorry—but I've got to go right now."

Tina waiting. He could *feel* her waiting.

"Go then," she said, and the phone went dead.

He looked at it.

"My god," he said. He felt it in his hand. Lifeless, it was.

At table, Tina was turning the pages of one of his happiness books.

"Here's what I think," she said. "To each person, happiness means a different thing. And happiness is just fine. It's good. It's essential." She sat back and was looking outside at the snow. "There's someone in the backyard. A dark figure, but I can just make him out. Isn't that the man you saw at Dick's?"

"What?"

"Isn't that him? Oh, my. He's up to his hips in snow."

"Who?" He looked. The man in black. That same man in black. He had followed him here, and he was now watching the window. If they moved to the living room, he would be watching that window. He would track him every day until one of them died. He was stuck with this dark figure of a man.

"Who is he, and what is he doing out there?"

"I don't know. He follows me, tracks me."

"But how would he know you are here? Was he following you in that car?"

"I don't know. I don't think so. He's always on foot."

She stood up and rapped at the window. "I would go out there, but the snow's half way up the door. I gave up on it. I stopped shoveling. Hey, you!" she shouted. She beat on the snow-packed window, rattling it. "Oh, I'll break it. No. I can't do that."

"I could go around," said Philip. "Go out the front and go around."

"No—we'll simply call the cops."

"Yes—that's a good idea."

"You haven't called the cops?"

"Not yet."

"Why in heaven's name not?" She was leaning over, her cup in her hands, and apparently bent on understanding him.

He didn't know what to say. "I really don't know why. I've tried to deal with it on my own—shouting, like you just did. I ran up to him, and I let him have it. Do you know what he said? He said I was 'in despair.' That's what he said."

"Are you?"

"No."

"Then why all those happiness books. Twenty?"

"Oh, that. That. Well, I got them from a man who insists I read everything he reads. A bibliophile, the man is. Reading the entire library. He needs company—another human to share his thoughts—or miseries, or whatever it is. And so, he had them all stacked and waiting for me. And so—"

She rapped at the window. "That man *cannot* be happy, standing out there in the dark like that. Perhaps we should invite him in. Do you think so?"

"No, no. Call the cops. That's what we should do—immediately."

"You think so?"

"Yes."

"Well, but consider. They would probably look at it this way: here's a man dressed all in black in this woman's backyard. At night. Standing out there just staring at her kitchen window. He's a trespasser. And more. He is . . . a window peeper."

"No, no. I wouldn't say that. He watches at various places. On the street, and so I wouldn't reduce him to a window peeper."

"There's no sense in calling the cops, then," said Tina. "They would undoubtedly end up in such a reductionism. After all, how could they not? It would have to be something that one could write on a form. A form is by its very nature reductionist. Name, address, phone number, email address, birth date, incident in question, time of incident—all such boiler plate details. Is what we see out there reducible to such details?"

"I have no idea."

Tina sipped tea. "I love this tea. Perhaps he would like a cup. I could carry a cup to him, go out the front and go around. But what a bother! I just feel so engulfed by snow!"

"That's awful," said Philip, "to be so engulfed by snow."

"Engulfed?"

"Covered."

"That's true."

And now he truly did want her. The word *covered* made him think of covers, and the two of them between the sheets and the covers. But then he watched as she set the tea cup down hard. And she grew morose, or something.

"I don't know. I just don't know."

"What? Don't know what?"

"Why my life is the way it is."

"What is it? How is it?"

"Oh, just miserable! Entirely, unequivocally miserable!"

"You're in despair?"

"No. I reject that."

"So do I."

"But why, why? Do you know that half of our life we ask the question *why*? Maybe there is no answer to why. Maybe it's all just *what*."

"No," he said. "No."

"I'm tempted to believe it. Your friend out there, for instance, is he a why or a what?"

"Pardon?"

"Can we understand him? Must we ask the question why? Perhaps the cops are right. It's all just a what."

"No, no," said Philip. "They would ask why too, wouldn't they?"

"And what would he say?"

"I have no idea. Other than what he told me."

"And what *would* he tell you? What would be the point of him telling you anything? I'm sure it just popped into his head. As so many things do."

"Maybe."

"We should decide to live our lives differently," said Tina. "I've said it so many times, but now I will. I will begin this very minute."

"How, then?"

"Yes, how. Don't dare ask me why. Please. I'm tired of why."

"I guess I understand that," said Philip.

"Sebastian is all about why. What's the nature of this, and why is it? Tommy is about what. What is it? He's already figured out why."

"Why?"

"Are you daring to ask *why* he's figured out why?"

"No, no—"

"You see, there is some disturbance, call it cosmic, call it preternatural, and we are all, every single one of us, out of kilter, and we must do, do, do to correct this imbalance. That's the why—the imbalance."

"I know—I gathered that."

"Do you believe there *is* an imbalance?"

"I don't know. Maybe. Sure, there probably is. Nothing ever works out perfectly. Everything's a bust, pretty much."

She looked at him, curiously. "Murphy's Law?"

"Well, yes."

"I'm with Tommy, and what I think it comes down to—if we're speaking of imbalances, and there are many—are principles. Perhaps moral. Perhaps scientific or mathematical. And we must use our reason to access these. Reason, Philip. We are rational creatures, and we need to use our reason."

"I agree with that. I wholeheartedly endorse that."

"I suspect you wonder why, then, the hole in the ceiling?"

"Oh, I guess you had your reasons."

"Equivocation, Philip. I mean reason that will hold up in *all* cases. Every single one. Reason that is logical and consistent. Would I normally put a hole through the ceiling? No, that was inconsistent, but you see I have my failings."

"Then Tommy is wrong?"

"I didn't say that."

"Well."

"But perhaps I jumped too quickly into it. You see? Do you? But I want to get at it. I want to get at so many things!"

Those gyrations!

Adam Most? Was she Adam Most? There was even a certain resemblance in her chin line, and he began to feel he was speaking to Adam Most, a *female* Adam Most, and he suddenly wanted to run.

She is different, he thought. *This is not Tina.*

"I have always been a creature of the emotions, but I'm working on my rational self. And, guess what, men don't like that. Men want women to remain entirely emotional. Well, buster, that's not me!"

Buster?

"Oh, but I don't mean to give you the impression—"

"Philip, honey, the 'buster' isn't meant for you—it's for all those Neanderthals at my place of work who have pegged me for a woman, only a woman. A woman who has two or three things in mind, in this order: getting a man, having sex with the right man, bearing his babies, making him lunch, feeding his kids lunch, keeping her figure, having sex and more sex, not getting old. For heaven's sake, do not get old!"

Two or three?

"Um."

"You don't feel that way, do you?"

"No—no."

"Well, I couldn't blame you, I suppose, if you did. Being socialized as a male. And females are socialized as females—into specific gender roles."

Blah, blah, blah—he'd heard it enough. Had professors drone on about it, ad infinitum. This one woman professor, especially. When, where, how, would he move this relationship along a notch—even *one* notch?

"I know exactly what you speak of," he said. "It's awful."

"Isn't it? But see, I value the reason, which many women value, but men, believe it or not, do not." She smiled at him.

"I know," he said. What could he say?

"But going on. The reason is the way to ethical decisions. And we must, Philip, become ethical creatures. There are so many, so many woes in this world, such tragic trials and tribulations for so many, and we must somehow forge a felicity that takes in the necessities or needs, oh so nuanced, of every person and nation."

God, why the alliteration?

"Have you been reading . . . ?"

"Oh, I've been reading, reading, and reading, Philip. And note-taking. Oh, believe me. I do wonder about those happiness books you toted over here. I do wonder."

"Wonder what?"

"Well, I do wonder if they call for a visceral sort of happiness. You know, grunt, grunt, that's good, feels good. Grunt. *My, how it feels so good!* That sort of thing. You know?"

"I don't know."

"Well, there's that type of happiness. We both, male and female, love our pleasures. But there are higher forms of happiness based on a more rational approach. It's not just 'Wow. Awesome!'"

"Oh."

"Haven't you thought about these things?"

"Yes, sure—sure I have."

"And what do you now think?"

Unfair! Right now, he was getting more and more excited. Sexually, that is, because she was no longer looking like Adam Most, but instead a curious blend of Lisa and Sophia. A curious, and profound, proportional, and pleasing pastry of a woman. Shapely, smooth, smelling so sweet—he caught her fragrance. He caught the sheen of her scrumptious blond hair and smelled it too. He wanted to put his nose in it.

"I haven't given it a lot of thought," he said. "But some."

"And what have you concluded—so far. What are your take-aways?"

Take-aways?

"Concluded? Well, that we must be a fair balance of reason and emotion. And go, go for life. Give it your all . . . or rather . . . that is, not miss a trick . . . I didn't mean to say that exactly . . . no. But what I mean is embrace it fully. Poetically!"

"Yes. But Philip, don't you see, I can't be part of a life that isn't taking me seriously. Do you see? Do you see that?"

"Yes, I do."

"I hope you do."

"Oh, but I do."

"Good. Because I'm trying to work out a system, I'm trying to understand my part and what I can give to acting justly, and honestly, and—yes, ethically. People hate that word."

"Does this, does it have anything to do with . . . you know, Sebastian?"

"Him leaving me?"

"Yes."

"I suppose. But then everything has to do with everything else, does it not? It snows, and we decide next year we'll put in a big flower garden. It rains, and we decide to buy a new computer. Our dog dies, and we sign up for a diet program. We are creatures of many impulses, and who knows just how they bank off each other—correct?"

"Yes."

"But, Philip, it is reason that must predominate, ultimately. You see?"

Reason, he thought. Reason.

"Yes," he said, but he wanted to say, *My impulses presently—mine! Please heed—*

"What I think happened is that as I was faulting Sebastian for being so rational, so unwilling to take something for what it was, or *is*, when he left, I decided to be ever so much more rational myself. Maybe because he couldn't respect me. And I couldn't respect myself. Yet, the pisser is: I was *trying* to be rational. I was reading stuff, *thinking*. Yes, dear old S.K.—how he hates him! But mostly he hates a thinking woman. He doesn't want that type!"

"And went for that bar woman? So you—"

"What's the difference—the genesis of the thing. I see the need now to be ethical. I'm doubling down! The need to develop a logical, consistent, yes rational method of deciding on what is the proper thing to do, how to live, how to conduct myself as a person in an ugly world!"

"We're all doomed?"

"Somewhat."

And now he took her hand. He squeezed it. Softly. How could he resist her? How?

She let him. But she seemed almost unaware of it.

He reached over to kiss her.

She let him.

He said, "You know, I am really . . . I think I'm in love with you."

She gave him a look, and pried her hand loose.

"Give it a little time, Philip. Let's give it a little time. Shall we?"

But he kept kissing her, on the mouth, on the cheeks, on the forehead. He was dying for her, for love. Rich, unadulterated, raw love. Raw sex. The rawest kind.

She backed away. "I'm not one of your sexual trophies, am I? I don't want to be one your trophies, Philip."

He backed away himself. "No, no, believe me, you're not—you wouldn't be."

"Good. I don't want to be the object of a game of love, or be reduced to merely aesthetic beauty of any kind. You don't see me that way, do you?"

"No!" But didn't he? Or did he?

"Let's have more tea, and then we'll think of other things."

"Yes—of course."

She'll come around. She'll come.

And pretty soon: "Philip?"

"Yes?" He wanted to say, *Yes, dear heart?*

"I must show you something. Perhaps it's a kind of postmortem on Sebastian. Or perhaps it's a shrine to my new take on the world." She beckoned him to follow.

She led him to the bookcase and motioned at the shelf of large binders with the neat looking labels.

"Here we are," she said. She removed a white binder. She held it up before him. "Notice."

"Logic," he said.

"Yes. A few items in it, notes, but that's all—at this point. But I'll be filling it soon."

She withdrew another binder, a fat black one. She fingered the nice, neat label: *Math.* "Math of all kinds," she said. She swept her hand at the other black binders. "All these, they'll contain everything I can absorb of algebra, geometry, calculus. One must think quantitatively, mustn't one?"

"Yes," he said. Only he didn't much care for all that math. He'd gotten it out of the way and been glad to do it.

"Philosophy," she said, taking out another binder, a blue one. "All the blue ones are philosophy. They'll be like lecture notes, you see." Then she grabbed up a red one: "Literature."

"Lots to do," he said. "Plenty—"

"Brown one here, *Papers of My Own*."

"So much, such a project," he said. "Myself—I've started a book of poetry—"

"How else should we spend our time?" she said, taking his hand, "being rational creatures? S.K. was very rational, but he wasn't. You know?"

"Right."

"I'm sort of down on S.K."

"Really?"

"Oh, not really. S.K. is S.K.!"

"Right," he said.

49

Outside it was snowing hard. Hard, hard.

He must show up at work tomorrow. It would be a long trudge through the snow, at least three or four miles.

Midnight was approaching, and Tina was asleep on the sofa. He went over to touch her, to see if she wanted a pillow. She looked up. "You're my boarder," she said, sitting up. She rubbed her eyes. "That is all. Until, or if things change. Is that clear?"

"Yes."

She sat there staring at him.

"We'll talk about this tomorrow. I've written a position paper on this matter—ever since losing Sebastian to that horrid bar girl. It seemed really important, or rather absolutely essential, to nail down my various thoughts on this subject—to organize them, that is, in a coherent fashion. To develop a cogent argument, well-documented. Being replaced as I was by that floozy! It's entitled 'Toward an Ethical Approach to Sex.' Would you read it?"

"Yes—I suppose so. Sure."

"I mean tomorrow, of course."

"Yes."

"Good. Then I'll give you this couch now, and I'll go back to my own room. But I'll bring you some sheets and covers and a nice pillow."

She patted his arm and left the room.

The couch was quite uncomfortable. He rolled over and rolled over and tried sleeping with his head on one end, and then chose the opposite. The pillow was too thick, like a huge marshmallow. Finally he found a chair and sat up and fell asleep. He awoke at four-thirty and went into the kitchen and turned on the gas and heated some water.

And then he sat up in the living room until dawn, drinking hot tea and resting his eyes, taking a moment to roam them over her books—and those bulky binders, white, black, red. Empty for now.

But perhaps filled soon. The filling already in progress.

He went to the window.

Outside, at the edge of the front yard, stood that man in black.

He got up, pulled open the door, and rushed out.

"What the hell! What the screwy hell! Do you have nothing, nothing in this world to do but stand around staring at me?"

He was right up next to the man in black now. He had him by the arm. He was hard on that arm, clenching it.

"Despair," said the man, pleasantly. "You must rid yourself of your despair."

"You got that right! Fucking A! I'm in despair! I got one, maybe two hours of sleep in that house there. I don't have my own place. I don't have a girl. She's too goddamned frigid to sleep with me. It's her in there in that bedroom with the door shut, and me out there in the living room, can't sleep, with that pile of books on happiness some absolute idiot pushed me into reading with a bunch of other depressing stuff like torture and war—yeah, I'm in despair. I'm really fucking A in despair!"

"As I've said," said the man in black. "As I've said."

"Oh, yeah? You got some suggestions, do you—huh?" He shoved the man. "Like how to get my girlfriend back, or how to get this one, this beauty in there, to cooperate a little and get a little romantic instead of touting the blessings of reason? Huh?"

"No, I don't," said the man in black.

Philip backed up a little. "What then?"

"You're asking me?"

"Hell, yes, I'm asking you!"

"Nothing to report, sir. Where's the center?"

"Huh?"

"Is not utility a floater?" The man in black headed off.

"Wait!"

But the man in black was trudging through the hip-deep snow down what used to be a sidewalk.

Philip went inside. Well, he thought, that dispenses with that one. *My life is about to get better, at least by a degree or two.* He felt a new, energizing sense of tranquility.

An hour later after he'd drunk a few more cups of tea, Tina arrived in a robe.

He wanted her. And in a whim, or was it a whirlwind of passion, he moved quickly toward her. "I want you," he said. "Now. Please."

"Don't you want breakfast?" she asked and patted his arm.

"No, I want you, and then I want breakfast."

"Philip."

"That's what I want. I must have you. I simply must."

She cocked her eye. "Well, all right," she said.

"Really?"

"If that's what you want. Do you?"

"I do," he said.

"Very well, then." She beckoned him back, removed her robe, and removed her panties. She stood entirely naked before him.

"Oh, god!" he said.

"You like what you see."

"I'd die for it," he said.

"Oh, Philip. Don't make so much of it."

"But I do," he said.

"Well."

He fell against her on the bed and took her right there, and pumped everything into her he had. He was so, entirely, he thought, lacking in the joy and fulfillment of this particular area that now, finally, he would have his fill. But afterwards, as she was fixing breakfast, he asked again: "Couldn't we? Before we eat? Just once?"

"Are you serious?"

"Yes. I am."

"If you wish," she said.

And it was the same as before.

"I . . . I think I am now fulfilled," he said. "Now, I feel good. Really good."

"Good."

"I just have such a need. It's unspeakably large." She seemed like a good ear to hear him, so he went on. "Is that natural? Is that okay?"

"I suppose so. I haven't given it much thought."

"Such yearning," he said.

"The will to live."

"Oh," he said.

They ate a pleasant breakfast.

"Now?" he said. "Again? Just one more time?'

"My god," she said.

"Please," he said.

"Oh, all right."

They did it again.

Afterwards, he nestled close to her. I want her. I want her, he thought. "Do you love me?" he asked.

"Pardon?"

"Do you love me?"

"I don't . . . exactly know you," she said.

"But could you love me?"

"I'm not sure. Maybe."

"I want to be loved," said Philip.

"Everyone does," she said. "Me too."

"What would it take?" he said.

"I don't know—it's a mysterious process."

"But not a rational one? You won't make it a rational one, will you?"

"Oh, about that," she said. "You haven't read my position paper yet. Let's get dressed."

Work, he thought. I must call in. I can't make it.

But he didn't want to call in.

He got up. He got dressed too. He suddenly had another urge as he saw her pulling on her panties, but he thought, no, no. That would be too much.

They sat at the kitchen table over her laptop. He began reading her position paper.

"Toward a sexual ethic," she said, stroking his arm. "Please follow the argument, if you will. And then, if you would, please restate the argument so that I am sure, proof positive, that my argument is valid, sound, and holds water in every rational respect. If you would."

Proof positive?

Her voice was level and yet not without emotion.

"Sure," he said. "I will do so."

He read and read. What a tortured argument.

But one must grant talent when one saw it. It was valid. It was sound. He went about restating it to her.

"Ah," she said. "That's it, that's it!"

"I saw a lot of *why* in there," he said. "Not just *what*."

"Of course you did."

"But I thought you said—"

"I'm very much interested in the why, Philip. Just not in Sebastian's continual inquiries and declamations. Perhaps it's simply jealousy. Or it's his stuffy, pretentious manner of doing it. But the why—I cannot give up the why. Not for the what."

"I thought you were going to do that."

"Not me, in spite of what I said."

"Oh."

"I suppose my inconsistency bothers you."

"I need the why myself," said Philip. "I'm tired of the what."

"Well, then, you must pursue it," said Tina, and she took his hand and squeezed it. "But pursue it with the most rational of inquiries. And methods. This ennobles us as rational animals."

"Yes, yes," said Philip.

"And love, it must be rational," said Tina. "It must have that component. It must be guided largely by that component."

"But how?"

"It must not be animal love only. Love is wisdom—a uniting of two hearts in a rational sphere of inquiry."

He wasn't sure. He didn't want the rational in bed that night. But he didn't dare suggest it.

"Don't play games," she said. "Don't make love a catch as catch can."

"Oh," he said. "No, no."

"Have you called into work yet?"

"No—I will."

She nodded.

He couldn't call in. But he could walk in. And so he left and trudged through hip-deep snow in the same direction the man in black had. There was sort of a path.

50

Professor Fellows wanted to know. "Where have you been? Where?"

"I had issues," said Philip. "Housing issues."

"Oh. Well, then, are you ready?"

"Ready for what?"

"A busy day—what's left of it, that is. A day made busy by data collection, and then later, this evening, or rather tonight, perhaps an all-night session of data interpretation—and then the graphing? We'll get hard at the graphing."

"All night?"

"These sessions *can* last all night."

He thought of Tina. He thought of her cold bed. He thought of her coming back from work to the cold house, him not being there to eat with her, and then the long, dark night alone.

"Well," he said. "Must I?"

"Time and a half," said Professor Fellows. "Zoomed right into your bank account the minute the session's over. When you leave, you will have the earnings from the data collection, plus the all-nighter. I love to call it an all-nighter because it makes me think back to my college days, grad school days, my dissertation days, and how many all-nighters I enjoyed back then, caffeine of one kind or another, coffee, NoDoz, pumping in my veins, and a young woman at my side, cheering me on. How about you, do you have a young woman at your side cheering you on?"

"Uh—yes," but apparently not tonight. Ah, how sad, how terrible. How could one miss a whole night? How, how?

Professor Fellows looked closely at him. "There *will* be young women here to serve with the all-nighter, to help us graph the data, and then to put this data into musical composition. You will surely find one of these young women to cheer you on. Don't you think? Don't you?"

"I suppose so. Are they—pretty?"

328

"Are they pretty? Are they beautiful? Are they sexy? Certainly *some* of them are. I am quite sure. And of course that matters. It does. And so . . . now it's time for you to get out on the collection route. Is it not?"

And he did.

He was to collect today, according to the instructions, at several corporate offices, and then a good distance away, on the edge of the district, several ordinary houses, it appeared. Ordinary citizens? Since he was getting a late start, he must save the private encounters for last. For the evening, after the company offices closed. Yet what private citizen would be willing to provide data on praise or panegyrics? If you knocked on their door, wouldn't they slam it in your face? Or sic the dog on you?

But perhaps they would want to do it anyway. Perhaps they would see in it access to something about their own being. Meanwhile, he would go about and get the data fed into his handheld device and imagine it winging its way to the university, accessed by the equipment sitting on Professor Fellows' desk, to be viewed later, to be graphed, and then listened to—music to the ears, indeed. Orchestral. Ultra-civilized. And of course the funds for all his efforts electronically shot like a bullet into his bank account.

"We'll eventually cover the whole city, the whole state, the whole country, and the whole earth if we can," the professor exclaimed when Philip returned, exhausted, that evening. "Imagine the vast number of musical compositions—the fine, distinctive differences. Capturing the human being in his or her deep mystery. Can't you just hear it?" The professor looked up and did a little dance. "Beethoven, maybe? Mozart? Debussy?" And then because he swooned, Philip had to catch him.

"Praise, you see, the mechanisms of it—we learn who we *are!*"

The professor was slinking in his arms. Would he totally expire?

"Um," said Philip.

"My days are numbered," cried the professor, "but I'll hear such sweet music yet! The sweep, the surge! The wild undulations, the artistic control! Ah, pure poetry!"

"Ah!" cried Philip.

When he told Tina about it after two consecutive all-nighters, explaining the whole business, the nature of the research and the musical output, and the amenities—that is, the young women cheering one on—she said, "It seems fitting, for you, anyway, though the professor himself seems to be tempting . . . well, he's on the verge of it, one might say."

She took him by the hand and sat him down. "This seems to be worth a position paper, Philip. I would like for you to do a position paper on this—with me. Are you interested? Are you game?"

Game?

"I suppose."

"I'm already buzzing with ideas," she said. She went for her laptop. "Aren't you?"

"Yes," he said, "yes, yes." And he took her by the hand and began kissing her neck.

"Not now," she said, gently pushing him away. "Later, much later."

"When?"

"The paper first. Finish the paper. Shall we?"

"All right," he said.

"Now," she said, "as to an ethical approach. Let us see . . ."

"Yes," he said. "Let us . . ."

But he was back to kissing her neck.

"Oh, god," she yelled. "Aren't you ever satisfied?"

"Me? No. Never."

She shook her head. "Well, then, let's move on. Reason, Philip. Reason."

Cell phone ringing. "I'll have to get that."

"Sure. You go ahead. Answer your call. Of course."

"I'll take it in the other room," he said.

"Of course. Privacy. Of course."

Sophia.

"Hello, Sophia."

"It's me, Philip. And I'm just convinced. I *am*, my dearest one."

"Regarding—"

"Who do you *think* regarding?"

Wasn't that *whom*? Or was it?

"Rod?"

"Yes, Rod. Yes, sir, honey, Rod."

"Of course."

"Gone, *gone*."

The door opened a crack, and there stood Tina. She whispered, "Just need one little thing. That binder . . . over there." It was on her dresser, the white binder: *Logic*.

She tiptoed over to get it.

She touched his arm just lightly as she left the room, gently closing the door.

His hand gripped the phone. He started to say something, but then his throat went tickly and he coughed.

"Are you there?"

"Uh, yes," he said.

"Well. It's time to collect on that little promise, Philip. That promise you made me, baby honey. And what a wonderful promise it was: to be here with your sweet Sophia. Here in my little apartment, and all our wonderful, glorious moments together. Me, an ice cream treat in the midst of all that wonderful whiteness, surrounding us—enclosing us! Isn't that a delicious thought? And the Hotel Horatio—when we can. You hear?"

"Yes."

"I'll be waiting, naked in bed for you. I'm so lonely. I'm so bored and empty without you."

"Oh, god," he said.

"You know it," she said.

"Uh," he said. Tina in the other room, singing to herself, laughing. A sweet laugh.

"Uh *what*?"

"Well . . . I've got to go. I must. But I'll call—I'll call later."

"Later?"

"Yes, later."

"You shouldn't," she said, "do this. Do this to me."

"Uh. Well . . ."

"Naked," she said. "Naked in bed, Philip. Your ice cream treat—all for you."

Tina waiting. His own Tina in the other room waiting.

"I know. I know. But later," he said. "I promise."

"Oh? And what do your promises *count* for, Philip?"

He had to ignore the plea. A woman with terrible emotional problems. He'd call her later—maybe. Or maybe he wouldn't.

"I must go," he said.

"Are you so weak?" she thundered, "that you can't do the right thing?"

"I want to," he said. "But I—"

Tina, sweet Tina, his new apple dumpling dish. Delectable—and so much yet to consume—

"*Okay.*"

"Okay?"

"Yes—you just go then!" she cried.

The phone went dead.

He went. Sophia in bed, naked? Was she perhaps *already* naked—and waiting?

But he showed up at the kitchen table, where Tina was working at her computer with the Logic binder and logic book open. Her fingers danced on the keys.

"Reason, Philip."

"Logic—I see," he said.

"That's right. And S.K. is wrong. We must not suspend the ethical. We cannot. Perhaps it's right, yet it sits uneasily with me, and so I *cannot.* I'm not my grandma."

"Oh, no," he said. "No, no you're not." Such powder-blue eyes, such—

"I mean wouldn't you be public enemy number one? Sure you would, just like S.K. makes clear."

"Uh, yes. I suppose so."

"You bet you would."

"Yes."

"And I can't do that. Stripping naked for all the world to see!"

"Uh—no," he said.

"Not me," she said.

For a second, he saw his pretty Tina as a granny, and it froze him. But this was the real Tina, young and in the flesh, and she wasn't her grandma. *No.* "But if you just *would*," he said. "*Now.* Because I'd be interested—so *interested*—"

"I know, I know," she said. "But reason, dear, reason is the key. Those urges—learn to control them."

"Well," he said. "But how—"

"*Reason!*" she said. "Please—do let us reason together."

"But I'm a poet!" he cried. He felt an electric surge in the very word.

"Sure. But are you ready?"

She was stroking the logic binder.

"I guess."

"Are you?"

"Well."

"*Are* you?"

Jack Smith's satirical novel *Hog to Hog* won the 2007 George Garrett Fiction Prize and was published by Texas Review Press in 2008. His novel *Icon* was published by Serving House Books in 2014. He has published stories in a number of literary magazines, including *Southern Review, North American Review, Texas Review, X-Connect, In Posse Review*, and *Night Train*. His reviews have appeared widely in such publications as *Ploughshares, Georgia Review, American Book Review, Prairie Schooner, Mid-American Review, Pleiades*, the *Missouri Review*, and *Environment* magazine. He has published a few dozen articles in both *Novel & Short Story Writer's Market* and *The Writer* magazine. His creative writing book, *Write and Revise for Publication: A 6-Month Plan for Crafting an Exceptional Novel and Other Works of Fiction*, was published in 2013 by Writer's Digest Books. His coauthored nonfiction environmental book entitled *Killing Me Softly* was published by Monthly Review Press in 2002. Besides his writing, Smith was fiction editor of *The Green Hills Literary Lantern*, an online literary magazine published by Truman State University, for 25 years.

www.ingramcontent.com/pod-product-compliance
Lightning Source LLC
Chambersburg PA
CBHW050549260626
47157CB00002B/491